Unraveled

Enveloped: Book 2 - Finale
Ava Milns

Line and Copy Editing By: Juicy Details Romance Editing
Proofreading By: All The Proof
Cover Design By: Naughty Nook PR
Formatting By: All The Proof

Visit my website for detailed lists of tropes and trigger warnings: avamilns.com.

Contents

PART TWO
HOPE

PART THREE
HELL

Author's Note (1)

This is a work of fiction. Please keep this in mind as you proceed. The themes in this book are approached with care and sensitivity, but the subject matter remains heavy. Readers are encouraged to make informed decisions about their comfort levels before reading.

This book features the following content:

Graphic and explicit descriptions of sexual activity, BDSM, angst and profound sorrow, emotional manipulation, a core theme of father figure and age disparity, sporadic use of profane language, descriptions of surveillance, portrayal of jealousy and obsession, raw presentation of addiction and consequences with a focus on healing.

- Self-harm and suicide: The third act of the book explores the aftermath of a suicide attempt and its devastating impact on those involved. While the subject is handled with care, readers uncomfortable with this theme may want to refrain from reading. Further points to note:

- The Act: Suicide and self-harm are not graphically depicted, but they are referenced multiple times in mild language. These mentions, though non-explicit, may still be triggering.

- Suicide Watch: The detailed portrayal of this process, though blended with creative liberties, retains a clinical and emotionally heavy tone that may affect sensitive readers.

- Restraints: As part of suicide watch, the use of restraints is mentioned repeatedly. Despite some narrative liberties to lighten the depiction, this element may still be triggering.

- Sedation: Sedatives, though used sparingly in the story, are described in the context of medical necessity and the potential reliance on medication. This theme may resonate deeply and/or negatively with readers sensitive to addiction or medication use.

- Feeding Tube: The use of a feeding tube is referenced multiple times in non-graphic language. Although it is unrelated to eating disorders or psychological issues, its repeated mention in a medical setting could be triggering.

Author's Note (2)

This is a work of fiction. No content in this book is intended to be factually correct. Neither I nor the team involved in creating this book are academic or legal researchers. It is my duty to inform readers of potentially sensitive areas that have been treated fictitiously.

Creative liberties have been taken to present a vivid description of an abject, dire situation the three main characters face. These events unfold in the trauma wing of a hospital. Please note:

- No patient could be hospitalized involuntarily anywhere outside of a psychiatric facility. A trauma ward is not a psychiatric facility.

- Doctors would not be legally able to surgically insert a feeding tube in a patient against their objections without a court order. Such an order would not be granted under the conditions portrayed, because no character was in imminent danger of starving to death. The court would also require the medical professional to try multiple, less-restrictive treatments first, including an NG tube.

- The doctors would not legally be able to keep a patient sedated and in restraints.

- It is unethical for therapists to see multiple members of the same family.

- There is no such thing as a tactile monitoring system.

Please also note that any harmful stereotypes characters might play into are unintentional and fictional.

Author's Note (3)

This book explores themes of suicide and its aftermath with care, but if you or someone you love is struggling, please know that help is available. You are not alone.

For support and resources, please reach out to:

United States

- **988 Suicide & Crisis Lifeline** – Call or text **988** (24/7, free, confidential)
  Website: www.988lifeline.org

- **Crisis Text Line** – Text **HOME** to **741741** (24/7 emotional support)
  Website: www.crisistextline.org

- **The Trevor Project** (LGBTQ+ support) – Call **1-866-488-7386** or text **START** to **678678**
  Website: www.thetrevorproject.org

- **SAMHSA Helpline** (Substance use & mental health) – Call **1-800-662-4357**
  Website: www.samhsa.gov/find-help/national-helpline

International Resources

- **Befrienders Worldwide** – Find crisis helplines globally
  Website: www.befrienders.org

- **Samaritans (UK)** – Call **116 123**
  Website: www.samaritans.org

- **Talk Suicide Canada** – Call **1-833-456-4566** or text **45645** (4 PM–12 AM EST)
  Website: www.talksuicide.ca

- **Lifeline Australia** – Call **13 11 14**
  Website: www.lifeline.org.au

- **Lifeline New Zealand** – Call **0800 543 354** or text **HELP** to **1737**
  Website: www.lifeline.org.nz

If you need help, please reach out. You are valued, and there is hope.

"There is always some madness in love.
But there is also always some reason in madness."
— Friedrich Nietzsche

To all who feel lost in the dark, may you discover the light of someone's memory, burning quietly for you.

PROLOGUE

Daddy,

I know you'll never read this, but I have to write it down—if only to make sense of the chaos inside me. I need to ask you something that's been gnawing at me since that night; since I left you.

Why didn't you hold onto me? Why didn't you fight for us? Why did you let me break up with you, just like that, and let me leave? You said you were just being a friend to Savannah, that she needed you, but I needed you too. You were helping her grieve the loss of her father, but did you forget what you said to me on the night you took me as yours forever? "You're mine, and I'll never let you go," were your exact words.

When we were arguing over the inappropriate contact Anna was making with you, I needed you to be honest with me, to fight for what we had, to show me that I was worth cherishing. Instead, you stood there, letting me walk away, letting our love fall apart without even trying to stop me.

I keep replaying her texts in my mind. Each word stabs me. You were so softhearted with her, so caring, and yet you didn't show me the same compassion when I confronted you.

1

How could you be so gentle with her while I was beside you, crumbling under what I had found? Why didn't you go to battle for me, for us, when it mattered most?

What hurts the most is that you didn't even try. You ordered me to accept your explanation, to move on, as if our love could be reduced to a simple command. But love isn't something you can control. It's not something you can order into obedience. I submitted to you willingly, trusted you without condition, and found freedom in letting you take control of me.

But love is messy, complicated, and requires work, attention, and sometimes struggle. When I asked you to put me and our love above everything else, you were divided. No, you *chose* her. You didn't fight for me. When I slipped away, you didn't cling to me. You just let me go.

Did you let me go because I didn't let you take command of me, Daddy? Did your little girl push you too much? What about that whore? She manipulated you, and didn't that go too far?

You were always my strength, my safe place, my protector. You knew how to take care of me and how to make me feel secure and loved. But in that moment, when I needed you to be my rock, you let me fall. How could you, the man who once made me feel like I was his entire world, stand by and watch as everything we built crumbled?

I wanted to believe you, to trust that our bond was stronger than anything else. But how could I when I saw the way you were with her? How could I when you couldn't even find it in yourself to embrace me when I needed you most?

I keep asking myself why you didn't fight for us, why you didn't do everything in your power to keep me from leaving. Maybe the answer is something I can't bear to face. Maybe you didn't because, deep down, you weren't willing to hold on to me. Maybe I wasn't enough for you?

The mere possibility of that breaks me. It makes me question everything we had, everything I believed about us. You've always been my strength, but now I don't know where to find that safety. I feel lost, like everything I believed about us has crumbled to dust.

I didn't want to leave. But in that moment, I had no choice. You left me no choice. You pushed me to a place where all I could do was run—run from the hurt, the confusion, the anger. And now, all I'm left with are these questions that will never be answered and a pain that won't go away.

I loved you more than anything, but I'm beginning to wonder if love was ever enough. If I was ever enough. And why you didn't think we were worth fighting for.

Alex

PS: *Who will take care of me now, Daddy? How am I supposed to live without you? Who will I rely on?*

I reread the letter for what feels like the millionth time. Once, I printed three hundred and ten copies of it—each one representing a day I knew him, from the first moment I saw him at the gym to the day I broke up with him. Then I burned them all in the kitchen. The flames licked at my grief, setting off the smoke alarms, and the sprinklers doused me with water. The alarms blared, but I stood there drenched and screaming louder than the noise, until my voice cracked.

Ted, Evie, and Mom were shaken out of their sleep, and their faces were pale with fear and confusion when they found me in the middle of the night, a shadow of the girl they once knew.

Today, as I wake up to a workday in Kiruna, Sweden—six months after I left Matthew—my gut-wrenching, soul-stabbing struggle continues.

What did you do to hold on to him, Alex? My genius brain—capable of understanding the Riemann Hypothesis at ten—demands an answer.

I crawl back under the sheets, not wanting to face that question. My thoughts fly as my mind replays my life with him. My body trembles as the tears and sobs start.

You gave him an ultimatum and walked away. Nobody likes ultimatums.

My sobs morph into a guttural wail as tears soak the pillow beneath me.

For all your intelligence, you might have just handed Matthew to Savannah on a silver platter.

My wails pierce the silence, echoing through the room as a thin line of midnight sun slices through the curtains, beckoning me towards the peace I cannot find.

PART ONE
DESPAIR

CHAPTER ONE

Alex: Echoes of Success

PRESENT TIME—EARLY JUNE
SIX MONTHS AFTER THE BREAKUP

The midnight sun bathes the city in a perpetual golden glow—a stark contrast to the darkness that has settled in my heart. I stand on the balcony of my condominium overlooking the bustling streets of Kiruna. It's early June—six months since I left Matthew—and while the world around me is vibrant and alive, I feel a constant ache that refuses to fade.

He humiliated me by choosing his whore ex-wife over me! Why the fuck am I still thinking of him?

Two days from now there's a grand celebratory event planned for Project GreenWind. Our trial power generation facilities, with their wind turbines and blades, have earned recognition from both the Swedish Prime Minister and the US Administrator of the EPA. Government funding is flowing in, and the Cunningham family is celebrating. NASA is also on board.

I should be in a celebratory mood, but all I can think about is Matthew. *He betrayed me! I gave him my body, my trust, my soul—and he let me leave like I was nothing. Despite that, I crave him like air. Why?*

Part of me wants to skip the celebration. I long for him—the one I truly want to celebrate with. I imagine every nuance of his presence: his words of encouragement and praise, the tenderness of his touch, his kisses, and the strength of his grip. I see his eyes filled with adoration, as if they're gazing at me even now.

The warmth of the sun—that shines throughout the day and night at this time of year—on my skin is a cruel reminder of the happiness I once felt with him. I try to push those thoughts aside and focus on the task at hand. I have a video call with NASA's geophysics department, and I need to be composed.

I glance at the clock and take a deep breath. This project is my lifeline, the only thing keeping me from drowning in my grief. I have thrown myself into my career, hoping it will help me forget the man who still haunts my dreams.

Lillian starts the meeting early, as usual. When I log in from my home office, it's just her and me. Her face is a blend of concern and softness, underpinned with a deep empathy. She knows my story—after all, I told her. As my brother James's girlfriend, she called me one day when I was spiraling. I didn't want to talk, but she insisted. In a moment of raw emotion, I spilled everything. I apologized for my bluntness, but her kind response agitated me further. I screamed at her, telling her I didn't want her pity.

Later, James filled her in on the details—how the family planned my move to Sweden to distance me from Matthew and help me heal. Since then, I've distanced myself from everyone—including the very family that's trying to help me if only I'd let them.

The video conference screen flickers.

"Hey, nice to see you," she says, her voice kindhearted, which irks me. I contemplate switching to audio. I don't want anyone's care, attention, or pity.

Then what do *you want, Alex?*

I force a smile, and after rushing through pointless small talk, I ask if she has the slides with the data handy. Lillian is a brilliant engineer, and her work is impeccable. During a recent episode when my hair was in knots and I couldn't speak without a snarl of insults—finding fault with everyone on my team—I scrutinized her code, designs, and documents, and couldn't find a single flaw.

Lillian looks around her conference room, lowers her voice and her eyes on the screen and says, "Alex, the mascara on your left eye is smeared and your lipstick is bleeding." She then clasps her hands. "I'm sorry, but I thought you should know. Please forgive me if I said anything untoward. I'm sorry."

For a fleeting instant, I reflect on why James loves her. She is beautiful, compassionate, and every bit a Cunningham in the making. My family loves her.

"Okay, I'll be back," I say and rush to my room, switching the vanity lights of my dresser on. My mom comes in and, seeing me fumbling with my makeup, steadies my shoulders. She holds me for thirty seconds while I take deep breaths. Then she fetches cotton buds and cleansers. In mere moments, she expertly applies light makeup to my face and tidies my hair into a ponytail. She straightens my outfit and hands me a few tissues.

"You're ready for the meeting, honey," she says, dabbing at a few spots on my cheeks. I don't respond.

On the call are Dr. Benjamin Whitaker, my Harvard professor and mentor; Dr. Natalie Harper, Deputy Director of Biosphere, Hydrosphere and Geophysics at NASA; and Dr. Evelyn Carter, Chief of Staff to the Administrator of the EPA. Several others are linked in via video, but those are the key participants. Lillian sets the agenda, and we jump in.

I ask if NASA's engineers have any feedback on the revised wind predictor models based on their review. Dr. Harper confirms that there's no additional feedback and outlines the next steps. She proposes expanding the models to include oceanic data, emphasizing that NASA has long identified oceans as prime locations for wind energy sites. Their earlier review suggested incorporating considerations like climate change and migration patterns. However, Dr. Harper now recommends we focus on evolving marine biodiversity patterns.

Dr. Whitaker chimes in, "Alex, considering the advancements in your predictive algorithms, I suggest integrating real-time data from ocean buoys and satellite imagery. This will enhance your models and provide more dynamic predictions. Additionally, analyzing marine biodiversity is crucial. We must ensure wind energy sites are sustainable and don't disrupt marine ecosystems."

The businesswoman in me takes over, "I appreciate your points of view. My team and I will create a new version of the predictor models focused on seas, oceans, and large lakes."

I note the hums and nods. But they haven't heard me yet. "That said, I have to ask. Is NASA prepared to support my team in the two pilot sites—the one in the US and the other here in Sweden? The sites were determined by the models I conceived, designed, and brought to life with my team. The wind turbine and blade designs were refined with the help of MIT and Harvard engineers. NASA's backing of our project would help me and the team innovate further."

Dr. Carter nods. "Alex, your initiative is impressive, and the team's energy is outstanding. The EPA is committed to providing the necessary resources and expertise to ensure their success. Furthermore, I propose we establish a collaborative task force that includes NASA, NOAA, and your project team to streamline efforts and maximize the impact of the agencies. This partnership will bolster the current project and pave the way for future innovation."

I'm not getting the response I want, so I slump in my chair and massage my temple with my fingers and a thumb.

"Go change the world, my little genius, my sweet Alex." Matthew's words echo in my mind, freezing me in place.

Dr. Harper's voice shakes me back to the present. She addresses Dr. Carter in a lively tone, "Evelyn, you and I haven't had a night out since that brawl at Brown. Give Alex a break here, will you?" They both laugh, and soon the others join in with college anecdotes, and laughter fills the room.

I stare at their faces, registering the dialogue, but my thoughts are on Matthew.

Dr. Harper shifts to a no-nonsense tone. "Alex, your project is the first of its kind in a long time—American innovation in something planet-changing, sparked by young minds. I am authorized to let you know that NASA is fully committed to supporting Project GreenWind."

I turn off the camera and microphone and press my face into the pit of my elbow, overwhelmed by the praise. Mom and Evie rush to my side, helping me regain composure. They hear the voices in the meeting praising me, my team, and our work. Mom steadies me, as always, while Evie consoles me. The three of us share a wordless hug as the conference continues. Mom gently reminds me it's poor etiquette to pause without notice.

I return to the call and apologize. "Thank you, Dr. Whitaker, Dr. Harper, and Dr. Carter," I say, looking at each screen. "Cunningham-Segal needs more than just verbal support. With NASA's backing, nothing can stop us. Please let us know the next steps—we need to fast-track the pilot sites."

Dr. Harper nods again. "Your dedication and vision are inspiring. Our next steps include establishing a dedicated task force to collaborate closely with your team on the technical and logistical aspects of the pilot sites. We will expedite the necessary approvals and coordinate with local authorities in both the US and Sweden. You can expect a detailed plan from us by the end of the month. Together, we can make this groundbreaking project a reality."

I notice Evie in the corner, giving me a thumbs-up. This is big. What Dr. Harper isn't explicitly saying is that NASA will also lobby the US government to clear obstacles and ensure the pilot sites are commissioned smoothly. While the detailed plans will take time, today's discussion is a milestone. My team is now free to innovate without roadblocks.

How proud and happy Matthew would've been of me in this moment!

I take a deep breath, feeling a renewed sense of determination. "Thank you, everyone, for your backing and commitment. Dr. Harper, your assurance encourages us. We look forward to receiving the detailed plans and collaborating with NASA to make Project GreenWind a success. Let's continue to push boundaries and innovate for a sustainable future."

As the meeting draws to a close, I notice Lillian giving me an encouraging nod from her video feed. She mouths, "You've got this!"

With a last nod, I say, "Together, we will make this happen. Bye, all." I click off the conference line, feeling the impact of my recent accomplishments and the immense possibilities ahead.

I sit back, letting out a long breath. Matthew's voice prowls my mind, and his unwavering support and belief in me are a source of strength. *How proud he would be of this achievement, and how I wish he were here to share in this victory.* Despite the circumstances and the pain of his betrayal, his specter continues to guide me, pushing me to be the best version of myself. I am left questioning, *Am I achieving professional milestones for myself, to escape him, or to make the man who trampled on me proud?*

I don't know what I feel anymore, but I'm not numb. The constant sting of his choice—to support his ex-wife over me—remains like a chronic ailment for which there is no cure. Yet a longing for him tugs at my heartstrings—*I don't have an identity without him.*

I go back to my grief. *He crushed me. I'm supposed to hate him. I do, but...do I, really?*

The world spins on. Time moves faster than I can. The future pulls me forward, dragging me into a place I don't want to go—a cave of loneliness cloaked in luxury, high society, and a business career. I'll be lumbering along elite corridors, haunted by the ghosts of my past in the shadows, ready to pounce and drag me into desolation. *How long can my family shield me from these demons?* It's not just emptiness—it's worse. It's a world where I'm a spectator, watching life slip by without me, powerless and unseen.

Will I reunite with Matthew? My mind scoffs, mocking me with cruel certainty. *Or am I destined for a hollow life, devoid of meaning, with no soul to power me forward?* The place I'm being dragged into is alive, breathing with my failures, and taunting me with all I've lost.

Will I be left standing on the sidelines, watching as Matthew builds a new life with a new woman—or worse, with that whore, Anna? The thought burns through me—sharp and acidic—and my chest drags me to the ground as I spill another river of tears.

CHAPTER TWO

Matthew: Aftermath

PRESENT TIME—EARLY JUNE
SIX MONTHS AFTER BREAKUP

The room in St. Gabriel's Community Center is filled with the quiet hum of murmured conversations and the occasional creak of the floorboards. I take a seat in the circle of folding chairs, and the familiar scent of stale coffee and disinfectant settles around me. I exchange smiles with a regular and lean back in my chair, crossing my arms.

The meeting begins, and I listen to the others share their stories. When it's my turn, I exhale a long-held breath and stand. "Hi, I'm Matthew, and I'm an alcoholic," I say, the words no longer foreign to my tongue. I talk about the progress I've made and the job I love, which I managed to keep despite hitting rock bottom. I don't describe it, but I try to confront and manage the feelings of hope that still linger for Alex's return. The heaviness in my chest tells me I'm not really managing anything.

Each day is a struggle, but today marks ninety days of sobriety.

After the AA meeting, I bid the regulars goodbye and step out into the golden light of a June evening in Manhattan, the warmth a stark contrast to the cold emptiness I've carried for months. By the steps of the church she waits—leaning casually against the building. Tall and toned, she stands with effortless grace, and the golden light casts her in a warm glow.

I approach, unable to look away. My steps falter for a moment as I take her in, and memories rush to the surface. She was twenty-three when I first met her six years ago, already mature beyond her years. That sharp mind and unshakable poise have only deepened, despite the hardships we have endured—separately and together—this past year. Physically too, she hasn't changed—her gymnast's physique remains as defined as ever in testament to how well she's always cared for herself.

I, on the other hand, am gradually regaining my physical and mental fitness.

She waves, tilting her head as if to ask, "What's wrong?" I shake my head and resume walking toward her.

"Evening!" Her smile reaches her eyes. Her raven-black hair traps the fading sunlight, and her presence brings a sense of calm.

"Evening, Anna," I reply, grateful for her support. We proceed to a nearby café, our routine of post-meeting coffee a small anchor in my tumultuous life.

"Hey, are you okay? How did it go?" Her tone is gentle and considerate.

"It was good." My voice reflects a mixture of relief and exhaustion. "I struggle to talk much beyond a few lines." I gaze up at the light reflecting off the windows of a tall building.

"But sometimes—like today—I do, and it helps."

She acknowledges with a nod.

We stroll a few blocks to a cozy café, one of those hidden gems that Chelsea is known for. Inside, the aroma of freshly brewed coffee mingles with the scent of pastries. I feel a pinch under my ribcage, a subtle reminder of the coffeehouse Alex used to take me to. This café isn't as upscale as that place, yet it stirs memories of what once was, leaving small, lingering pricks of longing.

Anna and I find a quiet corner and order drinks—decaf for me and a latte for her. We discuss our workdays, and the conversation flows easily. She tells me about a challenging project at Hudson & Greene, LLP, while I share my thoughts on a new piece I'm transcribing. Our interactions are a mix of comfort and lighthearted banter, a stark contrast to the heaviness of our personal struggles.

She listens to me intently, her nearly black eyes soft. There is something in her gaze, a depth of feeling that might reflect our present situation, the struggles we've been through, or a question about the future. I brush it aside, not wanting to discover what it might mean.

Finishing my decaf, I glance at my watch. "I should get going. The dinner crowd will expect music."

She smiles, though a hint of concern lingers in her eyes. "Play something beautiful tonight. I know you will."

I nod, appreciating her faith in me. "See you at the apartment later?"

"Of course," she says. "I'll make sure there's something ready for dinner."

With that, I kiss her cheek and leave the café, heading towards La Grand Élégance. The restaurant is a short walk away, and as I approach, I can already see the well-dressed patrons beginning to fill the luxurious space.

Inside, I settle at the grand piano, its polished surface reflecting the soft glow of the chandeliers. As I begin to play, the music flows effortlessly—classical and contemporary pieces that fill the dining area with a soothing ambiance. My fingers dance over the keys, and each note is a testament to my enduring love for music.

I say my usual prayer in silence, that nobody requests Alex's favorite piece. One time someone did, and I ended up stoned, on the streets, and unable to find my way home.

Despite my inner turmoil, these moments at the piano provide a sense of peace and purpose. As my fingers caress the keys, I think of Anna and the solace she gives me, and the promise of her presence waiting for me at the apartment—*a home*. It's enough to carry me through the evening, each tune a step toward healing.

After the performance, I leave the restaurant. The cool night air is a welcome relief as my mind lingers on the last notes I played.

The clientèle were generous with their applause and tips, but the real victory was finishing my set without anyone requesting Alex's favorite piece. That memory is one I don't care to revisit.

La Grand Élégance, a high-end French restaurant in Chelsea, attracts wealthy and discerning patrons, including Alex's family. I've been playing there since she and I were together, but I haven't seen them around—except for one night. Maybe they're avoiding the place because I work here. If the manager finds out, I'll surely be fired—no business wants to lose the Cunninghams' patronage.

I make my way to the subway, thinking of the dinner waiting at the cozy apartment Anna and I share. Our relationship, still undefined, is a source of stability in my recovery.

I try not to dwell on the future since that weighs me down. I take it one day at a time. Some days are impossible—the urge to drink overpowering—so I take those days one hour at a time.

As I ride the subway, the question nags me: *What have you become, Matthew?*

I can't answer. I've never depended on anyone. At eight, I took charge of my life. Even my parents let me lead them. At twelve, after my dad returned from deployment, I helped him set up his electronics repair workshop, working with him after school. I'd leave at six to cook dinner for my mom, who was at her second job. I handled the budgeting and planning for college while studying and practicing piano at night.

I felt invincible, growing in command and confidence every single day. I feared nothing. Even when it seemed I might not be able to afford college, I kept going, trusting in my musical skills. If college didn't happen, I'd help my dad expand his workshop and move it to Main Street. I smiled—always beaming—my teeth on full display.

My goal was simple: happiness. I believed it was mine to command, and I trusted it would lead to everything good and peaceful. I never needed extra money or things—being happy sufficed. That's how I lived, and I modeled this for others, though most didn't get my principles. Nothing—nothing at all—could faze me.

After Alex left, I turned to alcohol to cope, which eventually led to dysfunction. Now, I depend on Anna for my sobriety—and my stability—a result of six months of navigating grief. I didn't handle it well then, and I'm not sure I'm doing much better now. Six months of suffering broke me. When I hit rock bottom, I thought my life was over and all meaning was lost. I resigned myself to the idea that I could never be who I used to be.

While comforting Anna through her dad's death, I sank further into my own woes—until she pulled me out. Slowly, I'm starting to return to my original self, but she remains my crutch, offering a strength I can't seem to find on my own. She's been my anchor, helping me find a new lease on life. But I can't shake the feeling that I've lost something essential along the way.

So, to answer my mind's question, *I don't know what I've become.* I'm trying to be happy, but parts of me seem to have vanished, leaving a burning emptiness that screams to be filled. When I left Alex's penthouse and checked into a motel that Sunday, I was paralyzed—an unfamiliar, terrifying feeling that stripped away the confidence I'd worn like armor. That was the start of my downward spiral into unending pain. I began questioning myself, doubting my command and confidence.

Dreams of what-ifs consumed me—what if I had responded differently to Alex's demands? I regretted my choices that night, haunted by the knowledge that she was mine to hold, forever. Yet almost immediately I would convince myself that I had done the right thing—there was no way in hell I could leave Anna to grieve alone. The cycle repeated endlessly, spiraling into a tangled mess of confusion and heartache, drowned in alcohol.

Now was the right time to block this glum, dangerous reminiscing, as I have learned. Otherwise, I know I'll head to the corner liquor store for a handle of their cheapest vodka. I shut my eyes and exhale, routing my thoughts towards happiness, which—only for now, I hope—is not fully in my grasp. I repeat my mantra, "Be happy, everything will follow."

I start my walk from the subway to our small apartment, thinking of the warmth and aroma of a simple soup and Anna's unrestrained smile on her flawless face—her unwavering support a beacon in my journey toward healing.

The world spins on. Time moves faster than I can. The future looms relentlessly, pulling me forward when I want to stay in the past. My paternal instinct makes my heart leap with joy and dares to hope, *What if Alex comes back to me?* But the memory of how things ended, her stubbornness and hurt, quickly snuffs out that hope. And Anna, *Where are we even headed? Can anything I'm holding onto last, including my sobriety?* The thought of my life ripping apart again leaves me sick. The dreams I had of having a big family now feel like a cruel joke.

CHAPTER THREE

Anna: New York

PRESENT TIME—EARLY JUNE
SIX MONTHS AFTER BREAKUP

Grocery bag in hand, I walk toward our one-bedroom apartment nestled in a quiet corner of Hamilton Heights. The evening sun casts long shadows on the weathered brick of our building, its wrought iron fire escapes standing like old, wise sentinels. The place has seen better days, just like me, but it's still standing—tough, persistent, like a well-worn leather jacket that tells a story of survival.

I pause at the entrance, letting the familiar creak of the door greet me like an old friend. The sound feels like home, even if the building's not much to look at. It's a little battered, a little rough around the edges—but strong, sturdy. *Just like me.*

As I climb the stairs, the scent of fresh bread wafts down the hallway, mingling with the faint aroma of spices from someone's dinner. It's the smell of life going on, of simple and comforting routines. It contrasts the world I used to know—a sterile, high-powered world that feels far away now.

Inside, the apartment is modest, but it's ours. A place where Matt and I are trying to rebuild something—our lives, ourselves, maybe even...us.

I fumble for my keys while my mind drifts to him. He gave me his 30-day AA chip, and we had a hole drilled in it. Now it dangles from my keychain, a small token of progress—his, ours, and our shared resilience. I worry about him, of course, but I'm also proud. He's fighting for something, and I'm here to fight beside him. I hope I can keep being the support he needs, the way he was for me after my dad passed.

I think back to that morning at the police station. Seeing him hunched in that wooden chair—looking like a shadow of the man I once knew—knocked the wind out of me. My knees buckled, and if my lawyer hadn't been there, I might've collapsed right there. The man in front of me was a stranger. Only his viridian eyes—those eyes that always lit a fire inside me—told me it was him. Matt—my rock as I struggled with grief, carrying me with his uplifting voice and reassuring texts—sitting on a bench at the police station.

The apartment door swings open with a whine, and I step inside and set the grocery bag by the cooktop. The apartment feels like a blend of both our lives now—his chaos and my quiet—woven together into something that almost feels like peace.

After a quick face wash, I gather my long hair into a neat bun and secure it with a slender jade hairpin. When he returns, I want him to walk in to the inviting aromas of a warm, home-cooked meal infused with my love for him. In some cultures, they say the path to a man's heart is through his stomach. I intend to use every avenue—leave no path unexplored—to find and bring his heart back to where it belongs—with me.

MID-AUGUST LAST YEAR
ABOUT THREE MONTHS BEFORE ALEX'S AND MATTHEW'S BREAKUP

My first provocative text to Matt was unplanned, but it was a message I needed to send. Two weeks after my dad's passing, I was curled under his desk, the same place I'd hidden as a child during our games of hide-and-seek. He used to pretend he couldn't find me—calling out to God in mock desperation—until I'd burst out laughing, running to him and hugging his leg. Back then, I was safe. Back then, I was loved.

That night under the desk, I could hardly stand the memory. The ache of missing him was so sharp that it cut through me, relentless. I cried for hours under that desk, until my tears ran dry and my voice faded to nothing but the echo of silence. It was suffocating.

And then my phone lit up with a message from Matt. A small flicker of hope in the darkness.

Anna, you missed your check-in.

That one message shot through me like a lightning bolt. My mind raced, recalling the way he had held me, the way his body had made me float in ecstasy when we were together. It was the escape I craved. I needed it—needed him—desperately.

In robotic fashion—my mind in a trance—I crawled out from under my dad's desk, took a seat in his chair, and ran a hand through my hair. I bit my lips and crossed my legs. In that moment, I felt light—like a burden had been lifted, replaced with a strange warmth in my chest. I sent him the text.

Matt…I need the feeling of escape, like when you make love to me and my mind goes blank.

I closed my eyes, soaking in the sensation—a connection I was claiming for myself, something I felt was finally within my control. My heart leaped with a jolt, as if it had attached itself to something solid and started beating anew.

As I sent the text, anticipation and anxiety welled inside me. *Would he understand my desperation, my need for him to fill the void left by my dad's death? Would he see through my words, recognizing the depth of my emotional turmoil and the lengths I was willing to go to reclaim him? Would he even respond? Or would he ignore my struggle to avoid drowning and breathe?*

He responded with words of comfort and an order not to miss the check-ins. A belief arose in me, a feeling of purpose, as if I were on a path on solid ground—a lengthy and arduous journey to reclaim him. From that point on, I wore blinders—focused on the goal of having him back in my life, no matter the cost.

PRESENT TIME

The sound of boiling water startles me, dragging me back to the present. As I carefully pour the washed rice into the pot, my mind remains fixed on him. Though doubts consume me, I steady myself and reaffirm my commitment—*all* paths lead to him. Through his stomach, his eyes, his ears, his touch, his voice, his soul—and yes, my body. Nothing will be left to chance. *I'm patient. I'm persistent. I'm relentless.*

I know he's still tangled up in his feelings for Alex, but I don't care. This is a long game, and I've already decided—he will be mine again. Our lives are a complicated knot, but I'm determined to unravel it—thread by thread—until it's just the two of us, alone in our world. He just doesn't know it yet.

I think about her sometimes, about how she managed to capture his heart so quickly. I am jealous, of course, but she doesn't intimidate me. I am confident in my ability to reclaim him. He and I have history. We've shared things—moments, memories, an understanding—that she can never touch. And I will remind him of that. I'm slowly and deliberately weaving myself into his life again and I will continue, until he's so tangled in me that he won't need to escape.

I know the rhythm of this dance. Every text, every word, every glance, every touch—it's all part of my plan. And soon he'll see it. He'll realize there's no way out. Only me.

It's almost time for him to arrive. I can feel it—a tingle at the base of my spine like an electric pulse that urges me forward. I set the food on the small table for two tucked in the corner of our cramped apartment. It's small, yes, but it's perfect. He eats whatever I make with relish, but tonight I've put in extra care—ginger and garlic fried rice with vegetables and a touch of soy sauce. A dish that warms the body and the soul. His soul.

I slip into my pajamas and take one last look in the mirror, making sure my hair is smooth and my face is right. Perfect. Everything must be perfect for him. He deserves nothing less.

Settling on the sofa, I breathe deeply, attempting to calm the flutter of anticipation in my chest. As I wait for him, I whisper to myself, "Matt, I love you, and we'll be a family again."

The world spins on. Time moves faster than I can. The future rushes toward me, and I'm bracing myself to meet it head-on. I have him—well, almost.

Rebuilding his trust—our life—will take more time, but I'm prepared to do whatever it takes. No conditions, no limits.

I'm not naïve enough to think Alex is gone for good—far from it. If, or when, she comes back, she'll have to face me properly—no more hiding, no more games. She already hates me, and that's fine. She'll soon learn there's a difference between hate and fear.

I've worked too hard, sacrificed too much, to let anyone—especially her—take what I'm building with Matt. If she tries, I'll meet her head-on. And if she wants a fight, she'll get one. I'll do whatever I must to protect what's mine. *I'll kill her if I must.* The thought lingers, sharp and cold in my mind, and I hold on to it. She can't break what I'm putting back together—not again.

CHAPTER FOUR

Alex: Midnight Shadows

PRESENT TIME

The applause from the NASA meeting still echoes in my ears as I close my laptop. Another victory for Project GreenWind. My team is ecstatic, and I should be too, but as the noise fades, all I'm left with is the hollow silence of my home office.

I glance through the window at the midnight sun, its eerie glow stretching long shadows across the room. In early June, the sun never fully sets here in Kiruna. The perpetual daylight feels cruel, mocking the darkness inside me.

I walk to my bedroom, still in my work clothes, my heels clicking on the polished floor. The room—minimalist Scandinavian design—doesn't comfort me. I collapse onto the bed, still in my heels, too drained to change. My body feels heavy, pulled into the mattress by some invisible force.

I try to focus on my success—on the recognition from NASA—but my mind drifts to the past, to Matthew. His face fills my thoughts, with his intense eyes and his voice whispering, "I'll handle everything, Alex. You are the center of my world. Be happy, everything will follow." But the emptiness inside me clings like a shadow—an ache I can't shake.

I am irritable and frustrated. *Why can't I just move on? Why can't I feel proud of my achievements?* Instead, hopelessness spreads through me, making me feel unworthy of any success. On some days—despite Mom's attempts to wake me—I remain buried in bed, sleeping away the afternoon. Recently, I've cursed her—or Evie—when they try to pull back the curtains, as if the daylight could drag me from this dark place. On those mornings, I wish I hadn't woken at all. I imagine slipping into an eternal sleep, waking to find him beside me where we'd be together in peace.

I remember the day after I ended my relationship with him—the cold, sterile airport hangar where I boarded the plane to Sweden.

The first week after the move was surprisingly fine. My mom, Ted, and I settled into our luxurious condominium, and they marveled at the beauty of the Northern Lights from the windows. Their colors danced in the sky, but the beauty couldn't reach me. I told myself leaving Matthew was the right decision—after all, I was putting my well-being first. But guilt ate at me. I had chosen myself and left the man I loved, dragging my family into my mess. I convinced myself it was his choice. He wanted his manipulative ex-wife back. Who was I to stop him? I'd been lied to, betrayed, replaced.

But after the first week, reality set in.

The condominium's stillness felt suffocating in harsh contrast to the bustling days of unpacking. And then it hit me—he was gone. His touch, his voice—they weren't there anymore. The emptiness swallowed me whole.

Thinking I needed to revamp my entire lifestyle, I had decided I'd become a socialite in Kiruna's affluent circles. I knew my fame as a child genius and my status as the heir of Cunningham Energy Conglomerate—the world's largest—would attract people's attention. I started buying clothes—luxury designer outfits which had to be tailored to fit my frame, just as I used to with Mom in Manhattan. But no matter how many purchases I made, they didn't fill the emptiness inside me. They were distractions—fleeting, hollow attempts to patch the gaping hole left by him. When the tailors arrived to adjust and alter my outfits, Mom offered half smiles while her eyes scanned me as if trying to decipher what was wrong. Evie, ever the caretaker, patted my shoulder and asked if I needed help.

"Why? Don't you trust me to buy dresses on my own? You think I make the wrong choices?" I snapped, the words icy and sharp. Pride wrapped around me like armor—cold and unyielding—blocking out the pang of guilt that flickered in my chest as Evie blinked in surprise.

The guilt didn't last. It simmered—boiling over into anger—and I turned it on Mom next. She was standing too close, watching too carefully, and her half smiles grated on my frayed nerves. "Do you want something, Mom? Or are you just here to remind me how much of a mess I've made?" The words spilled out, venomous and unprovoked. Her expression wavered, but she said nothing. That made it worse. "No? Great. Then leave me alone." I turned away, retreating into my fortress of pride, or rather, an empty keep of escape.

In the days that followed, I continued attacking people—family and coworkers, my team. Even Lillian.

But the fortress wasn't as solid as I wanted it to be. Alone in my room, guilt clawed at the edges of my anger and whispered questions I didn't want to answer. *Why did you say that? Why are you so cruel to the people trying to help?* The questions burned, and I lashed out at the only person left—myself. I hated the version of me that couldn't handle this—that hid behind shopping bags and cutting words. But instead of facing the shame, I buried it in more anger. *They don't get it. They'll never get it. If they knew what I was really feeling, they wouldn't ask such stupid questions or offer to help.*

It was easier to blame them than to admit the truth: I was completely, utterly lost.

I tried to drown the silence—the stillness creeping into my fortress. I told myself I just needed to socialize, to make new friends, to fill the void. I even smiled at myself in the mirror, telling myself how silly I had been. *It will all be fine. I don't need him. I don't need anyone.*

I attended social gatherings, parties, and business meetings. I smiled and laughed, but each moment was hollow. The more I insisted I was fine, the more the emptiness echoed. But I told my family, "It's so refreshing. I'm back, and I'm fine without Matthew."

I was determined to believe it, clinging to the façade of independence. But in quiet moments my mind betrayed me, replaying memories of him and our time together. Ire simmered beneath the surface, directed at him for choosing her, at myself for still caring about him, and at everyone around me for not understanding the depth of my turmoil.

I would often stand in front of the mirror, practicing my smile, trying to believe that I was happy and free. Yet, the reflection staring back was a reminder of the fury I tried to suppress. I hated how easily I had been replaced, how quickly my world had crumbled.

In the solitude of my room—with nobody watching—I let the mask slip. I would collapse onto my bed, and tears of frustration and betrayal soaked my pillow. The rage was there—fierce and consuming—a fire I couldn't extinguish. I resented Matthew for not fighting for us, for letting me go so easily. I resented myself for caring so deeply, for letting my heart be broken repeatedly by the memory of him.

This was my battle—a constant tug-of-war between my inability to let go of him and my anger at everything. The struggle to find peace in my emotions became my routine. I knew I had to keep moving forward, although each step seemed like a betrayal of the love I cherished. But as time moved on, I couldn't escape the truth—he was gone, and I was left to piece together a life that felt unfamiliar.

The obsessive socializing lasted for about three weeks. Wherever I went or whoever I spoke with, every conversation seemed to circle back to love, romance, and relationships. It was as if the universe was taunting me. I began to find reasons to withdraw from events early, retreating to my room where the atmosphere weighed heavy, gloomy, and soul-wrenching.

Even a casual weekend trip to see the Northern Lights turned into one of the worst social events—and my last. As Ted, Mom, Evie, and a few colleagues from Segal—including the CEO—watched the spectacle unfold, they began philosophical discussions on nature and how small we all are. I couldn't take it anymore. Frustration surged within me and I snapped, launching into a fifteen-minute rant on the physics of the Northern Lights.

"The Northern Lights, or aurora borealis, are caused by solar particles colliding with the Earth's magnetic field," I began, my voice rising with each word. "They excite gases in the atmosphere—like oxygen and nitrogen—causing them to glow. It's not magic. It's science, predictable and measurable."

My explanation grew more intense, and my tone was acute and tinged with bitterness. "So, there it is. It isn't a big deal," I finished, my tone almost a shout. "There are unexplainable things, and those are what you should be bothered by. Have you ever had your heart ripped out? I suspect not—"

Evie dragged me away, preventing me from finishing. I yelled at her—agitation and bitterness spilling out—then burst into tears. She brought me water and kept hugging and pacifying me, helping me regain composure.

When I returned to my room, the complete stillness pressed in on me in an unrelenting reminder of my isolation. My mind raced—replaying the outburst—and my temper simmered beneath the surface. I couldn't believe I had unraveled that way and allowed that to happen, let my emotions pour forth for all to see. My feelings of worthlessness, self-loathing, self-pity, and vulnerability increased, as I had exposed my inner turmoil in embarrassing circumstances.

I stopped attending gatherings, functions, or outings of any kind. I retreated inward. I avoided anything that might remind me of Matthew or the love I had lost.

In the quiet moments of solitude, my refusal to accept my issues and my rage oppressed me. The logic and science that had previously offered comfort now felt hollow, unable to fill the void left by his absence. I realized that no matter how much I tried to prove otherwise, my soul remained shattered, and the pieces were scattered far beyond my reach.

I threw myself into work, hoping my professional achievements could fill the gaping crevasse left by the aftermath of my breakup with him. Long hours in the office and at home became the norm, followed by a collapse into exhaustion and at least eighteen hours of sleep. The cycle repeated, and I drove my team mad, demanding perfection and expecting them to match my speed, my brilliance.

Every review meeting became an opportunity to tear them down. "How else will they improve if they don't learn from their mistakes?" I asked Lillian. Her face was unreadable. I thought I was helping the team.

But when one member broke down in tears and sought help from Lillian, I realized the harm I was causing. I was pushing everyone—my team and myself—too hard. Yet, that realization didn't stop me. My obsession with perfection was too strong.

Project GreenWind moved forward—milestones achieved faster than expected—but emotionally I was collapsing. I closed myself off, only willing to engage with work. At the Segal office, I requested a space far from the team—one that looked onto the desolate Kiruna landscape.

In the solitude of my office, I questioned myself, *Was I truly dedicated to the project, or was I just using it to avoid my issues?* The urge to keep moving—to keep pushing—drowned out any answer.

At home, I shut myself away in my room, feeling the need to escape. *Escape? Hadn't I already escaped Manhattan and Matthew by coming here? Where did I want to go next?* These questions haunted me, but the answers were always out of reach.

I knew my behavior was unsustainable. My mind was a whirlwind of denial and anger—a ticking time bomb waiting to go off. I couldn't calm the storm inside.

Music—particularly classical solo piano—had been my refuge. But now every time Ted put on classical music I lashed out. I stopped listening to music altogether and deleted my playlists. Classical music had become a painful reminder of Matthew—the life we'd shared, the dreams we'd dreamed. Each note reopened old wounds I wasn't ready to heal.

My family didn't understand. Ted would quietly turn off the music, while Mom and Evie exchanged worried looks but said nothing. I could feel their confusion and their concern, but I kept pushing them away.

Classical music had been our shared language, a symbol of our connection. Now it was a reminder of everything I'd lost. I rejected it because rejecting it meant rejecting Matthew—pushing away the past. But the emptiness grew, and I found myself more isolated than ever.

One Sunday, I asked Evie to cut my hair. She hesitated, confused by the request. I shrugged it off, saying it was just because I hated pigtails. She didn't buy it, but she cut my hair anyway.

As she worked, I spoke, "It's amazing, Evie. In Manhattan, I thought Matthew was everything. Do you know what it feels like to be free?"

She didn't answer.

"It was just a phase," I added. "An infatuation. I'm fine now."

But memories of him flooded back—his touch, his desire, the way he adored my hair in pigtails. The memories twisted in my chest, but I pushed them away. I was done with everything that reminded me of him.

When Evie finished cutting my hair, I hugged her and apologized for my erratic behavior. Her embrace was gentle, but I felt her worry too.

I stared at my reflection—short hair, a symbol of a fresh start. But instead of feeling free, I felt more trapped. The haircut didn't erase the memories. The freedom I claimed felt hollow, like another lie I told myself.

When I drove to work, I talked aloud, trying to convince myself that he and I were never meant to be. The relationship had been doomed. It was better this way. I praised myself for staying strong and walking away from him.

One morning, as I lay in bed not wanting to rise, I fantasized about Matthew somehow finding me in Kiruna and appearing at my door. The image of him was so vivid that it pulled me further into emptiness.

I open the door and his six-foot-seven frame fills the doorway, so I step back. His viridian eyes catch and hold me, rendering me captive. I see his mouth move, but I hear nothing. A ringing begins, growing louder until it drowns out all the other sounds. His text conversations with his loathsome ex-wife flash in front of my eyes, pulling me from the trance.

"Alex, I've come to get you back. My sweet little one, I'm sorry. I am sorry for everything I did and didn't do." His husky baritone voice shakes my soul, and I grab a chair for support.

He hands me flowers, which I promptly throw to the floor. He tries to take my hand, but I pull away. "My baby, I've left her. You were right and I was wrong. I just got distracted. It's over. She and I are done and I mean done!"

His perfectly symmetrical face glows with a subtle radiance and sincerity. He doesn't have to do much. The endearment "my sweet little one" is enough. I collapse in his arms—tears streaming—as I cry, "Daddy!"

It was a dream, and I woke abruptly—caught between the ache of separation and a sudden, surging wave of hope. *He will be back to take me with him. He can't move a muscle without caring for his ward. This is only a phase. He will sever ties with the obnoxious ex-wife and come back to claim me, exactly as he did the first time.*

But as the days turned into weeks and then months, reality began to settle, burdening me. Each passing day without him chipped away at the façade I had built, revealing the cracks beneath. I clung to the fantasy, but a small voice whispered that it was time to let go.

This conflict reminded me of the battle between refusing to let go and embracing my new life. I wasn't ready to face the truth—to acknowledge that he might never come back. Admitting that seemed as though it would mean losing him all over again.

I lay in bed staring at the ceiling—the emptiness of the room reflecting the destitution inside me. This avoidance of reality couldn't last forever, but I wasn't ready to confront the pain beneath it. Not yet.

My mother had insisted I start therapy with Dr. Robbins—whose office is in Manhattan—and though the virtual sessions provided some relief, the void remained. The Cunningham family spared no expense, providing a private, high-tech virtual doctor's office with state-of-the-art equipment and privacy controls. Despite all of that, the therapy sessions couldn't alter the nihility inside.

My eyelids flutter open, and the line of midnight sun cuts through the curtains and casts a sharp beam across my face. It feels like a blade and I wince, closing my eyes then opening them again. I'm still in my work clothes, and the NASA meeting is now a distant memory—its success hollow without Matthew.

Tears sting my eyes but I squeeze them shut, willing the tears away. The fatigue in my body feels unbearable. Concentration is elusive—my thoughts drift during the most critical moments of my career.

A memory slides into my mind uninvited. His smile in Brooklyn Bridge Park, with the sunset casting hues of orange and pink across the sky. "I've got you, Alex. I'll take care of us," he said. It was so easy to believe, so easy to feel safe. Now that security is gone, replaced by a consuming ache.

I clutch the pillow—seeking comfort—but it's not enough. Part of me wants to reach out to him, to hear his voice, but Dr. Robbins' words echo. "Contact would prolong the pain." Yet the urge to check on him—to know if he's okay—pulls at me relentlessly.

What if he needs me too? What if the love we shared is still there, buried beneath the hurt and confusion? These questions ignite a flicker of hope amid the anger and defiance that I can't seem to shake. Another part of me is terrified he's moved on and left me behind in this liminal space.

His ex-wife's texts keep circling in my head. *What would I do if he's moved on with that whore?*

I can hear Dr. Robbins' advice echoing in my mind. I still struggle to suppress the desperate longing to dial his number, to break this deafening silence.

I know contacting him could unravel the fragile progress I've made, but the uncertainty around his well-being eats at me, leaving me unsettled—restless and adrift. *Oh, but excuse me, what 'progress' have you made? None.*

I'm caught between the fear of prolonging the pain and the overwhelming desire to hear him speak—to be reassured that he's okay—even if it comes at the cost of my own healing.

A painful sigh—stinging in the middle of my chest—escapes my lips as I stare at the ceiling while the unending daylight presses in on me. The success of the NASA meeting, the bright future of Project GreenWind, none of it matters if I can't find a way to fill my empty well. I take a deep breath, trying to calm myself. I need to focus, to keep moving forward, but the past clings to me like a constant shadow I cannot shake.

"Be happy, everything will follow," I whisper, the words a fragile mantra. Maybe—someday—I'll believe them again.

My thoughts are interrupted by a soft knock on the door. I don't respond, but the door opens anyway. Mom and Evie step inside, and their faces are lit by the soft glow of the sun.

"Alex, honey, the tailors are here to alter your dress for celebration night." Mom urges me. "Remember, we're celebrating? Two nights from now?"

Evie offers me a warm smile, gently coaxing me from my thoughts. "You've achieved so much with this project. It's time to celebrate."

I lift myself slowly, my frail body and psyche burdened by their expectations. The thought of celebrating feels foreign, almost impossible. But I nod, forcing a small smile. "Just give me a moment." My voice is barely above a whisper.

As they leave the room, I fill my lungs to capacity, trying to summon the energy to join their festive mood. The celebration may feel hollow, but I should do this as a show of respect for my colleagues, whom I have not treated well recently. Perhaps—surrounded by them and my family—I can find a flicker of the happiness I once knew.

CHAPTER FIVE

Matthew: Quiet Strength

PRESENT TIME

The subway ride home is short—just a few stops from Chelsea to Hamilton Heights. The usual mix of late evening commuters and city dwellers fills the car, and their quiet chatter and occasional laughter soothes my nerves.

As I walk toward the apartment, the city's familiar noise is a comforting backdrop. Three months of sobriety feels like a fragile peace. Anna already has my 30-day chip in her keyring. I gave her the 60-day chip next, but she—wanting to encourage me further—said she would wait for my 90-day chip. I have that now.

Tomorrow, I'll drill a hole in it before handing it over. I smile at the thought. She doesn't drink, and when we were together, I didn't either. Being with her helps me stay sober.

With? I shut my eyes. *Yes, we've become close.* We're living together—our relationship undefined but mutually beneficial. I support her as she grieves her dad's death, and she's embraced a simpler, more joyful life—walking away from her inheritance and the multi-million-dollar family business. If I influenced her decision to pursue happiness instead of worldly things, I'm not bothered—it's my rule, too—although I haven't been able to follow it myself since Alex left. *But I'm getting there. Hopefully.*

Anna and I provide each other emotional support and share rent, sex, and whatever else falls in between—intentionally leaving things undefined. *Wandering souls trying to heal.*

We've fallen into a routine mostly centered on our work and the apartment. She started as a receptionist and administrative assistant but quickly began handling IT tasks and using her programming skills. It's a far cry from her prior executive life, but she is thriving. She runs toward challenges and talks about them with the same intensity she brings to everything.

After my AA meetings, we go to the café and talk about everything—her work, mine, the music I transcribe as a freelancer, and my dinner sets at La Grand Élégance. It's a mix of moral support and lighthearted conversation, a welcome contrast to the heaviness we both carry.

At home, we've carved out spaces that reflect our needs. One living room corner is my practice space. A digital piano is hooked up to my laptop for easy transcription and arrangement. Sometimes I play for Anna while she relaxes on the sofa. Those moments remind me of Alex—her head on my lap as I played her favorite track on the piano she gifted me. I seal my eyelids shut tight and try to bury the hurt, and sometimes it becomes too much to handle. Then I look at Anna and take comfort in her presence—reminding myself that I'm not alone.

In the other corner of the living room, she has a workspace with dual monitors and docks for her freelance programming—a testament to her drive.

I've told her everything about Alex—the bond we had, her family, all the details of the breakup that were weighing on me. It was hard—each word tightened the ache in my chest—but Anna made it easier than I had expected. She listened with an open heart, offered neither judgment nor questions, and simply created space for me to speak at my own pace. As I talked, the burden lifted, and the release felt as rare as the relief I get in AA. With each story I shared, my chest felt lighter, as though I could finally take a real breath.

The freedom I felt afterward was unexpected—fresh energy surged through me. Whatever Anna and I have, it's stronger now—built on trust and vulnerability.

But there's one thing I kept hidden—Adam's murder. I couldn't share that with her, for her sake. Still, with that secret buried, the freedom I feel from revealing everything else remains.

Sometimes when I'm in the apartment, I stare at nothing, and the familiar heaviness in my chest returns as memories and unanswered questions swirl. In those moments, Anna instinctively nestles closer, as if trying to shoulder some of that weight. Other times, she quietly guides me to rest my head on her lap, offering me the comfort of her presence without saying a word.

As we eat dinner, her eyes soften with understanding. "I'm proud of you, Matt," she says, tracing the outline of my 90-day chip with her fingers. There's a radiance in her eyes—something sharp—as though the sky has brightened when the clouds drift away. The conversation flows easily. She tells me about her workday, the usual office politics, and a tricky programming problem she solved for a freelancing gig. I share a bit about the meeting and my relief at having another twenty-four hours of sobriety under my belt.

Later, as we settle on the couch with her nestled against my chest and my arm around her, I think about how much has changed. I close my eyes for a moment, taking in the quiet hum of the air-conditioning unit and the feelings of fondness and strength. I drift into the past...

LATE NOVEMBER LAST YEAR
SEVERAL HOURS AFTER THE BREAKUP

The rickety air conditioner growled, erratically spewing out warm air. Its temperature control knob was missing, and the red numerical display flashed some unreadable number. It was cold inside the room, forcing me to wear my heavy jacket as I lay on the damp, stale bed. There were only two lights in that poor excuse of a motel room—a dim one above me and another in the bathroom. Flickering neon lighting from the broken vacancy sign filtered faintly through the flimsy curtain. The air felt humid as I breathed in and out heavily. A stench from the bathroom hung in the thick air. I wondered if it had been cleaned before the uncaring receptionist gave me the room key without a keyring.

Still paralyzed, I tried to understand. *What happened? Did I really leave the penthouse after Alex ended things?* Only the repulsive sensory awareness of this motel room told me I was not in the bedroom of the penthouse where she had said the words that had stopped my heart: "Goodbye, Matthew." The tingling sensation in my chest wouldn't stop, and a heavy weight lodged in my chest—there to stay for a long while.

The flickering bulb above me became the only thing in my field of vision as I lay staring at the ceiling, unblinking. Beyond those two words, nothing lingered—just the repeated refrain. Eventually, the noisy air conditioner faded into a dull hum, leaving me in silence, still unable to process anything.

For two whole days I stayed like that—staring at nothing, waiting for my little girl to re-appear, to apologize, and to ask me to come home.

Hunger and fatigue finally pushed me out of bed. I wandered to the strip mall next door—lost—drawn to a liquor store with shelves of cheap bottles. I returned to the motel with a pint of bourbon, then resumed my position—eyes fixed on the ceiling, expression blank. On the third day I slept—thanks to the liquor.

Then the voices started.

"My precious girl is simply being a rebellious brat. But she loves me and will remember my lessons."

"She will return."

"My arms will always be open for her, ready to embrace her and hold her close."

"But I'll need to punish her, ensuring she won't repeat this mistake. She must never rebel against her daddy, who has given everything he has and is to her."

"She'll be here again. She just needs space to think and remember my guidance."

I only drank about a quarter of the bottle the night I bought it, but it put me to sleep. Gazing at what was left in the bottle, I began pacing—restless and uneasy. My stomach hardened and a painful tightness constricted my throat. I tried to take several deep breaths. My heartbeat slowed, and for a moment I considered calling emergency services. I slumped onto the bed, which made a cracking noise. My hand massaged my sternum, trying to assuage the growing pain. The voices crept in.

"No. The way she spoke to you was different. That was not your Alex."

"She wanted to hurt you. Your baby girl wouldn't."

"She was enraged and upset, but you tried to tell her you did nothing wrong."

"You didn't cross any lines. She refused to listen."

The pain surged sharply as the voices screamed, "She questioned your dynamic. She shouldn't be capable of that given the love, caring, nurturing, and protection you showered on her."

Then everything fell silent again, and moments later, I heard the muffled beats of my heart. The voices converged, taking a minatory tone. "You broke her, Matthew. She isn't coming back."

I spoke aloud for the first time since leaving the penthouse, my voice echoing to an empty wall, "Oh, Jesus." It felt as though God had completely turned His back on me.

I emptied the bottle and fell asleep an hour later. Thirst pulled me from sleep in the dead of night. I drank from the tap. Tossing and turning in bed, unable to sleep again, I landed on an idea—buy more liquor. *Instead of facing my problems.* The voices and chaotic thoughts left me unable to pinpoint what the problem was.

The next morning, the emptiness hit me in brutal, incessant waves. If my thoughts had been hollow the first two days, now they were a mess of fragmented memories—of Alex. While I was battling the never-ending pain of her loss, another image emerged from beneath the chaos: *Anna.*

I grabbed my phone and texted her to check in. She needed relief—as she was dealing with the loss of her dad, my friend—otherwise her mind would drift to dark places, something I couldn't allow. I was going to help her heal. She needed me. She texted back immediately, and a small smile crept across my face. Once I was sure she was okay, I went out for a burger and more liquor.

I lost track of time. A few days later I returned to work, but my off-work routine stayed the same for weeks—offering support to Anna during her grief while drowning myself in alcohol.

By the third week after Alex left, I was coming home regularly with a fifth of cheap liquor. I'd moved back to my cramped, rundown studio in the worst part of town—the same place I'd left when I moved in with Alex after my divorce. I couldn't afford to stay in the city, so I made the long commute to Manhattan. On my way back, I stopped at a corner liquor store in Jersey, near the studio.

Every night I replayed the past, starting with the first time I saw her at the gym and ending with the weekend she left me. I kept asking, *"Why? Why didn't you trust me, Alex?"*

That question turned to, *"Why me? Why am I suffering when everyone around me seems fine? Most people have someone, something. I have nothing. Why?"*

The anger and self-pity were toxic, constantly pushing me to numb the pain with more alcohol.

My routine shifted—no longer just buying liquor in Jersey, I started picking up a pint in the city. Soon I was taking gulps before boarding the ferry at Midtown Manhattan, then again on the walk to my studio—trying to shake the image of her penthouse as the ferry neared the Weehawken Terminal. Before entering my building, I'd stop for a fifth at the corner store.

Each night, the thoughts piled on.

Didn't I do enough to earn her trust?

Embracing her cost me everything—my teaching career, my calling.

What did I do wrong? What did I not do for her?

I even killed to keep her safe and avenge her. Fear gripped me every time I saw blue and red lights flashing.

I screamed into the pillow, drawing a couple of knocks from the guy next door. Meanwhile, the voices kept at it.

"Let her learn her lesson and come home to me."

"Nobody else can take care of her the way I did."

I texted Anna, ordering her to check in with me three times throughout the day rather than only in the evening. She agreed, adding a smiley face. I smiled and took a couple more gulps of the tasteless alcohol. As she managed her grief with my support, I set a detailed schedule on my phone, with reminders to regularly monitor aspects of her progress—therapy, meals, meditation, exercise, her return to work, family, home upkeep, and even her annual health checkup. *I got this for you, Anna. You're not alone.*

I didn't tell her about my breakup with Alex—I carried on as if everything remained normal for me. I was not planning to tell Anna at all. She eventually found out herself under the most miserable of circumstances.

A month later, I called Wyatt repeatedly until he answered with a sharp, "What?" I asked for help finding Alex. He sighed and said in a monotone, "She isn't in the country, and I won't tell you where she is. Stop calling me." He changed his number soon after.

That hit me like another stab in my already tattered chest. I sent more texts to her disconnected phone—longer ones explaining my actions. I called her phone over and over. I spent nights staring at my phone, waiting for a message, a call, anything. My inebriated mind tricked me into believing she'd walk through the door and apologize for her mistake. Each day of silence felt like a punch in the gut—a reminder that she was really gone. I kept sending messages and leaving voicemails she'd never listen to.

Every recorded message carried multiple mentions of, "I love you, Alex."

It took a miracle of willpower and a drowsy drift into intoxicated sleep to keep me from throwing my phone at the wall. The silence every morning was maddening. Frustration drove me to drink more, each unanswered message another reason to numb the pain. In due course, my tolerance for liquor increased, which led me to drink even more.

I began talking loudly—frustration and animosity spilling over—convincing myself that I hadn't done enough and that I wasn't good enough for her. My lowly job, nonexistent financial status, and current social standing didn't meet her expectations. Even my parents weren't spared. I blamed them for not creating a support system around me and for leaving me to grow up alone. I even held myself responsible for Anna's dad's heart failure.

I screamed at an imaginary Alex, "I'm your daddy. Why didn't you trust me?"

Heat flushed through my body. My heart pounded and my muscles quivered as I scolded her, "You brat, you rebellious little brat."

At the end of the year, a month after she had left, I set out to find answers. It was the week following Christmas, and the holiday crowds deepened my frustration. I visited the places she and I had frequented, hoping for a glimpse of her—the gym where it all began, the coffeehouse where we first connected, and the French restaurant where we had our first unofficial date. Each place now felt tainted by loss. In the city, I stood outside the restaurant where we had had our first official date, then walked along Fifth Ave—retracing the steps from that evening. Outside the French bookstore, I lingered, recalling her excitement on her first shopping trip there.

The holiday cheer around me only deepened my self-pity. Everyone seemed happy while my life lay in ruins. I couldn't afford to go inside the restaurants, so I stood outside—watching the patrons, hoping to see her face. When I didn't, my frustration grew.

I also sought answers from God in the night's stillness, but the heavens remained silent. My prayers went unanswered. The drinking worsened—my nights lost in a haze of alcohol.

Everything eventually turned inward. There was nobody else to blame. That deepened my dependence on liquor, which had become my crutch—a necessity, a friend I was desperate to return to at the end of each workday. It was my refuge.

After the New Year, Anna called, her voice brimming with excitement. I listened to her plans to forgo her inheritance and her share in the family business. At first, I thought it was a reaction to her grief, but it became clear her decision was based on careful consideration. She offered logical reasoning—answering questions I hadn't voiced but had silently wondered. Her plans centered on finding happiness and maintaining it. She said her dad would want that, and I agreed. She had this adorable habit of writing out scenarios and plans in a notebook, which she promised to show me later.

Be happy, everything will follow. I felt guilty for abandoning my own mantra, which was now buried under a mountain of grief with little chance of ever unearthing the essential drive that sustained me for forty years. *Maybe Anna will help me regain that.*

41

I commended her for showing strength and clarity. Stabbing pain pierced every part of my body and inward fury welled up all over again. *Why couldn't I be more like her?* I pointed out some immediate next tasks to get her started on her new life and assured her of my support every step of the way. She listened to me intently without saying a word, as if I were the authority on happiness. We ended the call expressing confidence and enthusiasm about the next phase of her future post her dad's passing.

I could learn from the strength she's built. I threw my phone to the floor and reached for the vodka bottle. Anger and self-pity drowned me further.

I resolved to be her strength—guiding her as she untangled her inheritance and business ties and helping her settle down in a peaceful, joyful life. My goal was simple: do that for Anna, then I could win Alex back. I would show her how my support helped Anna get over her torment and focus on the next stage of her journey. Alex would see the emotional care I gave Anna—navigating the tragedies that had hit her hard—to help her take on a new, fulfilling life overflowing with happiness.

While my drinking and self-loathing worsened, I still shaved, put on clean clothes, and met Anna to help her with things she needed. I hadn't seen her since the divorce. Following a few tears and a hug, she asked me to accompany her to a job interview. She landed the job the same afternoon. During the following two weeks, we searched for apartments in Hamilton Heights and eventually found the place we now call home. She had never established a home on her own, and I helped her with that as well.

There was something strange going on, but I didn't question it because it brought me comfort. Though she made no physical advances, her suggestive texts never stopped. I started looking forward to them, eager to respond. My physical needs—compounded by alcohol—took over. Sexual urges became hard to control. Save for a few fleeting moments during my twenties, I had never resorted to masturbation—never needed it. But I realized I had proven Alex right. Despite not texting Anna anything suggestive, my lack of control felt like a betrayal. I raged and cursed myself for my weakness. I punched a hole in the drywall and kept drinking.

I should have caught the red flag that would eventually destroy me, but in the haze of thoughts surrounding Alex—muddled by intoxication—I didn't. I started drinking during the workday. Hiding in the restrooms of the recording studio or behind trash dumpsters in the alleys of Chelsea, I downed shots of alcohol throughout the day. This was the next phase for me.

I remained firm in my decision to be there for Anna as long as she needed me, convinced that helping her rebuild her life would bring Alex back. Meanwhile, my respect, admiration, and cheer for Anna grew as I watched her take on her new challenges with the grace and sophistication that define her.

PRESENT TIME

Anna's head of smooth, silky hair slides down my chest and falls onto my lap, shaking me back to the present. Under the dim, warm lights, I watch her body rise and fall with each restful breath, and my heart slows down to match hers. In a gentle motion so as not to wake her, I get off the sofa and lift her in my arms.

Lying on the bed, I pull her close, gripping her a little too hard. My trip down memory lane unearthed some dark, dangerous ideas and moods. With effort, I redirect my senses to the present. If I don't keep going forward, I'll plummet down to unimaginable depths, undoing everything we've worked for. Anna shifts, settling into a comfortable position in my arms. I heave a silent sigh and the storm within me calms, if only for a moment.

The path ahead is still uncertain, filled with the daily battles of sobriety and the ghosts of the past. But with her here, I find a glimmer of hope in the darkness—a reminder that I don't have to face it alone.

Prior to the breakup I seldom worried. But now fear has become a demon lurking inside me—one I desperately need to exorcise. I'm not only afraid of what I'll become if I drink again. I'm also terrified of not being able to function without Anna. I still carry a sliver of hope that Alex will return—an obsession that once blocked everything else. Anna knows this, and she stays by my side. As strong as I am physically, I need mental support—an anchor to help me regain the Matthew I know. That foundational system revolves around Anna.

Since that fateful night in jail, I have many things to be thankful for—my music, my jobs, a comfortable place to live, a strong body, and the privilege of living in this beautiful city. But above all, I am thankful for Anna. She was there when I hit rock bottom, laying on the floor of a jail cell, discarded like trash—and she picked me up and helped me recover.

I hate feeling completely reliant on her. I've thought about walking away from this situation, but then I recall the dark abyss I fell into—if I leave, that's where I'll land. I know I will return to who I was before, so in this moment, I need her.

CHAPTER SIX

Anna: You and I

PRESENT TIME

I wake to the soft beep of my alarm at 6 AM. The apartment is quiet except for Matt's routine. He wakes at 5:30, always gentle with the door. Morning light filters through the curtains, warming my face, and I smile. No matter how tired I am, sleeping in his embrace fills me with energy that makes every morning a joy to greet. I savor the feeling for a moment, but today there's no time. Midweek at the LLP is always the busiest, so I rush to get ready.

He finds joy in his morning routine—making sure I'm prepared for the day ahead. He calls what we have "undefined," but I know better. *We're a couple again.* Emotional support, sex, sharing rent—this is what couples do. He's delusional or in denial if he thinks otherwise. We do more than that, too. We shop, run, grab coffee, and occasionally have dinner out—though we can't afford it often. I'm waiting for him to lower his shield and see what we share for what it is.

I've always been patient, calculated, and deliberate. Delays don't deter me. Soon enough, he'll realize he's all mine.

He communicates more through actions than words, and after a passionate kiss, he serves me breakfast, packs my coffee, and offers words of encouragement. He kisses my cheek, compliments my outfit, and tells me I'm beautiful. *That's some shield you've got, babe.*

Maybe he's working through his emotions and struggling with the idea of replacing Alex with me. That doesn't bother me—it's what I want, and it'll be permanent. I'm getting there. He's heading there too, even if he doesn't see it yet.

The subway is packed, and the usual delays make it worse. I stand gripping the rail with my other hand resting on my bag. His 90-day sobriety chip dangles from my fingers, catching the light. It's a small token, but it's ours—his journey, my role. I smile as warmth floods through me.

The train is filled with families; a few parents with young children. I spot a cute family—a mom, two little girls, and a dad. I make a funny face at one girl, and she laughs. Her mom smiles, then turns back to argue with her husband. I watch them for a moment, and my mind drifts—to a past that still feels fresh, the hurt stinging just as it did then...

We got divorced last year, about eleven months ago. Two weeks later, my dad died. But my journey through grief didn't begin with his death. It started a year before that, when Matt stopped talking to me.

I know I betrayed him by hiding my decision not to have children. It's something I prepared myself to live with as I pursued him, because I was irrevocably in love with him. I also had hope that he might change his view on wanting a family and align with my way of thinking. He embodied everything I dreamed of in a man when I was young—handsome, caring, confident, commanding. He saw me for who I was, beyond the sophistication and business acumen. Convinced he was the one for me, I lost my virginity to him.

Yes, I betrayed him. But when he refused to talk to me once I told him of my decision, that felt like a betrayal as well—like he had discarded me. I understand why he stopped talking—he respects a woman's choice, and he didn't want to discuss it further. He was upset, but he won't cross that line. I respect him for that, and it makes me fall for him a little more every time I reflect on it. *But was there really no other option? Why didn't he let me share my vision for our life? Couldn't we have discussed the future I imagined, where it's only the two of us in a world built on mutual understanding?*

I convinced myself he would eventually talk to me, that I needed to give him some space to think and gather his thoughts. *He loves me. He wouldn't leave me.*

I felt the sting of self-loathing and the heavy burden of being judged. Guilt made it impossible to focus on anything else. I retreated inward—withdrawing from all the things that connected me to the world—and I searched for any sign that he might be reconsidering. I went through the motions at work, but he consumed my thoughts. The longer he stayed silent, the more paranoid I became—convinced that he resented me, that he hated me.

He didn't leave the house. He stuck around. His silence was both a cruel hope and a torturous presence. There were moments when we almost spoke—our eyes would meet, we'd step closer, but then he'd turn away. The guilt, the hope, and the fear of losing him tore at me.

I blamed him for not letting me share the future I dreamed of, but deep down, I knew that wasn't fair. Before our marriage started falling apart, I had tried to share my vision, but it never felt right. It was the fear that kept me from telling him. I'd hidden my choice, terrified it would shatter everything. Each moment of hiding felt like an unraveling, but I couldn't risk losing him. I told myself I was hiding the truth for the sake of my love for him.

As he talked more about starting a family, I realized I was lying to him by omission. I clung to the fragile hope that something would shift, that I could guide him toward the future I envisioned.

My dream was to travel the world with the love of my life. The world itself would be our home. We'd take simple jobs, explore new places, and make love in the most romantic cities. My inheritance would fund it all.

I'd planned this from a young age. I didn't want children—the thought terrified me, and I wanted to preserve my body, which I treated like a temple. My dream was simple: to live with the man I love, no permanent home—just us. Not even my dad knew about this decision. And then I met Matt, two years after graduating from Yale.

After he stopped talking, I sent him voicemails, texts, and emails—apologies and declarations of love explaining why I had hidden my choice from him—all in a desperate attempt to reach him. He stopped reading my texts and emails.

His silent rejection of me was the first of many tragedies, a self-inflicted one. And with each passing day the life I imagined slipped further from reach—a dream broken.

I held him responsible for everything that had fallen apart. His silence made it easy to blame him.

I confided in my dad, who had started to notice the growing distance between Matt and me. My dad was my pillar of strength and the person I turned to with all my problems. I shared everything with him, and he held me close—offering comfort without judgment. With a heavy heart, he did his best to console me and lift my spirits, even shedding tears with me. Most nights, I fell asleep on his lap after crying—guilt destroying me for pulling him into the chaos I had created out of selfishness. But he never wavered in his unconditional support.

CHAPTER SEVEN

Anna: You and Alex

PRESENT TIME

The adorable family of four disembarks at Chelsea with me, their earlier argument having morphed into a cheery exchange as the couple guide their children out of the station.

I arrive at Hudson & Greene LLP, by 8 AM greeting my fellow receptionist with a smile. The office buzzes with early birds already hard at work. My workday begins with a barrage of emails and back-to-back meetings. I dive into transcribing the minutes of an early session, a tedious process that demands my full attention. As the conversation between the firm's lawyers and a female client unfolds, the topic of divorce stirs a bittersweet feeling. A small, involuntary smile tugs at my lips, but I quickly mask it. The mention of surveillance strikes a nerve, and I falter—briefly losing track of the discussion.

During a break, I refill the woman's coffee cup and offer her a half smile. She meets my eyes with a teary gaze and returns the smile. I hand her a box of tissues, then quietly close the door to the conference room to give her a moment of privacy, while I wait outside for the lawyers to return from a counsel-only huddle. Whether it's driven by a cold familiarity with what the client is going through or something else, I don't know. But the memories resurface—each one more painful than the last—as I slip back to that time, reliving it all over again...

Last January, six months after we had stopped talking, I noticed Matt was coming home later than usual. At first, I saw him in his gym clothes and assumed he had joined a fitness club. I was happy for him, thinking it might be a positive outlet. But it didn't take long for the unease to settle in. Since he had stopped using the gym at the house and the late nights had grown more frequent, a question gnawed at me: *Is he creeping closer to leaving me and abandoning the home we share?*

A few weeks passed, and he was coming home even later—often around half past nine. I mentally mapped out his day, accounting for his school and private classes and his new gym routine. But even with all that, there was still a gap—at least two hours of unaccounted-for time. Initially I brushed it off. But as the late nights continued, my unease grew until it became unbearable.

Hiring a private investigator to trail Matt was an agonizing decision. I kept it from my dad, not wanting to add to his growing health concerns. The guilt of not involving him tore at me, but there was no evidence of infidelity yet.

Ten days later, the PI delivered a report with photos and videos of Alex—at the gym, a coffeehouse, and dining with him. The proof was undeniable. A sharp, searing pain shot through my chest, and I struggled to hold back the tears burning my eyes. It was real now—he had replaced me with someone younger, someone who—it seemed—could give him everything he wanted.

My hands trembled as I gripped the edge of the table. My throat felt tight—each breath a struggle, as if the air itself had turned against me. I forced myself to thank the PI in a brittle voice and asked him to leave. Once alone, I collapsed onto the couch, clutching the stack of evidence as if it could somehow contain the storm raging inside me.

The night became a blur as I pored over the images and obsessed over every detail—her delicate hand on his arm, the way he leaned in, the way they followed each other around, him whispering in her ear, the soft smiles he gave her. My stomach churned and a hollow ache settled in my core. This wasn't just physical closeness—their intimacy was palpable, intense. She appeared to experience him in a dreamlike way that I had never felt.

She couldn't compare to me in beauty, grace, or accomplishments. I may not have been a child prodigy, but I went to Yale. Our family business may not have global operations, but Hunter-Ren leads the world in biomedical engineering. We were on our way to entering the pharmaceutical industry, and that would put us firmly in the billionaire league. It wasn't the details that bothered me—it was the intimacy of it all. He must have seen the future he envisioned—a family, a perfect life. She was everything I couldn't be.

Children and family. That's why I didn't confront him. It would've blown back in my face, bringing up the one thing that separated us—my decision not to have children. *No, I needed to play this strategically.* I planned to anonymously deliver the surveillance records to her father and strike her where it would hurt most—her business empire. I waited. If I confronted Matt, he would leave immediately, and I wasn't ready for that.

I kept hoping it was just a phase—a midlife crisis as he hit his forties. Surely, he would snap out of it. He was stronger than this—the strongest man I'd ever known.

When he didn't come home one night, it felt like my heart was being ripped from my chest and crushed underfoot. The hours dragged by—each tick of the clock a reminder of his absence. Sleep eluded me. I was haunted by images of them together, and the fear of losing him ate away at me. The emptiness of the house swallowed me whole.

The next day, he came home late, and the flicker of relief I felt vanished the moment I saw the cold, distant look in his eyes—something unfamiliar. As he passed me, a faint scent of perfume lingered on his clothes—a scent that wasn't mine.

I grabbed his shirt from the laundry basket and pressed it to my face. The smells of sex and Alex clung to the fabric. The blow stole the air from my lungs in a strangled sob. Tears streamed down my face, scorching paths of betrayal.

I collapsed on the floor clutching his shirt, as my body was wracked with uncontrollable sobs. My guttural cries echoed through the house—a desperate plea for the pain to stop. My chest heaved as I rocked back and forth, and the world blurred around me.

The salty taste of tears and the overwhelming scent of betrayal consumed me. My tears soaked his shirt, mingling with the evidence of his infidelity. The image of them together replayed in my mind, relentless.

As my sobs softened, I lay there broken. The love we had shared, the dreams we had built, crumbled around me. He was slipping away, and there was nothing I could do to stop it.

I was consumed by an overwhelming urge to strangle her. The temptation to hand the surveillance records to her father—to ruin her legacy—was almost irresistible. The PI promised to get more damning visuals from her penthouse. I waited, seething.

This discovery couldn't have come at a worse time. My dad, brother, and I were about to fly to the UK to finalize a crucial merger for Hunter-Ren—our first major step into pharmaceuticals. Dad thought the trip would be an escape, unaware that my world had already spiraled beyond control.

Our hearts shattered when divorce papers hit my desk on Monday morning, just as we were preparing to leave. My dad collapsed into a chair—pale and drawn—while my brother and I struggled to comfort him. The entire experience drained me. My brother assured us he could handle the merger, but we still had to go. We left for the UK with everything in shambles, as Dad's health worsened with every passing hour.

The cruel irony was that we were headed to clinch a merger on the same day my marriage crashed and burned.

Matt sent two emails: the first politely asking if I needed any further specifics, and the second urging me to sign the papers to bring our marriage to an end without conflict. *The audacity he had, to come to me with that request after cheating on me with an eighteen-year-old.* My blood boiled as I fired off a response, telling him I'd sign but that he was making a mistake.

A few days later, resentment ate at me for not having put up a fight. I wrote to him again, asking him to be fair and give me a chance to explain the life I had envisioned for the two of us. I didn't tell him I knew he had slept with Alex.

Deep down, I knew he had crossed a line that couldn't be uncrossed. He's not the kind of man to turn back—he would move on with confidence.

From me.

The evening after I returned to Manhattan, I spoke to him for what I feared would be the last time. I saw a man transformed—calm, composed, at peace—just like I used to know him. He wasn't angry. In fact, he empathized with me. That infuriated me beyond words. I mentioned her name and asked him if he was leaving me for her. He calmly reminded me of why he and I had separated. He remained unshaken, simply expressing a hope that I would heal and move on too. I cursed them both before storming away.

The divorce meetings were mere formalities—a process during which my heartbroken family and I huddled together while the lawyers handled the fine points.

Retreating to my room, I started to plot ways to eliminate her while the discussions continued.

My dad and the lawyers met with Matt's lawyers to finalize the details. I had signed what I needed to, but the thought of surrendering the surveillance records gnawed at me. I had planned to use them to destroy her, to taint her business empire and show the world what she was—a whore and a home-destroyer. But my dad, with the wisdom he always imparted, urged me to let go.

He quoted a Chinese proverb he lived by, "Repay resentment with kindness." He told me that to heal we needed to abandon hate, not nurture it. Reluctantly, I listened—because my dad always knew best.

Yet deep down, I couldn't let go. I resolved to keep an eye on Alex and Matt—to monitor them after the divorce once the dust had settled. They would slip, and when they did, I would be ready. Like a tiger lying in wait, I would pounce and reclaim what was mine.

On the day of the divorce, as I stood in the courtroom, all I could see were vivid images of Alex and him together, tangled in bedsheets. The judge banged the gavel. As I walked down the steps of the courthouse, anger surged within me. I cursed Matt to a long, painful death from an incurable disease and fled the court of torture.

CHAPTER EIGHT

Anna: You, Me, and Happiness

PRESENT TIME

The firm's meetings stretch far beyond the scheduled time, interrupted by breaks and hushed sidebar exchanges. I'm kept occupied well into the afternoon, when the grueling formality of divorce negotiations finally comes to an exhausting end, leaving a heaviness in the air.

I can't understand why, but the wealthy client pulls me close in a tight embrace after she shakes hands with the firm's lawyers. Maybe because I was the only other woman in the room, transcribing the meeting and helping with the documentation. Maybe because our eyes locked during certain moments of the meeting. I return her embrace and offer my best wishes—a quiet thrill running through me as her features relax in peace.

Before tackling my next task, I take a moment to check in with Matt. My lips curve when I notice his message.

Matt

Just wanted to say I'm thinking of you.

Anna

You have to explain that in more detail tonight. Or better yet, show me.

Text by text, touch by touch, moment by moment, I'm drawing closer to reclaiming him. There could be no sweeter taste than success—or revenge.

In my case, they are the same.

I spend the afternoon resolving a technology issue for a lawyer. He needs a specific report for a case, which involves some data mining and programming—nothing too complicated. I jump in immediately, settling into a quiet space. As my fingers drum out lines of code, my mind drifts to the sweet taste of revenge and success. I don't like what I did, but I did what was necessary to reclaim Matt. This time, the past comes rushing back—not just the pain and hurt, but also the sharp thrill, the fleeting happiness, and the stubborn hope that once burned through it all...

Little did I know losing Dad would open a door for me to get Matt back. Dad had gifted me with this chance, surrendering his own existence. Throughout his years, he constantly showered me with gifts, and he remained true to this when he passed.

On the evening of my divorce, my dad started having chest pains and palpitations. We rushed him to the emergency room, and he was immediately admitted to the hospital. He needed an operation to stabilize his heart. Initially, he showed signs of recovery, and we all had hope. Two weeks later, his heart failed again, and despite their efforts, the doctors couldn't save him.

I stood by his lifeless body—numb and silent—unable to process the reality of my loss.

Tears didn't cascade in a relentless, abyssal torrent until the funeral.

In the days leading up to it, I moved in a fog—sleepwalking, numb to the world around me. It wasn't until I stood at the cemetery surrounded by people I barely recognized that reality hit. The sight of the coffin, the droning of the priest's voice, the rhythmic murmurs of prayers—it all served as a haunting confirmation that he was truly gone. The rituals—the lowering of the casket, the faint smell of earth—were the final, undeniable proofs. My chest heaved, and grief tightened like a vise as I realized this was it. My dad's absence wasn't a nightmare I could wake from, but a cold, inescapable truth.

The sight of the wooden box descending into the earth broke something deep inside me. Tears streamed down my face and my body shook with the force of my sobs. It felt as if a crushing burden was pressed against my chest, making each breath shallow and painful. Each tear bore the memories of Dad's constant presence in my days—from when I was a child, until his last moments. As the dirt covered his coffin, I fell to my knees. My cries echoed in the silence of the cemetery, and my cornerstone shattered with each handful of soil that buried him.

He had been my rock, my confidant, and my guiding star. From childhood, we had shared an unbreakable bond—forged through countless late-night conversations and moments of quiet understanding. He was always there helping with homework, cheering me on at gymnastic meets, or simply sitting in comfortable silence as we watched the stars. His calm presence and steady support had shaped who I am today.

The week following his death was a disorienting journey. The days blurred in numbness and pain, and his absence hung over me with an unbearable heaviness. I moved in a daze—unable to find solace or comfort. The world had become hollow, with each passing second a stark reminder of the gaping void left by his passing. My heart throbbed painfully.

Another week later, I entered Dad's office in my childhood home. On the wall hung a beautifully calligraphed scroll bearing a proverb on friendship: "With loyal friends, even water shared shoulder to shoulder becomes sweet." I was reminded of his friendship with Matt. My brothers had adamantly opposed inviting him to the funeral, and it hit me—he wasn't even aware of my loss or his.

Before my marriage had fallen apart, he and my dad were close. I cherished having the two most important men in my life united by friendship. Their bright faces, joyful laughter, and hilarious conversations made me feel blessed in ways too overwhelming to bear.

My hatred for Alex is limitless, but that feeling never extended to Matt. I will never hate him. Despite everything, I had a duty to inform him of my dad's death and that the funeral had already taken place, so I sent him a text. Unbeknownst to me, I was taking the first step toward getting him back.

Hugs, consolations, comfort food, friends, family—none of it brought me any comfort. But his texts did. His words enveloped me in care and attention. I clung to him as though he were the only thing keeping me from drowning.

Neither my mother nor my brothers truly grasped the depth of my bond with my dad, or how profoundly his passing affected me—only Matt.

As I faced the next tragedy—my mother's mental decline and the doctor's recommendation of institutional care—he was there, supporting me with his texts. I relied on his steady reassurance as I navigated the paperwork, the endless formalities, and the heart-wrenching farewell to a mother who could no longer return my love.

Most of our business enterprises are headquartered on the West Coast, where my brothers manage operations. Mom, Dad and I had stayed in the New York City area to be closer to the financial and healthcare organizations on the East Coast. My brothers lingered for a while after the funeral, but they had their own lives, families, and children to return to. They endeavored to help me heal—putting forth their best efforts—but their presence only deepened my longing for Dad.

With Matt, it was different. I saw in him my dad following his passing. When we were married, he had taken care of me in the same way my dad did. He was the embodiment of my dad's love and more. Every morning had brought a sense of fulfillment and good fortune, knowing that these two incredible men were part of my life.

And now both were gone.

That realization unleashed fresh waves of guilt that tore through me un-hindered. My decision to hide the truth from Matt had ultimately proved catastrophic. Not just for me, but for everyone around me. It had led to him drifting away to Alex, the divorce, my dad's heart problems, and eventually his death. This guilt wasn't something I could shake off. It was something I'd have to learn to live with. I blamed myself for losing my dad—the anger inside me was too intense to direct anywhere else.

I poured all of this out to Matt in the texts we exchanged. He comforted me before gently reminding me to focus on the future.

Matt

> *Build monuments of memories to treasure and cherish.*
> *But look to the future, forward, always.*

My therapist alluded that I was trying to avoid facing my devastating loss by clinging to Matt, but he was helping me heal. Sessions with her left me convinced that everything wrong in my world was my own doing. I couldn't deny it, but acceptance didn't bring any relief, either. As I explored my past with her, it became clear that all the tragedies—my divorce, my dad's death, my mother's institutionalization—seemed to be on my shoulders alone.

I slipped into a routine where, once every therapy session concluded, I'd remain bedridden for several days.

Matt guided me gently away from the past—his affection a reminder that the future still held hope. It was something in the way he used the word *we*. He never said, "You should move forward." He said, "We," without exception. It reminded me so much of how my dad used to talk to me. In his honeyed voice, my dad would say, "Let's tackle this math test, my peanut." Although he intended for me to solve it on my own. He would sit with me—nudging me forward—and step in only when the pressure of the coursework threatened to overwhelm.

We can do this. I am with you.

Anna, treasure your memories. But let's keep moving forward. Memories can power us.

I need you to call me whenever those thoughts creep in.

So I kept texting. I kept the bond alive—vibrant and sustaining. By the fourth month we had graduated to talking. His words became the pulse in my veins—the very breath that sustained me through my darkest moments. I had never stopped loving him, and now my feelings for him only grew stronger.

My suggestive texts were a balm to my soul. The intimate language wrapped around me, making it feel as if he were there—right beside me—as if he belonged solely to me. It was as if he lingered around the house constantly, with each hour marked by the need to read his messages again and again.

What began as a desperate cry for attachment and intimacy—driven by an emotional need to feel loved and desired—soon morphed into something far more purposeful: *my master plan to win him back*. Alex faded into the background—a fleeting concern. My entire focus sharpened in on how I could reclaim him.

I never lost faith that their relationship would fail. The age difference, her status—too many factors weighed against them. At the time, I didn't know about their father figure/ward dynamic, but she was a volatile eighteen-year-old—bound to self-destruct and tear their relationship apart.

I continued texting and talking to him, inching closer to his heart piece by piece. My plan was in motion and there was no room for doubt. I was all in. And Alex? She no longer mattered.

My focus narrowed—every thought and every action aimed at perfecting my strategy. I dissected our communications, honing in on the smallest details and adjusting my approach to draw him back in. Precision was key—slow, patient, deliberate execution.

I was like a predator—waiting, watching, and ready to strike with cold calculation. Hour by hour, I perfected the art of pulling him back to me.

He—and the life we could have—was all that mattered.

PRESENT TIME

Occasionally, Matt surprises me by getting to the apartment early. He'll take the evening off from his dinner set at La Grand by asking a fellow musician who could use the extra money to cover for him. The subbing musicians are violinists or cellists—never another pianist. La Grand and their clientèle adore Matt, and they frown upon a substitute at the piano. The manager has assured him of a raise in the next cycle.

Tonight, the inviting aromas of dinner hit me as I walk in, and a smile spreads across my face. While he kisses me, his hands slowly undress me, and the moment stretches, deliberate, like we have all the time in the world. Then he massages me in the bedroom under soft lighting, with the comforting scents of white lotus, jasmine, osmanthus, and oolong tea candles filling the air. His hands—strong and sure—work their magic, easing tension from my body and mind. His words are soothing, but it's his touch—constant, affectionate—that truly melts away my stress.

"Relax, Anna...let me take care of you," he murmurs, and his deep voice sends a shiver through me. That and his touch draw soft moans from me as dull aches give way to pleasure. It's arousing and heartwarming, and I feel weightless. My thoughts drift, replaced by a blissful escape as I sink further into his care.

"You fill me with life...let my hands show you what that means," he says, his words benevolent yet powerful. They linger in the air and leave me wanting more.

I open my eyes with effort, drawn to the vision of him as he moves about the room. He's in shorts and an athletic T-shirt that clings to the sculpted muscles of his six-foot-seven frame. Despite our demanding work schedules, he stays in incredible shape. He does body weight exercises at night—countless push-ups, sometimes with me on his back in playful moments—and on some evenings and weekend mornings we run together through the neighborhood.

My heavy eyelids start to close again as the pleasure from his hands lulls me into a haze. I steal one last glance at his massive forearms and powerful hands as they return to me, ready to deliver the final strokes of relief to my aching muscles.

Afterward, he lets me rest while he draws a hot bath and finishes preparing dinner. Gently—as if I weigh nothing—he lifts me and places me in the tub, bringing the candles along. I soak in the warmth, basking in the pleasure of his care. With my eyes half closed, I watch him—gratitude and desire mingling in my gaze. He smirks and leaves me to enjoy my bath in peace.

He understands my decision to leave behind luxury and my elite circles. He respects my goals and my desire for simplicity, and he fully supports me. But more than that, he cares for me in a way I haven't felt in a long time.

CHAPTER NINE

Alex: A Night of Recognition

PRESENT TIME
EVENING OF THE DAY OF MEETING WITH NASA

The luxurious condominium buzzes with activity as Mom and Evie help me get ready for the celebration, while Ted occasionally reminds us to hurry. Losing her patience with him, Evie shuts the door on him and locks it. "Now, where were we?" She claps her hand thrice and smiles.

Mom fusses over my dress—a sleek black gown that complements the richness and charm of the evening—but I don't care. Evie adjusts my jewelry, making sure everything is perfect.

"Alex, you look stunning," Evie says with a smile and steps back to admire her handiwork.

I glance at my reflection in the mirror, barely recognizing the person staring at me. A pang of anxiety hits me, reminding me of how different my life has become since leaving Manhattan and Matthew.

Mom places a reassuring hand on my shoulder. "You deserve this celebration, honey. We're all so proud of you."

I wish my daddy was here. He would stand by my side, clapping and congratulating me till I am red in the face.

I am filled with nervous apprehension on the drive to Norrsken Plaza. My father flew in from Manhattan for the event, and my other brothers, sisters-in-law, and Lillian will join via video call. The thought of facing them all at once is daunting.

What was initially planned as a few months away from the country has stretched beyond six. Neither my family nor Dr. Robbins have opened the topic of my return to Manhattan. They just support me, even though a large part of my anger is directed at them. I can't explain it—it's simply my instinctive response to them. I have lost the ability to reason and analyze nonacademic, nonprofessional issues.

I am—and always have been—afraid of what awaits me at home. *What if Matthew has written me off as a foolish brat, never to forgive me? Why am I thinking of him when I should hate him and move on?* The more I fixate on him, the more my heart fears my family will also reject me. The dread of self-conflict and the slow-burning fear of failure wrap around me like a prickly blanket, suffocating and relentless. When I try to process these feelings, all I see is chaos, which scares me even more and paralyzes me.

Without a clear plan for what to do if I return to Manhattan, I remain in Kiruna, retreating further into a fog that numbs everything. My family has been bolstering me. Their presence is a constant reminder that I'm not alone, yet I've never felt lonelier. Mom and Evie fly between Manhattan and here, balancing their professional commitments with being available to support me. One or both are invariably around. When they're here they work from their home offices in the condominium. Ted stayed with me for three months straight when we first arrived, and then he settled into a routine similar to Mom and Evie's.

As the SUV surges forward toward the venue where we will be celebrating Project GreenWind's recent successes, I recall how my work helped me survive the past...

Work became my refuge, a desperate attempt to erase Matthew from my thoughts. I poured every ounce of energy into Project GreenWind, working with my team to transform my visionary concept into a groundbreaking reality.

The first major milestone came last year—when I was still with him—when we patented our wind pattern predictor models, which are capable of analyzing wind dynamics, human migration trends, and urbanization patterns to identify optimal wind farm locations. I remember celebrating the achievement with him—his warmth and love made me feel invincible, even though he'd silently endured his own job loss that day. Now the memory is a cruel reminder of what I left behind.

Our models pinpointed ideal pilot sites in the United States and Sweden, setting the stage for the design phase. Tailored turbine designs and partnerships with local firms brought our vision to life. The pilot sites—constructed with Cunningham Energy's financial backing—embodied precision and innovation, from the blades' lightweight composites to the turbines' placement ensuring maximum energy capture.

Test runs exceeded expectations, generating 30–40% more energy than industry standards. The project's success garnered global attention, from government funding to NASA's involvement.

My family is celebrating these wins—but my heart is laden, tethered to the blissful life and fulfilling love I lost. Project GreenWind is all I have left, my lifeline in a sea of grief.

PRESENT TIME

As we arrive, the grandeur of Norrsken Plaza takes my breath away, distracting from my inner tumult. The towering glass doors, the grand foyer with its shimmering chandeliers, and the expansive event hall all exude an air of sophistication and celebration.

The hall is filled with familiar faces. My father greets me with a warm hug, and I give him a half smile. He reminds me of home—an environment of control and protocol—which triggers the familiar sensation that I'm slowly sinking into the ground.

The room is filled with Cunningham-Segal executives, Project GreenWind team members based in Kiruna, consultants, the secretary to the Swedish Ambassador, and representatives from the engineering firm building the pilot site in Sweden.

High-definition video monitors line the opulent walls, connecting us to family across the Atlantic. I raise my hand to wave at the screens, only to realize that I am not waving at all. I force a smile, struggling to show my teeth. They all wave energetically, and my sisters-in-law and Lillian blow kisses.

As I mingle and greet the guests, the project's recent success flickers in and out of my mind. I ought to take pride in what I've achieved—laying the groundwork for future successes—but instead I'm left empty. *Matthew's not here.* I am adrift and unmoored, as if I'm being tossed by gusts. There's a void where purpose should be, and the motivation that once fueled me is painfully absent. My accomplishments are unremarkable, and I'm undeserving of recognition or praise.

The longing to hear him praise and hold me furthers in stinging waves.

Mark Hannam is here. As he approaches me, Evie and Mom leave, as if on cue.

"Congratulations. You look gorgeous," he says as he fetches a flute of champagne and hands it to me. *Not how Matthew compliments me.*

He stands six feet tall, his lean and toned physique emphasized by his tailored suits. His twenty-four-year-old face with those confident blue eyes is chiseled and framed by short, jet-black hair. Despite his exterior, there's an approachable warmth in his smile.

We clink glasses and I ask, "Why're you always here?" *He is not.*

He sips his champagne, and a soft laugh escapes his lips. "I'm not. I visit now and then to see you, and I don't miss memorable occasions. Congratulations, Alex. Well done." *Not how Daddy praises me.*

The son of a longtime family friend, Mark keeps his promise and flies in from his London office to visit me, as he said. He is practically a member of the family, tasked with taking care of me. But I am just not letting him, my family, Dr. Robbins, or anyone do that.

Urged by Dr. Robbins and almost forced by my family, I tried dating him. Disastrous is a mild way to describe the dates. All my eyes saw was Matthew. My attention drifted whenever Mark spoke. He was kind, cutting the dates short and driving me home.

When he dropped me off the second night, I asked him to fuck me, hoping sex would fix all my problems. *It wasn't the first time I had had that idea—there was another incident in a whole different context soon after I arrived in Sweden, which turned out to be calamitous.* He gently pulled away, referencing my vulnerability and his desire to take things slow. I drifted off and walked to my room in a daze.

Once there, a surge of guilt overwhelmed me. Asking Mark to sleep with me was a betrayal to Matthew, and my self-loathing was unbearable. I hated myself even more, and my actions pressed down on me until it felt hard to breathe, hard to move.

As the evening progresses, my father takes the stage to make a speech. He boasts about my achievements and Project GreenWind, his words filled with pride and admiration.

"Alexandra, you've accomplished so much, and we are all incredibly proud of you," he says, his voice echoing through the hall. "I invite you to share a few words with us."

How long will you continue to parade me around, Father? Fair or not, these experiences remind me of my childhood and college years, when my father showcased me at gatherings and events without private words of praise.

The room falls silent as I hesitate—my internal struggles threatening to overwhelm me. I take a deep breath and step forward, feeling everyone's expectations.

"I...thank you," I begin, my voice subdued. "This project means a lot to me, and I couldn't have done it without all of your support."

My mind drifts again. Matthew's face lingers, and my thoughts inevitably return to him. I hear his words echo, "You are my world, Alex." I manage a small smile, and the memory gives me a sliver of strength.

The applause that follows is courteous, though I'm more relieved than gratified as I step aside, and the noise fades as I retreat from the spotlight. Celebrations continue around me, but my soul is tied to him and the doleful journey that brought me here.

The night draws to a close, and we return to the condo with my father. He has decided to spend the next day with us before flying back to Manhattan.

As I lie in bed, the fateful weekend when I broke up with Matthew replays relentlessly in my mind. The journal on my desk beckons, its pages as empty as my resolve. I briefly remember Dr. Robbins urging me to write something each day, *There is nothing to write.*

She said that active participation in events like the celebration tonight is a step towards healing and recovery, but the road ahead still feels interminably long and fraught with uncertainty. I'm not convinced I've made any progress.

CHAPTER TEN

Alex: Friends with Him

PRESENT TIME
MID JUNE

Two weeks have passed since the celebratory event, and I have settled into a monotonous routine that reflects the hollowness I feel. Most mornings, I rise late, dragging myself from the covers with just enough energy to get to the office. I pour all my effort into Project GreenWind and neglect other ongoing initiatives, business-as-usual tasks, and everyone else.

I often sit without working—staring at my laptop, lost in thought. At first, my colleagues attempted to engage me with small talk and questions about how I was settling into the new place. Soon, only Ted did so. Now, nobody does. I moved away from the project area to a corner room of another part of the floor.

Some days I robotically rise from my desk, pack my things, and ask my bodyguard Lars to take me home. Once in my condo, I ignore the concerned gestures and sweet words of my mom and Evie and go straight to my room. I curl up in a blanket with my heels still on and fall asleep.

I zap through designs and pseudocode for the next version of our wind pattern predictor models—the ones that analyze winds over oceans and large water bodies. My team is breathless trying to keep pace with me. I work odd hours with no particular rhythm. I avoid team meetings in Sweden and online with the team in Manhattan. It is not by design or intention. I sleep most of the time, then work when I am awake and not lost in oblivion.

I do my work and the work of five other people on my team. The project is ahead of schedule. Lillian privately requests that I give some grace to the rest of the team and let them catch up, so they can contribute and we can accelerate progress together.

She is doing her job to perfection. She is a natural Cunningham. Appointing her as Team Leader for Project GreenWind stands among the best decisions I've ever made.

What about the decision to leave Matthew? Is that one of the best? Or chiefly among the worst?

My colleagues notice my disinterest and lack of focus on anything except Project GreenWind. The Chief Operating Officer mentions my lack of focus on the business-as-usual responsibilities, but I can't find the strength to care. Meetings on other renewable energy projects are a blur—I avoid them whenever I can. My disinterest is showing, and the symptoms of my despair are becoming harder to hide.

I don't have a fitness routine in Sweden. When I hit the home gym, I run on the treadmill as fast as I can, trying to shake the images of Matthew in the New Jersey gym where I met him. If I am not sleeping or working odd hours, I run. The exercise tires me enough to sleep again, with no need to call on my superpower to knock me out.

But the aggressive exercise and all that's wrong in my pitiful life are taking a toll on my body. I'm dropping weight, my periods are irregular, and I'm plagued by frequent headaches.

My appetite is nonexistent, and what I do eat, I struggle to digest. I switch to bland, unappealing meals, eating the same monotonous dishes every day. Most healthy foods don't taste good anyway. This routine lasts about two weeks before my appetite declines further. I'm avoiding food altogether because it reminds me of when he and I cooked together—the affectionate way he fed me, his touch warm and full of care.

My body is suffering, and it's getting worse.

The cold air in my room amplifies my awareness of my figure. My clothes hang loosely on my frame, a stark reminder of the muscle and fat I have lost. I catch glimpses of my reflection in passing—my skin is dull and sallow under the harsh lighting.

Dark circles under my eyes make me look perpetually tired, a shadow of the vibrant person I was. My once-thick hair that had brimmed with vitality is limp and lifeless when my fingers slide through the strands. The pronounced collarbone beneath my fingertips is a new and unwelcome feature—a testament to the stress and neglect I have subjected my body to. My hips, which used to have a soft, feminine curve, are narrow and unfamiliar.

My body fills me with a bitter mix of disappointment and self-loathing. *My body is Matthew's and I am not taking care of it!* I am a diminished version of who I was, trapped in a frame that reflects my inner turmoil . *Daddy won't like this skeleton, Alex!*

My teary-eyed mom sits me down to implore me to change my habits. She offers to take me to a physician for help and advice. I sit there as still as a statue of cold, unyielding rock, looking at her with a blank expression. Then I lose my patience with a quick, "Yeah, whatever you need," and walk away from the conversation.

Dr. Robbins' therapy sessions—held in the confines of the study-turned-consultation room in my condominium—have been an outlet. They are the only times when I can freely talk about him. When she's not gently asking why I'm picking at my nails—a nervous habit I picked up after the breakup—she proves to be an excellent listener.

Early on, I had thought of some ideas to bring relief and an end to my misery, so I discussed them with her.

"Can't I be friends with Matthew? I promise it will be nothing more," I asked, desperate for some connection.

Dr. Robbins shook her head gently. "Alex, you left him for a reason. You sought therapy and your family's support to get better. Reaching out to him now, even as friends, could put you in a worse place."

"But what if all I want is a courtesy call, to tell him that we can't be together, but I don't harbor anger, and I still want to be a good friend to him? He'll understand," I countered, my voice desperate.

"Contacting him would invite further pain and confusion." She leans forward with a concerned air. "You need to focus on healing and finding your own strength."

Her advice makes no sense, and the longing to reconnect with him has become an unremitting ache. The idea of never seeing him again feels like a relentless pressure, pinning me down.

Now and then, memories of sex with Matthew come back in vivid detail. The frequency is increasing. But I can't bring myself to self-pleasure. The longing for his touch is unbearable. When I think of him, all I see is his radiant face and all I hear is him saying, "You have a way of making me feel invincible." Trying to think of someone else or a fantasy to touch myself brings his image back quicker than a flash of lightning, and I can't continue.

I imagine myself in handcuffs, at his mercy, being hauled out of a closet like a fucktoy, the sensations of his touch and his hardness inside me. My heart races and then is quickly weighed down. I've lost all that. *All of him.* Pain builds and tugs at me.

The feeling of prolonged loneliness—combined with the distressing knowledge that I don't have his love anymore—lead me to rub at my wrists absent-mindedly at home, at work, and even in the shower. The skin there feels chafed raw. Even the handcuffs didn't do the damage that my rubbing does.

I snap at each and every thing—people, conversations, and minor inconveniences, too. I speak in short bursts, use minimal words, and my restlessness keeps me from sitting still for long. Watching television or having dinner without fidgeting or fretting is impossible. I spend most of my time in my room, unable to face the world outside.

One afternoon at the office, amid my emotional turmoil, Lillian brings welcome news. She video calls me looking more radiant than she has in weeks.

"Alex, I've been informally in touch with NASA. Their plans to endorse Project GreenWind and accelerate plant commissioning at the two pilot sites are likely to arrive earlier than expected," she says, her excitement contagious.

"Really?" My interest is piqued.

"Yes. I spoke to a few reps from NASA off the record. They're looking at increasing resources and personnel to advance the development process. They're impressed with our initial test results and want to capitalize on the momentum."

I manage a genuine smile. "That's amazing news, Lillian. What kind of backing are we talking about?"

"Additional funding, of course," she explains, "but also increased technical resources, personnel, and potentially a dedicated team to work with us on-site both in Sweden and in the US. They're really committed to getting this done."

She beams. "There's something else. Are you ready?"

I smile, hope flickering to life. "What more?"

"NASA will join forces with the EPA to lobby the government to fund and expedite plant commissioning—the full plants. With government backing in both countries, every obstacle we're facing will be removed!"

The conversation gives me a rare second of clarity and purpose. The fog lifts, and I feel a spark of the passion that once drove me. Project GreenWind is my baby and knowing that it's gaining the recognition and acclaim it deserves fills me with accomplishment and hope, even if just for a fleeting moment.

CHAPTER ELEVEN

Alex: Whisper of Danger

PRESENT TIME

The urge to run back to Matthew is building into a relentless pull that tightens my chest and sends my heart into a frantic rhythm. What's stopping me is the question why—or rather, my lack of an answer. *Do I want this because I can't bear the gaping void that refuses to be filled anymore?* The pain is destroying me bit by bit, like a slow, cruel erosion. Or is it because I'm still hopelessly in love with him, even though he let me go and chose his ex-wife over me?

My breath hitches, and tears prickle at the corners of my eyes. *What would I even do if I ran to him? Would I beg him to take me back, throwing away whatever dignity I have left?* My stomach knots violently at the thought of him looking at me with pity—or worse, indifference. *What if he's already moved on?* The question hits like a dagger—sharp and twisting—leaving me gasping for air.

Something must change...soon. I press a hand to my chest, trying to soothe the rising panic, but it intensifies. If nothing changes, I'm headed toward a mental health crisis, teetering on the edge of something I can't control. My brain whispers about self-respect, urging me to trust the decision I made to leave him, even if it feels wrong and unbearably painful. The ache in my heart protests, but I hold on to the small, flickering hope that moving on might somehow dull this endless agony.

So here I am—sitting alone and brooding over the shambles my private life has become—sipping coffee in my condominium on another dull morning. Ted finds me in the kitchen. "Alex, are you planning to keep the GT R you bought?" he asks softly.

Oh, dear God! I wish I could forget that entire week, not just that particular night, but it's all recorded in my memory in vivid detail for eternity.

LATE DECEMBER OF LAST YEAR

It was a month after we arrived here, as the year was ending and the world was wrapped in holiday celebrations.

My decision to leave Matthew hung over me, a gathering storm, gloomy and desolate. Every day in Kiruna was a battle against myself, and my emotions were a tempest of regret and self-doubt. The cold, stark beauty of the Swedish landscape offered little solace. It mirrored the emptiness I felt inside.

One afternoon—driven by an urge to do something that would make me feel like I was in control of my life—I was browsing luxury car websites. The Mercedes-AMG GT R caught my eye with its sleek lines and the promise of raw power. Without thinking, I clicked through the purchase process, and my heart raced with a fleeting sense of exhilaration as I finalized the order. The dealership promised delivery to Kiruna within a week.

When the car arrived, it sat in my garage—its matte black finish elegant under the fluorescent lights—every curve challenging me. The aggressive grille flanked by sharp LED headlights seemed to dare me to take control. But the thrill I'd felt when I ordered it evaporated. It was just another distraction—another attempt to fill the hollow space inside me. I turned away.

That night, the loneliness consumed me. I slipped into a shimmering minidress, its fabric clinging to my skin like a whisper of danger. I was already too drunk to drive, so I asked Lars to take me into the city, not sure what I was looking for—only that I needed to escape.

The hot disco was a chaotic refuge—neon lights flashing, bass thumping through the air. I went straight to the bar and ordered drink after drink. The air was thick with sweat and smoke. The pulsating lights blurred the faces around me. As Swedish house beats vibrated through my legs, alcohol fogged my thoughts.

I laughed and danced with strangers—movements frantic, desperate. When five men offered to take me with them, I didn't hesitate. My mind raced, thoughts blurry. *Fucked by five men?* I didn't care. Adrenaline surged as they led me to their SUV, my need to escape pushing me forward.

I didn't know that Lars had been tracking my every move. Concern turned to tension, and he'd called in reinforcements from Cunningham security. It took three more bodyguards and local law enforcement to stop the SUV and pull me back from the brink.

The ride home was silent. The suffocating weight of my choices pressed down on me. Lars's hard stare and the uncomfortable presence of the other bodyguards were grim reminders of how close I'd come to losing myself. I sank into the seat as the gravity of it all settled over me.

Back in my condominium, I collapsed on the bed, and the room's darkness swallowed me. I stared at the ceiling, while the events of the night ran in endless circles. The deep ache was relentless—the void unfillable—no matter how hard I tried. I had escaped one danger to find I was trapped in another—my own mind.

PRESENT TIME

"Hey, did you hear me?" Ted waves his hands in front of my face and pats my shoulder.

With a sudden jolt I shake off the haze with a few sharp movements of my head. "Yes..."

"The GT R, do you want it?" he asks.

Jumping off my stool, I shoot a look at him. "I have no use for the car. Do whatever you please with it." I head to my room.

He sighs, the tension and anxiety in his expression impossible to miss. "Alex, I'm trying to help. We're all here for you."

His assurances feel like needles pricking at the fragile surface of my composure. My anger surges. "I don't need anyone's pity! Leave me alone!" My voice rises, trembling with rage and frustration. "You think you're helping? You're making it worse!"

Mom and Evie rush into the kitchen. "Honey, calm down," Mom pleads, her tone a soothing balm that irritates my nerves further.

I scream—the words tearing from my throat like shards of glass splintering with each syllable. "I don't need any of you! Stop pretending to care!" Each word spills uncontrollably, venomous and sharp, cutting through the air. I storm off to my room and lock the door—my chest and soul hurting with rage and sorrow.

I fall on my bed, and the magnitude of my outburst presses on me, a force too heavy to bear. My family has sacrificed their personal lives to be with me, yet I keep pushing them away. The guilt and despair intertwine in a suffocating embrace.

That afternoon, I drag myself to the office. The contrast between my private and professional life today is obvious, especially with my attention on Project GreenWind. As I step into the conference room for a video call with Lillian and the team from Manhattan, I switch into business mode—my mind sharpening with a focus I can't otherwise muster.

"Lillian, it's good to see you," I say, my voice steady and composed, masking the turmoil beneath.

Lillian smiles. "NASA's formal plans have arrived. Let's review them."

We dive into the details. The plans outlined the points Lillian and I already discussed—additional funding, access to their resources, and a dedicated team to work with us on-site both in Sweden and in the US.

Ted calls for a meeting with Lillian and me. "NASA and the EPA have joined forces to lobby Congress to fund the rest of Project GreenWind. The Swedish Ambassador to the US is also lobbying the Swedish Government to follow the same path."

Lillian and I discuss the implications. "This move will eliminate all the barriers we've faced—pushback from local governments, lack of logistical support, and difficulties in speedy manufacturing of lightweight components," I say, feeling a rare surge of optimism.

Father joins on video for a few moments. "Meetings are now going on with the Congressional committee," he updates, his tone distant and business-focused.

His attention is on the business. Not once does he appreciate me as his child or express pride in private. My thoughts drift to Matthew, who would have done that first without regard to whether the project was a success. I miss hearing him encourage me, his embrace, and the way he valued me beyond my achievements.

After the meeting, Ted remarks, "You're so different in the office, Alex. How can I help with personal stuff?"

My shoulders slump, and the energy drains from me as I slip into the dark cloud that's become my companion. I refuse to meet his gaze, choosing to focus on the floor beneath me. "My life is absolutely fantastic," I mutter, the sarcasm sharp enough to cut. "Thanks to you, the family, and our wonderful society for making it perfect. You all drove me to leave Matthew. Thanks a lot." Without waiting for a response, I turn on my heel and storm out of the office. My footsteps echo my frustration, guilt, and misery.

At home, I join my therapy session in the study. Dr. Robbins' face appears on the screen, her eyes kind and patient.

"Alex, how are you today?" she asks, her voice tranquil and reassuring.

"I'm thinking of hiring a private investigator to follow Matthew," I confess, the admission slipping out before I can stop it.

Dr. Robbins raises an eyebrow. "Why would you consider doing that?"

I fidget, feeling a lump in my throat. "I need to know if he's okay. It will enable me to concentrate on my recovery."

"What makes you think knowing about his life will benefit you?" she probes with an easy air, her features intent and fixed.

"He has no one and nothing. He's been taking care of himself since he was eight." My voice trembles with angst and desperation.

Dr. Robbins nods. "How will the information from the PI help you feel better?"

"It could bring some closure, knowing that he is fine. Then I can focus on my recovery," I say, trying to convince myself more than her.

"What if you assume he is doing alright, since he has been looking after himself from the age of eight and he is forty-two now?"

Her question stings, and I shoot her a sharp look. "Why do you keep mentioning his age?" I rise to my feet, with my jaw tight and my pulse quickening. Dr. Robbins lets a few quiet moments pass, then coaxes me to sit down again.

As my temper cools, I glance at the sliver of midnight sun which peeks from behind the curtains as if it were a spear ready to impale me.

"I don't recall constantly bringing up his age. But let's focus on what you really want to know regarding him." Dr. Robbins, a steady rock in the middle of my raging ocean storm, stands unshaken.

A tense stillness fills the room, thick and suffocating. I freeze, and my pulse quickens as her gaze settles on me—kind, yet sharp and unyielding. *Does she know what I'm hiding?* My throat tightens and I swallow, while my heart hammers against my ribs. Her silence presses on me, pulling the truth from the cracks in my resolve.

Finally, I relent. My voice trembles, barely a whisper. "I need to know if he's back with that bitch." The words pour from my mouth, and each venomous syllable stings as I spit them into the air.

Heat flushes through my body, and jealousy makes my chest ache. The room feels smaller, airless. My fists clench on my lap—nails digging into my palms—a weak attempt to anchor the whirlwind of emotions coursing through me.

Dr. Robbins smiles, and compassion radiates from her soft expression. "If he is, it means he's moving on, and that's good for him. Shouldn't you move on too?"

Her question—more of a challenge than guidance—pushes me into a trance. Jealousy and rage swell at the mere thought of him with another woman, much less that leech. Dr. Robbins' repeated gestures on video and her voice over the conference line draw me back.

"Do you agree with that?" she asks again.

I mumble under my breath, forcing each word past clenched teeth. "Yes, I'm okay with that. I'm happy for him."

Inside, my stomach knots and my arms and fists go rigid. The mere thought of that attention whore makes my chest tighten—the heat of envy burns through me. My jaw aches from gritting my teeth, and a fresh wave of anger and betrayal churns within me even though I have no proof. My heart batters my ribcage as I struggle to maintain a façade of indifference.

Dr. Robbins closes the session with a homework assignment. "Imagine a future where you could be with someone and be happy. Try to journal your feelings and bring it to our next session."

I crash on the bed in my room. My mind is a tumult of despair, jealousy, longing for Matthew's touch, fury, and a deepening conflict over whether I made the right decision. With each moment I grow increasingly convinced I made a mistake, but I'm too lost to find the clarity I desperately need.

I cry as I fall into a fitful sleep, my body and soul spent.

CHAPTER TWELVE

Matthew: Rock Bottom

PRESENT TIME

A night behind bars forces a brutal reckoning with the choices that brought you there. Since that bitter, chilly night in jail nearly four months ago, I've been haunted by the reflection staring back at me from the cracked mirror of my existence. The journey toward sobriety has been long and tortuous, but along the way, it revealed the destruction I had caused in both my reality and my happiness. Nearly seven months have passed since Alex walked away, and it's time to regain control of my life.

There's a lingering hope that she will return. Then there's the mess I've made of my standard of living ever since she left. Whenever I try to sort through my unresolved, tangled emotions for her, I lose my grip on stability. *Spiraling beyond control—something I never thought could describe me.* Although I've remained sober for the past four months, my life still feels directionless—lacking vision, purpose, or a plan to anchor myself. Without a clear vision and purpose to ground me, I doubt I will stay sober. It's long overdue that I turn my attention toward them.

This evening, I need to have a tough conversation with Anna. I believe she's ready to take it on—eleven long months have passed since her beloved dad died. She has come so far in getting her life—a brand new way of living—together and paving a road to happiness. She is as strong as I have ever known her to be.

I've depended on her too heavily. I've relied on her strength for too long. It's time I learned to stand on my own once more. Rebuilding my world will take more work than I can imagine—forgiving Alex, forgiving myself, and finding a path to move forward without her. But it all starts with taking that first step.

I am Matthew, and I've been shaping my own route to happiness since I was a boy of eight. I will rise from these gloomy trenches and emerge as the man I once was—caring, confident, commanding, and in control. *Be happy, everything will follow.* It's time to revive the mantra that once defined me, to live by it once more.

The journey ahead is daunting, and I'm nowhere near safe, but tonight marks the first step forward. Tonight, I will talk to Anna.

I commute to the recording studio on a drenched morning in Manhattan. The rain is unrelenting—sheets of water cascade from the sky and pool in the streets. Raindrops seep through my coat, but I push forward, my mind already bracing for the demanding day ahead.

The downpour in Manhattan mirrors the storm raging within me. The rain blurs the cityscape—a bleak symphony of gray that resonates with my hollowness. The downpour wets my skin, a reminder of the void Alex carved in my soul.

Inside the recording studio the air crackles with tension. The film score we're working on is complex and taxing, and the director's relentless pursuit of perfection amplifies the pressure. The orchestra is assembled—their instruments poised, waiting for the cue. We've done multiple takes, each scrutinized by the music director. His vision is clear, but achieving it is a challenge. Each failed take stings—sharp reminders of my own faults in life.

"From the top," the director barks, his voice a whip cracking through the silence.

My eyes close, and with a deep breath, I let the music wash over me. The orchestra responds, a surge of sound that fills the room, each instrument a voice in the symphony of my turbulent frame of mind. We're so close, but close isn't enough.

At last—after what seemed like ages—the director offers a slight nod, a trace of approval flashing in his expression. "That's it. That's the one."

Relief sweeps over me, but it vanishes as quickly as it arrives. As the applause dies away and the musicians begin to pack, I remain, surrounded by the lingering echoes of their music and the unanswered questions that haunt me. *Why didn't I deserve Alex's trust? Why wasn't I enough?*

The recording session is a painful metaphor for my life. Each retake a reminder of my failed attempts to understand, to make amends. The unresolved chords mirror the dissonance of my broken heart.

ABOUT FOUR MONTHS AGO
MID-TO LATE-FEBRUARY

Not long after Anna settled into her new apartment, we spent an evening shopping for a television. While I helped her set it up, my gaze traced the contours of her body, and I felt a familiar ache stirring within me—longing I hadn't felt since Alex left. Before I knew it, a desperate hunger for intimacy overtook me—a need to feel something other than crushing pain.

Shame quickly followed. I felt like a monster for exploiting Anna's kindness and vulnerability—my weakness exposed after months of incessant drinking. Mumbling an excuse, I fled her apartment with self-loathing bitter on my tongue.

I had just betrayed Alex. Even though nothing happened, the thought was enough. Anger, shame, and regret twisted into a destructive spiral. I drank more, hoping the bottle would drown the darkness.

After that, I distanced myself from Anna. Offering support through texts and phone calls but avoiding face-to-face meetings. Each time I declined, conflict churned inside me—part of me was tempted, but the other part crushed those thoughts. My guilt deepened the self-loathing, fueling my worsening drinking.

I neglected my appearance. My conductor pulled me aside at the studio, telling me to clean up and shave. My day drinking continued.

The night I was arrested, I had been drinking shots nonstop, trying to numb myself.

After my set at La Grand, I ended up in a dim bar in Chelsea, nursing whiskey and watching a game on a broken television screen—my life fractured like the bar around me. The place was half empty, save for some regulars and a rowdy group at the back.

A girl, who had been watching me for some time, finally sat beside me. "You look like you could use company," she said, offering a warm, sorrowful smile. I wasn't in the mood to talk, but her gentleness softened me. We kept it light—talking about the game, the weather and the run-down state of the bar—both of us temporarily escaping our pain.

Then her ex-boyfriend appeared, shouting as he entered, "So this is how you move on?" he sneered, gripping her wrist.

I tried to keep calm. "We're just talking, man. No need for this."

He shoved me. "Think you can take what's mine?" he spat.

I snapped. I shoved him back harder than I meant to. He swung at me, but the punch barely landed. It set something off inside me—anger and pain exploded outward.

We hit the floor, fists flying. The girl screamed as I pummeled the guy, breaking his nose and mangling his lips. My punches came harder, driven by months of self-hatred.

Then came the sirens—the red and blue lights casting an eerie glow. I was already feeling the impact of what I'd done. Chaos spread through the bar. Someone called an ambulance.

My chest heaved as the adrenaline started to wear off. The girl looked at me with wide, frightened eyes, and her hands covered her mouth in shock. The bar was a mess.

I covered my face. Shame and regret flooded me. The ex-boyfriend was being helped to his feet, his face bruised and bloodied. The girl stared at me as if I were someone dangerous.

The police went around talking to people, and ordered me to stay where I was. I knew I'd hit rock bottom. This was not who I was, not who I ever wanted to be. My actions and their consequences began to sink in as I was handcuffed. The links clicked, and I was escorted from the bar—the biting night air bringing with it the need for change.

I was thrown roughly into a squad car. The ride to the station was a blur—my head pounding from the alcohol and the adrenaline.

The frigid night passed slowly in the grim, unclean confines of a jail cell. The floor was hard and unforgiving, and the smell of urine and sweat permeated the small space. The thin blanket they gave me offered little comfort against the chill. A dull, relentless ache pounded in my skull as I curled on the floor—pain radiating through my body.

The officers were indifferent, barely glancing at me as they processed the paperwork. My pleas for water were disregarded and my requests to make a phone call ignored. I didn't know who I would call. Wyatt came to mind, but he had changed his number. Hopelessness draped over me like a suffocating shroud.

Morning came when a harsh fluorescent light flickered on overhead. My head was still pounding and my mouth was dry and tasted of stale alcohol mixed with morning breath. The concrete floor had left my body stiff and sore. Rising slowly, I grimaced at the sharp pain throbbing in my head and behind my eyes. The cell door opened, and a guard barked at me to stand. I stumbled to my feet, my vision swimming. The guard led me to a small room where I was allowed to make a phone call. With shaking hands, I dialed Anna's number.

My voice wavered as I spoke into the mic, "Anna...it's me...I'm at the police station...please come..."

After a brief pause, she shrieked. As she scrambled to find words, her tears and cries were audible. "Matt! What happened? Where are you?"

"Chelsea Precinct...I need you..."

"I'm on my way. Hang in there."

An hour later, the officers led me out—my wrists bound in cold steel, the cuffs reinforcing the reality of what I'd become. A sharp gasp cut through the air, and I looked up to find Anna. Before I could hang my head in disgrace, she lost her footing, but the woman next to her helped her stand steadily. There was a man with them. They were the lawyers she had brought to secure my release.

The man squeezed my shoulder briefly before heading inside the police station with the other lawyer. The officer uncuffed me, roughly escorted me to a wooden bench, and ordered me to sit down. I slumped onto the bench, covered my face, and rested my elbows on my knees.

Anna sat beside me. Her tears fell silently at first, then gathered force as her body shook with sobs. After a few minutes, she wiped her eyes—composing herself—but pain lingered in her gaze. She reached for my shoulder despite the oppressive stench that clung to my skin—alcohol, sweat, disinfectant, and urine. I tried to pull away, but she didn't let go. Her hand found my arm again, anchoring me to something real.

She didn't ask for explanations. She just sat with me, and her presence was a balm to my broken soul. In that shared silence, we found strength—fragile, but enough to keep us from falling apart.

Thirty minutes later, the lawyers arranged my release. The DA—seeing no prior record—considered it a bar brawl and let me off with a warning. The girl and her ex hadn't pressed charges, which helped. My record stayed clean, but my debt to Anna was overwhelming.

She took me to her apartment and made me lie on her bed, tending to me in my vulnerability. Inside her apartment, I felt nothing—no emotions, no thoughts. I spent the day asleep while she rested on the couch.

On the second night, I told her everything. I shared every detail of my relationship with Alex, though I left out Adam's murder—I didn't want her implicated. I spoke of our bond, my grief over the breakup, and my spiral into alcoholism. I even told her about Alex's family, but when I reached the part about my breakdown and the bar fight, my voice went flat.

The next afternoon, I attended my first AA meeting. When I returned, I handed Anna my one-day chip. She looked at it and then at me, eyes filled with pride and sorrow. She pulled me close, and I held her tight, desperate for comfort. Her lips brushed mine, and in that kiss, everything reignited—passion, pain, and self-loathing collided.

That night, I made love to her with an intensity that felt like a reset—rebooting my mind and body, reviving me, like a rebirth. Passion and desperation flooded through me, tangled with shadows and fleeting images of Alex. But in Anna's arms, I found a fragile refuge from the torment.

I didn't regret that night with her—it was selfish, yes. I used her to cling to my sanity. A dark voice whispered that I was lost, a depraved soul. I didn't care—I needed something to hold on to—to know life had meaning, that it was possible to feel something other than the pain of Alex leaving me.

The next morning, I suggested we leave our relationship undefined.

PRESENT TIME

Later in the day, as I walk back to the soundproofed hall for the next recording session, I smile faintly. Anna and I both needed the escape and fell into an undefined relationship willingly. But now I see that I have swapped one dependency for another—a lesson that is routinely discussed at my AA meetings. I have used her as a crutch, and it isn't fair to her or to me.

It's time for this living situation to change. I need to reclaim who I was—the man before the addiction, before the chaos of Alex and my breakup. Tonight's talk with Anna is the first step. It can't wait.

It has to happen now.

CHAPTER THIRTEEN

Anna: Plum Blossom

PRESENT TIME

I am in the middle of organizing depositions when my phone lights up with a text from Matt.

Matt

> Hey! We're eating out tonight. I'll come get you at six.

Instantly, my face softens into a smile. He is regaining his confidence and control, step by step. He's not asking, but saying. Watching him steadily return to his former self fills me with quiet joy. I am thrilled to be part of that journey. I need that version of him—the man who can destroy obstacles and find pathways to happiness, no matter what gets thrown at him. He's getting close.

I considered texting him *no*, reminding him how expensive dining in Manhattan can be, but choose to leave it unsaid. *Let him take command. I'll keep track of the expenses and remind him if required.*

Anna

> Okay :) Can't wait.

As I compare him to the man I saw at the police station nearly four months ago, I realize something—I was in this same conference room the day I got his call from the police station.

I had just gotten to work. I was reviewing and categorizing emails related to a case when my phone rang...

LATE FEBRUARY
THE DAY AFTER MATTHEW'S ARREST

The sight of him in the police station pierced me, the sting lingering long after. I sat at his side, embracing him.

In that moment, words were unnecessary. Between us, there was no need for judgment or explanations. I hoped my caress, my warmth, and my presence provided a balm to his wounded spirit. In that shared silence, a bond formed, a connection forged in the crucible of adversity. We may have been broken, but shoulder to shoulder, we found a strength that would allow us to endure.

Two days later in the apartment, when he told me about his breakup with Alex, euphoria flooded me. I barely heard his words about the whore—my mind lost in a fantasy of jasmine gardens and waterfalls of champagne. Finally, I could picture a future with him—free from her shadow. But thoughts of her brought a bitter edge to my joy. I knew I had to tread carefully, but a dark satisfaction simmered within me. *I'd won.* The thing that stood between us was gone, and now he was mine.

After he finished speaking, he fell asleep without waiting for my response. I quickly grounded myself. The first step was done, but the actual work—securing a future with him—was far from over. I carefully plotted my next moves, ensuring every detail was perfect.

Then guilt hit me like a thunderclap. Tears fell as I realized I was the chief cause of his addiction. I thought of how much I'd manipulated him—how I'd drawn him closer through carefully crafted text messages and phone conversations—eventually leading to Alex leaving him. Though I was happy she had, remorse struck hard and fast—a ruthless blow that brought me to my knees.

I had unintentionally guided him toward his destruction through my careful manipulation. Although I'd required his emotional support following my dad's death, I had designed an intricate web of texts to draw him in and keep him close. The discovery of my texts by Alex had been a long shot, but as God would have it, she had made my job easier. None of that eases my self-reproach—*I played a part in his becoming addicted. I caused his pain.*

Whispering an apology and a prayer, I steadied myself. I had to help him heal—from the breakup and his alcoholism. For him, yes, but also for me. I needed the man he used to be.

When Matt left the next day, anxiety consumed me. Fear that I might lose him crept in, but I trusted him. When he returned holding the AA chip, my fear turned to tears of joy. I clung to him, and my heart expanded with relief.

As the embrace deepened, exuberance shifted into a raw, primal surge—an overwhelming longing that had lain dormant for two years. I reached for his lips, and he responded with a hunger I had never experienced from him before—a desire that matched my own, fierce and unrelenting.

He lifted me, carrying me into a dream, a paradise filled with the scent of jasmine and streams of champagne. Every kiss, every touch, felt like a revelation. His kisses held tenderness and intensity—a heady mix of aggression and reverence. He fucked me again and again with an animalistic fervor—each movement and thrust a dance of passion that sent shivers of ecstasy through me.

Though he had no tools, his dominance was in every contact, every breath, and every whispered command. His authority consumed me, and I surrendered fully, allowing him to guide me deeper into a realm where pain and pleasure entwined. My mind drifted between awareness and oblivion, only to be submerged again in ecstasy. Our bodies moved in perfect rhythm, a harmonious blend of desire and fulfillment. The sheets beneath us were soaked in passion, the air heavy with the intoxicating scent of our union.

As we finally collapsed—panting and spent—my body ached in the most delicious way. The intensity in our refuge grounded me, and my senses drifted in the here and now and the pleasure that enveloped us. The room was dim, and in the soft glow, I saw the red marks on my skin—painted reminders of the passion we had shared—proof of the exquisite torment he had inflicted.

He shut off the light and pulled me close as my whimper of contentment echoed the lingering euphoria that quivered across my body. Wrapped in his embrace, my pulse slowed and aligned with the steady beat of his heart. We drifted to sleep—lulled by the night's gentle whispers and the promise of a new day—while the echoes of our love lingered like the last trace of jasmine in the air.

Over breakfast the next morning, he confidently declared that he had no regrets about the previous night, and he suggested we not label our relationship. He said that since we were both still healing, introducing more complications would be unwise.

I smiled my acknowledgment. When he turned away, a smirk tugged at my lips. *Oh, my king, my heart-keeper, my sunshine—I'll obey you and dance to your rhythm. You may not want to admit it now, but we are a couple again. This time, I'll make it permanent.*

I have work to do. No, we have work to do, and I'm fully devoted to creating a joyful paradise for both of us.

We'll work side by side, babe. Though I played a role in your addiction, I refuse to let guilt consume me. Instead, I will give every ounce of my blood and sweat to help you reclaim your confidence, care, and command. You will reclaim control of your happiness, and I will stand beside you, sharing the joy we will build together.

PRESENT TIME

As the offices of Hudson & Greene LLP, empty, I retreat to the washroom for a final adjustment. Fixing my hair and dabbing at my makeup, I scrutinize my reflection until I'm satisfied. Every detail is flawless, carefully curated to please his discerning gaze.

He meets me in the lobby—his hand reaching for mine—and my voice catches in my throat. "Hey," I manage, my gaze fixed on his angelic face, his high cheekbones sculpted in the soft light. A familiar flutter dances in my chest, a reminder of that fateful Yale alum event six years ago when I first fell under his spell.

"Let's go," he murmurs, and his voice is a husky caress that ignites a wave of desire, intimate and secret. The same voice was restored—stronger than ever—When he returned holding his one-day AA chip.

We step outside to be greeted by a surprisingly cool evening for July in Manhattan. He leads and I follow—content—my heart expanding with quiet, fulfilling joy.

CHAPTER FOURTEEN

Alex: My Vision of the Future

PRESENT TIME—EARLY JULY
SEVEN MONTHS AFTER BREAKUP

W hat's going to happen to me once my project doesn't need me anymore? *I'll have nothing to hold on to.* When energy production starts and more power plants get built, it will be time for the design team to move on to other initiatives. Thinking about it sends a chill through me, amplifying the pain I'm already in.

The midnight sun will be gone in a few weeks, but now it's relentless. It's a cruel mockery, as if all my flaws are being exposed. This unending daylight feels as if the heavens are making fun of me, looking down with contempt and passing judgment that I don't deserve happiness. Or forgiveness.

The constant daylight could also be asking me to embrace hope instead of staying behind the shadows, but I am tethered to my past. Resolution, closure—nothing seems right without Matthew in the picture.

A nagging ache at my failure to adequately handle the breakup conversation and the aftermath of leaving him refuses to leave my chest. In the early hours of this endless morning, I direct my soul and energy to work, trying to silence the pain of missing him.

I'm struggling to prepare a critical presentation for the CEO of Segal on Project GreenWind. The House Committee for Renewable Energy in the US has approved government funds for full-scale construction at our pilot sites, moving the proposal to the Senate. However, in Sweden, progress remains slow and uncertain. The CEO will meet with Swedish officials in two days and requires a comprehensive dossier—ideas, designs, test data, cost projections, and analysis—to secure their support.

I try to focus—sifting through data—but my heartache crushes me.

A sob starts, sharp and relentless. I clamp my hand over my mouth, trembling with the effort to stifle it. My chest tightens, the ache almost unbearable as I stare blankly at the dim glow of my laptop. The project files blur before my eyes, meaningless despite the accolades piling up.

Memories of Matthew flicker like cruel taunts—each one twisting deeper and wringing me dry. Anger burns hot and brief, then fades into the heavy, unshakable weight of grief. I press a hand to my chest, desperate to fill the void.

The growing fear that I made a terrible mistake by leaving Matthew erodes my soul.

"Go change the world and make it better, my little genius."

"Show them what you're made of today, my sweet Alex."

"First, I need you to taste success with Project Green Wind. We'll have our children soon after." His praise, his directives, and his unwavering encouragement haunt me with the promises we made and the future we were meant to share. He fueled my passion for my career. I focused my efforts not merely to succeed, but to make him happy—to make him proud of me.

But what I miss most is surrendering to him—total submission—finding liberation in the safety of his control. His nurturing dominance was my anchor, my refuge, and the shield behind which I could truly be free. Without it, I've lost my identity. I'm untethered, adrift, and nothing if I'm not his submissive.

The ache of his absence presses heavily on my chest. The endless drift in this ocean of despair is breaking me, and I know it will destroy me if I can't find my way back to him.

Unable to bear the pain, I break into a wail which spirals, echoing off the walls of the condominium. Uncharacteristically, I allow myself to be comforted by Evie, not pushing my family away in my grief. I bury my face in her bosom, and as my weeping continues unchecked, she, too, begins to cry, and her tears mingle with mine.

"Evie...I love him, Evie...I can't live without him...I made a mistake, Evie..." My voice breaks with each confession, the words torn from the deepest parts of my soul. Memories of him flood my senses—his gentle reassurances, our moments of intimacy, and those damned texts from Anna that still burn like acid in my heart. My body betrays me as my tears mix with saliva—soaking Evie's dress—but I'm drained.

Anxiety grips my chest like a vise, squeezing until I can barely breathe. My muscles tremble with tension, and the overwhelming powerlessness and fear make my head spin. Nausea churns in my stomach, and the room blurs around me as I collapse onto the sofa.

Evie never falters. She holds me, her arms a lifeline despite my lashing out at her and blaming her for my breakup. She absorbs my anger and my grief, and stays unyielding in her affection. An hour passes with me lying motionless on her lap, staring vacantly at the laptop on my desk, while my grief stings and presses me further down the abyss.

But then something shifts in the haze. A sudden clarity pierces through the fog of despair, startling me and bringing focus. *There's an essential task I must do, but let me get my business stuff taken care of first.* I sit up abruptly, wiping my tear-streaked cheeks and hastily tying my disheveled hair into a bun. "Evie, I have work," I say, my vocal cords parched but tone resolute. "So, I'm going to be busy."

She nods, and her own face is streaked with tears as she forces a smile. Her voice trembles as she whispers, "Alex, everything is going to be okay. I'm here for you, regardless of what you decide in the future."

I embrace her, but my body is rigid, my expression blank. My eyes are dry now, and my tone hollow, but I cling to her as if she's the last solid thing in a world that's crumbling around me. I don't know why I'm holding on, but in this moment, it's all I have left.

After Evie leaves, I force myself to focus on the task at hand—finalizing the presentation for the Swedish government. Despite the chaos in my mind, Matthew's smiling face lingers—not any specific memory, just his presence—an indelible ghost haunting my every moment. My fingers move mechanically over the keyboard as I finish the documentation with robotic precision. The immediate praise from the CEO's executive team for my speed and thoroughness barely registers. It's just noise outside the emotional walls I've built.

Even as I organize my remaining tasks with practiced efficiency, the emptiness persists. My heart feels detached, each task an act of survival rather than purpose.

With the presentation complete, I pick up my untouched journal. Dr. Robbins asked me to envision a future and write about it, but the act of journaling feels foreign—a forgotten ritual buried in the haze of the past seven months. As is my practice before writing a new entry, I flip to an old one, searching for grounding in a memory from October of last year—a month before everything fell apart.

The words rise from the pages and strike me. My emotionless mask cracks as tears blur my vision. It describes a night Matthew texted me during his set at La Grand Élégance:

Daddy

Hey! Helena and Edward are here at LGE :)

Alex

Oh, dear God. Did they see you?

Later that night, as we lay entwined under the sheets, he recounted the scene with lighthearted cheer. His eyes glowed as he mimicked Helena's polite smile and Edward's deliberate indifference. His mischievous smirk made me laugh, but inwardly, my heart ached. He had lost so much—his teaching career, his passion, his calling—all because of us. Yet he never let those sacrifices weigh on me. He carried the burden with grace, lifting me with his unrelenting joy and love as though I were the sun in his sky.

Now that warmth feels like a distant memory, leaving a hollow ache. I close the journal, clutching it tightly as my tears fall, and his absence presses against my chest.

"You are my universe, Alex."

"When it comes to you, I don't gamble, my sweet little one."

"Mr. Cunningham, and family, Alex is the hub of my life."

As I grip the journal, his declarations echo, each a bittersweet reminder of what I've lost. My lips tremble, and I bite down to steady them, wiping away the glaze of tears that obscures my view.

With a deep breath, I turn to the blank page of the new journal lying open before me. *It's time to focus on Dr. Robbins' assignment.*

I pick up my favorite graphite and colored pencils, the familiar touch of them bringing ease. With slow, deliberate strokes, I begin sketching the idyllic world that Dr. Robbins urged me to envision—a destiny I've barely allowed my heart to dream of. In the center of the page, I write, "Alex plus someone." I embellish the lines and entries with intricate word art, surrounding them with vibrant colors and playful emojis, each detail carefully chosen to reflect the lifestyle I yearn for.

Around this central focal point, I doodle more words and phrases, each a piece of the paradisal future I'm trying to bring to life. I spend an hour decorating the focal words with meticulous care, letting the colors and shapes express the emotions I've kept locked away. In the next two pages, I record my thoughts and feelings on the elements of my vision.

I stop to admire what I've created. My eyesight clears, and to my surprise, my lips spread in a wide grin. There is a weightlessness in my chest I haven't felt in ages. The muscles in my cheeks stretch, feeling a new kind of tension as they adjust to the unfamiliar sensation. It feels strange, this smile, as if my face is relearning an expression it once knew instinctively. I massage my cheeks to relax them and get them used to this newfound joy, while my eyes drink in the good spirits that have eluded me for a long while.

I glance at each word and phrase, letting them solidify in my brain—each a tangible piece of the microcosm I want to build.

Peace, love, and happiness.

A deep yearning fills me—a desire for days to begin and end with contentment, where tranquility reigns.

Big family.

I imagine the warmth of many bodies hugging me, the laughter of children, the feeling of never being alone again. A longing for connection surges within me, a need to create a family of my own. My heart races at the thought of little hands in mine—my flesh and blood. I picture their faces and their smiles, and a fierce protectiveness rises in me.

An extensive property in the middle of nowhere.

The idea of a sanctuary, away from the chaos of the world, brings calm. I see sprawling fields—the freedom to breathe, to be ourselves.

Renewable energy-powered house.

I imagine a home that's not simply sustainable, but a beacon of our shared values—a commitment to leaving the planet better than we found it.

Electric sports car for me.

A thrill runs through me at the thought of freedom and speed, the wind in my hair as I drive down endless roads, the power in my hands.

Electric SUV for him and the children.

I smirk as I picture him behind the wheel, wrangling our children into the backseat while I'm off closing deals and running Cunningham-Segal. He's always been the steady one—the protector—and now he'll be managing the chaos of our kids while I continue to conquer the business arena.

Tons of sex.

My body hums with anticipation at the promise of intimacy and physical connection that binds us together in the most primal manner.

Cuddling with him by the fireplace.

A cozy warmth envelops me as I imagine us entwined, with the crackling fire casting a soft glow over our shared moments of quiet attachment.

Cuddling with him and our children.

My chest warms at the thought of our family safe in the circle of our love, where nothing else matters.

Going to sleep at night, wanting for nothing.

A deep sense of fulfillment engulfs me—the dream of ending each day in perfect contentment, my heart at peace.

As I look at the vibrant tableau I've created, my smile widens—a reflection of the hope and bliss I've longed for. The vision is clear, and for the first time in months I feel a spark of optimism, a glimmer of the future I want to claim.

As I gaze at the vivid tapestry of my envisioned life, relief enfolds me. The act of journaling, of putting these hopes and dreams onto paper, has been an escape—an avenue to momentarily exit the darkness and enter a sphere where everything is exactly as it should be. As if the sun is rising after a period of prolonged flooding and gloomy skies, I feel that happiness might be within reach.

I quietly thank Dr. Robbins for guiding me toward this exercise. She handed me a key to a door I didn't know existed. This simple activity has given me something I desperately needed—hope.

I've done the homework you asked me to, Dr. Robbins. I can't wait to present it to you!

As I make my way downstairs to head to the office, I glare at the GT R parked beside the car Lars uses to chauffeur me. The sight of it reminds me of that precarious night at the disco—a night where I nearly lost myself. My eyes shut as the memories flood my head, and shame submerges me. *How did I let things get so uncontrolled?* This isn't who I am...or at least, who I used to be.

At the office, with my tasks complete, I scroll through Cunningham-Segal's pipeline of proposed projects. For months I've avoided distractions, channeling every ounce of focus into Project GreenWind. As the project reaches its final stages, I know it's time to hand it over to Ted and Cunningham-Segal for global expansion using the data and insights from our pilot sites. My baby, *our baby*—Matthew's and mine—is nearly ready to release into the world, and the thought of letting it go sends pangs of emptiness and anxiety through me.

What will I do once Project Green Wind is no longer mine to nurture? What comes next? Ideas for wave and solar energy buzz faintly in the corners of my mind, but my unresolved emotions keep me rooted in the past.

I'm trapped, reliving that day we fought over the texts from his ex-wife. I never let him finish the sentence he started: "Our bond has survived…" Now his unspoken words echo, filling the silence with what he might have said: "Our bond has survived society's judgment, family's disapproval, and our own doubts." I can almost hear his familiar, affectionate tone as though he's beside me, his voice a gentle embrace.

The memory sharpens into pain, and I bite my lip too hard, as my eyes brim with tears. My chest tightens, and I can no longer hold back. Defeated, I call Lars to take me to the condominium.

In the car, my sobs spill over, raw and uncontrollable. Lars, usually stoic, glances at me in genuine concern. "Miss Cunningham, are you okay? Should I take you to a doctor?" he asks, his voice uncharacteristically soft. Shaking my head, I manage to request, "Just take me home."

When we arrive, Lars supports me to the door, his movements gentle. Inside, Evie is waiting, and I collapse into her arms as everything crashes down once again.

For two hours I wallow in my room, as my thoughts swing wildly between self-pity and anger. Desperate to convince myself that leaving him was the right choice, I shift all the blame onto him for not fighting to keep me. I retrieve the letter I wrote to him but never sent and reread it. When I finish, I pump my fist as if the physical action can somehow solidify my resolve.

Ten minutes before my therapy session with Dr. Robbins, I open my journal to the pages where I sketched my vision for the future, and suddenly the energy drains from my body. As I stare at the vision I've drawn, realization hits me—this is not solely my dream. It's the life Matthew always envisioned for us. *The utopia I envisioned is his.*

CHAPTER FIFTEEN
Matthew: Reins and Command

PRESENT TIME—EARLY JULY
SEVEN MONTHS AFTER BREAKUP

DATE NIGHT

I watch Anna season her bowl of noodles—each movement is deliberate, like an artist perfecting her craft. Her chopstick skills are graceful, a joy to watch. Despite her patient attempts to teach me, I stick to forks and knives, content to admire her honor of tradition.

The warm light of the restaurant casts us in a soft glow, and I see a familiar spark in her eyes. With a playful flick of her wrist, she tosses a packet of hoisin sauce at me, snapping me out of my musing. It lands in front of me, and I laugh—a sound that fills the quiet space, drawing the attention of nearby patrons. Their gazes pass over us, but I barely notice, too focused on her smile and her dancing eyes as I press my palms together in mock apology. She shakes her head, but her smile widens, and for a moment, everything feels lighter.

I wait for her to savor a few mouthfuls, watching her delicately handle each bite. I busy myself with the spring rolls, chewing thoughtfully. But the question has been hammering in my chest. I lower my voice—which is shaking slightly and laced with weakness. "Hey, describe the life you envisioned for us."

She sent me an email during our separation before the divorce, accusing me of never giving her the chance to share her vision—of a life without children or family.

For a moment, her chopsticks falter. It's as if I've struck a chord deep within her. The realization stirs regret and curiosity in me, and I glance away, giving her space. The silence between us is heavy.

When I meet her gaze again, her deep brown eyes—nearly black in the muted light—glisten. A strand of her hair falls loose, and she tucks it behind her ear with trembling fingers. She sniffs quietly and lifts her tea to her lips, fortifying herself.

As she places the cup down, Anna whispers, her voice trembling despite her calm facade. "Why are you asking this now, Matt?"

The question presses on my chest, but I know what I want. I didn't give her the chance to share her goals when we were married. Now I need to hear them. With a confidence born of our shared history, I respond, steady and deliberate. "Just tell me. I need to understand."

She sets her chopsticks down with practiced grace. Speaking softly in Mandarin to the waitress, she orders a fresh pot of tea. When she turns back to me, our eyes meet and I mirror her unruffled facade.

"With my new outlook on life," she begins—her voice cool and measured, "that vision is no more. I've let go of it. I don't intend to revisit an old, painful memory. Do you?"

Her words cut through me—a reminder of how much has changed in our lives, and how much still lingers, unresolved. The defensive wall she has erected is palpable, and I feel a pang of regret and the sting of a door closing on a past we never fully explored.

I've always admired this about her—how she mirrors me, no matter the situation. When we argue, we start off composed, laying everything on the table without letting emotions cloud our words. It's a dance of control—each step measured, each word deliberate. Then comes the phase where we allow our feelings to seep in and sway us. My dominance prevails, but it's always with the recognition that she's given something up for me—because she trusts me, because she loves me. Afterward, I draw her closer—physically and emotionally—vowing to protect the fragile balance uniting us, to make her life peaceful and comfortable.

But when it came to the issue that led to our divorce, that same approach crumbled. Even though she had hidden it from me prior to our marriage, there was nothing I could do after learning of the choice she'd made, a choice every woman has the right to make. I was powerless, stripped of my usual command.

And here we are facing each other again, navigating the complexities of what we were, are, and might become. I decide not to disguise my intentions with veils of carefully chosen words or calculated pauses. I feel a bit exposed, but I am not bothered, because at this point in my life, I have nothing to lose.

I take a deep breath, and my heart pounds in my chest as I look at her—her face so familiar yet somehow new in this moment.

"Take a good look at me, Anna." My voice is soft and steady but carries the weight of years gone by. I watch her gaze fix on me, searching. "I'll be forty-two soon," I continue, my voice faltering for a second as the reality hits me. "I haven't settled down, and I don't have a plan."

I pause and drop my gaze to the floor for a moment, then lift it again to meet hers. I sense a shared vulnerability in the air—which I can't avoid, which I don't want to avoid. "I have maybe another forty good years left in me. The dreams I once had...they don't matter anymore."

I swallow hard. The admission is freeing, and for a fleeting moment, heart-breaking.

"What matters now is the future." I lean closer to her, my hand brushing hers. "A future where I'm not alone."

She remains silent, her expression unreadable. My pulse quickens as I realize how much is riding on this moment. I need her to understand—the words, the emotions underneath, and the hope.

Her lips part, but I press on, my heart beating faster.

"You are my future. What I thought I wanted previously doesn't compare to this, to us. So please, tell me—where do you want to go?"

The question hovers, heavy with expectation.

I take a shaky breath and add softly, "Because wherever that is, I want to be right there with you. I've opened my eyes, and my mind."

My hand tightens around hers, and my voice grows firmer.

"As long as I'm with the woman I love, I don't care where life takes me."

She gasps—the sound sharp and raw—and quickly covers her nose and mouth. Her reaction draws the curious eyes of a small family seated nearby, but I pay them no mind. My focus is entirely on Anna, on the tears welling in her eyes, threatening to spill out. Every instinct screams at me to reach out—to kiss her—as if that would remove her pain. But I force myself to stay grounded, allowing her to process what I've laid bare.

I glance around, searching for something to anchor us. I grab a paper towel and hand it to her. She takes it, and her breaths come in quick, shallow bursts as she tries to compose herself. The surrounding air is thick with the mouthwa-tering scents of soy sauce and spices, but all I can focus on is her—the woman who once shared every corner of my world.

Her voice, when it comes, is barely a whisper, trembling with emotion. "What did you just say? As long as...what?"

111

Oh, God.

I hadn't intended to push her to this point. I had hoped she'd focus on my question regarding the future—where she wants to go from here. Instead, my words have struck a deeper chord, that neither of us can ignore. I cradle my head in my hands, pressing my fingers to my forehead, my thumbs digging into my cheeks. My words were a gesture of deep unspoken love and a feeling of helplessness about how to move forward. *She and I will figure that out together.*

When I lift my head again, I force a smile, trying to ease the tension. I can't help but think of how lost I'd be without her, how much she means to me. My appreciation for this small, intimate space—this tiny eatery where we're baring our souls—overwhelms me. I reach across the table, palm open, silently offering her the comfort she's always given me. She only hesitates for a moment. Our hands clasp and the warmth of her touch grounds me, connecting us with no need for words.

"Where are we going, Anna?" I murmur, gently massaging her fingers—each touch a silent plea for clarity, for connection.

She pauses, her gaze distant, and then I see it—the resolve in her eyes, the poise that defines her. She straightens, and her quiet strength radiates as she picks up her chopsticks, her movements once more fluid and purposeful.

"Matt," she begins, her voice steady but with an undercurrent of vulnerability. "I don't want to die alone. I want a family."

Everything around us—the dim lighting, the soft murmur of conversations, the rich aroma of spices—fades into the background. The world narrows down to her and me. My heart hammers in my chest, each beat echoing in the stillness that has fallen. When I am my confident and commanding self, I rarely zone out, but in this instant I'm lost—suspended in time, anchored by the depth of her words.

"I want your children," she states, her voice clear and unwavering. "And I want many of them."

I see her lips move, but her words take a moment to sink in, as if my mind needs time to catch up. Then the impact hits me, overwhelming and intense. My pulse races—my heart pounding with a mix of emotions I barely understand. In this quiet restaurant, everything changes. This is the moment that will define our lives.

As her words settle, a jolt of shock and disbelief courses through me. I stand abruptly as the need to escape overwhelms me.

"I...I need some air. Excuse...me," I say, my thoughts momentarily blanking, while I almost knock over my chair. A slight sense of vertigo hits me as I step out of the restaurant.

The cool Manhattan evening air brushes against my flushed skin as I step outside, wiping my face. My mind is spinning. Her words struck a nerve, taking me back in time to the pain and confusion of two years ago.

Her words challenge a core principle I've held onto, one I thought she knew. *How could she say this?*

I hear her footsteps behind me, light but determined. She wraps her arms around my torso, resting her head on my shoulder—a mild gesture that makes my chest ache. I quickly pull away, the warmth of her touch too much to bear. I guide her to a chair outside, needing space to think and breathe.

"Anna, please. Don't." My voice is tight with emotion. "You're aware of my stance on this matter. Your choice is yours alone. Please don't make me..."

She cuts me off, and her grip on my hands is unyielding. "My choice doesn't concern you," she says, her voice steady and filled with an intensity that makes my heart stutter. "I meant it when I said I don't want to die alone. This is driven by my new priorities—by what I want in life going forward. Neither you nor my dad persuaded me. It's my decision."

Her breathing slows, and her eyes take on a fixed, determined look. She raises her hands to her chest with palms facing outward as she states in a low, measured tone, "I'll repeat. This is not about you, or what you want and feel. Everything about this relates to me, how I feel, and what I need in life."

Several seconds of silence pass. We gaze at each other, letting our messages sink in and waiting for understanding to rise.

She's saying what I've longed to hear, yet the burden of doubt still lingers. I can't shake the feeling that her decision to revisit the idea of having children is influenced by me, her dad's death, or both. The thought claws at my conscience, and she senses it.

"Babe..." she says, her voice trembling, "Do you want me to sign a sworn affidavit saying my decision is mine? I'll do it. Take me to a lawyer right now!"

Her words hit me like a punch to the gut, and I tug her to me and wrap her in a tight hug, hoping to shield her from her own vulnerability. She buries her face in my chest, and her tears soak through my shirt as I hold her. We rise and I gently guide her to a quiet corner on the street, away from prying eyes. She takes a moment to compose herself, wiping traces of her tears with her thumbs.

"Listen to me," she says, her voice steadier but still full of emotion. "You—not I—wanted to discuss this topic tonight. I hid nothing—I told you exactly what I need. This is my truth. I want the life you've always dreamed of. Can we stop fixating on the past? Let's focus on making our vision a reality."

My body and mind undergo a seismic shift as I look into her eyes, and a carnal hunger slowly unfurls within me. I've seen how she has transformed her life, dedicating herself to the pursuit of happiness. What I hadn't grasped until this moment is that her definition of happiness includes children—our offspring. The realization fills me with gratitude, fulfillment, and a profound peace I haven't felt in months. It's as though the pieces of a long-lost puzzle have finally snapped into place, and with that clarity, my primal instincts surge to the forefront, taking control.

"Anna," I murmur, my voice thick with desire. "Before we discuss anything further, I want to tear you apart. Are you ready, gorgeous?"

Her eyes widen, reflecting the same craving that's consuming me. I act fast, pulling her into a fierce embrace—our bodies pressed together—preventing her from crying out. Her breathy sounds vibrate through my chest, fusing with my primal urges and fueling the fire that's burning between us. The blend of passion and love is intoxicating, blurring the lines between physical hunger and deep emotional connection.

I feel her heartbeat match the rapid rhythm of my own, and our breaths mingle in the cool night air. Slowly, I bring her back down from the precipice and head into the restaurant to pay and pack our food into go-boxes.

Silently, we make our way to the subway, descending the stairs as if we're taking refuge in the protective shadows of the city—a secret haven where the world outside fades, leaving just the two of us, attached and clinging to each other.

Anticipation builds with each step—a magnetic attraction drawing us towards the warmth and comfort of our home where we can finally unleash the torrent of emotion that has been building all night.

CHAPTER SIXTEEN

Anna: Bound by Shadows and Secrets

"Undress."

Matt's voice—deep and commanding—reverberates, sending shivers that ignite nerve endings in my sex and transmit dull aches of pleasure outward to all of my body. I've been wet since he called me by my nickname and promised to tear me apart. On the subway, I clung to his arm—legs crossed, trying to maintain composure. But now, in the warm, intimate confines of our home, I can't stifle my instincts—I obey, letting my clothes fall away, baring myself to him in eager submission.

My eyes reflexively flutter closed, and I take in a long shaky breath. My body trembles with a mixture of excitement and vulnerability as I imagine his gaze tracing my body from head to toe—intense, meticulous, and filled with a primal hunger. He seizes my wrists—pulling them behind me—and I gasp. The bite of rope against my skin makes me bite down on my lower lip, and a moan escapes my mouth as the tingling in my core intensifies and the pleasure builds.

The fibers dig deeper as he tightens the knots, making sure my hands are completely secure and unable to move. My world dims as he slides a blindfold over my eyes, and the pitch-black darkness heightens my other senses. When he ties the knot behind my head, the heat of his breath against my neck is a silent promise that I am safe in his command—safe within this chamber of exquisite care, tantalizing torment, and the aftercare he's mastered.

"Kneel."

His command echoes with authority. As my knees sink into the thin carpet, the sharp fibers bite at my skin, adding an edge to the pleasure and excitement swirling inside me. My senses amplify—I feel each wisp of air caress my exposed skin, noting each subtle shift in temperature, any slight draft, as if the room itself is alive and conspiring with him. My ears attune to the sound of his footsteps, tracking his movements as he circles me.

"Anna, stay perfectly still."

Yes, I will, my king.

Without laying a hand on me, the warmth of his presence cocoons me in comfort and desire. Wetness pools between my thighs as I wait, and my breath catches in my throat. A delicious blend of fear and longing courses through me—the thrill of the unknown, the anticipation of what he'll do next, of how he'll push me to new heights. Each encounter with him is unpredictable—a journey through the unexpected where fright and euphoria collide, sending electric excitement zapping across my body.

A soft but firm pressure on the sides of my skull cuts off the sounds of the outside world.

My increased awareness of the scents in our apartment overwhelms me. My senses sharpened, and I inhale the mingling aromas—the faint musk of our bodies, the lingering scent of freshly laundered linens, the remnants of breakfast, the recycled air from the conditioner, the subtle notes of his hair gel, deodorant, and even my lipstick. My senses are on fire as each smell amplifies the others, grounding me in the existence of our shared space. I taste the lingering traces of the tea and food from earlier, and my saliva is thick on my tongue, as if my body is trying to anchor me.

Then, I hear it—my heartbeat, muffled but relentless, drumming in time with the rapid pulse of pleasure building inside me. The sound is distant, as though coming from deep within a well, but it rescues me, tethering me yet leaving me adrift. My other senses are processing a million stimuli at once. My gasp is barely a whisper, swallowed by the heavy silence surrounding me.

Oh, dear God!

I can't hear anything other than my heart and scratchy breathing. The world outside has disappeared, leaving me alone with my racing heart and the surging heat within me. When he told me the advanced noise-canceling headphones gifted to him would serve other purposes, I thought little of it. I assumed he would use them for his freelancing projects or simply to listen to music. I never imagined this.

The headphones cover my ears, enveloping me in silence. All external noise vanishes, leaving the faint, rhythmic pounding of my heartbeat echoing in my skull and the distant, muffled sound of my own voice when I gasp. My head instinctively moves from side to side as the biting sensations from the rope and the roughness of the carpet beneath me intensify. The pain sharpens, and my breaths come faster, harder—but now I can't hear any of it.

My entire world is consumed by the heavy, tangible silence.

Without warning, he begins. His touch is deliberate and commanding, fingers rough as they carve patterns across my skin. I can't hear his movements, can't anticipate where his hand will graze or press—or when. My world shrinks to the unpredictable touch of his hands, alternating between tender caresses that make me shiver and sharp pinches that make me gasp.

When the unmistakable tip of a feather teases the curve where my butt meets my thigh, I feel the thrill. A rush of liquid soaks my pussy, and my muscles tighten, quivering under the intense, silent stimulation. The feather then trails the length of my spine and butt crack. The sensation leaves me longing for more of those avalanche-inducing tickles. My moans, my pleas—they drift and nullify in the void of his making.

A sudden, sharp slap stings my butt, followed quickly by two slaps on my hamstrings. The sting sharpens as he continues to spank me without mercy, blending with the constant bite of the ropes and the roughness of the carpet beneath me to create an exquisite symphony of excruciation that pushes me toward the labyrinthine corridors of rapture.

As I kneel there gasping and panting, I faintly hear my breaths, but no other auditory sensations register. My voice lost to the stillness that swathes me, I plead with the vacuum of sound. I know this is just the beginning. I'll have to beg him for release all night, caught in the blissful agony of torture and euphoria.

A sudden gasp fills my lungs as the feather brushes against the apex of my thighs. It traces intricate patterns on my clit—each stroke delicate and deliberate—in a design known only to him. My sex floods, and tingling sensations flutter in my groin and chest. My sanity unravels—coherence slipping away as I become a stranger to my own anatomy. My thoughts and voice are swallowed by the silence, even though I know I'm moaning and begging.

When he's had his fill of playing with the bundle of nerves that has me trembling, the feather glides up my midriff, pausing briefly at my navel. Each touch is a whisper against my skin—a light, teasing stroke that heightens the suspense. It continues its hunt, gossamer-light on the lower curve of my swollen breasts, sending shivers cascading through me.

My sounds are devoured by the headphones, and as the line between pain and pleasure blurs, my sense of self slips further under his control.

Pain sears through me as he pinches my nipples in a rhythmic pattern—each motion a testament to his mastery of time and his authority in pain. The metronome of torment pulses as fresh slaps fall on my butt cheeks, and each one sends shockwaves through the hypersensitive parts of my body. Tears of ecstasy drench my face—the line blurring between sensation and emotion, between pure lust and the need consuming me. My disconnected mind floats, only to be pulled back repeatedly by fleeting moments of awareness as he throws me onto the bed. The unforgiving bite of the ropes around my wrists digs deeper—a reminder of the exquisite affliction that fuels my bliss.

I brace myself for the next wave of torment, the part of his play I can predict with confidence—endless trips to and from the edge. My physical arousal, the pounding of my heart, my desperate gasps, and the fragmented cries that escape me—all are disjointed, each existing in its own space. I drift, seeking refuge behind the rising wall of pleasure as his graceful fingers slide into me. My wetness welcomes him as he thrusts into my pussy with technical precision. His other hand moves on my clit, his thumb tracing circles that send ecstatic paroxysms radiating from my sex.

The impending explosion builds, and my body teeters on the edge of release. Just as I wail—my voice swallowed by the void—he pulls me from the brink, withdrawing his fingers. I tremble in the aftermath, one done and a million to go. He leans in, and his lips suckle the delicate junctions between my thighs and folds, deliberately avoiding the center of my need and leaving me yearning for the sweet roughness of his tongue there.

His mouth and nose replace his fingers, resuming the merciless edging. He starts by sucking on my labia as he would my lips—gentle yet command-ing—before parting them with his tongue. His nose rubs my clit side to side, bringing me to the brink of release again. His tongue moves with metronomic accuracy, darting in and out, up and down, and tracing circles that push me further into a haze of sensation as he sucks me.

I shiver, and my core throbs with delight—each one teasing me with the promise of an orgasm that remains just out of reach. Two, three, and...I lose count as he continues to edge me—his control resolute—leaving me gasping, moaning, and wailing in silence. My body arches in response to the unpre-dictable external stimuli. The torment of his skillful touches taunts my sex, leaving me on the precipice again.

Finally, he shows me mercy. His strokes become deliberate and focused, holding a promise of release. He thrusts his fingers into me, and his thumb circles my clit with relentless exactitude. My body responds, and a monumental wave of pleasure and heat crashes, sending shudders through me. The orgasm shreds me with a force that leaves me gasping for breath, and my frame writhing under his command. He continues to thrust, drawing a torrent of my juices, and savors the moment before indulging—licking and lapping my release, his tongue cleaning my thighs and sex with practiced attention.

My psyche wavers between moments of clarity and disorienting dissonance. In a swift, controlled move, he flips me onto my stomach, bringing my legs together before straddling my hips. He adjusts the headphones and deprives me of further connection to the outside world by pressing my nose to the sheets and burying me in the mattress. My breath comes in shallow gasps, just enough to sustain me as I howl at feeling his thickness enter me. My drenched pussy invites his cock in, and rapture surges in my core. His other hand firmly pins my hips to the bed as he begins to drive his hard length into my slit, slowly and deliberately at first—each movement a calculated torment.

I ascend the mountain of arousal again, and his pace quickens as he pummels me with unbound passion. My sobs, whimpers, howls, and moans blend and create a chaotic symphony of need, none of which reach my eardrums.

"Matt...oh, God! Yes...there, right there...harder, babe...fuck me harder." The words dissipate into the soundless abyss. Fire sears my butt cheeks—the pain so intense that my mind abandons the search for a source, surrendering instead to the euphoria that follows.

Each minute is an eternity in the silence. Each time I near the brink, he pauses, leaving me teetering on the edge and denying me the sweet surrender I crave. My body quakes, drenched in sweat and muscles coiled tight with unspent energy. My mind spins, caught in a dizzying whirlwind of frustration and desperate arousal—as my nerves scream for another release that eludes me.

He eases his grip on my head, offering me a brief reprieve. Then he pins me with renewed force—my hips and skull locked in his unyielding hold. His thrusts accelerate in a frantic rhythm. When my release comes, it's a climax so intense that my body spasms and I shatter into a million pieces. The orgasm rips me inside out, long and overpowering—my juices bathing his cock, worshipping his member, and surrendering entirely to his possession.

In the midst of my climax, he removes the headphones, and the sudden flood of sound hits my eardrums with the roar of a thousand thunderclaps, amplifying the intensity of my release. The growl of my own voice fills the room as I give in completely to the euphoria that consumes me.

I convulse—lost in the throes of rapture—but he holds me steady, guiding me as he finds his own release. "Oh, Anna, my Anna...My angel, my beautiful Anna..." His voice—compassionate and reverent—is the sweetest sound I'll ever hear, and his words are a balm to my soul. He removes the blindfold, and as I open my eyes, the world rushes back to me in a flood of color and sensation.

His warm semen fills me with a profound sense of belonging, of being claimed and cherished. Tears of pure joy flow over my cheeks as I howl in the afterglow, my body and heart utterly drenched in the overwhelming emotions.

When my paroxysms ebb, he transitions to worship with thoughtful and methodical care. Gently, he unties my wrists, and his fingers massage soothing lotion into the raw marks left by the ropes. Each stroke of his hand is full of care, erasing traces of pain from my frazzled body. With a tenderness that melts my heart, he lifts me and places me on the bed—handling me as if I'm the most delicate thing in the world.

"Shh, my gorgeous," he whispers, his voice a balm to my nerves. The sound of his words calms me, grounding me in the safety of his presence. He fetches a warm cloth and meticulously wipes away the sweat and other remnants of our intense session from my skin, his touch considerate and loving. His hands knead my shoulders and neck, massaging away the tension that still lingers.

Then he wraps me in a warm, soft blanket, cocooning me in its soothing embrace. Finally, he lies beside me, drawing me inside the shelter of his arms. He strokes my hair with reverence, and his breath is warm and steady against my forehead. "You did so well," he murmurs, his voice laden with praise and unbridled affection. "I'm so proud of you."

Still floating in the lingering euphoria of my release, I nuzzle closer to his chest, feeling the beat of his heart against mine. The intensity slowly dissipates, replaced by peace and contentment that settle over me like a soft, comforting mantle. In his grip, I am safe, cherished, and utterly loved. The gentle rhythm of his heartbeat lulls me into a tranquil sleep, as the afterglow of our shared intimacy shields me in an envelope of love and serenity.

The next morning, as I sip my tea, I catch him regarding me—his eyes tracing the contours of my face. His gaze pierces me, making me feel delicate, like a petal in the cradle of his hands. My cheeks flush, and I instinctively cover my face in a futile attempt to hide. He smirks, and I playfully smack his forearm. But when his lips curve into a stunning smile, I freeze. His cheekbones, his perfect teeth, his entire countenance—he is a radiant work of art that leaves me breathless.

I close my eyes, inhaling deeply and savoring this moment.

"What's step one, gorgeous?" His voice is casual, effortlessly shifting the conversation back to where we left off last night. He seems unaware of my crumbling composure—no, he knows exactly what he does to me. I let a few seconds pass, relishing the journey from last night to this morning. It's been more than two years since I felt this swoony, smitten, and completely satisfied.

Finally, I draw myself together, smoothing my hair and straightening my posture. After a long breath, I clear my throat and reach for a notepad and pen.

"Today's Saturday. How about we visit the property my dad gave me when I turned eighteen? We can start sketching plans for a small house to build. It's all we can afford for now, but there's room to expand..."

"That sounds fantastic." He sits straight, and his shoulders broaden while his chest puffs slightly. His raspy voice barely conceals his eagerness. It's my turn to smirk, but he meets it with a piercing look, as if he's trying to read my thoughts. I close my eyes and sigh, brimful with satisfaction and a hint of anticipation.

"But that's not step one." His steady voice brings me to the present minute.

I snap my eyes open, tilting my head as amusement, curiosity, and fear rush through me. *Is he about to say something that could hinder our blossoming relationship? Nah, why would he?* My heart flutters in suspense, but as if sensing my unease, he squeezes my palms, and his eyes never leave mine. I smile warmly, reassured by his contact.

He stands and walks to his desk, returning with a small envelope. The air shifts around us as his expression turns serious, and melancholy darkens his gaze. His voice is somber as he gives it to me.

"Anna. This is a letter to Alex. She'll never read it. I told her that I've forgiven her, and that I'm moving on."

He takes my hand again—his grip grounding me as my mouth opens. Tears well up and spill over as warmth spreads through my chest, still tinged with the anguish of old wounds. The flood of profound happiness feels surreal. I try to smile, and my hand rubs my breastbone, massaging the spot to calm my emotions. The relief and joy bubble up, and I can't repress a stream of tears, my heart raw and full of delight.

"There's more, darling," he says, voice steady—a stark contrast to the emotions raging within me. His composure feels almost like a gentle mockery, and it breaks me. With a sob, I leap toward him, twining my arms around him as if he's the root tethering me to this earth—my source of life.

His muscular arms adjust my position slightly, still giving me space to cry and let the emotions flow freely. He removes the bracelet—the one the whore had gifted him, a symbol of everything that once was. Without hesitation, he places it in the envelope alongside the letter. In a deliberate, almost ritualistic gesture, he seals it, the moisture dabbed on the flap final.

"Take this and do what you want with it," he says, extending the envelope to me.

Tears blur my vision as I place it on the table, and my limbs tremble with this moment. Remnant pain and elation crash together in a deluge of emotions. The euphoria from the removal of emotional agony is a different kind of high—contentment and energy fill me.

Suddenly, I reach for his lips with a fury I didn't know I possessed—my kiss urgent and desperate—as if the world might end any second. Lust surges through me, consuming me as I kiss him with all the passion and need that's been building inside me for so long.

He holds me close, settling me in the warmth of his embrace, and his touch grounds me as he gently wipes away my tears. "What next, gorgeous?" he asks, his voice soft with affection, treating me as he would a fragile plum blossom.

A lightness fills my heart, lifting the weight off my shoulders and sending a rush of adrenaline through my veins. I am energized, as though I could conquer the world. An idea crosses my mind, and I grin at him.

"Why don't we go for a run on this beautiful morning?" I suggest, tugging playfully at his callused fingers.

He smiles, and we walk to our small wardrobe. With gentle hands, he dresses me in a cross-back sports bra and shorts, and his touch lingers in a way that sets electricity crawling up my spine. We lace our shoes and share a lingering, impassioned kiss that leaves us both breathless.

Reluctantly, we pull apart, chuckling as we speculate about whether the neighbors heard us last night. Hand in hand, we step outside, and the cool Manhattan summer morning greets us. The wind brushes our faces as we run side by side, with the future stretching ahead like an open road.

PART TWO

HOPE

CHAPTER SEVENTEEN

Alex: The Mistake - Fear

My therapy session with Dr. Robbins starts in a few minutes. Instead of walking her through my vision, I decided to email her detailed pictures of my journal half an hour ago. I have no desire to talk to her about the future Matthew and I visualized together. That dream is sacred to me—a cherished fragment of what we shared—and the idea of unraveling it with her is unbearable. *She's going to judge me.*

Dr. Robbins can read me like an open book, and she always does, which fuels my frustration. She sits there psychoanalyzing every word and breath, getting me to say things I'd rather keep locked away. It's infuriating.

Why doesn't she just say what she thinks of me? Or what she assumes I'm thinking? Better yet, why doesn't she simply hand me a list of things to do? At least then I could decide whether to trash it or execute her recommended actions. But this endless dance of psychotherapy is grueling. Her sessions leave me feeling helpless—more worthless than before.

Yet I keep going to her because...it's the only place I can talk about him and my past. *A past I don't want to let go of?*

I join the online consultation room early, staring at the big monitor in my study, tapping my fingers restlessly on the couch. As I try to distract myself with a magazine, the images of the smiling women and happy families in the ads evoke a nauseating sensation. I toss it aside, stoking a familiar bitterness. Dr. Robbins arrives shortly after, taking her time to settle in with her notepad, pen, and glasses—*the tools she uses to scrutinize me and jot down judgments.*

I sit on the couch, my gaze locked on Dr. Robbins. She watches me as if I'm a puzzle she's determined to solve, but I don't want to be explained. Her calm demeanor—coupled with that composed, steady, and soothing voice—grates on me as she begins the session. "Hi, Alex! How are you feeling today?"

Apparently, I'm broken, and Dr. Robbins is here to fix me. I can see it in her eyes—the way she's assessing me as if I'm a car in an auto shop for repairs. *Tighten a handful of screws, change the oil, and I'll be good as new. But I'm not a machine, and this isn't a simple fix. There are no repair manuals for me.*

I nod and force a smile. "Good." The word tastes bitter on my tongue as I force myself to continue the motions of this unpleasant exchange of pleasantries.

My throat tightens and my stomach knots as I watch her prepare to pop the hood and take me apart. In the back of my mind, I chant, *You can do this. Try to think straight.* I keep repeating, *Focus,* silently willing my thoughts to align and steady.

Dr. Robbins offers me a brief, practiced smile and holds up the printouts of my journal pages. "Your vision is important because it shows us what you want for the future. But we must understand how it connects with your current feelings, especially after everything you've endured."

I nod again, but inside I'm boiling. She's completely missed the point. This isn't merely what I want—it's what Matthew and I dreamed of. I glance at the vision I painstakingly drew, which she's so keen to analyze. Every detail was something he and I imagined and explored. I know he's not with me, but his absence doesn't mean I have to change what I want. *Him.*

Her words carry a quiet weight—an implication—a delicate reminder of his absence and its supposed impact on my plans. Frustration grips my chest, tightening with each replay of the vision I drew in my journal and the endless conversations he and I had about what lay ahead for us.

My fingers run through my hair in a futile attempt to soothe the tension building inside me. I shake my head, my posture rigid as the simmering anger finally erupts. My voice quavers as I exclaim, "This isn't a mechanic's job of putting me back together!" The words escape before I can stop them. "It's not that simple! Matthew's absence doesn't mean I have to dismantle my life. I'm not some car you can repair and send on its way."

Dr. Robbins meets my outburst with a soft expression, her voice gentle but firm. "I'm not here to mend you. You're not broken. What you're feeling is valid, and it isn't something that can simply be 'repaired' like a faulty machine. But I am concerned that you're holding on to him in a way that might keep you from healing. Can we discuss that?"

Her words land heavily, hitting me deep. *Of course, I'm holding on to him. He's all that still makes sense—the one proper relationship I had until it ended. There is no fix without him back in my life.* He understood me, controlled me, gave me purpose and direction. He showered me with love, and I basked in submission. *And this doctor expects me to simply let him fade away?*

Frustration wells up, and I slam my clenched fist onto my lap. Sharp pain shoots through my hand and leg, but it pales in comparison to the deep ache of being misunderstood.

He is the engine that still drives me.

I think Dr. Robbins is a robot programmed to act calm and collected, come what may.

"Alex," she continues, her voice steady yet soft, "he remains a significant presence in your world. I'm wondering how much of this plan is truly yours, and how much echoes what you had both dreamed of once."

See, I was right. She knows everything. Maybe she's aware that Matthew was my daddy.

The anger rises in me again, hot and suffocating. *How do I tell her I want him—that he is all I need to get out of this torment that I have been in for the past seven months?*

She falls silent, her eyes never leaving me. Her gaze pierces—scrutinizing—as if she's trying to see right inside my soul. I know what she's thinking. She believes I'm too fixated on him, that his memory continues to dictate my actions despite him being far away. But she fails to understand.

Of course, it all circles back to him! But does having an engine equate to obsessing? What kind of psychiatric science or psychology is that? How can I move on without the person who understood every part of me—the spirit that kept me going?

The burden of her gaze and the reality she's trying to push on me crush my defenses. My shoulders slump under the unbearable pressure of it all. Betrayal washes over me—Dr. Robbins has betrayed me too.

Heat blurs the world as the unshed tears cloud my sight. The sobs come, muffled and heavy, as I struggle to contain the emotions surging within me. I want to scream, to shout out my pain and frustration, but I can't. Instead, I direct all my hurt into my tear ducts, letting the tears flow freely, silently screaming out the agony I feel.

Dr. Robbins gives me a few moments to collect myself. I dab the tears—avoiding her gaze—while the relentless midnight sun glares mockingly through the window. Another sharp pulse of anger rises within me, the urge to throw something against the glass growing stronger.

She heaves a deep sigh and sits back, her posture certainly not the poised, composed façade I've always seen.

She says something—her observations and concerns that I'm not letting myself heal—but her words barely register. *She can keep trying to patch me, but what if I don't want to be fixed? What if I'd rather stay here, a broken car in this garage, pretending that Matthew is still holding me together?*

She leans forward, her eyes locking onto the camera, her voice low and steady—the tone that both soothes and grates on my nerves. "I'm not here to fix you, and you don't need repair. But I worry that clinging to him may prevent your progress—there's room for healing, forgiveness, and other possibilities we can explore."

Judgment #4592—Alex is obsessed. Dr. Robbins believes the solution lies in forcing me to forget him, but she fails to grasp the depth of our bond.

The session ends, and I leave feeling even more isolated. Dr. Robbins thinks she's helping, but all she's done is make me realize how much I need him—how deeply I long for him, even after everything that happened. I step onto the balcony, the midnight sun stinging my skin, and a truth slams me. *I'm not ready to let him go. Not yet. Maybe never.*

By mid-July, Project GreenWind reaches a major milestone as full government funding is allocated for the US and Swedish pilot sites, signaling a global commitment to renewable energy. The results from the initial installations are staggering—turbines are producing 40–45% more electricity than industry standards—far surpassing our expectations. With a fraction of the turbines installed, the output already exceeds the test results by an additional 10–15%. Full-scale construction is underway, and the excitement inside Cunningham-Segal is electric.

The success has transformed my "proposed little project"—as Ted ridiculed it once—into a cornerstone of our business empire's future. The turbines, blades, and facilities—offered as open-source designs—have been celebrated globally as a revolutionary step towards a greener planet. While scientists and media outlets clamor for interviews, I send Lillian to handle the spotlight. The world may see triumph, but I only feel Matthew's absence—the hollow ache of grief overshadowing every achievement.

Cunningham Energy's proprietary wind pattern predictor models remain tightly controlled, providing the intricate analyses needed for wind farm expansion. These models—the backbone of our success—ensure firms seeking customization must engage with us directly, cementing our dominance in the renewable energy sector. Yet, even as these victories pile up, I sink further into despair, drowning in shadows that no professional triumph can dissipate.

My baby. Our baby.

A new dread seeps into me as each day brings us closer to the operationalization of Project GreenWind. The operations and facility management teams will soon step in, eventually taking full control of the running of these power plants. In a few weeks, my team and I will have little left to do with the project.

The thought terrifies me. Without a purpose, I may never escape this abyss of sorrow—trapped in an unending maze of despair. My outlook is bleak, like a road leading nowhere in a barren landscape.

At the end of the seventh month since our breakup, I'm almost convinced—almost—that leaving Matthew was a mistake. My brain keeps fighting, arguing that leaving was the only path forward—the best decision—despite the hardship that lies ahead. But my brain can't feel what I've endured—the anguish, the torture, the guilt, the fear, and the anger that have become my constant companions.

My brain is wrong. It can't comprehend the torment of walking away from the man who was my universe.

CHAPTER EIGHTEEN

Alex: The Mistake - Realization

I made a mistake.

As I lie on my bed, that thought loops in my head—an anthem that's been playing for weeks. No matter how hard I try, I can't reconcile my feelings about the breakup with the love I still have for him. The longing to be back in his arms is an unbearable ache. I love him, and I miss him with every breath. I hate him for choosing his ex-wife over me, but I can't cast him from my heart.

I'm lost without him.

Every action I've taken since the breakup has proven this. Over seven months have passed, and though the destructive impulses have dulled, the resolution I desperately crave remains elusive. I'm a time bomb, ticking away, ready to explode at the slightest provocation.

If I still feel this way after all this time, how can I be sure leaving was the right choice? What am I missing? Should I give it more time? Another few months? A year? How much longer can I endure this?

Evie is a godsend—always there to listen, to calm me when I'm lashing out in fury or sinking into agony. She never judges or offers advice unless I ask. But that's the problem. I get no answers from her, no resolution. She can't understand what I'm going through—not really. Her care is comforting, but she can't save me from my troubles.

There are things about my relationship with Matthew that I can't tell her or my family. Things she wouldn't get. Things no one could. That he's not just my lover but my father figure and that I crave my submission to him—the dynamic isn't something you can casually explain. It defines me, and without understanding that, no one can fix me. I doubt even family would understand.

Mom's support is different—conditional. She'll back me as long as it doesn't go against the family's interests. If I choose a path she doesn't approve of, she'll offer lukewarm support from afar—just like when Matthew and I were together. Her loyalty lies with the family legacy, the business empire, the expectations of society. And if I can't fit within that mold, she'll nudge me back into therapy, where everything feels like an exercise in futility.

Which brings me to Dr. Robbins. When it comes to the topic of my relationship, she and I got off on the wrong foot from the start when I went to her after Adam. She asked if I wanted to explore my relationship with Matthew, to dig deeper into it with her help. Then she theorized—though it seemed more of a declaration—that a relationship with a man more than twice my age was unhealthy. That was when I first yelled in her office, storming away and slamming the door behind me.

Now, I talk about him in our therapy sessions, but I can't shake the feeling that she sees me as some broken object to be fixed. Our sessions leave me drained and more abandoned than when I started. She keeps suggesting I try dating other people—Mark Hannam, specifically. I've tried. Several times. But I can't get past Matthew, memories of his touch, the words he said and the things he did to me in and out of the bedroom. He's all I see, all I feel. Nothing else works.

I suspect Dr. Robbins knows more than she's letting on. She asked me once if I was using him to replace something—or someone—in my life. Her words were so pointed, so carefully phrased, that I almost let the truth slip. If she knew Matthew was my father figure, she wouldn't help me find a way out. It's been over seven months, and I'm no closer to healing than I was when I started therapy. I wonder if I'm her first failure—the one patient she can't fix.

If I had someone who understood me beyond doubt, someone I could lean on, talk to—someone whose familiar voice could comfort me, whose chest I could cry on...

The noise in my head stops. My ears fill with an overwhelming silence, expanding and suffocating. My racing thoughts come to an abrupt halt, as if time itself has stopped. Darkness envelops me as I jolt upright on my bed, staring with a blank expression. Everything blurs, and my attention spins with disjointed thoughts. I sit motionless, my hands buried in the mattress, grounding myself in reality.

Then, from oblivion, a voice emerges—faint and distant—reminiscent of an echo carried by the wind.

"She's trying to find comfort in a familiar voice," I recall Matthew saying.

The words come closer, then retreat in a cruel twist of Doppler's effect. They hit me from all directions, bombarding me with echoes that grow louder, until they shatter the fragile confines of my psyche. The realization crashes—the tightness in my chest building, and a pain pressing in the back of my throat. Self-loathing creeps in again as I replay what he said, making it bigger in my mind.

Matthew tried to explain what Anna was doing, but I didn't listen. I couldn't. All I could think about was how much I wanted to hurt her, to kill her. Her pretty face, her grace—I wanted to burn it all. When I wasn't consumed by rage, I was obsessing over how he had lied to me, how he must still have feelings for that bitch. I couldn't see past my pain and his betrayal. Not once did I consider that his explanation might be plausible.

Today, after seven months of tempests and countless trips through the bowels of grief, I understand what he meant—at long last. His words, which I had ignored, have broken my impenetrable walls of jealousy and rage. I now realize that I'm in the same place she was—desperate for comfort, clinging to the familiar, haunted by the ghost of a love lost.

The echoes in my head become brutal blows, landing hard in my gut and chest. Stabbing pains sear in all parts of me, igniting a fire of realization that burns hotter with each breath. In the end, I understand what she was doing. Though I will never approve of her methods—she will forever be a whore—I comprehend her actions. I understand her, because I feel the same way.

"I can't deny someone support during the darkest, lowest, and most desperate time of their life."

His words echo in my mind, each one a punch that hits hard and drains me. I break into a wail, the sound reverberating in the emptiness around me. I've become her. I am Anna, lost in this dark and frightful abyss, reaching for the solitary soul who can shine a light and pull me from the pits. Even if that soul is the one who sent me down there. Because that soul understands me.

Anguish sweeps me with ruthless force as I realize how deeply I hurt him—and, by extension, her—by dismissing her sheer desperation and grief, by trivializing the support he gave her. I disparaged her pain and belittled the comfort he provided, all while ignoring that he was doing what I now long for—being there for someone when they need it most.

I hurt him further when, in the heat of our argument, I weaponized his age and questioned our special dynamic—the very essence of our relationship, the core of what we meant to each other. The thought of how deeply that must have wounded him makes my stomach twist in knots, the pain sharp and unforgiving. My self-loathing is a pressure that refuses to let up. Tears cascade down my face, soaking my skin, my cries tearing through my throat as I am consumed by the agony of my actions.

I realize it now. It was my worst mistake—unforgivable, the kind that haunts you for a lifetime.

"No, it wasn't."

Yet again, everything comes to a standstill. I'm engulfed in a void, where the only sound is the persistent chatter of my own brain. Matthew's voice is replaced by the cold, detached tone of logic, spouting a line that echoes painfully in the hollow space where my heart should be, *"You did not make a mistake."* The words reverberate within me, countering the sharp pains that twist in my belly.

The line fades, replaced by my brain's uncompromising reasoning, *"Even if you had realized then what you think you realize now, you would still have acted the way you did. Your jealousy, anger, and murderous rage would have always prevailed, regardless of Anna's grief."*

I sit there stunned as my rational intellect presents its case—cold and clinical.

"So it doesn't matter. Relax. Accept your decision and move on. You've got everything you need. Your family's sacrificed everything for you. Dr. Robbins has been trying to care for you, treating you like a child. Mark Hannam's been a gentleman. Your colleagues have tolerated your behavior. NASA, the EPA, they've all been helping you. You, Alex, have every resource in the world to improve your life."

In rapid succession, memories replay in front of my eyes—plain and indisputable. Each flash is an epiphany, a series of signs I'd ignored. I grasp for alternate explanations, resistant, eager to disbelieve the cold logic.

The reasoning stings. My heart fights the cold rationale, but the logic is relentless, pushing me to accept what I've done. The dissonance between what I feel and what I'm supposed to accept rattles my bones.

And yet a small, terrified part of me wonders if maybe, just maybe, my brain is right. That all this pain—this regret—was inevitable. That there was never another path. He hurt you, rejected you, and humiliated you by choosing her over you.

But as soon as that thought starts to take root, the storm inside me rises again. It thrashes, demands to be felt, to be acknowledged, to be reckoned with. What about me? I hurt him too. I didn't listen to him, trust him. And as much as I hate her, I minimized the grief Anna felt after her dad's death.

The pain and crushing weight in my chest shift. My ribs go rigid, and a cold shudder shakes my torso, a slow-moving frost spreading inside me.

My reason doesn't relent. "Fix yourself. I will assist you. Stop complaining, because you aren't getting closure. You don't want to."

An eerie calm settles over me. It's a bizarre sensation. But in that calm, a warmth begins to build within me, akin to a faint ember slowly coming to life. A delicate ray of hope rises from the depths of my despair.

It's the feeling I get when I'm on the verge of an answer to a complex physics problem. It's near, yet out of reach—hidden somewhere in the shadows of my intellect. But I know the answer is there, waiting for me to discover it. It's not in my logical brain—it's buried somewhere in my emotional landscape. I can almost touch it.

A small yet potent envelope of positivity surrounds me, igniting a spark of promise. I leap off the bed, my body suddenly light, my mind clear.

Just as I do when I'm studying a difficult problem, I talk aloud to my brain—trying to unravel the layers—confident the clarity is buried in there.

"I need a few quiet moments to think. I've heard your points. It's clear I've committed a serious blunder, I'll find a resolution, and you'll partner with me. I must be patient and organize my thoughts, catalog them in neat folders, ready to be accessed. The answer is waiting for me."

"Alex, stop. You're regressing. There's no other way you would have acted. It doesn't matter. Move on."

"No," I say firmly, my voice unwavering. *"It was a severe error in judgment. I could have reacted differently."*

"How? Prove it."

"I will."

I am surprised by the calmness that washes over me. After months of emotional turmoil, serenity takes hold. I smile to myself—a quiet, confident smile. The answer will come to me. Or I will find it.

I'm drained right now. Battling my brain—on something nonacademic, so personal—is the hardest fight. But I'm driven by the conviction that I'm on the brink of something crucial. I started the day feeling lost, trapped in darkness. But now, after an endless stretch of time, I sense something brighter—something promising—not too far away.

As exhaustion takes over, I call on my superpower—letting sleep claim me before any doubt can take root. Moments before slumber takes me, my mind whispers a single truth.

I made a mistake.

CHAPTER NINETEEN

Matthew: The Plan

Dear Alex,

This letter has been a long time coming, and it's difficult for me to write. But I owe it to you and us to finally put into words what has been weighing on my heart.

From the moment I took you into my life, I vowed to protect, care for, and shield you from anything that might hurt you. I told you to let me handle the world so you could sit back and breathe easily. I meant every word. I wanted to be the one who could give you everything—your strength, your peace.

But love is complicated. It's not merely about protection. It's about knowing when to let go. And as much as I wanted to hold on to you, I've come to understand that genuine love sometimes means releasing the one you care about, even when it breaks you.

There were misunderstandings, and we both could have communicated better. But fixating on that won't change anything. What matters is letting go and finding our paths forward.

I forgive you for leaving. I forgive you for walking away

from what we had. You needed to find your own way, and I needed to let you go, even though I lost a part of myself.

I'll always treasure the memories we made and how you made me feel when you were the center of my world. But I can't keep living in the past.

I took you to be mine, but now it's time for us both to move forward and find fresh paths that don't involve holding onto what once was.

So, this is goodbye—to you, and to the part of me that was enriched by who I was to you. I'm letting go, and I hope you find the peace and happiness you deserve.

Take care of yourself and know that I'll always remember you with love and gratitude for the time we shared.

With all my soul,

Daddy, who once was, and is past

This is my new modus operandi, a ritual of liberation. Whenever memories of Alex rise in me, or when an incident reminds me of her, I breathe in a lungful and exhale. Then I recite every word of the letter I wrote. It takes two minutes. I don't have her photographic memory, but I am a pianist, and memorization comes from practice. So I etched that letter into my mind, note by note, until it became a part of me.

Tonight, a wealthy patron at La Grand Élégance requests Alex's favorite Chopin piece, Nocturne No. 1 in B-flat Minor. The instant the request is made, my mind drifts to her—our music room, her head resting on my lap as I played, her eyes closed in contentment. Then the memories turn dark: pint after pint, shot after shot, a drunken stumble through the alleys and streets of Manhattan, aimless wandering, a cop ordering me to trash my open bottle of bourbon, begging someone to help me find the subway, curling up by a building's heat vent to survive the night.

Yet as my fingers touch the keys, my limbs take over, playing the piece to perfection. The patrons rise to their feet in applause, showering me with generous tips.

But as I make my way home, the memories and melancholy threaten to drag me back into the shadows. The familiar heaviness creeps in, tightening around my chest.

I implement my plan and recite the letter through my teeth. Twice. When my eyes open, I find myself smiling. My breathing has steadied, and my entire body feels lighter. *I forgive you, and this is goodbye, Alex.*

Anna has been burning the candle at both ends for the past two weeks. Late nights at work—assisting the legal team with a high-profile case—have become routine. She gets home around half past nine, diving into a freelance project while she eats. By the time she crawls into bed, it's already one in the morning, and her alarm blares at half past five, signaling the start of another grueling day.

But tonight is Friday, and I'm determined to give her the comfort she deserves. Humming softly, I prepare her favorite dinner and set it on the table, surveying our cozy apartment with satisfaction. When she walks in, she heads straight for me, wrapping her arms around my neck. I kiss her with a fierce need that's been building for days. She melts into me, her tension easing with every second. The kiss is electric. But tonight isn't about my needs—it's about giving her a reprieve.

I guide her to the table, feeding her small bites as I trace the lines of her face. Her eyes are heavy, her usual vibrancy dulled by exhaustion.

"Hey...can you turn off some of these lights? It feels like a stadium in here," she murmurs, her voice tinged with fatigue.

"Shh, my darling, eat," I whisper, feeding her with touchy-feely care. But as I watch, her eyelids weaken, and her head wilts forward—exhaustion pulling her down.

Oh, no you don't.

I grasp her chin gently but firmly, tilting her face upward. A few light slaps—the last one a little too hard—to her cheek jolt her awake, and her eyelids snap open in surprise. The sudden alertness in her gaze sends a thrill through me, igniting a fire that was smoldering beneath the surface.

"Hey, Anna! Stay with me," I coax, with command and affection.

She blinks, her eyes wide and disoriented. "What...oh, babe...I'm sorry, I'm drained...But I'm awake now."

I smile at her, my tone softening as I assure her it's okay. I continue to feed her, savoring the intimacy of the moment—the way her lips part to accept the food, the trust in her near-black eyes as she looks up at me. But after a few bites, she places a hand on her stomach, shaking her head.

"I'm full, Matt. Can we go to bed?" she asks in a soft plea.

I lift her with a firm, not-so-gentle touch, noting how her eyelids lower again as she drifts back toward slumber.

A bit more force this time, maybe? Yes. I give her feeble cheek a slap.

A startled yelp escapes her as I carry her to the couch, where I flick on the television—the burst of light and sound filling the room. Flipping to a sports channel showing a game replay, I crank up the volume, the commentator's chatter and the crowd's roar echoing around us.

She curls into me, her voice barely a whisper as she pleads for the television to be turned off. But I'm not done yet. As her head nestles into my chest, I tilt her chin, pulling her face toward mine. Our mouths meet and I feel a satisfying throb in my chest and groin as her weary eyes snap open. She moans against my mouth, and I take advantage, deepening the embrace, tasting her, claiming her. She trembles, but I steady her, holding her close as the noise from the television surrounds us, a chaotic symphony keeping her from slipping back into sleep.

She groans in frustration, pulling away and slumping into the couch. I keep a watchful eye on her, ensuring her eyes remain open, then stand and undress, stripping down to my boxers. The sight of me sparks something—her face brightens, and she moves with newfound energy to kneel before me. But when she reaches for my waistband, I slap her hands away, my own desire barely contained.

I lift her back onto the couch, sit beside her, and draw her into an embrace that offers a hint of rest. I can feel her respirations slow and deepen as exhaustion takes hold anew, and I wait, watching the game with one eye and keeping the other on her.

When her breathing grows too calm, I rouse her afresh with a few light slaps to her cheeks. "Hey, gorgeous. Hey, Anna!" My words are firm and commanding but laced with fondness.

She jolts awake, a low, mournful sound escaping her as she reaches for me, clinging to my arms and shoulders. I get off the couch and haul her up with me, her figure limp in my grasp. She seems disoriented, her head jerking slightly as she tries to focus, finally lifting her gaze to meet mine.

"My angel," I whisper into her ear, letting my nose brush her earlobes. Her response is immediate—a low, yearning moan that stirs me, making my cock harder. Her desire echoes my own, but we'll both have to wait. Our experience has to be perfect—every sensation heightened, every contact deliberate.

With careful precision, I unzip and unhook her pencil skirt, my rough hands grazing her smooth skin. She inhales sharply, her breath sizzling through clenched teeth. I set the skirt aside, my gaze never leaving hers. Her stare, once sharp and focused, now sags, exhaustion pulling her toward sleep. But I'm not ready to let her drift away.

When her eyelids begin to slump again, I place one hand on her firm breast, my other arm steadying her against me. Her eyes snap open, a gasp leaving her lips. I press gently, feeling the warmth of her skin through her shirt. Her hand slams onto mine, urging me to squeeze tighter, but I resist, instead pinching her nipple through the fabric of her shirt and bra. She cries out, the sound a blend of pain and pleasure that sends a thrill through me.

Holding her close, I lower my mouth to her other breast, tracing it with my tongue, teasing her until she cries in desperation. "Matt...babe! Please...please fuck me. Now."

Her pleas are a sweet symphony to my ears, but I won't give in. Not yet. I press her to my chest, feeling her body relax before she starts to drift off. With a swift motion, I flip her limp form as her strength ebbs away, and begin undoing the buttons of her shirt, one by one. Each button undone is a victory, as she jolts awake with every movement.

Before I remove her shirt, I take my time tracing patterns on her midriff and letting my fingertips dance around her navel. She shivers, her skin alive with anticipation. I squeeze her hips gently, feeling the tension in her muscles, then swiftly remove her shirt. She moans, trembling, as I wrap my arms around her, caressing her butt with slow, deliberate movements.

I pause, taking a second to admire her in the red lace underwear that cling to her curves. My dick hardens and throbs—the ache of restraint almost unbearable—but I force myself to hold back. Not yet. This is for her, and I must draw it out to make her feel every second. My hand wraps around her neck, gently but firmly, as I circle her, inspecting every inch, taking in every detail of her body.

She's nearly spent, her exhaustion palpable as I lift her and let her legs wrap around my waist. Her head falls onto my shoulder, her breathing slowing, growing quieter. But I'm not letting her rest yet. I carry her to our bedroom, laying her down in the center of the bed. Her eyelids flutter, the drag of sleep too strong to resist. But I'm ready for this—I deliver another series of light slaps to her cheeks, just enough to jolt her awake.

She covers her face, trying to shield herself from the bright lights I deliberately left on. I pin her wrists to her sides, holding her in place, watching as tears spill down her cheeks. Her eyes threaten to close again, sinking into the depths of slumber.

I trail my fingers down her midriff, navel, belly, and further, tracing her clit through the thin lace of her panties. Her eyes snap open, glowing with a sudden, intense awareness. I smirk, feeling the wetness seeping through the fabric. Her back arches as she reacts to my touch with unfiltered need. She gasps, her breaths coming faster, her chest rising and falling in a frantic rhythm.

I tighten my grip on her neck with enough force to keep her present and grounded. She trembles beneath me, a quivering mess of anticipation and desire. I can see the desperation, the longing, the sheer exhaustion on her face and it only drives me further.

Then, with a deliberate, measured pace, I step off the bed, leaving her howling, moaning, and begging as I retreat into the living room. My ribcage pounds, desire clawing at my control. I sink into the couch, running my hands across my face, trying to regain my composure. The sight of her—splayed out on the bed, wrapped in that red lingerie, trembling with need—nearly broke my resolve. The urge to shove her panties aside and plunge my cock into her soaked pussy almost overpowered me.

However, experiences beyond succumbing to primal urges await us this night. It's about control, about pushing her—and myself—to the limit. I inhale and fill my lungs, steadying the fire inside me and letting the heat simmer without bubbling over. I wait, counting the seconds as they tick, allowing the anticipation to build anew.

When I return to the bedroom, her breathing is shallow, her head lolling to the side. I know the time is right. Leaning down, I whisper into her ear, my speech a soft caress, "Hey, my angel...my darling, hey..."

She stirs, her head moving slightly, but she's on the edge of sleep. I give her another series of light, considerate slaps, rousing her again. This time, she wails, the sound pleading, as she forces her eyes open. My heart clenches at the sight—her effort, her willingness to comply with my needs, her surrender to my dominance. "My baby, my gorgeous, you're doing so well, dear." My words are praise and encouragement, meant to soothe her even as I push her further.

I freeze as a fleeting but forceful realization—a confrontation—hits me. The words *my baby*. I used to call Anna that when we were dating and married. After I met Alex, the meaning of the word changed for me—it became an expression of the special bond she and I shared. When Anna and I got together the second time, I had stopped calling her that. But now, unexpectedly, the word tumbles out of my mouth as I caress her. Stitches of pain travel under my ribcage and I struggle with focus, as memories and images of Alex—our lost bond and our time between the sheets—play in random loops.

I've not let go of her. Will I ever? Truly?

My frame shudders and jerks, and with effort but swiftly enough, I recite my letter silently to myself and regain my focus: Anna. *I need to check myself whenever the word "baby" crosses my lips.* I wonder if Anna noticed that I had stopped calling her by that nickname. I fix my gaze on the beauty lying on the bed, floating off to sleep again.

With as much tenderness and care as I can manage, I shock her fully awake by slowly sliding her panties off and stroking her clit, my eyes locked on her tired face as she wakes to sheer, exquisite elation. Her moans, soft at first, quickly grow louder as my fingers delve into her soaked pussy, one by one. "Ooh, ooh, babe...yes...Matt, oh, God...there, there, keep going, Matt...oh, God," she moans, her voice a sultry blend of exhaustion and need. The sensation of her wet sex around me is something I will never tire of—her pussy responds to my thrusting fingers with a fervor that ignites every nerve in me.

I kiss her navel, sucking on her soft belly as my thumb circles her bundle of nerves, eliciting sharp gasps that fuel my desire. Her back arches off the bed—straining toward release—but I push her down, denying her the satisfaction she so desperately craves. I can feel her teetering on the edge, her figure taut with anticipation. Just as she's about to climax, I pull away, cupping her face and pressing my mouth against hers to muffle her protests, her cries, her pleas.

She calms, her breath evening out as she teeters on the brink of sleep another time. But I'm not done with her. I slide down her frame—my lips and tongue suckling, nibbling—trailing heat over her skin until I reach her pussy again. Her shrieks fill the apartment as I lick and worship her clit and folds with my lips and tongue, my hands steadying her thrashing torso as I devour her.

She clutches the sheets tightly, knuckles white with the effort of holding on as I use my tongue—teasing and tasting, driving her wild with need. I know how my nose brushing her clit drives her to the brink, so I press down and deeper, reveling in the way her cries turn into loud, desperate moans. I kiss, lick, and suck her labia—savoring the sweet taste of her—then pause long enough to relish the sound of her wailing, begging for the release I continue to deny her.

"Babe...please, please make me come, Matt...I'm dying...please, babe," she pleads, her tone a strained whisper, her bloodshot eyes glistening.

She's endured enough torment—two weeks of relentless overtime, grueling freelance hours, and nights of scant or nonexistent sleep, all culminating in this carefully orchestrated crescendo of sensation and restraint. Before granting her the release she craves, once again I indulge myself, descending between her thighs to savor her juicy, intoxicating pussy.

My mouth claims her, tongue dancing on her most sensitive spots, drawing out muffled cries that resonate deep within me. She responds in kind, hips bucking, hands clawing at the sheets, a symphony of surrender. Satisfied, I let my fingers assume control, plunging deep, curling right where she needs them, sending her spiraling into a long, quaking orgasm. She twists and convulses, ecstasy crashing inside her as my relentless thrusts push her over the edge.

A sudden gush signals her release, her essence spilling forth, and I shift, steadying her as she squirts, her ecstasy painting the sheets. Her eyes, once heavy with exhaustion, are wide and wild, head jerking violently. She reaches out, trying to grasp my neck to yank me closer, but I have duties yet to fulfill.

I dive down, my mouth lapping up her juices, cleaning her thighs and the intimate spaces between with deliberate, languid strokes of my tongue. I moan, relishing the taste of her, the act fueling my arousal and painfully hard cock—a sensation I know I'll never tire of.

Finally, she collapses onto her back, chest heaving, limbs limp from the rapture. But our night is young. Desire courses through me—an insistent pulse in my groin that demands satisfaction. I reach for her, positioning myself to claim what is mine.

"Oh, my angel...oh, Anna," I moan, voice thick with ecstasy as I guide my cock into her, feeling the wetness and warmth of her pussy envelop me. The sensation of her drenched, welcoming folds fires every nerve in my body—a sensation I can never get enough of. Our bodies move in perfect harmony as she finds the strength to match my rhythm, her desire fueling her resolve.

Tonight, I choose a different path. Instead of taking her on endless trips to the edge, I slow my pace—savoring the moment and drawing out the pleasure. At the end of every stroke, I ram deep into her pussy. She groans beneath me as she urges me to go faster and harder, but I resist, diving deeper and connecting with her in every way. My admiration for her increases with each deliberate thrust—her strength, grace, elegance, perfectly sculpted form, and mesmerizing eyes that reflect every emotion she feels.

Then it happens again—an echo, slowly building in strength. A fragile, yet sultry voice moaning, and weeping, in sheer ecstasy, *"Daddy...fuck me...harder...please, please don't stop, Daddy!"* I falter for a moment, but Anna doesn't seem to notice.

Spasms of guilt stall me. An image of Alex—bound and bruised, red marks all over her skin—lying on her stomach as I pound her, takes root. A sting in my chest grows sharper. Anna shifts under me and attempts to open her eyes.

With immense fortitude, I remind myself of the letter, again, and silently apologize to Alex—and Anna—as I shift my focus.

I run my eyes and hands all over Anna, handling her breasts too forcefully. A shout escapes her lips as she arches her torso, and something within me snaps—maybe remnants of guilt—and my fervor to make up for my lapse intensifies.

I grab her neck and impose my mouth on hers, pulling her into a greedy and unapologetic kiss as I increase the force with which I ram into her drenched pussy at the end of every thrust. Her body tenses, a telltale sign of her nearing release.

Relenting, I pick up the pace, responding to her pleas with renewed intensity. Faster, harder, deeper—I give her everything she craves. She quivers, then shakes violently as she explodes into a powerful orgasm—her voice breaking as she cries out my name again and again. The intense warmth of her pussy, her release, and her clenching flesh drive me wild. Her delight feeds my own—pushing me to the brink—and I finally let go, climaxing deep inside her.

We moan together, our voices intertwining as I claim her lips, the warmth of my release mingling with hers. Even as I continue to move within her, the feeling of her wetness wrapped around me—her juices coating me—drives me further into an intoxicating frenzy. I keep going, emptying every drop of my semen inside her.

When I finally pull out, she shrieks as more of her release spills forth, her body caught in the spasms of a lingering orgasm. I can't resist the urge to taste her a second time, and I go down on her to lap up every drop, cleaning her with slow, deliberate strokes, my tongue tracing every curve and fold.

She writhes—her hands clutching the sheets, fingers digging in as she twists and turns—lost in the aftershocks of exhilaration. I move to her side, wrapping her in my arms and holding her close, caressing her tenderly with a soothing whisper in her ear. Our passion subsides, leaving us wrapped in a warm, peaceful afterglow—golden nuggets of time in pure connection and fulfillment.

"Shh...my darling...I'm here..."

"Oh, Matt..."

"Anna, oh, my sweet angel..." I murmur, planting warmhearted kisses on her head, face, and hair. Slowly, her trembling subsides, and her breathing evens out. I soothe her with a gentle massage, feeling her muscles gradually unwind. Her whimpers tug at my heart, and she murmurs, "Matt...oh, babe...I love you." Her voice is a soft echo of the euphoria still coursing through her.

I press a kiss on her earlobe and whisper, "I love you, gorgeous." The words comfort me. I can do this, despite my earlier lapse when I was reminded of Alex.

As Anna soaks in my aftercare, enveloped in the warmth of our shared passion, I cocoon her in a blanket. As I'm about to step away to fetch some water, she surprises me with a burst of strength, grabbing my forearms and pulling me back to her. Our session of torment, pain, fatigue, and liberation concludes with a lingering kiss that speaks beyond physical desire to deep, abiding love.

She falls asleep in my arms, her body melting into mine, and I hold her close, unwilling to let go. I watch her sleep cuddled in my arms, my lips brushing over her head and hair as I whisper assurances and tender notes of care, though I know she can't hear me.

Finally, I recline, wrapping her securely in my embrace. Our bodies sink into the quiet of the night, swathed in the remnants of euphoria and the silent promises of peaceful rest. Before sleep claims me, my cheeks stretch faintly as a thought lulls me.

I love you, Anna, and I'm ready to fill this world with our beautiful children.

CHAPTER TWENTY

Anna: The Commitment

I tilt my head, caught in a haze, and watch the children leaping with unbridled joy. Everything else becomes a blur. The band plays a cover of a pop hit, a favorite among the kids, and their ecstatic cheers fill the air with pure, infectious happiness. Older children and adults join in, and the crowd is swept up in the magic—dancing, holding hands, swaying to the beat, and singing along.

"Hey, you okay?" Matt's voice shakes me out of the daze as his arms encircle me, keeping me steady. I snap out of my reverie to beam at him, and warmth floods my chest. I take his hand and steal a quick kiss before we both lose ourselves in the vibrant energy of the audience, cheering the band on.

Central Park is alive with color and movement—the green expanse of the lawn stretching out under the fading light of the day. The tall, stately trees form a natural canopy around us, and their leaves rustle softly in the evening breeze. The scent of freshly cut grass mixes with the faint aroma from nearby food vendors, adding to the rich symphony of sensations. The city's skyline peeks through the trees, a reminder of the world beyond this oasis of music and joy.

Free concerts in Central Park always remind me of my dad. Even though we had access to VIP boxes and exclusive lounges, he often brought me to these free performances. It was his way of escaping the high stakes, high-energy corporate world that consumed him—a chance to breathe in the simplicity of life. For me, it was pure joy—jumping up and down with other children, screaming and singing, and feeling the thrill of the crowd. I remember the warmth of his shoulders as he lifted me high, my legs dangling over his chest. As I grew older, he told me it was his way of showing me life's simpler pleasures, reminding me of the humble roots from which he and his father had built a world-leading company.

Tears sting at the edges of my vision, and a knot tightens in my throat. My body softens, my breath steadies, and memories drift in, surrounding me with calmness. Time slips away as I replay those cherished moments with my dad—a bittersweet longing filling my heart.

Today I'm here with Matt, the love of my life. He senses my nostalgia and draws me close in a tight embrace. His lips press gently against my forehead, replacing my pain with comfort and happiness. His actions seem to transfer my burdens to him, leaving me filled with a peaceful energy.

"My gorgeous."

He says it with a sunny smile—his high cheeks lift, and his lush black and gray hair sways gently in the evening breeze. His viridian eyes shine affectionately, and I am mesmerized, lost in the depths where I'm content to remain captive and resting.

As the band plays on, the skies above us display a symphony of purples, oranges, and reds, casting a warm glow over the concert. The crowd's cheers crescendo and children's laughter blends with the music, creating its own joyful rhythm. Matt and I join in, swept up by the flow of the evening. Beneath the lively energy, a quiet connection ties us together—a calm that makes the evening intimate, as if we're alone in a sea of people.

As we ride home on the subway, I wrap my arms around his and rest my head on his shoulder with my eyes fixed on the untidy floor of the car. My mind drifts, lost in a whirlwind of thoughts. Memories of my dad, my childhood, the laughter of children in the park, and images from the last year spin through my head, taking me on a rollercoaster emotional journey—until my feelings finally settle into a restful rhythm of peace, love, and happiness. Each memory brings its own sensation to my body—a stab of pain, a second of lightness, a thrill, a shiver—before everything aligns in soothing harmony.

In the apartment, we settle down to a simple takeout dinner. The familiar comfort of the space wraps around us, a stark contrast to the emotional whirlwind during the subway ride.

"Babe, when do I go off birth control?" I ask, breaking the silence. I'm not one to ease into serious topics, especially with him, but I can tell I've caught him off guard. He chokes slightly on a spoonful of fried rice, needing a second to sip water and compose himself. He covers his mouth with a fist as he swallows before meeting my gaze. His face is relaxed, with a soft glow that makes his already perfect features seem even more ethereal. His brows furrow, and a crease forms on his forehead before it quickly smooths away.

"What are we waiting for?" I ask quietly, squeezing his forearm—my voice barely steady. He continues eating methodically, as if weighing his words. He rises and walks over to the window, staring out at the night. I stay at the table, hand trembling as I stir my spoon, tracing slow, exaggerated circles. The tension is unbearable.

When he finally returns, he takes my hand. His touch grounds me, but it's also electric. "I want to marry you first. Well, again," he says, and his smile widens, warmth radiating from every inch of his features. His words strike like a lightning bolt, knocking the air from my lungs. My heart stutters, then pounds painfully in my chest. The world tilts, everything blurs, and time stands still. I'm lost in the rush of it all.

A tug on my fingers pulls me back to the present, and I gasp, pulling my hand from his. The intensity of my emotions threatens to spill over. A desperate need to escape—to breathe—overtakes me. I stand abruptly and move to the window, pressing my hands to my face, trying to steady my racing breath. My heart pounds faster, and my thoughts are a tangled mess. I'm on the verge of panic—everything is crashing down on me.

I want to run. I want to disappear. I feel so exposed, so unmoored.

He approaches me, and his calm presence is a stark contrast to the storm inside me. He gently turns me around, lifting my chin to meet his gaze. His soft eyes promise that everything will be okay. But it doesn't feel okay. His voice—low and soothing—rumbles in my chest.

"Everything will be okay, gorgeous," he murmurs, and I shudder at the timbre of his words. His grip tightens, grounding me, but all I can feel is chaos.

I collapse against him—holding on tightly—my gaze vacant. My arms tighten around his waist, desperate for the comfort and security he offers. His fingers move mellowly through my hair and down my spine, and his touch is a balm to my frayed nerves. He kisses the crown of my head, leaving his lips there as if anchoring me in the present.

I wasn't ready for the bomb he dropped—marriage. I thought I had prepared for everything—stopping birth control, moving into a bigger apartment, even discussing the future of his job. But I hadn't prepared for the panic and strange thrill that consume me. I was so sure, so calculated, and now I'm anything but.

He shot through all my plans and calculations with a simple, casual statement. As I meet his gaze, my perception of his want shifts—it's no longer a simple desire but an undeniable, profound need. I lock lips with him, pouring all my love and devotion into a long, desperate kiss, trying to express the torrent of emotions inside me.

"Matt...I..." My throat feels parched, and I struggle to find the words. My mind is slowly emerging from the fog of uncertainty. Still clinging to him, I shift, searching his eyes, trying to ground myself in the calm strength I always find there. I clear my throat—my voice barely above a whisper. "Why do you want that? I don't think I'm—*we're* ready. And...you don't have to do that for me—"

He doesn't let me finish. "It's what I need. I'm not doing it for you. For us, perhaps, but that comes later," he says, and his voice is calm and unshaken

"It's time to settle down, Anna. I may be saying this selfishly because I'm forty-two now. But we've found each other again." His gaze brims with serene confidence.

"What we went through...it's strengthened us. Trust, do not doubt." His words resonate with quiet determination. Warmth spreads through me, soothing the tension that had coiled in my chest.

He smooths my hair, and his fingers are gentle as they tuck loose strands behind my ear. His touch is asthenic, almost reverent, as he grazes my brows and cheeks with light strokes of his knuckles. "Anna, I can't wait to fill this world with our beautiful children. But I must marry you first, again."

His words jolt me. I watch him take a step back. I shriek, gasping and howling as frantic breaths escape me. I cover my mouth tightly, trying to contain the flood of emotions. My heart slams against my ribcage as I watch him lower himself on one knee.

Shaking my head violently, tears spill, released from the deepest recesses of my love and fear. "Matt...please...babe...no, I don't have the strength...please, Matt...don't..." I can barely speak—my voice breaking as I heave and pant, and my entire body trembling with the force of my emotions.

But none of it fazes him. He remains serene, as if my unraveling doesn't disturb him. His expression is unwavering and his gaze steady as he kneels before me. And then a smile—his brightest one—spreads across his angelic face, a vision of pure love and joy. His cheeks lift, and his perfect teeth flash—every feature of his flawless face a symphony.

I'm crying. My tears are cascading down my cheeks, trailing along my neck, pooling in the hollow of my collarbone. My hands tremble as they move between a praying pose, covering my nose and mouth, and clutching my head, as if trying to contain the explosion of emotions surging within me.

"Savannah Mei Ren…"

I yelp as euphoria finally breaks through, flooding me with pure, unbridled joy. Every cell in my body comes alive, celebrating this man, this love, this shared experience.

After a pause he continues, his voice resolute.

"Savannah Mei Ren, you will marry me."

In a blink, I'm on him, closing the distance and grabbing his face. I crush my lips against his—my kiss trying to absorb his words, make them part of me, and let them mingle with the elation tearing through my veins. My fingers dig into his skin, clinging to him, trying to ground myself in this reality that feels almost too wonderful.

I take a shaky breath to complete the formalities and whisper, "Yes, my king." My voice trembles—the words come out dissonant—but my resolve and submission are unwavering. He calms me down in stages, then asks me to fetch our original engagement ring, the one I've kept safe all these years. It's a simple band with a single, unassuming diamond—a symbol of clarity, purity, and now, renewed love.

As he slips the ring onto my finger, he speaks confidently, but this time there's passion underlying his words: "Both of us have been through struggles the past year, unimaginable yet real."

I nod—my heart swelling as I reach for his lips, unable to contain myself. I steal another quick kiss, craving the connection, needing him close.

"I believe our bond has stood the test of time. Both of us have become tougher. This ring on your finger—it's a testament to that."

His words sink in, and my tears spill over as I replay memories from over six years ago. I remember the moments of doubt before we started dating—when I almost lost hope—pursuing him with all my heart while he gently fended off my romantic advances, steering us toward friendship. But once he gave in…well, the rest is truly history. A history that has shaped us, strengthened us, and prepared us for the future, exactly as he said.

My mind fills with positive thoughts, and lingering fears of the future dissolve. Contentment and a profound sense of ease envelop me, and everything glows with a newfound brightness. Questions fade away, replaced by answers that have never seemed more straightforward. My hand tingles in his grasp as a warm current pulses through my chest, filling me with a deep, abiding safety.

I nod once more, and we come together in a silent embrace—the connection grounding me as the world revolves around us. In this instant, I am completely in sync with the universe, no longer alone but bound to Matt, now and forever.

"Let's be happy. Everything will follow, gorgeous," he whispers, and his voice is a silky caress. He restates his mantra—the living belief guiding us—as we walk together toward the bedroom as if this apartment were a garden of blooming flowers, flowing champagne, and endless sunshine.

CHAPTER TWENTY-ONE

Alex: The Midnight Sun - Rising

THIRD WEEK OF JULY, ABOUT SEVEN AND □ A HALF MONTHS SINCE THE BREAKUP

PRESENT TIME

E ndless sunshine greets me as I throw open the curtains in my bedroom. The floor-to-ceiling windows invite a flood of warm, soothing light. I breathe deeply, letting the sunlight permeate my skin, and my lungs expand with each inhalation. The warmth invigorates every cell, filling me with renewed energy.

I step onto the balcony. "Good morning, sunshine," I say with enthusiasm to the miracle of nature which fills the world with light and hope. My smile grows wide, mirroring the brilliance of this celestial wonder—the silent guardian around which everything revolves.

Blowing a kiss to the never-ending light in this part of the Arctic Circle, I swear the glimmers brighten as if they are reaching for me, whispering, "I've got you."

I twirl around, humming my favorite tunes as I tidy my room. As I enter the bathroom, I catch my reflection in the mirror, but I don't let it deter me. "Oh, don't you worry, Alex. I'll make you over," I say chirpily and get to work.

For the next ninety minutes, I devote myself to self-care, undoing the neglect I've subjected my body to over the past seven months. A long, indulgent shower washes away the remnants of sorrow, and I carefully fix my hair. My skin glows from the meticulous grooming, and though I need little, I apply a light touch of makeup. The girl standing in front of the mirror is a far cry from the one I saw yesterday. *Daddy will love the new Alex.*

"Top of the morning to you, Teddy, Evangeline, and Mommy! How are you all on this blessed morning?" I flutter around the living room, where three stunned statues stand frozen in disbelief. My laughter ripples through the air, shaking them from their trance.

"Breakfast?" I ask, dancing into the kitchen as they take their seats at the counter. My cheeks lift as I hand them plates of toast, savoring their reactions as they absorb what they see.

"Honey, dear God—you look so bright and beautiful," Mom stutters, her eyes wide and glassy as she struggles to process my transformation.

Evie rushes to me, inspecting every detail—my meticulously styled hair, smart business attire, and radiant expression. She retreats a step, covering her mouth. "Sweetie, I'm afraid to hug you. You're stunning, and you sound so...delightful," she says, more composed than Mom.

"Hey, I'm happy to see you like this. What happened?" Ted, ever the inquisitor, searches for answers.

I walk over to him and grab his elbows firmly. "Eldest brother, I'll explain everything before the day ends. And to you too, dearest Mom and Evie. But work awaits. I must get to the office at once," I say with verve, planting kisses on their cheeks. Mom's plate slips from her hand, clattering onto the countertop, and I laugh.

"See you at the office, Ted? I need you there today. I've called an important meeting." I wave to them before grabbing my purse.

As the elevator descends, I peer through the glass windows and greet my new friend, the sun. Speaking earnestly, I whisper, "Dear Sun, I have the answer, and I have a plan. Just as you illuminate everything, I've discovered where I went wrong. Inspired by you, I won't let my mistakes defeat me. I'm going to confront them with confidence and determination. I know what I have to do." Blowing kisses at the light, I meet my bodyguard, Lars, for my ride to work.

"What do you mean you're done?" Ted snaps, throwing a stack of printouts on his desk in his corner office, which is illuminated by the sun and overhead lights. He wanders a short distance towards the windows, pauses as if thinking, and returns to the desk. Lillian, who's in Kiruna for a site visit, touches the base of her neck and scratches her temple. Her expression is blank as she rubs her forehead.

My calm demeanor infuriates Ted, but I remain composed. In a steady voice, I continue, "Okay, maybe 'done' wasn't the right word. I'm handing over the reins to Lillian. She's been leading Project GreenWind as the Team Leader. I'm simply transferring any remaining responsibilities I have to her. She's more than capable of managing everything."

I stand, back straight and chest out, crossing my arms. My gaze shifts back and forth between them.

I linger on Lillian for a moment. I reflect on the past year—how I created my informal cohort during my internship at Cunningham-Segal in Manhattan, with her among them. What started as a small group grew into a world authority on wind energy. I introduced her to my youngest brother, James. Now they're a couple, and their public appearances make them a media sensation. I made Lillian the project's Team Leader after Adam 'disappeared.'

Lillian places a hand on my elbow, squeezing gently. "Alex, you're the brains behind this. Even if we manage the designs, the wind pattern predictor models are your—"

"I've collected all my pseudocode, sketches, and designs in one place," I cut in. "Two hundred and fifty pages of documentation. It's uploaded to the cloud, only accessible to you," I say to Lillian.

They both listen carefully, foreheads creasing. A sharp tug pulls at my chest as I hand over my baby—the ideas I conceived when I was with Matthew—to Lillian. "You just need a decent physicist-mathematician. I've asked Dr. Whitaker from Harvard to recommend someone. Find them, swear them to secrecy, and you're good. Until then, I'll help with the models."

I step toward the door, signaling the end of the conversation.

Ted slumps in his chair, leaning on the backrest as his hands scrub his face. Lillian offers me a reassuring nod, which I return, grateful for her calm. She settles in her chair—her composure a contrast to Ted's obvious distress. Lillian can handle this.

Ted leans his elbows on the desk and lifts his chin, and his voice is clear but tinged with fatigue. "What about this thing with the president? You know, the president of the United States?"

My smile remains as bright as it's been all morning. From the windows in Ted's office, I glimpse the midnight sun hanging high in the sky, and I can't help but break into a wide, toothy grin. Gesturing with outstretched arms, I declare, "You've got this, guys. You're it. Cunningham-Segal, the project, and the prospects for wind energy—it's all in your hands from this point on."

Ted is referring to the invitation from the president's office, asking me to join the US delegation at the Global Summit for a Sustainable Future in London next month. The president intends to showcase Project GreenWind as a prime example of young American innovation and the country's commitment to renewable energy.

I know they expected me to lead the presentation.

Ted pleads, "Alex. Project GreenWind is your baby."

This discussion has dragged on long enough. I grab my laptop, and my tone sharpens. "That's enough. You're professionals. Start acting like it."

As I make my way to the door, Ted moves to block my exit. His tone is soft, his manner delicate and kind. "You've changed. I'm happy to see you like this. God, the last seven months...but never mind that. What's going on?"

Lillian steps beside him, and in an instant, this becomes a warm, comforting family moment.

I steal a quick glance at the midnight sun outside, then turn to my brother and future sister-in-law. With the same radiance, calm, and composure I've carried all day, I address them with quiet confidence. "I've found clarity. I've mapped a path forward. I'm going to be happy. All I need is your support. Start by taking the project to the next level."

I hug them, planting a kiss on both their cheeks. As I step away, I heave a contented sigh of relief—my positive smile never wavering. With a last nod, I turn and leave Ted's office.

A single tear escapes my eye as I reflect on the fact that I've just handed over our baby to Cunningham-Segal. But I quickly brush it away and lift my chin. From here on out, my life will be more rewarding than any professional achievement. *I've played a part—not my last—in securing a sustainable future for the world. But now, my destiny—Matthew—shines even brighter.*

CHAPTER TWENTY-TWO

Alex: The Midnight Sun - Shining

At home, I sit down with Evie and Mom for a much-needed heart-to-heart.

Wishing I could go back and change what happened, I tell them, "Mom, Evie, I owe both of you an apology for the destructive and abusive behavior I've exhibited over the past several months. You put your lives on hold for me—sacrificing so much—and all I did was push you away and treat you with disrespect. I took you both for granted, and I'm truly sorry." My voice is low and steady. Anxiety threatens to bubble up, but I collect myself. I'm determined not to cry. I must stay strong—for the future I'm building.

They sob, embracing me firmly. For a second, my resolve falters as their cries pierce my tightening chest, threatening to drag me down. It takes all my strength to hold back my tears, even though I know theirs are from the joy of seeing me transformed. I pull away gently, letting them see the brightness in my face, the broad smile I've worn all day.

"Alex, honey, don't apologize. You're my baby," Mom says, wiping her cheeks. She lets out a shaky laugh, pressing her palm to her heart. She smiles and sits up, straight and alert.

"Sweetie, that's what sisters are for. And we don't do apologies," Evie adds, wiping away her tears and attempting to lighten the moment with another shaky laugh. She relaxes and wears a joyous expression.

I laugh with them, giving their arms a playful shake. I tell them what I told Ted and Lillian—that I've found clarity, a resolution. I promise to share my plans with them at dinner.

Evie and Mom speak in bubbly voices and reassure me that they support me entirely, and that I can lean on them whenever I need to. For a fleeting moment,

I see them exchange puzzled and concerned looks. Then they smile, open their arms wide, and embrace me again.

I jump up from the sofa, bouncing on my feet a few times. In a cheery tone, I say goodbye and dance out of the room, leaving their smiling faces behind.

"Alright, you ready?" I ask aloud, preparing for the final debate in the matter of Alexandra Mary Cunningham vs. her intellect—a battle to explain with conviction why I'm certain I made a mistake.

I shut the door to my room, ensuring no one can hear my voice as I speak aloud. Then I draw the curtains wide, inviting my new companion, the midnight sun, to flood the room with its light. The golden rays fill the vast bedroom, bringing strength.

I take a few deep breaths to solidify my composure, letting calm wash over me.

My frontal lobe is still processing, and after a brief silence, it restates a familiar logic. "You are aware of my reasoning. You would have reacted no differently—driven by murderous rage, jealousy, and anger. You would have left him, regardless of what you think now. Accept that and move on."

I close my eyes, letting peace soak me like a soothing balm.

"Here's how I know I made a mistake," I begin, steady and confident. "Instead of walking away, the smart choice would have been to insert myself into their life. I should have played Anna's game. I should have used you, my dear brain, to stay close to them."

"We're going in circles," my logic retorts with a mocking laugh. "You couldn't have done that. You weren't strong enough to restrain yourself and think as you're doing now."

I nod, acknowledging the truth in that. *Agreed*. But I am strong now.

Two nights ago, I spent hours tearing myself apart over this. I could have handled everything so differently. With calculated precision, I could have slipped into Anna's and Matthew's dynamic—his support for her and her expert manipulation—monitoring them. I could have pretended to care and asked her to join him and me in *our* lives, even if the thought of befriending that bitch churns my stomach. I could have started small, maybe by inviting her to dinner—a simple show of solidarity. I could have put her on the defensive, rattled her.

My intellect remains silent, offering no rebuttal.

I could have done countless things to enter their bubble, slowly unraveling the bitch's twisted plan to seduce him and win him back. I could have played her game and outmaneuvered her.

My thoughts continue to be quiet—no counterarguments.

Instead, I walked away, giving her exactly what she wanted—him, alone, vulnerable to the web of lies and manipulative texts she spun around him. I might as well have handed Matthew to her on a silver platter, just as my brain warned me some time ago.

My brain starts to see my counter-logic and responds. "Alright, alright. I concede. Your reasoning is solid, but what if…"

For a fleeting second, I lose my composure, and panic grips me. I understand what my logic is hinting at—*what if they're already together now?*

I catch my breath and exhale a sigh of relief. I know Matthew. I've always been the center of his world, and that won't change. He's the strongest man I've met—in heart, mind, and body. He'll wait for me. He needs his ward just as much as I do my protector and caretaker. *We were connected from the instant I first saw him at the gym.*

I laugh—a dry, mirthless sound—at the absurd suggestion. Unable to find any other flaws in my reasoning, my intellect resorted to this baseless theory—that he could have wavered in his commitment to me.

By now, he's likely helped her grieve and heal. He's not stupid—he knew her lewd texts and casual advances were wrong, but he couldn't just cut her off and let her spiral down into the depths of her despair. Not the way I spiraled, after abandoning the one person who could hold me together.

I close my arguments with the assurance that my brain will help should I call upon it. It's time for action.

He's thinking of me, and he's waiting for me. I have to hurry. I can't keep Daddy waiting.

My next stop is Dr. Robbins.

As the session begins, she appears stunned, standing for a few moments as she takes me in. She takes her time settling in her chair with her gaze fixed on me. She waves, and her eyebrows furrow and then release. She leans forwards, and a slow smile creeps across her lips. She pushes her glasses up and blinks. I wave back and smile with enthusiasm and confidence, letting her see the broad, genuine beam on my face that she's never seen in our therapy sessions.

"Alex, you look radiant," she says, her voice filled with spirit, though I notice the careful selection of her words. *Thank you for not asking me how I feel today, as you usually do.*

"Dr. Robbins, this will be our last session," I announce, getting straight into it—my tone vibrant with energy, matching hers.

Her brows knit, her lips curve subtly, and there's a trace of hesitation in her expression. In her usual calm and collected manner, she responds, "It's your decision, of course, but I'd love to know what's changed in your world." Her features soften further—her eyes warm and attentive—and her words are chosen with meticulous care.

"I've decided to return to Matthew. I let everything slip through my fingers when I should have held on tightly. It's time I fixed what I broke—me, him, and the life we had." I sit up straight as I meet her steady gaze, bracing myself for any challenge she might present.

"Would you mind sharing more details with me?" she presses, and her kindness feels like a gentle nudge—a subtle manipulation.

There was a time when I felt a deep sense of comfort, a bond, with her, especially when we discussed Adam's assault. Out of courtesy, I briefly share my reasoning. A surge of clarity and purpose washes over me. I straighten my posture, and my voice is steady and clear.

"Instead of managing the issue, I chose the easy road—walking away," I say firmly, meeting Dr. Robbins' gaze through the video feed. "When I could have stayed strong and monitored his interactions with Anna, I removed myself from the picture."

Dr. Robbins' pen pauses mid-note, and her brow lifts slightly. She adjusts her glasses and leans back in her chair, observing me intently. I press on—the words flowing, each one infused with a conviction I haven't felt in months.

"She's playing a game, but I should have played it too." I gesture emphatically—my hands punctuating my words. "My thoughts weren't in the right place then, but they are now. I see everything clearly. I've suffered, and I know he must be suffering too."

Dr. Robbins tilts her head, and her lips curve into the faintest hint of a smile. "Go on," she says, her voice calm and inviting.

I take a deep breath, leaning slightly forward as my energy builds. "I have to get back to him. It's not about clinging to the past—it's about fixing what's broken. We were good together. Better than good, and I know we can heal. Together."

She makes a few notes—possibly more judgments—before looking up, adjusting her glasses again, and offering her signature attentive gestures. Her usual rituals don't bother me as much, given my upbeat mood. Finally, she closes her notebook and places it on the side table.

A fleeting pulse of pain and pressure touches my chest. After all, in the last seven months, I've talked to Dr. Robbins more than I have to my family. She might not have helped me in the manner I wanted, but she listened to everything I threw at her, enduring all my tantrums and crying. With our sessions ending today—and this being the last time I see her—a bittersweet mixture of goodbye and anticipation at my renewed bond with Matthew fills me.

Her expression shifts to one of formality. Clearing her throat, she betrays a current of concern, "I wish you well. My door is always open to you." She smiles, but there is a hint of shadow on her features.

Without further hesitation, I bid her goodbye, exchanging the usual pleasantries.

But as I end the call, I think: *I won't be needing your door ever again, doctor. I'm going to my safe place, where Matthew will take care of me, and I will hold onto him with all my might.*

The monitor goes dark as I clap my hands together, feeling a sense of finality. *Dr. Robbins, check. Done.*

CHAPTER TWENTY-THREE

Alex: The Midnight Sun - Setting

My final stop is dinner with my family. With no preamble, I lay out my plan, "I'm returning to Manhattan. Please don't judge or worry, but I'm going back to Matthew."

They stare at me, facial muscles slack, and their heads swivel as they glance around. These three people—my constant companions here in Sweden, my family—who endured months of torture with me, blink their dull eyes slowly.

"I understand this isn't what you want to hear, but I've made this decision after careful consideration."

Ted gets up and paces around the table, shaking his head. He stretches his hands out wide and then relaxes them. He crosses his arms and says, "Alex, that's how all the mayhem started. You ended up hurt and went through seven months of hell," he says, voice tense.

My mom's face contorts as she leans in. She raises her eyebrows and purses her lips. "What changed, honey? I'm happy you've transformed yourself, but you can't run toward something that might leave you traumatized and emotionally bruised. Honey, my heart will break, and I might not recover if I see you like that again..."

Evie rushes over as Mom's voice quavers and a tiny stream of tears escape. I remain rooted, just observing them. *I must stay strong. I can't let myself be bothered by their worry.* I appreciate all they've done for me, but I have to face my issues alone.

I feel the urge to offer them something—more reassurance without divulging details—so they don't think I'm jumping off a cliff.

"I made a mistake—a huge one—when I misunderstood what Matthew was doing. He was trying to protect me, and in a fit of anger, I insulted him and left.

I overreacted, and then I was too stubborn to see my mistake. Only when I was away from him did I see everything clearly."

Their demeanor doesn't change. They still, and their eyebrows draw together—concern etched deeply on their features.

After several moments of uncomfortable silence, Evie sighs, squeezes my shoulders, and smiles—the curve of her lips not quite lifting. She blinks sluggishly. "What are you going to do next, sweetie?" she asks—her tone kind but beaten, reflecting the toll of my struggles and reckless behavior.

Her tone reflects what Ted, Mom, and the rest of my family have borne, standing by me. I feel relieved knowing they can return to Manhattan and resume their normal lives. No amount of gratitude could ever repay what they've done or the strength they've shown.

I stand and place my hands on the table, my gaze shifting between Mom, Evie, and Ted. Shutting my eyes briefly, I gather my thoughts, then speak with quiet confidence. "I'm flying to Manhattan tomorrow. Is there a place I can set up base in the city?"

It's been too long, and I must leave as soon as possible. Matthew needs me, and I need him even more. I want our renewed relationship to begin in a new place—not the penthouse in Weehawken where I broke up with him. That place would remind me of my mistakes, and of Anna.

Ted offers the penthouse on West 53rd, but quickly adds, "Alex, any chance you'd reconsider this decision?" Mom's eyes mirror the question.

I give them a poised smile and shake my head. "No. I've never been more certain."

I shut my room door behind me, and immediately slump on a chair, cradling my forehead in my palms. I replay what happened with my family, magnifying the expressions on their faces, their mannerisms, and their actions. My thoughts fill with self-loathing, knocking me off my pedestal of composure. I hadn't expected them to capitulate or agree to my decision so easily. They pushed back and asked questions, but what I saw in them brings a pain to the back of my throat. My skin's sensitivity heightens, and the midnight sun feels prickly.

In their faces, bodies, and speech, I saw overwhelming fatigue—from the shared journey through my grief. They walked in agony with me. Now they're drained. Their shoulders sagged, their limbs were sluggish, and their voices were strained

I did this to them. Time slows down.

As I sit on the chair with my head bowed, the rays of light bathe my skin and lift my spirits, as if they are beckoning me to the life that awaits in Manhattan. I wipe my tears and face the sun.

The best way I can make up for the damage I did to my family is to live a life filled with purpose and joy. Though they still might not accept Matthew—I doubt they ever will—seeing me spiral into depression is worse. They'd rather see my smiling face, even if I am with the man they all hate.

I resolve to do that for me, for them. Jumping up off the chair, I stand, back straight and chest puffed out.

My dear family, I am filled with gratitude for all of you, for standing by me, and accompanying me as I navigated hell. My guilt hurts, but it's not about me. I will make sure you see me happy, content, and at peace for the rest of my life.

With Matthew by my side, guiding me, that will be a sweet journey.

As the days in Kiruna grow shorter, I notice the midnight sun's relentless brightness beginning to soften—the once all-consuming light gradually fading beyond the horizon. It's as if the sky itself is granting me permission to let go, urging me to embrace the darkness I've avoided for so long. The endless daylight that once mirrored my frantic, unresolved emotions now yields to the quiet of twilight—a reminder that not everything has to be illuminated to find one's way.

I stand by the window, watching as the sun dips just below the edge of the world and leaves behind a soft glow that lingers but no longer overwhelms. A sense of peace washes over me after so long in turmoil. The light remains, but it's no longer blinding—it's guiding. This transition, this gentle fading of the midnight sun, feels like a metaphor for my own journey. I've been trapped in the harsh glare of my mistakes, unable to think beyond the pain. But as the season changes, as the light softens, I can finally glimpse the path forward.

It's time to leave this place and return to where I belong. *To whom I belong.* The sun is setting on this chapter of my life, and my doubts and fears are retreating into the shadows.

As my private jet soars out of Swedish airspace, I open my journal, feeling the urge to capture the moment. Today, I am flying toward the light, and my heart is at peace. Unlike when I left him, there isn't a shred of doubt in my mind. This decision is the right one.

Begin Journal Entry

My Reunion with Daddy
I can clearly visualize it as if it's unfolding before me. When I enter our world, I'll feel the warmth of his presence, the love that never wavered, even when I did. I'll walk through the door, and there he'll be—standing tall, his viridian eyes filled with that familiar mix of strength and tenderness.

At first, I'll hesitate, my feet rooted to the floor as guilt and regret threaten to choke me. But then, as he senses my fears, his face will soften and he'll take that first step towards me. His arms will open wide and I'll rush into them, unable to restrain the tears that have been trapped inside for so long.

"My precious girl," he'll whisper, voice thick with emotion. "You were lost, but you're home again."

In his embrace, all the darkness, all the pain of the past months, will melt away. I'll cry on his chest, feeling the safety and love that only he can give. I'll tell him everything—how sorry I am for leaving, how wrong I was to think I could ever live without him. And he'll listen, holding me close, his heart beating strong beneath my cheek.

But this won't be an occasion of despair or mourning what was lost. This will be a moment of pure joy, a reunion. Because just like in the story of the prodigal son, I'll have returned home, which is something to be cherished, not lamented.

"We must celebrate," he'll say, his voice full of joy that echoes through the walls of our new home. "For my little girl was lost, but she is now in my arms."

I'll look up at him, my tears drying as I take in his happiness. And in that instant, I'll know that everything will be okay. He'll forgive me—he already has. He'll welcome me back into his life, his heart, and together, we'll rebuild what was broken.

We'll laugh, we'll comfort each other, and we'll celebrate this miracle together. Because that's what he and I share—love—a miracle that transcends everything, even the darkest of times.

Matthew will welcome me with arms spread wide open, and the connection will be stronger than ever. I was lost, but now I am found. And this reunion, this homecoming, will be the beginning of a new chapter in our lives—one filled with forgiveness, love, and endless possibilities.

End of Entry

CHAPTER TWENTY-FOUR

Anna: Eagle

I've been keeping tabs on Alex since shortly after Matt's arrest. The night we made love and started a new life together marked the beginning of our commitment. I focused my energy on protecting him from her, in case she ever resurfaced. Without a full-time investigator, I took matters into my own hands.

During his recounting of the breakup, he mentioned speaking to her bodyguard, who told him she was out of the country but divulged no further details. She was far away, unable to interfere with our life. But I couldn't relax. I needed to prepare for her return, should it come.

Every day on my subway ride to work, I sift through Alex's digital footprint. First, there were two weeks of inactivity after she left Matt. Two weeks of silence followed by a barrage of sarcastic comments on happy couples' posts with sour hashtags: #LoveIsBland, #StaySingle, #HeartbreakIsFreedom. But a month after the breakup, her activity spiked—frequent, impulsive, emotionally raw.

A selfie:

> "Fading into the night...Who even needs the morning?"

An empty wineglass:

> "Cheers to love—it's another empty glass. #LoveIsBland."

A mirror selfie with smudged lipstick:

> "Trying to hold it together...but maybe falling apart is easier."

Over four days, she posted nearly thirty times—desperation in every image and comment. Her final post from a nightclub showed her with a group of men, captioned:

> "I'm done playing it safe."

Then, silence. No more posts or replies to the concerned comments that followed.

I check for updates daily, but there is nothing new. Part of me feels relief—she's spiraling, proving she's not the one for Matt. But another part feels pity for her, knowing how much pain she's in.

I exhale, grateful he doesn't use social media. He barely uses email, preferring face-to-face contact. It's something I admire about him.

He doesn't know about Alex's meltdown, and I'm relieved. If he did, he'd want to reach out to her, but he can't. She's not right for him. I'm the stable partner, the one who keeps him grounded. Unlike her, I didn't fall apart, and I won't. *Well, but isn't that because he supported you? What would you have done if he wasn't around for you?*

That thought is a reminder. *I'll never take him for granted.* But I am the one he deserves.

As I lock my phone, satisfaction and unease wash over me. Her unraveling proves she's unreliable, but her reckless behavior also hints at tenacity. When she wants something, she goes all in. The silence now makes me nervous—she could be planning something drastic, a dramatic return to reclaim what she lost.

As if I'm going to stand on the sidelines and watch that happen. Matt is my king, and I will guard him and our love with everything I have.

At night, when he is asleep and I'm working on my freelance projects, I take breaks to scan scientific journals, always on the lookout for mentions of her. Even if she's not active on social media, I refuse to relax. I can't afford complacency—not when he and I are rebuilding our future.

Tonight, I find three articles in different journals—all mention Alex and Project GreenWind. Each one makes my heart skip, a sharp pain building in my chest. I hide it well, but the worry eats at me. She doesn't scare me, but I'm deeply concerned about what her potential return could mean for us. I'm not afraid of the fight, but I'm tired of it. This time, I'll be prepared. That's why I research her—why I won't let my guard down.

The articles also mention Lillian Hearne, the team leader, and Ted Cunningham, the CEO of Cunningham-Segal. I follow Project GreenWind's progress closely. The latest buzz is monumental—the president herself has praised their innovation. I can't help but admire Alex's brilliance, but a deep resentment simmers beneath. Her success is a bitter reminder of the life Matt and I had, and how easily she disrupted it.

I try to rationalize my feelings, telling myself, *if she's focused on work, maybe she's moved on*, but the thought offers little comfort.

With steady hands, I pull out my notepad and start listing scenarios—what I'll do if she comes back, how I'll talk to him, and how I'll protect what we've rebuilt. My heart tells me he will never stray, but I can't afford complacency. I won't be caught off guard—not now. I've fought too hard, and I won't lower my defenses. True strength isn't surviving the blows; it's seeing them coming and rising stronger to face them.

I'm not afraid of her. I'm prepared to face her. My confidence isn't pride; it's knowing I'm the right one for him—the lover, friend, and guide who understands him, supports him, and protects him. The strongest alpha needs someone to care for him, and I'm here to cherish and protect him.

In the morning, as I get ready for work, I stand in front of the mirror, preparing for yet another conversation with him on an important topic. I've already tried talking to him twice. I inhale deeply, steadying myself and rehearsing what I'll tell him. The right words, the right timing—this is delicate, but it's for him. It's for us.

I know how much his teaching career meant to him, how badly he was hurt when it was taken from him because of her. But he must refresh his professional career, working where he belongs—the highest stages of academia and musical performance. I can't rush this, but there is no time like the present. It's been a year since he lost his prestigious teaching job at Ellsworth-Harrington Preparatory. We have a stable income, we're engaged and preparing to conceive our first child. The timing feels right to me, and I'm going to make him understand as well.

I can't let his past stand in his way.

He's already at the table, sipping his decaf as I pack my bag. I pause, feeling the weight of the moment. I must be strong this time. With a steady voice, I ask, "Hey, did you apply to the Philharmonic?"

He drops his head slightly, rubbing his eyebrow—a slight gesture, but it speaks volumes. I abandon my things and slide onto his lap, needing his strength to power my own resolve. I trace his face with my fingers, gently coaxing him. "Babe, you lost your teaching career almost a year ago. Forget that. You deserve to perform on the biggest stages in the world. Please, apply again to the Philharmonic."

He gives me a dreamy smile. Then he bites the tip of his tongue at the corner of his lips. I momentarily lose myself and close my eyes. Yearning washes over me, and a blush creeps into my cheeks.

Gathering all my strength and fortitude, I jump off his lap and assume a rigid posture, although my knees are failing, and the wetness between my thighs increases. I assume a stern tone and cross my arms tightly. "Matt, please. Approach them again. Inform them that you're engaged and the thing with the young girl is in the past. They'd be stupid to pass on a talent like you. You can't deny that. Please?"

I prepare to continue to beg, urge, and encourage to help him regain his vocation. As principal pianist in the Philharmonic, he would teach and mentor other performers, including graduate hires. He would be on one of the world's premier stages—where he deserves to be.

He approaches me with a playful smile. I strike off his advancing hands once, and then I give in. He swoops me into an embrace and a passionate kiss as I lose my footing and submit to him. My insides melt as I pull him in for another kiss. Minutes later, he lets go, much to my chagrin.

Without further words or argument, he simply agrees.

"I'll make an appointment for tomorrow and talk to them," he says.

Although I take a few moments to regain composure after his hypnotic kiss and embrace, I manage to put together words in as steady a tone as I can. "I love you."

He kisses my forehead and cups my face. His deep baritone shakes my foundations, and my sex pools with moisture. "I love you, gorgeous," he says before walking backwards towards the door, his gaze focused on me.

As the subway car rattles and snakes over the underground tracks, I perform my ritual of scouring Alex's digital footprint. Not finding anything new, I turn off my phone and rest my head against the cool glass of the subway car. The world outside blurs, but inside, a storm is brewing—a tempest of anger and resolve.

She didn't merely break his heart; she dismantled his core being. She ripped apart his livelihood, stripped him of the professional identity he'd spent years building, and reduced him to a shadow of the man he once was. The world no longer saw him as the prodigy, the maestro; they saw him as a scandal—a man who lost everything for a girl too young to grasp the consequences of her actions. It wasn't fair. It wasn't right.

When Matt told me everything after his arrest, I was the one who held him as he questioned his worth, who witnessed the toll it took on him—the man who once commanded respect reduced to whispers and rumors. I can't help but think that was one of the demons that drove him to drink.

I remember those nights, the way he tried to mask his pain, pretending to be okay when his eyes told a different story. I would pull him close, reassuring him he was more than what others thought and that his value wasn't diminished because of societal judgment. But deep down, I knew the damage was done, and it all pointed to her—the career-destroying whore.

Today, as I stand on the brink of reclaiming our life together, that anger fuels my resolve. I won't let her take anything else from him—from us. I won't lie down. Not anymore. He deserves to rebuild and rise from the ashes of what she left behind, and I will be his loyal partner to ensure that he does.

"Alex," I whisper, "if you return, you'll have to go through me to reach him. And I will shield him with every breath in my body."

Day by day, as I gear up and prepare for the potential battle ahead, a speculative flicker creeps in—a whisper that maybe she is already defeated—that she has given up. But I shove it aside, refusing to allow the thought to take root.

181

Complacency is for the weak, and I've come too far, endured too much, to falter now. I will protect what's mine, no matter the cost.

CHAPTER TWENTY-FIVE

Alex: West 53rd

As my private jet enters New York airspace, my heart syncs with the subtle vibrations of the aircraft, beating in perfect rhythm. Following a brief but restorative sleep, I'm wide awake, leaning forward in eager anticipation. From the panoramic windows, I watch the sun dip below the horizon, a scene that echoes what I left behind in Kiruna. It's surreal—the dark landscape below is dotted with the scattered lights of small towns, while the sky above fades from deep blue to soft gray, the slender arc of golden light gradually giving way to the soothing embrace of night as it descends over the East Coast.

My heart steadies, matching the tranquil grace of the night as the world below slows in preparation for rest.

I am prepared too, though not for rest, but for action—action that's long overdue. A smile tugs at my lips as I mentally review my carefully organized thoughts and plans. *My reunion!* A shudder of quiet pleasure ripples inside me as I close my eyes, savoring the memory of his arms around me, my head pressed to his chest, my arms wrapped securely around his waist. *Soon, I'll feel that embrace again.*

I have so many things I want to say to him, and I've committed them all to memory. Every word will be infused with positivity, hope, and a focus on the future, acknowledging my mistakes and the pain we've both endured. He's always been a good listener, content to sit back and hear me talk for hours, and I imagine the myriad ways his smile will dance as he hears me out. The thought of his expression fills me with a comforting warmth, like a soft embrace that wraps around my heart.

My immediate plans are simple. I'll land in Manhattan around midnight and settle into my new penthouse, letting the city's familiarity ease me back into the life I left behind. After a few hours of sleep, I'll meet him at his recording studio. A call or text won't do. Our first contact must be face-to-face, where I can see him, touch him, and make him feel the sincerity in every word. We'll talk, then I'll bring him to the penthouse, where we'll start over. There may be tears, anger, and confusion, but I'll turn them into hope and anticipation, my confession clear: *Daddy, I made a mistake.*

I can't wait to see Wyatt. His presence will bring a sense of normalcy, a connection to the past. Wyatt won't help me find him—my brothers will have taken care of that—but I'll be prepared. If Matthew's not at the studio or La Grand Élégance, I'll call him directly. If he's changed his number, I'll hire a private investigator. No matter what, I'll find him.

I've planned for every scenario, even one where he's moved out of state. For a moment, doubt creeps in, and I bury my ,ace in my hands, tears threatening. If only I'd been this focused and steady when I found those damn texts from his ex-wife.

But then I hear his voice in my mind: *"Be happy. Everything will follow."* I repeat it aloud, steady myself, and force a smile. The solution lies in building something new, stronger than before. My focus is on creating a future brighter than the past.

My plan isn't just for tomorrow. Healing will come first. I'll share my journey—my reckless nights, my desperate social media posts, and the grief I've processed over the past seven months. I won't delete my posts, selfies and comments, even if I once wanted to. He needs to see how far I fell, how close I came to losing myself.

But this time, it won't be all about me. I'll coax him into sharing his struggles, his anger, and his pain—whatever he needs to release. No part of his experiences will go unacknowledged. We'll confront it all together.

I'll tend to his wounds, showing him my devotion to his healing. We'll revisit the places that nurtured our love, rebuilding and strengthening what we had. We'll go on vacations to new and romantic destinations, where we can continue to bond and nurture our new life.

He always said I was the center of his world, but now I will make him the center of mine. My mission is to undo my mistakes, step by step, until he is fully healed.

At the right time—perhaps during a vacation—I'll share my vision of the future and bring up the topic of children. That moment will be pivotal, the point where he and I shift focus to building a family. I want his children, and the yearning for the first one is unbearable. We will resurrect the plans to build our dream home on the plot of land we bought last year.

My carefully crafted plan will ensure that these crucial conversations happen at the right time, once we've both resolved our issues, from the darkness to the light.

This new chapter isn't about mending the past, but about creating a new life together. I'm not returning to pick up the broken pieces. I'm returning to build something even more beautiful.

As the plane touches down, the jolt ignites a deeper resolve within me. My determination flares, pushing me to pack my things with hurried efficiency. The engines hum to a calm as we taxi toward the private lounges and reception areas. I feel adrenaline surge, quickening my pulse in anticipation.

When I see Wyatt, I throw my arms around him in a tight embrace, savoring the rare sight of his smile—only the third time I've ever seen it. "Welcome home, Alex," he greets me in his usual professional tone, though it can't fully mask the happiness beneath it.

"It's good to be home," I reply, smiling back at him. Before slipping into the armored Mercedes-Maybach S 580, I close my eyes and lift my chin high, inhaling the New York City air. It's the smell of home, the invigorating scent I've missed for far too long, and it fills me with renewed energy.

Though I already know the answer, I ask Wyatt about Matthew and whether they've stayed in touch—careful not to mention Adam. Wyatt shakes his head, his expression betraying nothing. I probe a little further, my last attempt, asking if he knows where Matthew is. I don't feel a flicker of suspicion or worry when Wyatt hesitates and deflects. Instead, I gently but firmly remind him, "He and I are meant to be together, Wyatt."

Wyatt remains silent as he guns the car toward midtown, and the shimmering lights of the vibrant city fill me further with energy and resolve.

My new penthouse occupies the 76th and 77th floors of a high-rise on West 53rd. I've been here once before. My family has always preferred the seclusion of our Upper West Side estate. From here, I can see that estate's towering columns.

The private elevator lacks the glass windows of my Weehawken penthouse, but the breathtaking interior makes up for it. The 360-degree views—from Central Park to the iconic city skyline—feel like a perfect reflection of my vision for a future with Matthew.

I step inside and feel a wave of satisfaction. The living room, with its soaring floor-to-ceiling windows, frames Manhattan like a living painting. I picture him here—his presence filling the space, his laughter echoing in the rooms. This is where we'll build our future.

The open-plan design invites possibilities. I picture quiet mornings with coffee in the gourmet kitchen, where sunlight casts a golden glow. The primary bedroom will be our sanctuary—a place to reconnect and rediscover each other. I can already imagine us entwined in a passionate embrace with the city lights sparkling outside.

As I gaze at the panorama, purpose settles over me. These rooms aren't just for living—they're the foundation of new things—a family of our own, fresh memories, a bright future.

Sebastian had the place cleaned and stocked with supplies. I spend the next few hours settling in, making sure everything is perfect. If all goes according to plan, Matthew and I will spend our first night here together. The hybrid piano I bought for him will arrive before the weekend, completing the space. There's already a grand piano in the living area, but I need my first-ever gift to him to be part of our renewed life.

The recording studio opens at ten, but I know he won't care about rehearsals once he sees me. I plan to arrive a little after ten thirty, giving us the time we need.

I set my alarm for nine, confident and ready. With everything in place, I fall asleep, content.

At nine in the morning I rise, stretching as adrenaline pulses through me. Four hours of sleep—just enough. I rush to the windows, throwing open the curtains to greet the city. With a click, I part the rest, letting in the light. In the shower, the sting of my mistakes hits, but I channel it into resolve. Everything's on me now—I broke it, and I'll fix it. No excuses. I'm ready.

How do you elevate already soaring confidence? I let out a silly grin and snort. The answer is simple—a beautiful summer dress.

But first, I carefully part my hair and scrupulously braid pigtails, ensuring every strand is perfectly in place. A surge of lust courses through me as I recall the long hours he used to spend playing with them—he could never get enough of my pigtails, or my hair as it is. My cheeks are warm and the mirror tells me I don't need any blush, but I apply a light touch of makeup anyway. I choose a mid-length belted shirtdress in white, his favorite. Five minutes of inspection, nuanced adjustments, and gentle touchups later, I am ready. Ready to meet him.

To comply with his instruction to always go out with a full stomach, I prepare a light breakfast with memories of him in the kitchen every morning flashing before my eyes. I laugh aloud, recalling the morning I begged him to spank me with the spatula he was using to make me an omelet.

As I chew my breakfast, I visualize the reunion with unwavering confidence. Matthew will forgive me and welcome me with open arms. My focus is on making the reunion as perfect as possible, with my apologies and meek surrender.

On the ride to the recording studio, joyful anticipation fills me. He will punish me—and I look forward to that—but not before forgiving me. I know he already has, so we can proceed to the punishment. He can keep punishing me for as long as he wants, and I will willingly submit to everything he says, commands, and does. We will return to our natural roles—he as my father figure, and I as his devoted daughter—the basic instincts that define us.

Wyatt pulls into the recording studio's parking lot, and I step out with a spring in my heart and a lightness in my step. Before heading inside, I pause outside the frosted glass doors, smiling serenely, knowing that today is the day everything changes for the better.

CHAPTER TWENTY-SIX

Anna: West 148th - Home

The shower bathtub in the apartment's tiny bathroom is barely big enough for one person, let alone two. But that doesn't stop Matt from pulling me in with him, his arms strong and unyielding as he lifts me off the floor and presses me against the tiled wall. The warm water flows across our intertwined bodies, mingling with our laughter as I wriggle in his grasp, trying to find a comfortable position in the cramped space.

"Babe, we barely have room to breathe in here!" I giggle, feeling his chiseled, firm body pinning me against the cold tiles.

He smirks, his lips brushing against my ear, sending currents down my spine. "Who said anything about breathing?" His voice is a deep, commanding whisper that makes my heart race and my pulse quicken. Even in this cramped, modest shower, he's the dominant force I fell in love with.

I gasp as his hands roam over my wet skin, his touch fond and possessive. The heat between us is palpable, and the warm water increases the temperature. He bites gently on my shoulder blade, making me yelp in surprise, and his smirk widens. "You think I need space to make you feel good?"

"Matt—" My protest is cut off by his mouth covering mine. His kiss is hungry and demanding, stealing away any discomfort. His body presses harder against mine—leaving me no room to move—but that's exactly how he likes it, how we like it.

I try to wrap my legs around his waist but the narrowness of the shower makes it awkward, and I accidentally knock the shampoo bottle off the shelf. It clatters to the floor, the lid popping off and spilling shampoo everywhere.

He chuckles, his eyes gleaming with mischief. "Making a mess already?"

I swat at his chest, but he catches my wrists and pins them above my head, his grip firm but gentle. "Focus, Anna," he murmurs, his voice low and imperative. "I'm just getting started."

The water pours, mixing with the remnants of body wash as he shifts and adjusts my frame slightly—his body controlling mine effortlessly. His other hand slides down my thigh, lifting it to his hip, and in one swift motion his hard cock is there, filling my pussy and finding every depth inside me. I gasp at the welcome intrusion, my slit clenching around him as he thrusts his dick deeper, his breath hot against my ear.

"My angel, you belong to me," he growls, and his hips move in slow, deliberate thrusts, pushing me harder against the wall. The pressure of his body and the way his length fills me so wholly are overwhelming, indulgent, and euphoric. Every nerve in my body ignites as he moves within me, and his rhythm intensifies as the confined space forces us closer, more intimately connected than ever.

I can feel his strength and power in every plunge, but there's something more—something profound. As his lips find mine again, I realize it's not merely physical. He's grounding me, claiming me, and filling me with a sense of safety and belonging. This tiny shower, this small apartment—it's ours. It's where we love, where we argue, where we live. And in this minute, it's where we become one.

The tiles are cold against my back, contrasting the passion between us. His hands tighten on my hips, his pace quickening, and each movement sends pleasure through me. I cling to him, my fingers digging into his shoulders as I surrender completely, letting him take me where he wants. His growl of approval reverberates through me, and the sound vibrates in my chest, adding to the sensations.

"Matt...oh..." I moan, my voice trembling with the intensity of it all—how he's pushing me to the edge, as he always does. He knows me, knows exactly how to make me fall apart in his arms. As the tension in my core coils tighter, I feel the familiar rush of release just within reach.

"Let go, Anna," he commands, his voice rough with his need. "I've got you."

And I do. I let go—every muscle in my body tensing as the orgasm crashes over me, powerful and consuming. His name falls from my lips in a breathless cry, and my body arches against his as I shatter in his arms. His grip on me tightens, and his release follows—a guttural sound escaping him as he pulses inside me, filling me with his warm semen.

For a time we're both still, and the water soaks our gratified bodies, mingling with sweat and the remnants of shampoo and body wash. Then he looks at me and his eyes soften, the dominant edge giving way to something more tender.

"You're my everything, Anna," he murmurs as his lips brush mine in a gentle kiss—a stark contrast to the intensity of seconds before.

I smile against his mouth, and my heart expands with the certainty that *we* are what truly matters. Not this tiny bathroom, the small apartment, or the world we live in. "And you're mine, babe. Always."

We stand there for several seconds, letting the water bring us to earth. The sound of the shower, the feel of his arms around me—it's all so simple, so perfect. This cramped space is home. It's not the size of the shower or the apartment that matters—it's the fact that we're in it together, making every tick count, whether we're laughing, loving, or simply living.

As we're about to step out, I hear a muffled knock on the wall from the neighboring apartment. He raises an eyebrow and his grin returns. "Think they heard us?"

I laugh, a light, carefree sound that echoes in the tiny bathroom. "Probably. But hey, at least we didn't break the tap this time."

He chuckles and pulls me close again, the water still drenching us. "Who cares? As long as I've got you."

And at that moment, I know that no matter where we are, as long as we're together we'll always find happiness in the simple pleasures.

As I serve him breakfast in the little nook, and my heart swells with warmth and pride when he casually mentions, "Hey, I'll be going to the Philharmonic first before heading to the recording studio. The HR guy wants to have a casual chat—which I reckon is a screening interview." He chortles, and the sound is rich and comforting.

I can't contain myself. I drop everything and rush to him, showering him with kisses—first his lips, then his face, hair, and lips again. He is on the brink of reclaiming his career and professional dignity. Today will be a step towards that. I also expect the HR executive will want to ensure that the chapter with the career-destroying teenaged whore is closed, and I'm confident Matt will navigate that with grace. He has me now, and together we are unshakable.

"Do you want a picture of you and I, showing the engagement ring, to present to the interviewer as proof?" I murmur, my arms wrapped around him as I try to steady the mix of nervousness, excitement, and worry bubbling inside me. I have no doubts about his musical prowess—his talent is unmatched. However, the shadow of his past relationship with Alex and how society views it lingers.

But all that's in the past. The present and future are bright, and I silently pray for today to be the beginning of everything for him.

His laughter fills the room, light and heartwarming. Seeing him have fun—cheeks rising, dimples flaring, and vivid eyes sparkling—is such a joy. The sight sends me spiraling into a blissful haze as I slump on the rickety chair opposite him. "Anna, I have you, and I'm confident in my skills. It will be fine, gorgeous," he says, his voice firm and filled with aplomb. As he leans forward, his hand brushes against mine, and it's as if he's reaching for my very soul, touching that place where all my fears and hopes converge.

With some effort, I keep my tears in check and smile at him. He, my sunshine, has me in his grasp, treasuring me. My body is primed with thrills and waves of safety and comfort. All those feelings curl up and settle low and deep between my thighs, urging me to seek his closeness, his skin, his touch, and his command.

But I restrain myself. Today is an important day for him and his career—I need him focused and ready to face whatever challenges the HR executive at the Philharmonic might throw at him.

I close my eyes and inhale deeply, letting my lungs fill. I kiss him one more time, lingering just a little, savoring the connection, the bond we share.

As he prepares to leave, I tease him with a smile, "Go charm the Philharmonic, babe. Don't forget to mention you've got a top-notch admin assistant-slash-tech support at home who can take care of everything else."

He chuckles, playfully tugging my ear, and we share a lighthearted moment before the seriousness of the day settles in.

His words, actions, and smile fill my mind as I softly close the door to our modest little sanctuary. My heart fills with love and pride, knowing that no matter our challenges, we'll face them together.

CHAPTER TWENTY-SEVEN

Anna: West 148th - Alert

I slump on the sofa feeling weak and drained, but my muscles are relaxed and my breathing is easy. A sensation of lightness envelopes me in comforting quietude. I think about Matt, feeling blessed that my path led me to this place, to him. A deep urge to earn the privileges—of being desired, valued, treasured by him—rises all over again. Having found *the one* is uniquely fulfilling. I long to improve myself for him, to protect him, to ensure that I never give him the slightest reason to be unhappy with me. *I will never fail him.*

I've taken the day off to work on a freelance gig that challenges me and pushes me to the full limits of my technology and programming skills. It calls to me, but I choose to bask in this sensation of pride—of being valued, and the satisfaction that comes with it—for a bit longer.

When he opened up about his breakup and his life with Alex over dinner after my lawyers got him released from jail, his words settled between us with a weight. His voice—steady but vulnerable—laid bare their complicated history. As he spoke of their relationship—the paternal figure and ward dynamic entwined with romance—and how that bond had deepened over time, I felt a rush of emotions. I didn't judge him. I understood that sharing this was hard for him.

I was surprised and curious, but also oddly stirred. I pushed it aside and chose to listen, absorbing the pain and love he entrusted me with. I saw how much it hurt him to relive those memories, but I viewed it through the eyes of someone who loved him deeply.

The term "father figure" echoed in my mind, but it didn't define what he was to me. Yes, he'd taken on aspects of that role, but he was far more than that—he completed me. I loved him not just for reminding me of my dad, but for his

197

personality, his divine looks, and his understanding of me—fragile yet strong, devoted, and in control when needed.

As he finished speaking, I reached for his hand, offering reassurance. "Matt," I said softly, "I'm not here to judge. You are my world, and I love you for all that you are. I understand why you care for her and did what you did. I'm here to love and support you, no matter what."

At that moment, I saw him—not a reflection of my past, but the promise of my future. Our love wasn't defined by the roles we played, but by the deep connection we shared.

While I wait for news from him regarding the Philharmonic interview, I research Alex and Project GreenWind. The complete list of the delegation accompanying the US president to the Global Summit on Sustainable Future in London is posted on the White House's public relations website. I scan through the various names of individuals and organizations until I land on Cunningham-Segal. Alex isn't listed.

A flicker of worry and unease courses through me before an eerie, cold calm replaces it. The Chaos Queen might be planning a return. Why else would she not be part of the delegation—especially with the president? That question and a growing conviction that she is headed to Manhattan put me on alert.

I open my notepad and flip to my plan to protect him and our relationship. Methodically, I review the scenarios and my planned responses, and my confidence rises as I read each potential situation and carefully calculated response strategy.

I read the battle plans I've written. I glance through the scenarios: Alex appears at Matt's workplace unannounced and refuses to leave. She befriends a mutual acquaintance—maybe even his parents—and stirs up trouble. She attempts a public confrontation, ugly and dramatic. She spreads rumors or lies. She fabricates a personal crisis—using it as an excuse to reconnect—or worse, threatens suicide or self-harm if Matt doesn't get back together with her. She sends unwanted letters or gifts. She stalks us. She bombards our cellphones with calls and texts, or she hacks into our phones and emails. She shows up at my workplace to sabotage my career. She hires shady people to stalk and scare us or a private investigator to dig up dirt on me.

I pick one scenario and review our response plan. If she sends letters or gifts, step one is to discard the items without engaging. If it escalates into harassment, I know exactly which forms to fill out and how to file for a cease and desist letter. Working at a law firm has its benefits. Matt might be upset, but not for long. I'll remain calm and supportive, reminding him of the life we're building .

I revisit each scenario, making subtle adjustments and finetuning our strategies. *Bring it on, Alex. Whenever you decide to show up in Manhattan, I'll be ready for you.*

Matt and I had briefly discussed these plans, but he didn't want to delve deeper—the topic clearly disturbed and disoriented him.

"Anna," he said in a weary yet steady tone before heading to the bedroom to lie down, "All I know is that I'll face whatever happens. I'll meet whatever is thrown at me, with you at my side."

My chest warms as I replay those words in my mind. It's the right strategy and guiding principle. My responses to whatever the home-destroyer might throw at us are centered on him and me acting in unison. *Perfect!*

An odd warm feeling creeps up when I think of Alex as a child who needs care and nurturing. My cheeks flush with a budding maternal instinct, which leads me to think about my conception of our first child. I've not gone off birth control yet, since he asked me to wait a few weeks before marriage. I feel ready to be a mother. The urge to create and sustain, the drive to nurture, and the thrill of having a living symbol of my union with him overwhelms me with joy.

Alex is a child—someone Matt and I need to take care of. Although a burning part of my heart hates her with unbridled anger, the other part feels compassion. She's a nineteen-year-old girl who needs help and guidance—which are themes in some of my planned reactions to her intrusion on the world he and I have built together.

As the clock strikes five, I finish my workday and prepare to receive him when he returns from his battles—interviewing, working, and hours playing the piano.

I head to the bathroom and groom myself to his liking, determined to welcome him with warmth and love.

After a long, hot shower, during which I recall our morning shower sex with a smile, I put on a simple summer dress in white, his favorite. I prep ingredients for dinner, ensuring he is treated to a comforting meal when he comes home.

As piano music softly streams from the smart television, I settle onto the sofa with a book, but my thoughts drift. In slow, purposeful tones, I murmur inward, "We're going to be okay, babe. I'll make sure of it. Just come home, my king. I'm here and I'll always welcome you with open arms—without expectations. You gave me your heart, and you deserve the world. I am yours."

CHAPTER
TWENTY-EIGHT

Alex: Opulent Cage

I inhale deeply, fill my lungs to capacity, and then slowly exhale, centering my mind and body as I push open the frosted glass doors and enter the recording studio. My heart races, and I smile from ear to ear. As I step inside, I'm greeted by the soft hum of the studio and the offices.

"Hi there!" I venture in a childlike tone as I approach the receptionist, a kind-looking woman. "I'm here to meet Matthew—Matthew Michaels, the pianist in the orchestra? I've just returned from a trip and want to surprise him. Would you mind calling him for me, please? Just say a visitor is here to meet him?" I tilt my head slightly—letting my baby face work its charm—and flash a smile, blinking in a way that melts hearts.

The receptionist's expression softens, and her demeanor is warm and accommodating. "He's running a little late, miss—unusual for him, but I'll let him know he has a visitor." Her reassuring smile heightens my anticipation, and I nod gratefully.

"He must have gotten stuck in subway congestion or some other traffic," I speculate, trying to quell my nervous excitement. *Daddy will be here soon.*

As directed by the sweet receptionist, I head towards the small conference room in the lobby area. The walls are lined with more frosted glass on one side and concrete walls on the others, creating a sense of privacy. As I settle in, I browse catalogs of shows and events in Las Vegas—a destination I've already planned as one of our first vacations together. My thoughts drift, and I can't help but picture his reaction when he sees me, imagining the warmth in his expression and the way his smile will illuminate the room like it always does.

But underneath it all, there's a subtle tension—a nagging doubt that I quickly push aside. *Everything will be fine.* The chant echoes in my mind, steadying my nerves. This reunion will be perfect.

Around eleven, the doors to the conference room swing open. He steps in, and his hand lingers on the door handle as it slowly clicks shut behind him. My heart skips. I spring to my feet, and my eyes take in the familiar perfection of his face—his flawless features framed by black and gray hair, a blend of maturity and timeless beauty. His nose is just as I remember it—every detail a masterpiece. Everything about him is as it was, and a warmth fills me at the sight, like finding home after a long, cold journey.

But then, the moment hits me—the months apart, the uncertainty of how he'll react. I feel myself unraveling, like a tightly wound string snapping under too much pressure. My body is weak, but I'm rooted to the spot, staring at him. My mind is blank, as if it's stopped working altogether. But beneath that fog, memories crashes.

I remember the nights he held me, enveloping me in his warmth. The gym where our connection first sparked. The stolen moments on the riverfront, kisses shared with the Manhattan skyline as our backdrop. His touch, the echo of his sweet words, the sharp bite of ropes and restraints that turned pain into something sweet, euphoric. The music room where we built our private melody. The family interventions, the punishment, the delicate aftercare. Every sensation jolts me awake, only to retreat into the shadows of the present.

Here he is, standing before me in the flesh. My chest tightens as I struggle to reconcile the past with the present—the man I love with the man before me now. I know this moment is crucial—what happens next could change everything.

Another realization hits me, and it is unbearable. He isn't smiling. His arms aren't wide open to receive me. He's just standing there, expressionless. When our eyes met, his head drew back quickly, and his eyebrows squished together. Then he froze, as he is now. His mouth is slightly parted, and his breathing is slow and steady. His viridian eyes—once so full of fire—seem dull, calculating, as if he's thinking of something else. *But what?*

I want to shout—to tell him I'm right here, and he doesn't need to think or doubt. I'm here, ready to make things right, no matter my past mistakes. Instead, vertigo disorients me. My heart pounds, and the world around me feels distant. The sharp ringing in my ears drowns everything out, and my eyes burn as they stay locked on him—the man who holds the power to redeem me.

My limbs grow heavy, betraying me. I stumble back, collapsing into a chair. The jolt of my fall shakes me awake, and I lurch up again, but my composure is slipping.

With the door shut behind him, he continues to stand frozen.

At long last, his body moves. His broad shoulders slump, and the vibrant energy that surrounded him drains away. His face is a mask and his eyes are empty, lacking the intensity they once held.

"You've prepared for this, Alex. This is number five on your list. Calm down and execute the plan. Talk to him," my brain commands, stern yet supportive, attempting to clear the chaos in my mind. I am grateful for its relentless focus.

"Daddy..." I say, and my voice trembles, barely more than a fractured whisper. I force myself to move toward him, but my steps falter and my hand grips the backs of the conference room chairs for support. Something is terribly wrong. I expected him to invite me into his arms with a sad but definite smile, welcoming me home. But he stands motionless, save for the slightest shift—a subtle, almost imperceptible step back—that deepens my confusion and dread.

I cling to the plans and preparations I meticulously crafted, and rush toward him. Before I can reach him, an iron fist grips my shoulders, halting me in my tracks. My chest heaves and my heart pounds at a frantic pace, and a piercing pain ricochets between my chest and stomach as I try to wrap my arms around him. His firm and unyielding hands stop me cold. The electricity that normally would have surged through me at his touch is replaced by icy pressure that travels the length and breadth of my body, paralyzing me.

He retreats, raising his hands, palms out like a wall. His chest rises and falls with measured breaths, but his gaze is cast down, avoiding mine. A chill—more severe than anything I've felt before—arrests me in place.

My mind desperately searches for answers. I feel exposed and judged, as the warmth and security I expected from him is stripped away. Heat floods my body, my chest tightens, and I shake my head. I blink rapidly and swallow hard, as confusion wraps around me like a suffocating fog in the presence of the man I believed would share the clarity of my newfound life.

I lunge toward him again to be met with an even firmer, almost harsh grip on my arms, followed by a slight push that leaves no room for doubt. I fumble, struggling to regain my footing, while the conference room chairs spin away, offering no support. I turn away—momentarily defeated—trying to gather my thoughts. I can't breach his resistance. I hadn't prepared for this—this rejection, this distance. All my plans were built on one unwavering belief: that he had already forgiven me and would welcome me without reservation, then everything else would fall in place.

Then his familiar voice travels through the room's silent and frigid air as I slowly turn toward him. "Alex," he begins, his husky, deep baritone heavy with emotion. "How are you? You...you look well..." He trails off, and my brows knit together, my forehead wrinkling as my mouth drops open. I clutch my head, trying to make sense of what's happening. Then with full force, I dart toward him and throw my arms around his waist, burying my head in his torso—desperate for the comfort I've missed for so long.

"Hey, no..." he says a little too loudly and pushes me away with a hard grip. The strain in my forehead deepens—my brow furrows as I try to comprehend this unexpected coldness.

"Matthew...I...I'm back. Please..." I stammer, still moving with purpose toward him, yearning to bridge the gap between us. But he withdraws further, halting me with the palm of his hand—my fingers just graze his, but the contact is fleeting and cold.

My brain primes for action, urging me to keep it together and stay calm. I obey, closing my eyes and breathing into my palms as I try to analyze the situation. But through the disorder in my mind, one thing becomes clear—there's a truth I need to express, a confession he needs to hear.

I clear my throat and meet his eyes. "Matthew, I made a mistake," I say in the calmest voice I can muster, pausing to observe his reaction. He remains calm, and his gaze is unwavering in focus and intensity though his breathing is still heavy. I continue, scrambling to find a path to his heart, "I was wrong to leave you. But I am home, having realized the enormity of my blunder. I am here to make amends, to heal you, and to build a better future for us."

I fall to my knees—the energy it took to say those words draining me completely. He begins to step forward, as if to reach for me, but stops himself—I know his every muscle, every move. He shuts his eyes for a second, and his appearance is a mixture of concern and calm that only he can project. Without offering his protective hand, he motions for me to rise. The gesture feels foreign and distant—a version of him I don't recognize.

I remain on my knees, wanting to see how long he will let me stay down, silently pleading for him to pull me up and return us to the way we were. "Alex, please." His steady voice, with an unfamiliar softness, again urges me to rise.

Please? He's not supposed to use that word. My forehead wrinkles painfully as all reason, memory, and knowledge disperse. That word has a place in our dynamic, but only I use it. His job is to command, and I obey. It's my duty to plead, and his to provide, pamper, and coddle me.

Please? A frustrated breath escapes my open mouth. He's always ordered, placated, and handled me with unwavering authority—never needing to ask or say please—and I've instinctively submitted. The word feels wrong, a betrayal of the control I've always relied on him to exert over me. Unease washes over me, solidifying the disorientation that has been building since he walked in.

He turns away so his back is to me as he faces the wall, pressing his hand lightly to his forehead as though searching for words. He's always said he's not good with words, and part of me clings to the hope that his use of "please" is a symptom of that—nothing more, nothing less.

When he finally turns to face me, his posture is rigid and his gaze unwavering. He sits at the head of the table, his expression tight and controlled. He motions for me to stand again, but this time there's no warmth, no gentleness. The snap of his fingers is sharp, an echo of the authority I know, but it's muted now, restrained.

I stand, my body trembling beneath the silence between us. I move without thought—my legs shake—but I obey. He pulls a chair out for me, one seat away from his. The space between us feels like an abyss. My body crashes into the chair as the distance settles into my bones, suffocating me.

The next few moments stretch like hours, and each second is heavy with unspoken words. I can't tear my eyes from him as I search for any trace of the warmth I remember, anything that might remind me of who we were. But his gaze is an unblinking, relentless stare. His face slowly hardens into a mask of calmness that mocks the turmoil inside me.

"Alex," he begins, sounding strained as he clears his dry throat and swallows hard. "I'm not sure why you returned, but I don't need to know. You look well, and I'm glad. But that's the extent of it."

My chest tightens, and the sting of his words cuts deep. Tears spill over and fall down my cheeks in a rush. I can barely breathe through the pain, but I force the words out, desperate, pleading. "Matthew...I'm here. I was wrong to walk away, but I'm home now. I swear I am..."

The words falter and break on my tongue, lost in the emptiness between us. I search his face for anything—a glimmer, a crack—but his expression remains set, unyielding. He raises his right hand in a silent command for me to stop, and that's when I see it—or rather, don't. *The bracelet. The one I gave him. It's gone.*

The realization hits me like a physical blow, and I stagger, clutching my chest. The absence of it is a wound. It's a symbol of something lost, something I can't fix. My stomach twists with a cold, hollow ache that spreads like wildfire burning through me.

Everything I'd imagined for this moment—the reunion, the forgiveness, the warmth—crumbles in front of me. I try to hold on to my sense of control, but it slips.

I try again, and my voice trembles as I force the words out. "Please, let's go to my penthouse. This room...it's suffocating. I can't breathe in here..." Before I finish, he leans back in his chair, covering his nose and mouth as if shielding himself from my desperation.

Moments stretch into infinity before he lowers his hands and turns his gaze back to me, but it's still cold, unfeeling.

My body acts before I can stop it—before I even know what I'm doing. I lunge, knocking over chairs in my frantic rush to reach him. I throw myself into him, pressing my lips to his in a desperate attempt to reconnect. But his response is immediate, forceful. His powerful hands grip my arms—lifting me as if I were weightless—and he sets me back in my chair.

My body crumples. I break down completely, as everything crashes down on me. A cry escapes me. He turns away, clutching his head with his hands—his back to me as he moves toward the wall, as though seeking stability from its unyielding surface.

He suddenly snaps toward me, his expression stern as he puts his index finger to his lips. "Shh, this is a workplace. Stop."

I scramble to obey, pressing my mouth tightly with both palms. The gut-wrenching pain seeks release, but I rein it in—causing further pain in my throat and the back of my eyes. I heave and pant, trying to stifle my wails. He brings his palms together over his lips, nodding slightly as if in silent approval.

Several agonizing moments pass, and I'm still choking on muffled sobs. He hands me a box of tissues, which I clutch tightly, unable to even think about using them. His calm demeanor returns, solidifying his expression—his glare steady and stiff. When he speaks again, he is unhurried—too tranquil. Every word is like a spear slashing my chest and stomach.

"The first thing I want you to know is that I forgive you—for everything, unconditionally, without any reservation or anger."

YES! This is the foundation of my plans, the lifeline I've been waiting for. I attempt to rise from my chair, to reach for his heart and bridge the gap that has widened between us. But with my energy already drained, I fall back.

"But..." he starts again, pausing as he sees me struggle. "But I want you to know...I'm engaged."

My brief attempt to stand again fails, and I slump back down with even greater force, as if this place were a swamp pulling me under while I fight to grasp the root of a nearby tree.

Every movement in my body halts, including my breath. The suffocating room closes in further, the walls pressing against my chest. The stillness and the crushing realization manifest as a nauseating wave, and I convulse, but nothing comes out of my mouth—only empty releases of air.

I retch again, and he moves forward to pacify me, but I collapse on my knees, and my entire body trembles, unable to hold on. He recoils and turns away, facing his beloved white walls once more.

I press my hand against my breastbone and throat, each heave and pant inducing nausea and dizziness. Sharp, cutting pains sear my chest, mercilessly overpowering me.

My palms hit the cold floor as I hunch over. He returns to his seat and buries his head in his hands. When I scramble to stand, he jumps to his feet with concern etched on his face. He offers me his hand, but I am shivering—paralyzed and confused. My brain struggles to process, to signal my limbs, as thoughts scatter like dead leaves in a gust—leaving me incapacitated. Bile churns in my belly as I recollect what he said, and I hit his palm away.

He watches me with that familiar mix of care and concern, but I'm too shattered to respond. He massages his temples, elbows resting heavily on the conference table. I finally manage to drag my body onto a chair. My vision is blurred by tears, yet his eyes still reach me—a beacon.

"Alex," he says, his intonation steady. "I've moved on."

His words hit me like thunder, a tsunami of vibrations crashing over me. The nausea intensifies, and this time bile rises from my stomach, spilling onto the pristine conference table. I retch again, the bitter taste burning my throat. He quickly grabs tissues and reaches for me. I strike his hands away and collapse on the floor again, curling into myself, drawing my knees to my chin.

He cleans the table swiftly and then crouches beside me, and his presence is both suffocating and tormenting as I recall his words. When he touches my head, it triggers another wave, and I retch violently. A sharp sting pierces my stomach as I lie on the floor, depleted.

Then, I lose lucidity. My coherence and strength slip away as I stay collapsed on the floor, with the world spinning around me. The hollow walls of my mind echo with the desperate scream of "*Daddy*," but no sound escapes my lips. The faint creak of a door opening and closing registers, but it's distant, like a memory. My vision blurs as I struggle to find my footing, and my trembling hands graze the rough fibers of the commercial-grade carpet.

I feel his familiar hands—strong and gentle—lifting me and placing me in a chair, but my head crashes onto the table with a hard thud. The impact jolts me, but it's like stirring embers in the cold ashes of a long-dead fire. I stare at the blackness that swallows me whole, leaving my senses drained and my body numb.

I feel another set of steady hands pulling me. Through the muffled haze in my ears, I hear a sound—pleading yet steadfast as a mountain amid a raging storm. "Wyatt, take her home, please."

Unfamiliar hands wrap around me—firm yet devoid of warmth—carrying me out of the building. The distant rumble of thunder echoes in my mind, and my body shudders, prompting the hands to tighten their grip and hold me more securely.

"Alex, I've got you. I'm taking you home," Wyatt's ever-professional, robotic tone slices through the tempest raging within me. I float into the armored vehicle, only to realize that no amount of protection can shield me from the maelstrom of shock and the tornado of humiliation he—my protector—unleashed on me without a shred of mercy.

The car's vibrations do little to soothe my churning heart and stomach. I retch several more times. Each time, Wyatt breaks his professional exterior, offering me comforting words that barely register. I need Wyatt today as he guides me to my building and up the private elevator.

He walks me to the sofa in this luxurious yet empty penthouse and mumbles something I can't quite catch. I hear fragments—"Your mother...sister-in-law...brother..."—but they're meaningless, lost where my thoughts and emotions used to be. My limbs lie flaccid on the sofa, just as Wyatt left me, abandoned to the silence.

I stare at the skies beyond the floor-to-ceiling windows of this opulent cage to see the clouds darkening. A lone silver lining fades behind a dark gray cloud as the heavens roar. White streaks of lightning cut across the sky, as if to protect the gods of wrath poised to unleash an unforgiving torrent on this city.

The city is resilient, having withstood centuries of merciless weather. But I am not. The torrential cloudburst mirrors the deluge of raw, unfiltered truth Matthew poured over me during our reunion—a reunion I had naively believed would be as bright as springtime sunshine nourishing the blossoms of a new beginning.

CHAPTER TWENTY-NINE

Anna: DEFCON-2

S omething is wrong.

I can see it in his eyes and feel it in the movements of his body. I know them all—every muscle, sinew, joint, and bone. But today, his face seems slightly puffed, the flawless features downturned. His eyes, usually so vibrant, are dull and tinged with a faint redness that dims the incisive green of his irises. A slack expression tugs at his angelic face, and he walks with heavy, deliberate steps. The sigh that escapes him as he places his wallet and keys on the side table is more than exhaustion. Something is wrong.

But what truly tells me something is wrong is the silence. The absence of his voice, the way he always calls me gorgeous the moment he walks in, before the door even closes. Usually, the echoes of his playful tone linger, only to be replaced by more of his tender care and attention—both spoken and unspoken.

This isn't just wrong. Something terrible—something deeply disturbing—has happened. He's not the kind of man to be shaken by an interview with the Philharmonic, even if the result wasn't positive. He would laugh it off, as his confident, commanding nature never lets him lose control. He lives by his mantra.

Some disturbing incident is etched on his expression, and the usual warmth he radiates is nonexistent. It's probably why he didn't text or call me after his interview—something far worse has stolen his joy.

While deeply concerned, I am determined to be the rock he needs. My mind flies, trying to piece together what could have happened in the morning interview at the Philharmonic or afterward at the recording studio, but I rein in my racing thoughts and stay calm for his sake. My grip tightens on the armrest, and my pulse quickens, but I manage a warm, reassuring smile as he slumps beside me on the sofa.

I can feel his distress, and I jump to care for him. Without hesitation, I wrap my arms around him, holding him close. His body surrenders, his head falling onto my shoulder as if seeking refuge. I stroke his back, and my fingers thread gently through the lush black and gray strands of his hair while I plant soft kisses on his head. He doesn't need to explain anything right now. My presence, calm and nurturing, will soothe him. If he chooses not to speak, that's perfectly fine. I'm here to give, not demand.

"She's returned," he says, and his tone is dry, cutting through the comforting silence of our embrace. The words hang heavy in the air. I listen, feeling a whirlwind of emotions—anger, fear, and a fierce protective instinct. For a fleeting moment, I go completely still as the shock of his words freezes me in place.

But then all my senses snap into sharp focus, and my mind recollects the plans and scenarios I've meticulously prepared, all stored in my head and notepad. I remind myself that my priority is to be here, in this moment, for my king. I close my eyes briefly, steadying my breath, centering myself for the battle ahead.

I'm ready for you, Alex.

She may have appeared out of nowhere and gone straight to him, catching us off guard, but now it's my turn. I need details, but I take my time—careful not to rush him—even though my heart and determination are racing ahead, ready to defend what we've built.

I hug him tighter, pressing my lips more firmly against his head, letting them rest there, sending him comfort. I can feel his heart is heavy, but I'm here to ease that burden. He has me, and I will carry his troubles. Simply give them to me, Matt, and let me shoulder them. You can relax, and I'll take care of everything.

After a moment, he straightens, but his posture is heavy with exhaustion as he leans forward, elbows resting on his knees. I watch him—my gaze soft, my heart aching, but calculating. He wipes his face, and the weariness in his expression is almost too much to bear.

I slip away quietly, preparing the hot tea I know will soothe him. It's a simple gesture, but I've learned the art of making him feel cared for in every way.

When I hand him the cup, I make sure my touch lingers a fraction longer than necessary—my voice soft, coaxing. "Take a few sips. You need it." I observe his every move, knowing the warmth will settle him, make him more pliable. He obeys, bringing the cup to his lips, slowly and deliberately, and the tension in his shoulders eases with each sip. The tea works its quiet magic—calming him—until the cup is finally lowered with careful intention.

When he speaks, his tone is low, shaking with the weight of his words. As he recounts the painful details of what happened, I listen, every part of me focused on him. I hide my emotions—though it's a struggle whenever he mentions her touching him. My stomach tightens, and a hot, burning sensation spreads from my core to my chest. A flare of jealousy, a flash of rage. But I keep it contained, as I always do. I'm in control, even when my jaw clenches at the mere thought of her hands on him. Anger bubbles just beneath the surface, but I can't let it show.

I focus on him instead, reaching for his hands, locking my gaze with his as he tells his story. His exhaustion is palpable, and his confession hangs between us. When he finally collapses onto the sofa with a sigh, I move to sit beside him, careful to maintain the right balance of proximity—close enough to be comforting, but not so close as to seem desperate. I need to be calm, be the strength he relies on. He interlocks his fingers and places his hands behind his head, closing his eyes to retreat into his thoughts.

I allow him the silence, but my thoughts are spinning. Each mention of her burns me. Violence flashes through my mind—sharp and vicious—irrational fantasies of punishing her, stabbing her repeatedly, erasing her presence from his life. I push down the dark corner of my mind to focus on the task at hand. I need to make sure he's whole again, and that means keeping him away from distractions—especially her.

The nausea in my stomach, the dizziness in my head, and the heat rising in my chest—though discomforting—are all good, because the more I soak in these feelings, the more driven I become. I take a strategic step away from him, seeking a moment of privacy. I press my hand to my throat, willing calm. I need clarity now.

I know what must be done. Alex is a problem, but a problem I'm prepared to deal with. She's nothing but a distraction, and I'll show her that. I don't want to fight her, but I will, if necessary. A part of me almost wants to help her—guide her, teach her what she needs to know. After all, she's just a girl, a victim of her own desires. Learning that Matt has moved on is like a second breakup for her, and I understand. I sympathize with her, in a way. But my priority is clear. It always has been. I will protect him and everything we've built, and if she interferes, she will have to face me one-on-one.

I let the thought settle, a smile curling as I rejoin him. There's a renewed purpose inside me, the next steps in my strategy forming with each beat of my heart. Our wedding is set for the Mid-Autumn Festival, which is a date my dad cherished. It was Matt's suggestion—something I knew he would want, something that would link our future to my dad's memory. We have two months to prepare, and I know that, with the right moves, we can handle anything she might throw at us.

When I return, he looks refreshed, and a hint of light returns to his features. The sight warms my heart. I bring my notepad and sit beside him on the sofa. He pulls me in for a kiss, a half-smile playing on his luscious lips. Before I can begin, he speaks first, his voice carrying a note of reassurance, "Everything is going to be okay. She needs to learn, and it will be tough, but she'll be fine." The confidence and command in his tone break through a lingering layer of melancholy.

He strokes my hair, playing gently with a few strands. But then his tone dips again, and the sadness seeps back in, revealing how deeply this situation affects him in ways I can only imagine. "My heart broke, seeing her collapse like that," he says, pulling me closer, my head resting against his chest. I listen to the steady beat of his heart as he continues. "My instinct was to lift her, to care for her. The paternal drive was almost overwhelming. But I had to force myself to stop, because this is a battle she has to fight on her own."

His heartbeat steadies, and his breath is slow and deliberate, as if each inhale requires effort. Revulsion and unsteadiness hit me at the thought of his hands touching her with care. I force the irrational fear aside, focusing on his calm embrace, synchronizing my heart and lungs with his steady rhythm.

"What do you have there, Anna? Is that...the scenario planning stuff you showed me a while ago?" he asks, and his gaze softens as he motions to the notepad on my lap. I nod and show him everything again—the refinements and fine-tuning I'd been working on. My speech is steady and a bit too clinical as I lay out response strategies. He listens, with an expression that moves from flat to melancholic to amused.

As I speak, his tension melts away, and his worry fades into a smile. My methodical approach—my ability to think ahead—mirrors his confidence and command. We share a quiet understanding, with no words needed.

His face brightens, and warmth spreads across his features, sending a thrill through me. If he were still weighed down by the pain he carried when he walked in, I would be broken. There's nothing more agonizing than seeing him struggle.

When I finish, he laughs unsteadily, shaking his head with affection. He motions for me to sit on his lap, and I do, wrapping my arms around his neck. We share a kiss, and his touch grounds me as he murmurs, "I hope we won't need any of those plans, angel."

The energy he sparks in me settles into a steady voice. "No secrets, no unspoken doubts, babe. We'll face everything together. No concern is too small. No burden is too much as long as we're in this together." I kiss him again, the rising desire unmistakable as I see his expression return to the one I always yearn for.

In that moment, we reinforce our bond. Our relationship is a fortress—unbreakable. Hand in hand, we're stronger.

"Together, gorgeous." His raspy intonation returns—deep and full of emotion—as his hand squeezes my waist. The combination of his words and touch sends a pulse inside me, intensifying the tingling and throbbing desire building within me.

He mentions being hungry, a sign his burdens are lifting. We move to the kitchen to begin preparing dinner together, and our conversation shifts to lighter topics, occasionally drifting back to Alex. Calm confidence fills the air as we talk things through, preparing ourselves for whatever she might throw at us.

Over dinner, he mentions wedding plans—another sign that her return isn't totally consuming him. But soon, we're playfully arguing about the scale of the wedding. He insists on a big celebration, fondly recalling our first ceremony, which I had meticulously planned. It was perfect.

I calmly repeat my preference for a simpler affair, and he teases me, riling me up before pulling me close, his warmth comforting me. It's reassuring—he's back to being the playful, loving man I adore. After dinner, I jot down ideas for a simple, meaningful wedding with a modest budget.

Outside, thunder cracks and rain patters softly against the window as we settle into bed. Contentment fills me as I reflect on how far we've come. I feel more vital than ever, ready to support him in reclaiming his career and shielding our relationship from her.

He wraps me in his arms, fingers playing with my hair. As we drift to sleep, he whispers, "By the way, the Philharmonic wants to proceed with the selection process, my darling."

My heart swells. I kiss him softly and whisper congratulations, already planning how we'll celebrate when he gets the job. But for now, I just want to hold him close and share this moment of peace.

CHAPTER THIRTY

Alex: Echoes - His Words

M y eyes snap open. The golden morning light bathes Central Park, and the emerald lawns and trees shimmer with the remnants of last night's rain. Droplets cling to the leaves, sparkling like jewels, and puddles reflecting the sunshine dot the peaceful refuge below—a blatant contrast to the emptiness within me. Sun floods through the giant windows of the penthouse, attempting to reach the darkest corners of my soul, as if my friend the sun is trying to heal me. *Don't bother, dear sun. I'm a failure—certainly not your first, but chief among them. There are some darknesses that even you can't penetrate.*

A failure.

In the past, I was rejected by my family and cast aside as a rogue teenager who embraced a forbidden relationship—maybe they maintain that opinion, given I'm pursuing Matthew again. I'm a colossal loser—the first disgrace in a long line of prestigious ancestry. My last therapy session with Dr. Robbins confirmed yet another disappointment—I'm her greatest failure—the one patient she couldn't save.

But none of my failures sting and burn as acutely as failing to be what my daddy wanted—a good, obedient little girl who trusted in his unwavering love and attention. One rash decision and I sent our lives spiraling into chaos. Now, here I am, piling loss upon loss, and failure upon failure. I'm perfecting the art of ruining my life—getting better at it with each passing day.

The serene view of Central Park... *Wait, what?* My bedroom windows don't open toward the park. I jolt upright only to realize I'm on the floor of my living room. I must have fallen asleep here last night, too exhausted from the battle raging in my mind to make it to my bed.

My thoughts return to the conference room. The choking feeling and nausea surge again, and bile churns in my stomach. With great effort, I drag myself to the bathroom. My appearance is a shambolic mess. I reek of vomit, sweat, and the neglect of self-care. My once-beautiful summer dress is soiled, and my hair is sticky and matted. *As if I needed more proof that I'm worthless and pitiful.*

Moving in slow, robotic motions, I force my limbs to act and clean my body. I end with a long, scalding shower, hoping the heat will burn away the layers of shame and despair clinging to my skin.

Slumped on a stool in the eat-in kitchen, I try to drink a bottle of juice to soothe my churning stomach, but it worsens. Dizziness clouds my vision, and my skin prickles. Time stretches, warping around my confusion. The clock reads a little after eleven—my latest woes started at this time yesterday. I replay our meeting in my mind, convinced that I must have imagined it. It can't be true. *Who is he claiming he's engaged to, anyway? No! It can't be true.*

I grab my phone and dial his number. He doesn't take my call, so I try again, my heart pounding. This time, after several agonizing rings, he answers.

"Hello." His deep, husky voice floods my frail senses and fragile body.

I think I'm speaking but realize I'm not when he says hello again. Snapping out of my daze, I clear my throat. My voice trembles as I struggle to steady my nerves. "Daddy, this trick you're playing makes me uncomfortable. It hurts. Please, do something else to punish me—stretch me and tie me up for days, put me in a closet, deprive me of sunlight and food and sleep...anything you want..." The words spill faster and faster, laced with desperation—a plea for him to show me some glimmer of hope.

He is silent and I continue, my voice breaking in short bursts, frantic and desperate. "Anything but this. I'll obey you...as a puppy does. But please stop what you're doing. It hurts. It hurts so bad, Matthew!"

He's silent, but only for a few moments. "It's not a trick. It's the truth. I know it hurts. But you're strong. Work with your therapist, lean on your family. They'll take care of you. You'll be all right. It takes time, that's all. Please...give it time."

My throat constricts, and my stomach and chest tighten as if placed in a vise. Irritation flares within me. Even the carefully regulated air in the penthouse feels spiky against my skin. Sudden heat flushes my body, and I lash out at him, as my voice rises to a desperate pitch. "Why the fuck aren't you calling me your little girl? Your precious girl? What, I'm not yours anymore? Why are you saying please? Did you cast me away? Throw me out on the street..."

He doesn't respond, and the silence is deafening. Shock and disbelief crash over me. I leap to my feet, pacing frantically through the kitchen and the living area, moving from room to room as if searching for something—anything—that will make sense. The motion does little to calm me, but somehow I manage to propose a desperate solution. "Matthew...I think you're confused. You waited, and I didn't come. I hurt you. You struggled to get back on track.

You made some impulsive decisions in a very confused, disturbed state. I get that. Believe me, I do."

I hear a sigh, and then his voice steadies and becomes stern. "Alex, stop."

I can't stop. I am driven by a frantic need to make things right. "I'm here now. It's on me to fix what I broke. I will fix my mistake. Trust me to fix us. Come home, please. I sent you a text with the address of my new penthouse. I'll come pick you—"

"I'm in love with Anna. That's everything you need to know. I love her."

His words strike like a physical blow, and his unruffled tone delivers a slap that reverberates, deafening me. Then the world plunges into silence. The floor becomes my refuge, and I collapse onto the plush carpeting of my living room. Paralysis grips my limbs, which feel leaden and useless. The ringing in my ears returns briefly, only to be drowned by the muffled pounding of my own heartbeat. My thoughts flip between blank emptiness and chaos, spinning so fast it's impossible to keep up.

My brain retreats behind the shadows, abandoning me. Vertigo pulls me down when I try to stand, leaving me numb—devoid of any feeling, physical or emotional.

Disjointed, fragmented lines and words from my dialogues with him echo, cutting through the oppressive silence and alternating with the relentless ringing in my ears—driving me to the brink of insanity.

"I am not good with words. My actions will show what you mean to me."

"Tell me you love me, Daddy."

"I'll always prove my love for you, every single minute. I love you."

"Mr. Cunningham, and family. Yes, I love her."

"My sweet little one, you are the center of my world."

"I'm your daddy, Alex, and I will always love you."

"I love you. Always have, always will. My only job is to protect and sustain us."

"You have power over me. Something no one else has."

The echoes grow louder, closer, more personal, as if the voices are right here in the room with me.

He loves her? That snake? Matthew and Anna? No way!

Where's the phone? I am lying on the floor of my bedroom, but I made the call in the library. *How did I get here?*

Matthew and Anna? Wow! This is a second rejection, a second dismissal—and it's worse than my first breakup. *Perfect, Alex.* Two breakups in less than a year. *Add that to my long and glorious list of failures.*

221

A loud, primal wail escapes my throat, as the torment that has been building within me erupts. I heave and pant as my tears soak the carpet. My screams are an outpouring of hurt, anger, and self-pity, as the darkness and shadows of heartbreak smother the luxurious yet empty penthouse. The pain intensifies as I curl into my torso, clutching my stomach and chest, wailing as time slips away...

When my eyes snap open again, the penthouse is dark, and the fading glow of the evening casts subtle tones of yellows and oranges, stretching shadows across the room. I am curled on the sofa, my body stiff from hours of lying in the same position. My stomach growls—a stark reminder that I haven't eaten anything in nearly two days. Walking into the bathroom, I glimpse my reflection in the mirror and barely recognize the pale, hollow-eyed figure staring at me.

Desperation claws at me—a frantic need for anything that can numb the piercing feelings of rejection, hurt, and anger tearing through me. The bar beckons, and I make my way there, grabbing a bottle of whiskey and pouring a stiff glass.

The first sip burns as the liquid fire sears my nasal passages and throat. The whiskey is too strong, and I'm not used to it. *Great. So, is even the whiskey rejecting me?* I won't let it. I hold the drink in my mouth, forcing my senses to endure the stinging burn before I swallow it in one go. The fiery sensation returns—scorching my throat—but this time it feels good. My body jerks as the strong drink courses through me, burning away my old self, making way for someone new to emerge. *Excellent. It feels good. And oh, look at that—Alex can handle whiskey after all. Scratch that off the list of failures.*

I open my laptop and begin typing furiously. I sip the whiskey between keystrokes, and my fingers drum out the dialogue and actions between Matthew and me during and after the failed reunion. Every word and action is extracted effortlessly from my photographic memory. I print the pages and make a detailed analysis. *There, another thing I'm good at—analysis. Or am I? Should I add that to my list of failures? At this rate, that list is going to be full when dawn arrives.*

As I analyze his words—dissecting every syllable he spoke to me—I search desperately for something—anything—that might give me a glimmer of hope, some hint that he's undecided or confused. I break down his actions, the way he touched me, scrutinizing each detail. *"He's moved on. He couldn't have been clearer,"* my brain insists. *No, there must be something, some tiny detail that I missed, something that could give me hope.*

My brain is right. The truth hits like a sledgehammer, and I scream. The sound echoes off the walls, the only response in this lifeless space. I scream again and again until my voice is hoarse and my throat burns. Whiskey will help with that. I take a few more sips, then refill the glass, pouring generously so I don't have to keep going to the well-stocked bar.

An image of Anna flashes in my mind—one he showed me at the gym, from a picture taken in Times Square by a street photographer. They looked so happy, but that's not what I focus on. I trace her beauty, her elegance—tall, lean, just over six feet, matching him perfectly. Her poise is striking—her flawless skin, her near-black eyes and jet-black eyebrows are mesmerizing, almost dangerous. She is a snake. Her long, black hair falls past her hips, thick and shining. And that face, her perfect nose—symmetrical, sculpted—mirroring his. Perfectly proportioned.

The familiar burning sensation sears me inside as my stomach hardens. My pulse elevates and adrenaline gushes through me. The image of the snake won't leave my mind. Desperate to rid myself of it, I scream and hurl my tablet at the eighty-five-inch television in the living room. The dull thud of impact reverberates and the screen cracks, glass shards falling to the console. *Perfect. A visual of how my life is shattering.*

Knowing sleep will elude me, I stagger to the medicine cabinet and swallow a sleeping pill with whiskey. The burn of the alcohol mingles with the bitterness of the pill as tears stream down my face. I twist in agony as my mind loops one question: *Why did you throw me away?* I whisper it, a prayer to a God who's stopped listening. As sleep drags me under, the question morphs: *Why me? Why am I suffering when everyone else is happy?*

This is great. Until now, I didn't appreciate how alcohol could improve brain function and pump me up for a busy day. I have a lot to do. I take another gulp of whiskey—*or was it bourbon? Who cares?* I review the information I've written on a crisp sheet of paper. It's not much, but it's all I have to offer to the two private investigators I'm about to hire.

I can't meet them directly, so I've scheduled a couple of video conferences. The first one will start soon. Wyatt would stop me from visiting a private investigator in person—it's against my business empire's security policies, specifically mentioned in the list of don'ts. If anything or anyone needs to be monitored, they handle it themselves, as I've seen time and again. *But their stupid rules can't stop a determined Alex.*

"Matthew Michaels, age forty-two...umm...says he's engaged, but is single as far as I can tell, two postgraduate degrees from Yale. Here are his qualifications and job details..." I start cheerfully, rattling off the basics to the first private investigator .

"Ms. Cunningham, I can get you what you need—his whereabouts, daily routines, his work and social contacts, other places he visits outside of his habits, his...his partner, and the same set of information on her as well," the PI assures me confidently.

I give her two thumbs up, beaming so widely my cheeks hurt. I quickly turn off the video and take a gulp of my drink before returning to face the smart-looking woman sitting at her desk. She is in what appears to be a scene straight from a witness protection movie—a rather dark room with blank walls and no sign of a window. A lone table lamp illuminates her face, which is devoid of makeup.

"But, Ms. Cunningham, I need to know how you plan to use this information," she says, her tone polite but direct and firm.

She talks about ethics and aiding criminal behavior, but none of it registers. I'm too focused, too determined. I shift to my businesswoman's tone, crisp and unyielding. "That's private and privileged information I can't share with you. I'll double your compensation and agree to a waiver that frees you of any ethical or moral consequences—even criminal liabilities. Draft whatever you need and send it to me. I'll sign it."

That satisfies her. Perfect. Step one is complete. Using the information from the PI, I will ensure I am always around him. He'll understand that I'm still in his life, that he can't shake me off—not with words like love and Anna.

The mere thought of her makes my jaw clench and my face go rigid, trembling with barely contained rage. A sharp pain stabs at the top of my skull, hammering a warning—but I don't care. If I am to die of the unhealthy harboring of intense jealousy, so be it.

The next meeting should help me take care of her. I finish my glass of whiskey and take the call.

"Dirt on a Ms. Savannah Mei Ren, from Hunter-Ren, the biomedical-slash-biotech company?" the PI asks, smiling as he interlocks his fingers and rests his forearms on the table. His office is more polished, with windows and certificates hanging on the wall behind him.

"Uh-huh. Yup. Anything you can find on her. The more damaging the information, the higher your compensation. Mmm hmm." I nod at him more times than necessary, my body floating on a cloud.

He smiles and begins to speak, but I cut him off, trying to imitate the cool tone of a movie hero. "You're going to ask why I need this information, but allow me to tell you. I want to hire her for a crucial, personal role, so I need more than a background check." I lean in my chair, swiveling slightly, and place my hands behind my head.

I give him the other piece of information I have on her—her email address. The burn in my chest and stomach stings as I recall the email she sent Matthew during his divorce. *This is good.* If I can show him that Anna isn't who she claims to be, he'll thank me, dump her, and then thank me again. Then we can proceed with the plans I originally made for our reunion.

Pleased, I decide to take a nice bath. More whiskey, combined with the warm water enveloping me, is an even better idea.

As I soak in the tub, sipping more drinks, I scroll through the text conversations he and I had when we were together, desperate to feel closer to him, as if he were still within reach. Memories of pain, laughter, and amusement flow freely through me. The way his sparse words wrapped around me like this warm water, his "dirty" texts that confused me, leaving me reeling with anticipation for wild and intense BDSM sessions.

The pain of the double breakup stabs at me, burning with each recollection of his words: "I love her." Tears of anger and self-pity overwhelm me as I take a few more sips, letting my head fall back and sinking deeper into the tub. My phone slips from my tired hands, dropping onto the tiled floor.

A familiar voice cuts through the haze, pulling me from the depths as I jolt upright and send water cascading onto the floor. My intoxicated mind struggles to grasp what's happening, and I scramble for footing, my hands flailing for leverage.

"Oh, Alex, honey, hey...have you been drinking?"

I still can't tell who it is or if I'm caught in a dream. A few gentle slaps land on my cheeks, and soft yet firm hands grasp me, keeping me from slipping under the water. My body goes limp, sagging into the supportive grip. "Mom...Mom...he left me for her, Mom..." My wails reverberate through the enormous bathroom, threatening to shatter the glass as I'm slowly pulled from the tub. She grips my petite frame with both hands, guiding me toward the closet. But then, she senses something and immediately rushes me to the toilet, where I vomit uncontrollably. She holds my head, rubbing my spine as I retch, the minutes—or hours—blurring together.

The rest of the...is it afternoon? Evening? Night? It's all a complete blur. The last thing I feel is my body, now clothed in something soft and comforting, collapsing onto my bed.

CHAPTER
THIRTY-ONE

Alex: Echoes - Together

I've never had a blackout before. My friends in college described it to me, but I was too young to drink or go to parties, so I never experienced one. Last night was my first. *Go ahead, add losing control when drinking to the ever-growing list of my failures.*

The smell of coffee is refreshing, but the breakfast aromas churn my stomach, threatening nausea. I took a pill for my headache when I woke up in a stupor earlier, slept, and then rose again. The pain has dulled, but it's not completely gone. Now I sit on the sofa in the living room with the curtains drawn, holding my head in my hands. Mom brings me a plate of fluffy scrambled eggs, toast, and orange juice. She also hands me my coffee, but her expression is stern, arms crossed, standing tall. She will not budge until I finish the plate.

The food helps settle my stomach, but with it comes the return of familiar pains and unresolved feelings, tears welling afresh.

Wyatt. He must have given my family quite a report, because here they come, one by one—Ted, Evie, James, and Sebastian, filling the penthouse, smothering me. *A family reunion, I guess. At least this appears to be one, unlike the catastrophe in the conference room where Matthew renounced me. Father isn't here. Oh, right. He sent his people to take care of me.*

Evie sheds tears when she sees me curled, pale, and limp—a mere sliver of the person I was over a year ago. Mom consoles her, but I can see her tears glistening as well. *I must get these people out of the penthouse so I can execute the plan I've devised for this evening.* It's about noon now, so I have a few hours to talk to them and get them to leave.

My strategy is to stay calm, even though I feel like shattered glass—pain poking at me in every part of my body. If I lash out at them—and I want to—or crumble and cry again, they'll never leave. I notice Mom's brought a small suitcase with her. *Oh no, you're not staying here, Mom.*

"Everyone, please. I'm asking for a few days. There are some issues still unresolved between him and me. I need to discuss them with him. Then I'll accept my fate and move on. Or at least, I'll start removing things that remind me of him from my life, bit by bit," I say, faking my calmest and steadiest tone as I sit upright on the sofa.

Not a word of what I said is true. It's the opposite of what I plan to do.

"Unresolved? Things seem clear to me. He's engaged—God bless the couple. Let's all be happy for him and remove ourselves from the picture. Let's make this peaceful and simple," Sebastian, the Manipulator-in-Chief, offers. There is sympathy in his features, but not in his tone, which remains flat and detached.

I restrain my anger and continue to fake my poise. "Sebastian, for me it's not that simple. For the family, maybe it is. All I'm asking for is a little time. I'm saying I'll leave him be—a change from what I said earlier."

Taking turns, my family members—including Ted—offer me words of comfort and gestures of solidarity and support. If I maintain this attitude and false reasoning, I think they'll leave.

"I haven't been able to speak to him because I collapsed when I heard what he had to say," I say and pause, struggling to suppress the bile and burning rage stirring in my gut. "I think I deserve a last chance to speak to him calmly, with words, trying to keep the emotion at bay as much as possible."

Yes! Their faces shift—a faint glimmer of understanding showing. Sebastian is nodding too. *Time to deliver the final blow.* I stand and face them, chest thrust forward, shoulders straight, and arms crossed.

"It's time I handled this as an adult, on my own. After all, I created this mess, didn't I? Please give me a chance to make it right. Let me learn to do this the right way," I say, lacing my steady tone with a carefully measured hint of pleading.

I can tell my mom and Evie aren't buying it. They shake their heads and mention my drinking. I nod, admitting my fault, and quickly point them to my life in Kiruna, Sweden, where—aside from three weeks—I never needed alcohol to soothe my nerves or drown my sorrows. I remind them of the exemplary work I did with Project GreenWind, hinting that I might work on a new project soon.

Lies. Lies. Lies. Way to go, Alex, lying to your own flesh and blood.

It's starting to get uncomfortable. Their support is both soothing and suffocating. They engage in heartfelt conversations—trying to comfort me—offering a stark contrast to the darkness brewing within me.

Finally, I lash out at them, hoping it might drive them away. "All I'm asking for is a chance to fix myself and leave this situation in a way that works for me. If you keep intervening, or if you drag me to our mansion, I might regress. Please, try to understand," I demand as I fall on the couch, staring at the view of the Empire State Building bathed in the surreal glow of the late afternoon sun.

They have to leave now if I'm going to make it to La Grand Élégance to see Matthew.

Eventually they all leave, but not before making check-ins with Evie and Mom a requirement—twice a day, and video calls only. I hastily agree to everything, watching them exit. *Thank God Edward, The Enforcer, wasn't part of this intervention.* He wouldn't have folded. He would have assigned an in-home caretaker to boss me around inside the penthouse and made reporting to work at his company mandatory.

"Where do you think you're going?" The sound booms across my private garage as I open the driver's side door of my Porsche Taycan.

My bodyguard has never spoken to me in such a tone. I turn to Wyatt and give him an amused stare, a slight smile playing on my lips, my forehead wrinkling, my brows furrowing. "Excuse me?"

His professional tone, laced with concern—and maybe pity—hits me as if it were a slap. "You heard me, Alex. Tell me where you want to go, and I'll take you there. But I'm not taking you anywhere near Matthew."

My smile drops, replaced by a cold, hard edge. "Wyatt, you have no business interfering in my personal life. I need you to respect boundaries. I am an adult, and this is my car. You can follow me, but you can't stop me from going wherever I wish."

Not bothering to wait for a response, I get in the car and switch it on—the low hum of the electric engine barely audible as I speed onto the streets of my beloved city. A rush of adrenaline surges in me, and I squeal and hoot as the car glides effortlessly around corners. Since I can't drink in public—including the private areas of a high-end exclusive establishment such as La Grand Élégance—I took a few shots of bourbon before driving. I'm dressed to perfection in a sleek cocktail dress—an organza sheath with sophisticated grommet embellishments. *The dress—no, I, will be pleasing to Daddy's eyes.*

I turn the valet mode of my car on and hand over the keys before entering the luxurious, princely interior of the restaurant. The manager approaches, and I notice heads turning as the youngest Cunningham makes her entrance. But I'm unfazed—my focus is entirely on the rich notes of Ravel drifting from the concert grand piano in the corner, which is flanked by massive floor-to-ceiling windows overlooking Chelsea Piers. After exchanging pleasantries with the manager, I hurry toward the piano, but the lid is blocking the view . My heart races faster than the butterflies in my stomach as I take quick steps toward the source of the music. The manager asks which table I prefer, and I request a chair by the piano as I round the huge instrument and finally face Matthew.

He looks at me with a barely noticeable jerk of his head. He maintains his composure as his fingers continue to dance effortlessly across the keys, not needing to look at the keys. I sit on the chair, crossing my legs and resting my chin on my hand with my elbow propped on my knee. A smile breaks across my face, and I tilt my head, beaming, letting my gaze linger on him. The butterflies settle, but my pulse quickens, and my heart pounds as I'm filled not just with the beauty of his music, but with the overwhelming comfort of being near him again, knowing he's only an arm's reach away.

As soon as he finishes the piece, I stand, tipsy and clapping enthusiastically, and my shrill voice rings out above the ambient noise. "Matthew Michaels, everyone—the best pianist on the planet!" I declare. My heart inflates with pride, but a sharp sting punctures it, knowing that his career and professional identity were shattered because of his love for me. *The Philharmonic will not refuse a check of a million dollars with additional monthly donations. On top of what my family is already sponsoring.* I'm here to fix everything, to create a better future for him and me—one with no regrets. Though he's resisting, I trust he'll let me fix us soon.

For a moment, his face goes rigid, his eyes tilting upward while his head remains slightly bowed toward the keys. His forehead wrinkles, but the rest of his face remains serene.

"Amazing, Daddy," I compliment him, taking a step closer, but he rises in a flash and engages the fallboard, which closes over the keys in a slow, calibrated motion. Without glancing in my direction, he strides toward the manager, exchanging a few words I can't hear from where I stand, and then he exits the restaurant—leaving me standing near the piano, my heart sinking as he walks away.

Not bothering to walk or move gracefully, I dash out of the restaurant to find Wyatt grabbing Matthew by the collar with one hand, his other hand raised, ready to strike. I shriek and rush toward them, desperately trying to pull Wyatt off him.

"She was fine until you came into her life, you asshole!" Wyatt shouts, and his words are filled with fury.

I scream at him, my voice rising in frantic desperation. My compact frame struggles to pull a trained ex-soldier out of an assault stance. The scene erupts into chaos as valets and security rush to intervene, and onlookers gather to witness the turmoil. Wyatt shoves the valets aside and orders security to back off. Matthew, towering over him, grabs Wyatt's fist before it connects with his face and gently pushes him away, far calmer than Wyatt.

My chest heaves with jagged breaths, and tears stream down my face. I cry out, yelling at Wyatt to stop. My voice is laced with panic as I try to get him to control himself.

Then it gets worse. A matte brown G65 AMG pulls into the parking lot, and I spot Edward stepping out, his eyes narrowing as he takes in the commotion. Without hesitation, he lunges at Matthew and lands a few brutal punches on his chin. My heart drops, and in desperation, I throw myself at Edward's back, grabbing him around the neck, using every ounce of my strength to pull him off Matthew while I scream.

Matthew takes a moment to compose himself—rubbing his chin where the blows landed—then, without a word, turns and walks away, heading toward the subway.

I drop to my knees and my twelve-thousand-dollar dress scrapes against the rough asphalt—the fabric tearing as I crumble. Tears pour from my eyes as I gasp for breath and clutch my chest with one hand, while the other is pressed to my face, trying to hold everything in. My mascara streaks down my cheeks, and my hair falls in messy tangles. *What just happened?* The anger, the jealousy, the pain from the breakup—everything fades into the background, replaced by numbing shock. I can't process what just occurred.

Edward towers over me, and his shadow looms large as he takes my hand and forces me to stand. Once on my feet, I yank my hand away—clenching my teeth and glaring at him—my head trembling. He seethes, leans in close, and in a low, menacing tone, he threatens, "There, you saw it. Approach him again, and I will make sure he ends up in the hospital."

He gives a devil's pause as his red-rimmed eyes harden, before he says, "Or worse."

I stay rooted, further stunned, as his words sink in. He continues, "Do we have an understanding, Alex?"

My first instinct is to get away from The Enforcer, but I must give him a piece of my mind first. "You rogue, rowdy fool. Control me all you want, but if you lay a finger on him again, I'll make sure you regret it." Rage spikes, and I want to strangle my own brother to death.

He steps closer—his face inches from mine and his intonation a deep, threatening growl. "Challenge accepted. Test me. You have no idea how far I will go." His face is a mask of anger, and his eyes burn with a terrifying intensity that makes my breath catch in my throat.

Edward calls for my valet, and my Taycan is brought around. He hands me the keys, saying in a cynical tone, "Here you go, my dear sister. I expect you in your penthouse no later than thirty minutes from now. You will call me on video once you arrive. If you don't, I'll send a group of not-so-nice people to his apartment, and I will come talk to you myself. Is everything clear?"

I sniffle, wiping my nose and tears, trying to steady myself. My heart is heavy with guilt at the pain and anguish this incident must have caused Matthew. The thought that this might cost him his job at the restaurant bites my heart. Though I could never have predicted Wyatt would act the way he did, or that Edward would arrive with aggression on his mind, it's still all my fault.

Another addition to the list of reasons I'm a failure—shattering Matthew's routine, disrupting his life, and potentially causing him to lose his job and income.

But my current focus—so that Matthew's night doesn't become more miserable—is to do exactly what Edward says.

I get in the car and drive, noting Wyatt in the S580 following closely. He must have called Edward, thinking he was protecting me, or maybe Edward instructed him to—I don't know. I purposely jump a signal, gunning the car to put some distance between us, and momentarily lose Wyatt. But he quickly catches up, and I enter my building. I disregard him and head straight to my private elevator, feeling his stare on me as I ascend to my penthouse.

Once inside, I take a couple shots of vodka, letting the burn settle in my throat and steady my nerves, trying to calm my trembling body. In a matter of minutes—despite his attempts to prolong the conversation with probing questions—I finish my video check-in with Edward. My heart swells with fresh anger. I never imagined anyone in my family could be so violent.

Last year, when Edward threatened to harm or even kill Matthew, or even when he visited the Weehawken penthouse and grabbed him by the collar, I hadn't taken him for someone with violent tendencies. But now, seeing how unhinged he truly can become—how he has an unpredictable, dual personality—my first instinct is to protect Matthew from him and his goons.

I take a breath and collect myself, but I feel the need for another shot to steady my resolve. The next call I make is critical—it's a small step toward fixing the mess—the latest in a long series that I've made.

After a couple of rings, Matthew's voice comes through, low but firm. I take a moment, waiting for my heartbeat to slow, before I speak. The words catch in my throat, and my voice cracks as tears streak down my face. "Hey, I'm so sorry for Wyatt's and Edward's behavior. I swear, I had no idea they would go after you, or that Edward would even show up. I just—I couldn't bear another moment away from you. I had to see you, so I came." My voice breaks as I sob, struggling to control myself. My chest feels as though it's being torn open.

The line goes silent—no background noise, no sound at all coming over the headset.

"Are you there?" I whimper, the sound fractured and laced with desperation.

"Don't worry about it. They acted from pure, genuine care for you. Don't hate them for this." His speech is clean, poised, unbroken—a calm, straight line. I'm relieved by his generosity, his grace in forgiving my guardians and brushing it off, but there's a weight pulling me under. *Is he going to send me to my family, ask me to find comfort and healing in them? Why?*

The hurt manifests again, searing my stomach and radiating outward. But I stick to what I intended to say, the original reason I went to see him at the restaurant.

"Matthew, come home? Please? This pain is unbearable. Please? I need you," I beg, my vocal cords and body trembling, the words trickling in short, broken bursts between sobs.

There's no response. I hear nothing—only the absence of sound, the line eerily mute.

A sudden chill travels from my head to toe, and a surge of adrenaline kicks in, flooding my system. The pain recedes slightly, replaced by a relentless pounding in my ears. An edgy, twitchy feeling overtakes me, and my pulse races wildly. My breathing is rushed, my throat dry, but I clear it, pushing through the adrenaline that's making my body quiver and my thoughts scatter.

Steady at first—not too loud but filled with determination and anger—I ask, "Are you really engaged to that bitch, Anna? Are you? To your ex-wife?"

Again, no response. The line is mute. "Are you there? Are you engaged to her?"

The lack of response pushes me to the edge. "Are you listening?" This time, I scream, juddering at the meaning of the words I'm about to unleash. "Are you fucking her, Daddy? Huh? Are you fucking that whore?"

As those vile but justified words leave my mouth, my mind spirals, conjuring images of hurting her, of seeing her blood spill, of standing over her gravestone. These twisted thoughts soothe me momentarily, then they fuel me, making my anger burn hotter. Right now I can't focus on anything else.

A desire for vengeance clouds my heart and mind. I can't be chosen over that snake, that bitch. I've been mistreated, misunderstood—despite my flaws—and she's the reason. Matthew, who is commanding but also forgiving, must have been brainwashed, twisted by that poisonous leech. *My energies could be better spent planning her murder, which will clear all impediments to my reclaiming him.*

The silence is broken by an ominous hiss.

"Hi, Alex. This is Savannah. We haven't spoken, and I'd like to. May I request you kindly try to relax, please? I want to talk to you."

Her venomous, yet...sweet-sounding voice cuts through my thoughts as a sharpened knife would butter, slicing the darkness with a calm, unflustered tone that leaves me stupefied. Silence hangs in the. The ringing in my ears intensifies, mingling with the muffled sound of my heartbeat. A sense of paralysis creeps over me, leaving me numb, frozen in place.

Every word I'd use to describe his caring, confident, and commanding tone could apply to her. Over the phone, she seems soothing—more so than Dr. Robbins, more compassionate than Mom, Evie, or even Matthew.

I hang up, and the ringing in my ears continues as I stay rooted to the spot—my phone slipping from my hand and clattering to the floor.

Should I also be stunned that they were on speakerphone—tackling the issue of my contacting him—together? As a happy, loving, all-sharing, no-secrets couple?

A peculiar calm settles over me. I crank up the La Marzocco to brew a potent blend of coffee, hoping caffeine will clear the alcohol-induced high of the past several hours. Then I take a long drink of cold water and feel the chill slide down my throat, grounding me. I heat a bowl of frozen food in the microwave. As I wait for the food to warm and the coffee to drip, I reflect on how her speech reminds me of Matthew's—so unnervingly similar, a female version of his.

I know now, beyond doubt, they're together, and he isn't confused. Neither is she.

The fresh coffee drips into the decanter. Each drop feels like bits of dark energy, fortifying the rage building inside.

I'm going to make her life hell. I'll even hurt him if I must. He can take it, but I apologize in advance, Daddy.

The microwave chimes—its tone blending with the sound of dripping coffee, further soothing me. My breath evens, returning to a normal rhythm.

She will have no choice but to escape the pandemonium I'll create. She'll regret this—her choices, her audacity.

The steam from the hot food mixes with the rich aroma of coffee, placating me. My heart is still racing from the heavy drinking, but it will settle once I've rested for the night.

I must be refreshed, powered, and healthy—body and mind—so I can go about freeing Matthew from Anna.

I turn off all the lights in the penthouse, save for the soft glow in the eat-in kitchen, and settle in for a warm meal and much-needed coffee.

Once he's free of her, I'll have him. All to myself.

I sit in silence, eating slowly, the food and coffee overflowing my already full tanks of sheer determination and resolve.

He'll understand me once he's free. After all, I am his little girl.

CHAPTER
THIRTY-TWO

Anna: Radar - Blip

The weekend hadn't come soon enough for Matt and me. The past week has been a whirlwind of stress—Alex's intrusion, long hours at work, and wedding planning. I've started considering a job with fewer hours, one that lets me leave at five without exception. When I first took the administrative assistant and receptionist role, I thought I could balance work and life, but I hadn't accounted for the high stakes cases at Hudson & Greene LLP. My tech expertise makes me indispensable. When things heat up, it's all-hands-on-deck, no matter how late. I do like the company, though—the people are kind and supportive, and they gave me a raise midyear, which deepened my loyalty.

Still, my life with Matt comes first. With our wedding just six weeks away, I've decided to hold off on making any career changes until after the big day. I think about this as I lie in bed on a hot Saturday morning, wishing the facilities team would fix the air conditioner—it's stuck at a sweltering seventy-seven degrees.

A hand glides toward me on the bed, not quite touching me but close enough to send a shiver of anticipation through me. My sex tingles—desire building—and I crave to be ravished. The last few times we tried, her texts and prank calls interrupted our passion, leaving us discussing defense strategies and whether to change our numbers. She has resources, so finding our new numbers would be easy. He suggested blocking her, but I argued she'd just use new numbers. Instead, we decided on do not disturb' mode when she contacts us, and though it helps us sleep, it puts off our lovemaking.

His hand draws nearer, grazing the small of my back. My wet pussy throbs with need—anticipation amplifying the sensation. In one swift motion, he lifts me off the bed and strips me of my nightdress. I yelp, and a laugh escapes as I meet his dreamy gaze, intense and decadent. My wetness pools, and I reach for his mouth as hunger overtakes me. But he has other plans. He fends off my advances, but his lips are hovering near my ear, sending jolts of electricity through me.

"You know what I admire about your gymnastics background, gorgeous?" He whispers in my ear, sending vibrations from head to toe.

I blush, trying to hide it, but the heat in my cheeks betrays me. His powerful arms snake around me from behind, grazing my breasts, then sliding lower with a featherlight touch that barely brushes my groin. The tenderness contrasts with the exquisite pain he often inflicts—a promise of mind-altering euphoria that has my pulse racing.

A shiver runs down my spine. "Umm...my flexibility to your needs? If you get my meaning?" I manage, my voice shaky as his hands roam over my body with practiced precision. Each touch sends waves of pleasure, gentle yet agonizingly slow.

He knows every inch of me, every place where a touch can convert gentle pleasure to aching lust. His lips find my neck, suckling as I moan in exquisite delight, and the arousal turns me into an animal with a need to consume him. And for him to consume me.

His mouth travels across my nape next, planting kisses. He expertly traces artful caresses on my chin, then up to my earlobes. Each suckle sends a jolt through me, as if he's setting off a series of demolition charges within all the sensitive parts of my body. My lungs falter, and a long moan escapes me.

Then he breathes in my ear, and his fiery words are laced with dark promise. "No. It makes me creative, so I find unique ways to torment you."

His words send arousal coursing through me, and my heart pounds in my chest as fear and excitement flood my body. I brace for what's coming—his creativity in causing pain has always left me trembling and bruised but wallowing on the border between ecstasy and torment. But it's not the physical affliction—it's the way he takes control, the way he pushes me to my limits, knowing exactly how far I can go before I break.

In reaction to his words, my pussy clenches, as a delicious ache and heat spreads within me. The warmth of his nose on my skin, the way his palms explore my skin and muscles with calculated intent—it's all too much, yet not enough. I crave more—I need him to push me further, to that place where pain and rapture blur, creating one overwhelming sensation.

But he's not in any hurry. He savors the way I tremble under his touch, the way my breathing quickens with each fresh sensation. He knows he has complete control over me, and he's going to make sure I feel it.

As his hands continue their exploration, I close my eyes, sinking into the moment, surrendering to the storm he's about to unleash. My thoughts scatter, replaced by the overwhelming desire to be his—to let him shape me, mold me, break me, and put me back together again, piece by piece.

"Creative, huh?" I manage to whisper, betraying the itch that's building inside me. I try to maintain my composure, but it's futile—he knows exactly how to unravel me.

His fingers glide lower, tracing the curve of my hips before sliding around to my stomach where they pause—his fingers pressing to remind me of his control. "Yes, Anna," he murmurs like silk wrapping around me. "And now, I have something tormenting in mind."

Before I can respond, he spins me around, face to face with him. His intensity leaves me breathless, and I submit, begging to be pushed to my limits. He leans in, his lips hovering so close that I can almost taste him, but he doesn't kiss me—not yet. He lets the tension build, and the ardor between us is palpable.

He takes my wrists and with a swift motion pulls them above my head, pinning me against the wall. The cool surface contrasts with the heat radiating from him, and I gasp as he binds my wrists with a soft, unyielding rope he produced from nowhere. The knot is secure but not tight enough to hurt—yet.

"Your flexibility, my creativity," he says, his voice low, dark, and full of promise. "Let's see how far we can take this."

He retreats—his eyes drinking in the sight of me bound and at his mercy. My pulse races as I realize how vulnerable I am, and yet there's nowhere I'd rather be. The anticipation is almost unbearable, and I bite my lip, trying to contain my desire.

He takes his time, moving with deliberate slowness, letting the moment stretch. He knows that the waiting is part of the torture—the sweet agony of not knowing what comes next. Finally, he reaches for a small leather flogger, its tails swaying ominously in his hand.

My breath catches as he trails the soft leather across my skin from my collarbone to the swell of my breasts, teasing and taunting. He watches my reaction closely, smirking as I arch toward him, desperate to begin.

"The rules, my angel," he says, his tone both commanding and considerate. "Tell me your safe word."

"Lavender," I whisper, the word slipping from me almost involuntarily. It's our secret, the single word that holds all the power to stop this, but I have no intention of using it—I never have.

"Good," he purrs, and with that, he brings the flogger down in a quick, sharp snap against my thigh. I feel a fleeting second of numbness and then the sting, accompanied by scorching fire. It's the kind of stinging which—after I brave it enough to send me past the threshold—induces a rush of endorphins, a heady mix of pain and pleasure that leaves me breathless and wanting more.

"Are you going to use your safe word?" His tone is a low, dangerous whisper, and his eyes gleam with desire and dominance.

"No..." I barely manage to respond, trembling as need coils tight within me.

A slow, dark smile spreads across his face. "You are such a sweet angel," he murmurs, and the nickname is laced with both affection and promise.

Without another word, he steps back, his presence still looming as he picks up the flogger again. The leather tails sway ominously, and my heart pounds in a frantic rhythm that matches the adrenaline flooding my veins. I close my eyes—my heart pounding and pulse racing.

He doesn't waste time. The next strike is harder than before, landing across my thigh with a sharp crack that reverberates around the room. The sting is meteoric, searing from end to end akin to flares of fire laced with electric shocks, but the suffering awakens something deep inside me—something dark and primal. A moan escapes me, the sound uncontrollable, and I bite hard on my lip, refusing to cry, refusing to give in.

I know he's watching me closely, and his eyes darken with satisfaction when he sees the fire in my eyes. He knows I'm holding on—pushing through the pain because it's what he wants, and what I require. The flogger lands again, and this time the blow bruises across my stomach—the leather biting with a force that makes me wail. I gasp and jolt between the crying, the agony spreading, but instead of retreating, I arch, craving another.

My skin screams, asking me to call, *Lavender!* but I refuse.

"You please me, gorgeous," he praises in a low growl that sends a thrill down my spine. "You can take it. I know you want more."

The next strikes come quickly on my butt, thighs, and stomach again, followed by another round, and another, each one harder than the last. The blows rain on me in relentless rhythm—each crack of the flogger echoed by my sharp intakes of breath, and the sound of my moans and wailing grows louder with each strike. My skin burns, a thousand flames igniting with every crack of the flogger, and yet I'm desperate for more, desperate to be pushed to the very edge of what I can endure.

Is today it? The day I find my limit and use the safe word?

"What did you say, my darling?" he taunts, dripping with dark satisfaction as he watches me writhe under his control.

"Nothing...I need...Babe, hurt me again...please..." I gasp, my resolve unbroken, even as pain threatens to overwhelm me.

He chuckles darkly, the deep baritone dripping another round of arousal down my thighs. "Such an angel," he murmurs again, but there's a sinister edge to his tone now, a hint of the darkness he's about to unleash.

He drops the flogger and steps closer, and his hands are rough as they grip my hips, pulling me toward him with a possessive force that claims and owns me—I am his, completely and utterly. He spins me around, pressing me face-first against the wall, my bound wrists above my head as I submit. The cool surface is a cruel contrast, and my pulse races—my frame trembling with a heady mix of fear and desire.

His palms roam my form, exploring the tender flesh he's flogged, and I can't help the moan that leaves my lips, and the sound of my surrender fills the room. He's rougher now—his touch no longer gentle, but commanding, demanding.

"You're beautiful," he whispers, his breath hot against my ear. "So perfect when you're at my mercy."

He pushes me to my limits, knowing exactly how far I can go, knowing exactly what I crave.

Without warning, his hand lands hard on my butt—the slap echoing and bouncing around the room, followed by the delicious sting that spreads inside me. I cry out, the sound more a howl than a scream. The hurt is sharp and biting, but it's the kind of spasm that heightens everything else, making every nerve ending in my body come alive.

He doesn't give me a moment to recover. His hands are everywhere—gripping, pulling, twisting—his touch punishing and intoxicating. My body is on fire as each novel sensation pushes me closer to the edge—the pressure and heat building in my pussy until they're almost unbearable.

"Do you want me to go on, gorgeous?" he asks, in a low, seductive growl.

"Yes, please...ruin me..." I beg, my voice trembling, the desperation clear in every word.

He presses against me, a solid wall of heat and power, and when he finally fucks me, it's with a fierce, unrelenting intensity that leaves me gasping—the sound of my moans and his growls filling the room. He pins me—face and chest against the wall, bound wrists above my head—as his hard cock enters me from behind, traveling the length of my soaked pussy and beyond.

The pain and pleasure meld together in a dizzying haze that sweeps me up and carries me away, until there's nothing left but the raw, primal connection between us.

He pummels me with his thick dick—deeper, harder—until I'm teetering, and the world is spinning around me as I climax, shattering into a thousand pieces only to be pulled together by the force of his embrace, by the power of his will.

It's a deliciously long orgasm, and my juices are dripping as he rams his cock faster into my pussy. My howls of ecstasy echo through the room, mingling with his deep, primal grunts as we reach the peak together—the intensity overwhelming, all-consuming. The whole exhilarating experience is sweetened by the feeling of his semen as he pumps into me.

When we've half recovered from the blissful assault of euphoria, he unties my wrists. His touch is gentle now as he gathers me in his arms, holding me close as the aftershocks ripple through me and send me quivering in his grasp. I'm spent—my mind a blissful blur—but there's a deep sense of satisfaction, of completeness, that fills me as I lie in his arms, knowing that I've given him everything, and that he's taken it all.

"You're mine, Anna," he murmurs into my hair, pressing a soft kiss to my temple. "And my heart is forever yours."

I smile, dipping in the comfort of his embrace as the last echoes of our shared sounds fade and the rays of the sun cast a golden glow on our entwined bodies. With him, I am exactly where I'm meant to be—both in his arms and at his mercy, the warmth of the sun echoing his declaration.

It's been ten days since the violent incident at La Grand Élégance.

The thorn still lives in my heart. Someone dared lay a hand on my king because of her, and I won't let that go unavenged. I won't resort to physical violence, but I will break her. I'll teach her a lesson so severe she'll have no choice but to leave us alone. I'm lying in wait, like a tiger hungry for the kill.

Every time we take our phones off 'do not disturb,' we brace for the onslaught of missed calls and texts. He gets the bulk of them and I occasionally.

We sit together, review them all, then delete each one. He suggested we delete everything without a second thought, but I insisted we examine each message. No detail is too small. I'm learning about her mind—she's not just a disturbed girl on a path to self-destruction. She's far more dangerous. I won't underestimate her. My dad always said, "Do not underestimate anyone. Respect everyone, even your enemy, and you'll act accordingly."

In the past week, the texts to Matt have escalated from love notes and pleas for forgiveness to desperate demands for him to return to her.

Alex

> I miss you, Matthew. Can't we go back to how things were? Just us, just like before.

> You're my only safe place. You know that, right? I'll wait forever if I have to.

> Do you think about me? Or has she already erased me from your life? Tell me it's not true. Please.

Each call is akin to her flailing her limbs while drowning, reaching for a lifeline, twisted with desperation and obsession—attempts to pull him deeper into the darkness she created. She sobs and sometimes wails in her voicemails, and her cries move him as he steps away for a few moments, needing to compose himself.

"Matthew, I need you...I can't breathe without you. Please...just come home."

"I'm so sorry for everything, for ruining us. But I can't let you go, I won't."

Her voicemails are manipulative, sometimes laced with threats, and filled with more weeping.

"You said you loved me. You promised we'd build a future. Why are you leaving me alone in this hell? If you don't come, you're leaving me to die lonely and miserable."

"You belong with me, Matthew. I'll wait forever, but I know you'll come back. You'll choose me over her. You have to."

245

"I know she can't love you the way I do. I'm the only one who truly sees you, the real you, my father figure. I won't let her take you from me."

Each contact is a window into her unraveling mind, which fuels the fire in me to protect what's mine.

I get maybe two prank calls a day—sometimes from her number, sometimes from an unknown number. I must confront her at some point, but I'm waiting for the right moment, so I don't answer.

Her messages to me are fewer—maybe three or four a day—each one contains a single character: a full stop. It's as if she's trying to command me to end my relationship with him. But I don't give her the satisfaction of a response. I delete the call records and texts calmly, methodically, without letting her see the storm she's stirring within me.

I'm not immune to feelings of jealousy, hurt, and rage. Irrational thoughts and behaviors lurk in the shadows of my mind, waiting to pounce. But I've learned to control them—to keep them at bay—knowing that nothing constructive comes from acting on impulse, driven by those emotions. Yet I struggle to maintain my composure when wave after wave of jealousy and anger storms me, triggered by the texts in which she reminds him of the "good times" they shared.

Alex

> Matthew, please. Remember the nights you held me as if I was a glass sculpture.

> I'm the center of your world, always. You will realize that soon.

> Remember the commitments we made in London? I can't wait to have our first child.

> I love you. I can't overstate that. Please forgive me. I will keep begging.

> *I made you proud, Daddy. Here's a link to the president's address at the London summit. Project GreenWind is a world-acclaimed success. I came here to be with you, instead of going with the president.*

> *Hey! The evenings by the riverfront. Our serene moments by Manhattan Bridge. The story we've written. It's waiting to be continued. You can't simply ignore what we've built.*

> *Who will look after me, Daddy? One mistake, and you throw your daughter on the street? I am all alone, and I need you.*

And so on...

Each message is a dagger, twisting deeper with every word. My irritability heightens, and my muscles quiver with barely contained rage as I read her attempts to manipulate him, to remind him of their bond.

I sit a little away from Matt so he can't see the tension tightening my body or feel the rapid pulse pounding my veins as my impetuosity knocks at the door, urging me to do something—anything—to lash out and silence her once and for all. The fantasies come unbidden—violent, dark visions of what I want to do to her, what I could do if I let myself.

But I don't. I can't. Nothing constructive can come out of it. It'll destroy us.

I force myself to remember the long game. This is not a battle to be fought with reckless actions or hasty decisions. No, this requires strategy. I have to be methodical, to bide my time until the moment is right. Then, and only then, will I deliver the final blow.

She's doing this on purpose. She knows he and I are facing her together, reviewing every word side by side. Each message is a calculated reminder of what she meant to him.

Her strategy is obvious, mirroring what I once did to Matt when I was drowning in grief after my dad's death. My guilt strikes, but the life I've built with him—our life, forged from the ashes of our past grief—is stronger. It transcends the darkness we knew.

Her texts are designed to hurt me, and they do. Each word is a stab, a wrenching reminder of the agony I felt when I learned he'd slept with her while still married to me. He may have considered us separated, but I hadn't. That betrayal pierced me deeply.

It's painful to confront the intimate bond they shared, and it dredges up feelings of insecurity I thought I'd buried. I can't help but think that, at one point, he held her above me—she was the center of his world, as she claims. And though I now occupy that place, I can't be sure unless she is gone. Their relationship had a complexity ours doesn't, heightened by their special dynamic and her youth.

My unease grows, but so does my confidence in my strategy. There will come a moment when either she or I will force a confrontation. Until then, I won't fall into desperation. I won't bite at her bait. *I am Anna, Matt's shield, and I know how to protect him.* Not with violence—but with patience, cunning, and the unwavering strength that comes from knowing exactly who I am, and that he is mine.

CHAPTER THIRTY-THREE

Anna: Radar - Mass

The woman snaps her head away quickly, sinking her phone into the pocket of her yoga pants with practiced ease. She pulls on her hoodie—covering her profile—adjusts her earplugs, and taps her fingers on the handrail as the train surges forward. It's the kind of behavior that blends in with the mundane chaos of a subway car—easily overlooked.

But I notice her. Yesterday, it was a man. They alternate, like players in a twisted game.

I can't shake the feeling that Alex hired shady people to stalk us. Her goal? To scare me—a blend of proximity and psychological assault designed to wear me down. When I wrote this scenario down in my plan, it didn't feel as scary as it does now. The woman steals another glance and turns away, chewing on her bubble gum.

I've heard of it happening to others—relationships broken under the pressure of obsessive stalking by ex-partners. The thought chills me. I casually mentioned it to a lawyer at the firm, who offered support and legal advice. It was comforting, but not enough to calm the jittery fear growing in my chest.

Every time I spot the man or woman watching me, an icy dread settles in, and my stomach hardens. I've even considered pulling the chain to stop the train and disappearing into the tunnels, where I might feel safer than under the gaze of the unknown forces at play. The fear creeps in slowly, but it's becoming overwhelming.

Matt has noticed someone following him too. At first he thought it was just coincidence, but tonight, after I share my experience, his face changes. He tells me about a man lingering outside the recording studio, possibly with a camera. The same car parks outside La Grand Élégance on his route to the subway. The realization hits us both—we're being stalked. My stomach churns, and my chest tightens with anxiety.

He is determined. "Next time, I'll check the license plate or confront him," he says, but the idea worries me. I admire his courage but fear what might happen.

I place a hand on his arm, and my voice trembles. "Please, don't. I don't want you to get hurt or caught in whatever trap Alex is setting. What if she's waiting for us to slip?"

His eyes soften, but I can see the conflict in them—the need to protect me, to take action, warring with the possibility of making things worse. The modest living room feels heavy with unspoken tension. The unknown presses on us as we try to navigate this twisted game she's playing.

He looks at me for several seconds with disquiet. His viridian eyes, usually so calm, are now bloodshot—a reflection of the restlessness churning inside him. Without a word, he reaches for his phone and dials her number, turning the speaker on. I wince as frustration and anguish mingle in my chest, and I whisper a protest, but he silences me with a stern look and a finger pressed to his lips. *I don't want him to rile her up further.* The commanding authority in his gaze leaves no room for argument, and I know better than to fight when he's assumed a controlling stance.

She answers on the first ring. "Daddy?" Her voice is thick with emotion, and we can hear her shallow breaths. Then she sobs, unmasked and raw, her throat occasionally hitching—as if she's been drowning in her own despair waiting for his call.

He is direct, cutting through her tears with steady intention. "Alex, if you've done something foolish like hiring private investigators, or worse—having someone stalk Anna to frighten her—I'm asking you nicely to put a stop to it. Do you understand?"

There's no response, only sobbing. I tug at his hand, my alarm rising as I whisper another plea for him to hang up. This might provoke her further, and while my heart swells with warmth at his protective stance, this is a moment for strategy, not confrontation. But he gently pushes my hand away—his grip tender but secure—and motions for me to obey him and sit down. Reluctantly, I slump on the sofa, clutching my temples as the tension in the room crushes me like a heavy steel compactor, relentless and pitiless.

"You care about that whore that much, huh?" She is loud, scratchy, and venomous—her outburst laced with pain and anger. "I'm suffering here, with no one to look after me, and you call me to talk about that snake? That poisonous leech? Fuck you."

I shake my head, silently pleading for this conversation to end, but he remains unfazed. His voice is the deliberate, measured tone I've always known, steady as a rock against her fury. "Listen to me. Unleash your anger on me. I can handle it. But I need you to leave her alone. Do not even think of harming her."

"Or else what?" she snaps, her voice trembling with palpable desperation and defiance. "You'll hurt me? Please do it. You deserve to discipline me, show me your fury. Punish me for the mistake I made. Come home and punish me. But stop talking about her. I am yours, not her."

Her words hang in the air—a twisted plea that chills and irritates me. I can feel the tension radiating off him, but he remains composed, dropping to a low, ominous tone. "You heard me, Alex. Cease all actions you're taking—or even thinking of taking—against Anna. Focus on your healing. Do not make me repeat this."

With that, he ends the call, and the silence that follows is oppressive. I lift my chin to meet his gaze, and my heart pounds. The line between protecting and provoking is razor-thin, and I can only hope that this confrontation won't tip her further into darkness, escalating the damage.

But one thing is clear—his resolve is unbreakable. As much as it frightens me to think of what'll happen if he were to lose his resolve, it also reassures me. We're in this together, and no matter what obstacles she throws at him and me, he'll stand by my side.

Then, in a fit of rage I rarely see, he slams his fist on the rickety old chair at the small dining table, shattering it in two with a violent crack. He's about to unleash the same fury on the drywall when I rush to stop him. "Babe, no. Please," I plead, wrapping my arms around him and pulling him close as tears stream down my cheeks. My sobs quickly become a wail, the sound muffled against his shirt, as I feel his body trembling—his limbs quivering with barely restrained anger.

I can't hold back any longer. The soreness in my throat and lungs intensifies, and my chest and limbs tighten under our shared despair. I cling to him with all the strength I can muster, but hopelessness, guilt, and dread crash over me, paralyzing my mind and body. A suffocating thought takes hold: *we will never escape this moment, never be free from Alex's shadow, and the pain we're enduring will be eternal.* I wail into his chest, soaking his shirt with tears, feeling as if we're both drowning in this endless torment.

For several moments, we stand locked in shared grief. Finally, he moves, and his steady hands wrap around me, pulling me close. His touch is a lifeline, grounding me as he kisses my hair and forehead, and each gesture pulls me away from panic and despondency. In silence, he leads me to the kitchen where he begins preparing dinner with deliberate, almost meditative movements. The quiet soothes me, as the storm inside me slowly subsides.

I retreat to the bathroom, where I wash my face and apply a light touch of makeup to erase the tear-streaked remnants of my breakdown. When I return, I rejoin him in the kitchen. We cook—no words spoken, the silence now one of understanding.

It was a bad moment—a stark reminder that we must remain unshaken, no matter the hand we're dealt. He let anger take over, and I let despair consume me. I chastise myself, vowing to plan better for these emotional surges. I know he is doing the same. To navigate the minefield of Alex, we must be steady, while she remains the unpredictable force trying to tear us apart.

We settle on the sofa, eating slowly in silence. He flips on the TV, and we watch a basketball game, the rhythm of it offering a brief escape from her intrusion.

After dinner, he lifts me into his arms and carries me to bed. He spends an eternity kissing me—lips, head, hair—his touch gentle yet firm. He holds me with a fondness that contrasts the earlier chaos, and his grip is protective, as if silently vowing never to let me go. It's his way of showing me without words that he'll protect me from her looming presence.

But as much as I appreciate his protective gestures, I am his shield—the one who must defend our relationship from external forces. It's on me to end her invasions of our future, to strike when she least expects it, and to do so in a way that leaves no room for recovery. The right time will come. Until then, patience is my ally.

"My darling, my gorgeous," he finally murmurs into my ear, and his affection is a soothing balm. His words melt my heart, and the warm sensations make me feel weightless. The dull, aching pleasure of his affection spreads across me in a slow, comforting wave.

We sit on the bed, still wrapped in each other's arms—the intimacy of the moment grounding us.

"I'm thinking of filing a restraining order," he says, his tone measured but serious. I blink in surprise, a slight jerk of my body betraying my shock at such an extreme measure. Before I can state my concern, he continues, his reasoning thoughtful and deliberate. "But we'll never be able to tie these people to Alex.

If they're PIs or hired muscle—they're all trained escape artists, prepared for situations if we ever try to confront them. It would only make things worse."

His words resonate, and I relax, reclining on his chest as I nod in agreement. The path to resolution lies in peace, not in further escalating the situation. We both recognize that, deep within, even as the impulse to protect what we've built tugs at us to react with drastic action. Personally, I'm fine with taking drastic action. I'd start with a cease-and-desist letter before taking out a restraining order, but I'd need the proof first, which as he said, is difficult to obtain.

In the same serene tone, he finishes his thoughts. "It's the same with the texts. The police or lawyers would dismiss them as the actions of a heartbroken teenage girl. But I'm jumping ahead, along a path we deliberately chose not to take—not unless we must. Our strategy isn't to meet aggression with aggression."

Yes, my heart-keeper, I think, feeling a renewed sense of clarity.

We sit upright on the bed, facing each other, gazes locked. Taking turns, we reaffirm our commitment to the original plan, reiterating the approach and guiding principles with quiet determination.

"We will treat her as a child who needs help. We will always redirect her to therapy and her family," he says, his declaration steady.

"Our wedding is the sole focus, and we won't allow any incident to disturb the peace we've worked so hard to build," I add, my resolve firming with every word.

"We'll ignore her advances, responding only when necessary, and always with kindness," he continues, his gaze holding mine, a silent promise traded.

"Treat her with respect, empathize with her, as we know and understand the grief she's navigating," I echo, feeling a deep sense of purpose settle over me.

"Share everything with each other—no secrets, nothing goes unreviewed, together," we conclude in unison, our voices a shared vow.

In this moment, we're stronger together in a bond fortified by the challenges we've faced and the challenges yet to come. The darkness that surrounds may be daunting, but as long as we remain united, we will navigate it with grace, with love, and with an unbreakable commitment to each other.

In the third week since Alex invaded the placidness of the life Matt and I are building, he beckons me over one evening, and his tone is somber, carrying a weight that immediately makes my heart skip a beat. "Hey, I don't want you to see this, but we agreed on no secrets."

A lump forms in my throat, and my heart stops altogether as I try to anticipate what he might be about to show me. My vocal cords catch, and I stammer, unable to find the right words. Dread surges within me, tightening my chest.

But when I see his calm demeanor, I force myself to restrain the fear, to bury it deep where it can't reach me. I nuzzle into him on the sofa, trying to draw comfort from his presence even as dread lingers at the edges of my thoughts.

He hands me his phone, showing a series of texts with pictures Alex had sent him throughout the day. The images appear in sets, each one more provocative than the last. She's dressed in expensive, revealing lingerie, and her poses are deliberately seductive, her cerulean eyes locking onto the camera with boldness. It's as if she's staring straight at the viewer, inviting a destructive response.

My body goes rigid, except for my fingers, which automatically scroll through the pictures. Bile churns in my stomach, quickly turning to searing heat that spreads through my chest. My jaw clenches, a slight twitch betraying my composure. He reaches for the phone, but I swat his hand away, desperate to absorb every detail. I go over the images again, top to bottom, searching for something—anything—that explains what she is trying to achieve.

The pictures rekindle the worst of my nightmares. They clarify my thoughts since I discovered he slept with her before the divorce. These images fill in the gaps, painting vivid pictures of him entwined with an eighteen-year-old in her luxurious bedroom. Every curve of her perfect body, flattered by designer lingerie, fuels the fire burning beneath my ribs. My stomach tightens, and my breaths are shallow and erratic—my vision flashing as it all presses down.

She's ten years younger than me. Her youth radiates from every inch of her body—smooth skin, flawless and firm, framed by perfectly styled brunette hair and piercing blue eyes. Her lingerie flaunts her body, a cruel reminder. Her petite, yet sensuous frame—a body anyone would envy—tightens the knot in my chest. I feel the pulse in my ears, wild and out of control, as if I'm suffocating.

But it's not just envy. It's something darker, more unsettling. Nausea rises, and my body is drenched in sweat—my vision swimming. A deep inadequacy takes root—irrational, but real.

Alex isn't just any girl. She's the one who had Matt and held his heart in a way that I'm now beginning to understand. And today, she's reminding me of that, trying to pull him back into her orbit.

The air feels thick, too heavy to breathe. I want to dismiss the emotions, to remind myself of his love, of the strength of our bond, but the pictures won't let me. They linger, a reminder of the constant threat she poses—not just to our relationship, but to our fragile peace.

She knows I'll see these pictures.

I try to push my feelings down, but they cling to me, impossible to shake. He doesn't seem to notice, unaware of the growing disturbance in my mind. I feel it bubbling, ready to explode.

I won't let her win. I won't let her break me. This is her game, and I need to be stronger, more resilient. But as I hand the phone to him, I wonder—how much longer can I keep this up before the cracks start to show?

"Anna, hey...hey?" His prompt clears the haze of envious rage consuming me, and his hands are firm as he pulls me away from the edge. He holds me, grounding me with his presence. He lifts my chin gently, attempting to meet my gaze, but I look away as my lips curl in resistance. Tears blur my vision, and my lips tremble as I bite hard—struggling to stem the sob in my chest, desperate to escape.

He turns me and cradles my cheeks and chin in his hands, and the touch is tender and insistent. I sniffle, fighting to keep the tears at bay, struggling to swallow the painful sob lodged in my throat that threatens to break free at any moment.

"She knows you'll see these pictures. It's a mind game she's playing with us. Alright, Anna, my sweet angel?" He pacifies me, as if commanding me to settle. The tears slow, though they don't completely vanish, and stillness struggles to replace the anger, hurt, and jealousy locked in that painful sob, which claws at my throat, refusing to be silenced.

"I'm deleting these," he says, his tone resolute. "And I want to reaffirm my commitment that I won't let her actions disturb what we have. Do you hear me?"

His tranquil voice, the serenity on his angelic face, and the intensity in his eyes continue to pull me away from the dark thoughts and intentions that had begun to harden. The sobs recede as he lets go of my cheeks, allowing me to nuzzle him for comfort. He deletes the texts and pictures, and I manage to speak, my speech dry and raspy, "I'm sorry I slipped into a dark place, Matt." I clear my throat and say it again, this time undeniably steady and articulate.

"That's why we're doing this together, gorgeous," he murmurs, planting firm kisses on my head, and his touch anchors me to the present.

Yet, even as I cling to his warmth, something is off—an unease that settles deep in the pit of my stomach. Despite the intimacy he and I share, the thought of Alex casts a dark shadow at the edges of my mind. It feels as though every smile Matt gives me is tinged with a flicker of doubt, every caring touch a reminder that she is still out there, lurking on the fringes of the life he and I are nurturing—a ticking time bomb of unpredictable obsession.

I try to push these thoughts away, to focus on the here and now, but they cling to me, tightening their grip with each passing day. No matter how close he and I get, no matter how much we reassure each other, Alex hovers—the darkest cloud—a constant reminder that the peace we've cultivated is fragile, and the resulting happiness is threatened by forces beyond our control. All we can do is respond and chip away until it's time for me to meet her.

CHAPTER THIRTY-FOUR

Anna: Radar - Raid

In the next few days, her texts become more intense—closer to explicit territory. The pictures she sends are more provocative, and her poses are calculated to enflame, to unsettle. She's in lingerie, but now the images are darker—she's in restraints: handcuffs, loosely bound ropes, blindfolds, and gags. Her hair is always styled and braided into pigtails, a twisted play on innocence.

One picture shows her lying on her bed with her body arranged in a way that screams vulnerability—on her back, wrists bound behind her, knees bent and legs spread wide. The room is dimly lit, and the darkness is broken by the soft glow of sixteen candles—eight on each nightstand.

The caption reads:

> *Remember this night? The day you moved in with me?*
> *Please come home, and we can have a wilder one.*

Another image is her bundled in the corner of a coat closet, bound and blindfolded, her figure small and submissive.

The caption taunts:

> *Remember when I disobeyed you? Come and punish*
> *me again, Daddy. This time, tie me up and closet me*
> *for days, however long you want to. But please come*
> *home.*

Then there's the image of her lying on her stomach, her hips pressed to the bed, legs tightly together. Red palm prints mar her buttocks, and a whip is lying menacingly beside her. Her hands are folded behind her in a display of surrender.

The caption stings:

I never knew which part of my body was your favorite, but come, show me?

And the text messages and pictures continue to arrive.

Each day, we delete the pictures, trying to erase the growing sense of violation and disgust. But it's no use. The images are seared in my mind—the captions echoing when I'm alone. My composure is fraying with every new message. She's relentless, chipping away at the wall of strength I've built, inch by inch. He's struggling too. I can see it in the way his jaw tightens when he deletes the photos, the way his palms linger and press on mine, as if straining to reassure me, to anchor himself.

"Anna," Matt begins, his articulation low. "My dynamic with her was different. You're aware of that. The love she and I shared, the father figure and ward aspect...it led to things and behaviors I can only hope to explain. I don't want you to see these, but I also don't want to hide anything."

His words hang heavy in the air, a bitter reminder of the history that ties him to Alex—a history that threatens to unravel the life we're building. I nod, swallowing hard against the bile rising in my throat. He's being honest and laboring to navigate this nightmare with as much transparency as possible. But it doesn't make it any easier to bear.

I'm trapped in a cycle of dread as each new message tightens the noose around my heart. I can feel myself falling flat—my carefully maintained composure slipping away, piece by piece. She isn't merely testing his resolve—she's testing mine too, and I'm terrified of what will happen if I fail.

As he deletes another round of pictures, I can't help but wonder how long we can keep doing this. *How long before the strain breaks something inside me? Or worse, inside him?* I cling, desperate to keep us together, but the shadow of Alex looms, threatening to consume our humble existence.

He deletes a recent round of pictures, an explicit set, and he gives me an apologetic gaze, showing how disturbed he is by the messages and images hurting me. He opens his mouth, and I stop him, reaching for him, mashing my lips onto his with a fraught need to reassure, to take some of his burdens onto my shoulders. Our kiss is long and passion-filled—a silent exchange of strength and support. We hum and murmur through stolen breaths, and our lips move as if to seal commitments to one another, to remind ourselves that, no matter what she throws next, we are stronger together.

He gently pushes me, only to quickly pull me onto his lap. He holds me close with one hand resting firmly on my waist while the other caresses my cheek. A shadow of melancholy and strain veils his otherwise faultless face, and his bloodshot eyes look straight through me—full of care, concern, and a tinge of exhaustion. His deep baritone cracks as he struggles to maintain his usual tranquility. There's a hesitation, a stammer in his words that I rarely hear from him.

"I think—I think I know what you're feeling when you see these pictures, but I can't fully understand—I'm not a woman, I'm not you. But Anna, look at me. Only look at me, and channel everything at me."

At that moment, the darkness fades, his voice lifts, and the sight of his striking viridian green eyes overpowers the strain. His features glow with a divine transformation, and the radiance of his love and commitment permeates me. He's telling me without words that we are each other's—for eternity. No shadow of the past, no specter of Alex, can break what we've forged together.

My heart swells, and the heaviness lifts as I bask in his glow. We hold each other, no more words needed, only the comfort of connection.

After that, her texts escalate. Naked pictures of her, with and without restraints, flood his phone. Each caption recounts their sexual exploits, laced with pleas for forgiveness and love. She mixes in demands for him to come home to her penthouse, over and over.

I force myself to act desensitized. I laugh, coaxing him to join me as we review and delete each message. It's a charade, a façade I wear like armor, shielding us from the corrosive effect of her relentless intrusion.

But inside the fire intensifies with every text, every image. My anger is harder to control. The searing pain in my stomach and chest lingers, invading my work hours. Her texts, her pictures, the vivid descriptions of their past—an incessant loop of torment. The physical toll is terrifying—gut-wrenching tightness, a clenching jaw, throbbing headaches, trembling limbs. I can't keep this up. If I break, it will destroy Matt, and our future will suffer.

I find myself glancing over my shoulder more often, listening for footsteps that might not be there, feeling unseen eyes watching me. My relaxed façade begins to crack, and the fissures deepen with each unsettling text, with each time I sense a stalker's presence in the subway or on the street.

Her presence, though not physically near, feels like a storm gathering on the horizon, and the tempest is coming for me, threatening to tear apart the fragile peace Matt and I have fought to build.

I know we'll soon reach a breaking point. Although we're ready—I'm ready—the uncertainty of when the breaking point might occur leaves a persistent doubt that's growing, threatening to darken and destroy the walls I and Matt have built.

Something has to be done.

With the wedding date about six weeks away, we must attend to preparations soon. I can't allow the shadow of Alex to hang like a cloud over us. This can't go on. I must find a way to end this, for both our sakes.

Something has to be done.

Now.

The evening is eerily quiet as I step off the subway. The air is crisp, and the streets are deserted—the usual sounds of the city muffled, as if the world is retreating. I pull my coat tighter, trying to shake off the unease of the day. A figure from the subway flashes in my mind, the one I've seen too many times this week. Always at a distance, always just close enough to notice but never close enough to confront. I try to dismiss it, telling myself it's paranoia, but the feeling clings.

As I walk through Hamilton Heights, the comfort of the neighborhood offers little solace. Every shadow stretches longer, and every sound is amplified. I glance over my shoulder—there he is, barely fifty steps behind me, the figure from the subway. His hoodie is pulled low, his face obscured, and the faint glow of his phone casts an eerie light.

Panic surges in my chest. I quicken my pace, my shoes thumping hard against the pavement. His footsteps match mine, echoing in the silence. I glance behind, and now he's too close. My breath hitches. He's following me.

I turn down a side street, and my heart is pounding so hard it smothers everything else. The streetlights flicker, casting a sickly yellow glow on the empty sidewalk. I can hear his footsteps gaining on me—the rhythm of his steps matches the frantic thudding of my heart. I'm almost sprinting now.

What does he want? I can't let him catch me. A fresh wave of terror crashes through me, and I run, my breath coming in ragged gasps. The sound of his footsteps is louder now, pounding in my ears, and I realize he's chasing me.

"Matt!" The name bursts from my lips—a desperate cry swallowed by the vast, uncaring city. I force myself to keep going even as my legs are about to give. I'm a few blocks from home, but it feels like miles.

I round the corner and there it is—the apartment building, a beacon of safety in the darkness. It gives me a burst of energy, and I sprint the home stretch, fumbling with my keys as I reach the apartment door. My hands are shaking so badly that it takes three tries before the key slides into the lock. I wrench the door open, slam it shut behind me, and collapse against it, my chest heaving as I gasp for air.

But the horror doesn't go away. It's inside me now—a cold claw that refuses to let go.

"Anna!" His voice cuts through the fog of terror, and he rushes toward me, eyes wide. I try to speak, but the words stick in my throat, and all that comes out is a broken wail. He reaches me in an instant, and his strong arms pull me close. I cling to him as my body shakes uncontrollably.

"He was...he was following me," I choke out, my vocal cords wobbling, and I quiver as the words leave my mouth.

He stiffens, his muscles tensing as the full weight of my words sinks in. He pulls away slightly, just enough to cradle my chin and cheeks, and his gaze searches mine. "Are you hurt?" His tone is a mixture of alarm and anger, and his thumb brushes away the tears that streak down my cheeks.

I shake my head, but the terror lingers, shrouding my heart like an infernal blanket. "He chased me...I thought..." I trail off, the words too frightening to say loud.

His expression darkens, and a fierce protectiveness dominates his composure. "Stay here," he says, his intonation low and determined. "I'm going to find him."

"No, babe, don't—" I start to protest, but he's already out the door and I hear his footsteps echoing in the stairwell as he races outside. Fresh agony grips me as I think of what might happen if he were to locate the stalker. As much as I want the individual to be punished, the possibility of Matt getting hurt in the process stings. I cry quietly—the confines of the modest apartment and pieces of furniture my only companions until Matt returns and envelops me.

As I stand there, the cold reality of what just happened crashes down on me. I collapse on the couch and pull my knees to my chest, trying to hold myself together. Every sound makes me jump—every creak and groan of the building sends trepidation through me. I can't shake the feeling that he's still there—in the neighborhood, in this vast city—waiting, watching.

Time stretches before I hear the door open. Matt's expression is grim as he hurries in. He says nothing but crosses the room in a few quick strides and takes me in his arms again. I can feel the tension in his body—the anger simmering beneath the surface—but he holds me gently, stroking my hair, soothing my tears.

"I couldn't find him," he says after a long moment, and his speech is tight with frustration. "He's gone."

A shudder runs through me, and I bury my head in his chest, clinging to him as if he's the only thing keeping me from falling apart. "What if he comes back?" The question hangs in the air, heavy with dread.

Matt is silent for a moment, and when he finally speaks, his voice is unruffled. "It might be some thug...attempting to rob a vulnerable woman walking home late. An isolated incident."

"But what if it's not?" I whisper.

He steps away slightly, piercing me with his soft yet heightened glare. "We'll involve the police. I'm ready to go there."

His words are meant to be reassuring, but I can see the worry etched on his features.

And then, as if the thought just hit him, his expression hardens. "I'm calling Alex."

He grabs his phone, and his fingers move quickly as he dials and puts the call on speaker. The anger rolls off him in waves, and the room's atmosphere shifts to something darker, something more dangerous.

He paces the room as the phone rings—his free hand clenched in a fist. She answers at once, saying, "Matthew?" all too eagerly.

"Did you do this, Alex?" His demand is sharp, cutting through the silence like a knife. I glimpse the bulging veins and quivering muscles in his forearms.

There's a pause on the other end of the line, then she responds in a confused tone, devoid of any other emotion. "What are you talking about?"

"Don't play games with me," he snaps. "Someone chased Anna tonight. Scared her to death. Was that your doing?"

There's a longer pause this time. "I wish I had thought of that. Thank you for the idea." Her mocking tone drips with malice, and new anger mixes with my terror. "But no, it wasn't me. Although I wish it had been. It's a shame."

"Don't you dare touch her," he growls.

"Oh, don't worry," she says, her tone sickeningly sweet. "I wouldn't want to get my hands dirty. But you know what they say—accidents happen."

His expression tightens. He ends the call with a sharp tap and slams the phone down on the dining table. For a moment, the room is silent—the tension thick. Then he turns to me, eyes blazing.

"She's lying," he says, his voice severe. "But I'm not taking any chances. Let's talk to the police tomorrow, even though we don't have proof. Let's hear what they have to say."

I nod, striving to contain the tears that threaten to spill again. He pulls me close—his arms shielding me—and I melt, finding safety in his embrace. But apprehension gnaws at the edges of my mind, whispering that this is far from finished—we're in a maze, left to find the path to home. There is a simple solution to this problem, which is my next—and perhaps final—endeavor. If I play it right, Alex will have no choice but to leave.

"Give me the address of her penthouse," I say as we sit for breakfast, my request steady and composed. My ask might become a demand if he protests. I'm trying to present a placid front.

"Anna, we talked about this last night. I can't let you..." his refusal trails off as he stiffens, and his gaze is cold as he stares at me.

"Yes, we did, and we also agreed this was necessary. What changed? What happened to facing things together? You talked to her a few times, and nothing came of it. It's my turn." I cut him off, but I soften my tone enough to coax him, needing him to step aside so I can handle her.

Last night, after I had calmed down with a long, hot shower and a warm meal, I decided. It's time for me to meet Alex face-to-face, woman-to-woman. In bed, I broached the idea, and we argued for an hour. At first he refused to engage, saying it's too soon. But I wore him down, slowly persuading him until he finally agreed.

My argument was simple and genuine. "Let me try. I'm only going to talk, with no agenda. I'll help her in any way I can."

But this morning he's protesting once more, and I must remain mild to get him to agree again.

"Babe, what's the worst that could happen? She shows me the door? Things stay as they are? We're not losing anything." My tone is gentle, carefully crafted to coax him.

He rises, shaking his head in frustration, and walks to the window. I follow and throw my arms around him from behind, pressing my cheek against his back. "Matt, you know me. I'm calm and confident—traits you've strengthened in me. Trust me, please?"

He turns to me, gently cupping my cheeks, saying nothing. He doesn't need words. He envelopes me in an aura of care, comfort, and protection.

"The wedding is in six weeks. After that, she'll have to cease her actions, or her family will step in. What could go wrong with my meeting her now? Nothing. Allow me to try." My speech is casual, but deep down, I have a desperate desire to do this—for him and me.

He rubs my cheeks tepidly with his knuckles. *YES! He's going to agree.*

"Alright, angel, but I'm coming with you. I'll wait street-side. And I need you to return in less than an hour, no exceptions," he commands, his words laced with soft caring.

I beam. My heart lifts, and confidence and resolve roar to life within me.

With easy breaths and a lightness in my chest, I take his arm and step onto the street.

As we transfer to the F line, heading for the 57th St station—the closest to her penthouse—I reflect on the conversations he and I had last night and this morning.

Matt, I'm sorry I lied. I do have an agenda, and I'm not merely going to talk. I'm going to make her understand why she needs to cease her intrusion on the life you and I are nurturing and leave forever.

Today I might hurt her, and it will be for her own good. I am going to help her see that, but I won't be giving it my all.

CHAPTER THIRTY-FIVE

Alex: Forged in Hell

"Hi, Alex, it's Savannah. Good morning. May I come in, please?" Her sweet and steady voice lilts over the intercom—a discordant melody that chafes at my nerves. It cuts through the stillness and leaves an ache in its wake.

The high-definition monitor in front of me captures her perfectly—every detail sharp, her flaws nonexistent. The camera's wide-angle lens distorts her slightly, but it's her. The snake and whore. The poisonous leech, Anna.

As I stare at her, my familiar companions rise inside me. I'm a boiling pot that never runs out. My muscles tense, my chest tightens painfully, and the air around me feels hostile. My fingers twitch, itching to claw at something, anything. Flashes of violent thoughts punctuate my desire to hurt her, to eliminate the source of my torment. The sheer force of my fury obliterates all other thoughts.

Why did she refer to herself by her full name and me by my nickname? Is it a tactic to assert dominance, to make herself appear larger, more significant than me? Is this a power play, an attempt to undermine me right at the threshold of my own home?

For a split second, I consider switching on the 'Do Not Disturb' sign, but that would give her the satisfaction of knowing she rattled me. And she does—her grace, her beauty, her elegance—everything about her makes me feel inadequate, like every flaw I've ever hated about myself is magnified in her presence. Her being at my door is a violation of the one place I still feel safe.

But this is my house. *I won't let her intimidate me.* I remind myself who I am, the gifts I was born with. *I am Alexandra Mary Cunningham.*

This isn't just a confrontation—it's an opportunity. I'll use my mind to find cracks in her perfect armor and uncover the flaws she hides beneath that polished exterior. Everyone has weaknesses, and if there's even a sliver of vulnerability in her, I'll find it. Tomorrow, the private investigator's report arrives, and with it, ammunition to dismantle her piece by piece.

My next texts and calls to Matthew will be about her, the serpent.

If she tries to boss me around or intimidate me, I'll kill her with one of the knives in my pristine kitchen. Simple. And that'll be the end.

In a frenzy, I clear away the lights, cameras, and lingerie scattered across the living room. I shove everything into my closet and throw sweatpants and a hoodie over the designer underwear I'm wearing for the pictures I was about to send him.

"Hi. I just want to talk." The snake hisses on the intercom, her voice slithering into my ears. Bile churns in my stomach, acidic and hot.

Without a second thought, I press the green button and bark at the microphone, indifferent to the words leaving my mouth. "Come on up." *Welcome to hell, bitch.*

I undo my hair, tucking it under the sweatshirt. I glance in the mirror, noticing the confident look on my face. It's not the makeup, but the sharp focus I've cultivated—intellectual readiness. *Thanks, brain.*

My heartbeat quickens. When the elevator doors slide open and she steps inside, my chest and stomach flush with heat, and my skin burns as I come face-to-face with the woman who destroyed my relationship.

She smiles, her serene gaze locked onto mine. For a moment I am overwhelmed by the emotions choking me. Pictures don't capture her beauty. The images of her on his phone were nothing compared to seeing her in person. Taller than me by a foot, graceful, commanding—she exudes confidence. Her cheap summer dress and block heels can't dull her allure. Her porcelain skin shines, and her dark brown eyes sparkle with cold intent. Her long hair cascades below her waist, effortlessly perfect. She is flawless, and I know I'll never match her grace.

Everything moves in slow motion as I watch the snake twist toward me with that warm smile still plastered on her face. My brain jolts me from the haze, reminding me to focus. *Remember your strengths, Alex. She can't make your grade. You're a genius.* I stand rooted as she approaches. I blink a few times, trying to ease the tension in my cheeks and around my eyebrows.

She's mere feet away. "Can we sit somewhere to talk?" she asks, her tone firm and dripping with poise.

I turn around, trying to regain my composure. My forehead wrinkles as I close my eyes and exhale slowly, forming an 'O' with my mouth. *You got this.*

I walk toward a corner of my penthouse where three designer couches surround a small table, offering an unobstructed view of the Empire State Building from the floor-to-ceiling windows. *Take that, bitch. You may be a millionaire, but can you provide Matthew a home with that view? Your companies may be at the forefront of biomedical engineering, but you're not billionaires.*

She doesn't acknowledge the view or the furniture. Her serpent eyes remain locked on me, a wicked but serene smile still carved on her mouth. She sits on the couch with effortless grace, and I take the opposite one, locked in a silent challenge. *Let's see who breaks first.*

"How're you feeling today, Alex?" she casually asks.

Who are you, my mom? My therapist? Or are you here to patronize me? The muscles in my face tighten as irritation boils. My response is rigid. "What do you want?" I scowl, a sharp contrast to her composure.

"I'll get straight to it. I want to walk you through the experiences Matt had—from beginning to end—when he was alone after you left him."

Direct and nonconfrontational, her tone is a mix of kindness and matter-of-fact clarity with an undertone of businesslike detachment. It catches me off guard, and the way she casually refers to him as "Matt" makes me seem like an outsider, as though she's the rightful owner of his heart.

I peruse her words, my stomach already grinding. *'Alone' 'Left him' Is she reading from a script designed to condemn me? What does she mean by 'end.'* The word hangs in the air, cold and final, and it chills me. *My story with him is not over.*

Noticing my silence, she prompts me again, "Would you like to hear that? If nothing else, it could be a conversation starter."

Conversation? With you? I'd rather jump off this building and be done with it. I long to learn about that part of his journey—it was part of my plan—but hearing it from her is akin to swallowing broken glass. *Play the game, Alex. Find her weaknesses.* I suppress my morbid instincts and prepare to respond.

But she doesn't wait for my reply, her blasé voice starting a narrative that I can't help but be drawn into. "A run-down motel..." she begins.

She recounts his story in agonizing detail—the night he left my penthouse after I broke up with him, the cramped studio where he hid from the world, his struggle to function. The days bleeding into nights of emptiness, silence, and loneliness. His spiral into alcoholism—drinking to forget, then drinking to cope with the pain of not being able to forget. The bottle became his only friend as his life crumbled. Drinking to function which led to dysfunction and collapse, hitting rock bottom.

My breath hitches, and I inhale sharp bursts of air as her words dig deeper and hurt. Suddenly there's silence—she's not talking. I hadn't realized I was sobbing, hadn't felt the tears or the mascara staining my cheeks, until the stillness took over. She watches—her black eyes cold—as I unravel, crying uncontrollably as my hands shake, smearing makeup across my face.

Tightness in my chest crushes me as my heartbeat falters and becomes irregular. Numbness creeps into me and drains my energy. Pain in the back of my throat increases. But these feelings pale beside my self-loathing. *I caused this. Everything I touch is a disaster. His world exploded because of me.*

A suffocating heaviness settles over me. Negative thoughts crash relentlessly. *I'm a fool. I destroyed his world.*

Amid my despair, my mind processes her words. They're deliberate, surgical. *Forget you, lonely, alcohol was his friend.* Each phrase twists the knife deeper.

Her smile is replaced by wincing, and a slight *tsk* sound escapes her lips when they curl. *Is she pitying me?*

Then she's unmoved, indifferent to my tears, and her calm demeanor grates against my nerves. She seems unaffected by the devastation she's causing. *Is she mocking and pitying me? God, this is humiliating.*

"I understand you were also grieving at the time. You were also in pain."

Another pause. A sudden, sharp pain stabs my heart. Her motherly, therapist attitude—bordering on patronizing—riles me further, driving me to the brink of insanity.

"Are you okay? Do you need a break?"

She does it again. Her cunning inquiry, calm and soothing, slices me, and the concern in her tone heightens the searing pain. I'm unable to react, forced to endure this psychological torture. I drop my head into my hands. My throat is dry, heaving with emotion. "Just...go on..."

Unfazed, she carries on with his story as if my breakdown is background noise. *Did she intend to placate me when she asked if I was okay, seeing me spill my guts?* There's emotion in her countenance, modulation in her voice, and an air of caring about her—but none of it seems directed at me. *As if I need this bitch's care.*

With extraordinary effort, I shift my focus from her to Matthew's story. She tells of his bar brawl, his arrest, the way her lawyers swooped in to get him released without a record, then ends with a mention of them living together. Each word from her mouth feels like a fresh wound, bleeding me dry.

Blame and guilt pile on, draining me by the second.

My body stiffens—my eyes locked on hers, my breath coming in heavy bursts. She doesn't flinch. Instead, she moves on, unbothered, and shifts the topic to their shared life.

She delivers another blow, casually repeating what she said but in a different form, and each syllable is carefully designed to pour fuel onto the flames within me.

"We started our life in a modest one-bedroom apartment."

Her audacity is staggering. She maintains eye contact, offering me a half smile as she says it. My rage surges, and I feel an overwhelming urge to lunge at her, to mangle her appearance with my bare hands, to see her blood stain my pristine carpet. *I know you're fucking him, you whore.*

My body goes rigid, and my unblinking eyes fasten onto hers. A strange sensation of increased strength courses through me, exhausting itself in the quick, heavy bursts of my breath. But to my annoyance, she shows no acknowledgment of my state of mind and body. Instead, she shifts the topic, not lingering on their shared living situation.

She talks about how she relinquished everything—her career, her inheritance, her stakes in her companies—to lead a lifestyle of simplicity and joy.

With pride, she says, "I chose to be happy, knowing everything else would follow."

She pauses and beams.

"My net worth is practically zero, but I now have a happy, peaceful future with Matt."

She has been exact in choosing what to say ever since she started her malicious discourse. She repeats herself, sitting upright and smiling at me. "All he and I have is a fulfilled, tranquil life with each other."

I sit, rooted on this luxurious couch, staring at her with my mouth open.

His mantra. She is living his mantra, demonstrating it, practicing it. And I am not. How much more worthless can I get?

That feeling rises to the top, as if the heart-crushing guilt and self-loathing weren't enough to make me an emotional disaster.

She pauses, her gaze never wavering from mine, and I look away, focusing on the Empire State Building, hoping I can somehow draw strength from the steel and concrete of the urban jungle. But it's futile.

She embodies him, living the values he holds dear. How could I ever compare myself to her?

"Are you following me, Alex? Should I repeat or clarify anything? How about taking a pause?"

Stop mothering me, you harlot! The trembling returns as I inhale and exhale in rapid bursts through clenched teeth, and my eyebrows narrow as pure rage fills me. The burn in my stomach intensifies as dark fantasies of harming her resurface, filling me with twisted satisfaction.

For a fleeting moment, she glances at the Empire State Building, and a gentle smile plays on her lips before she turns her pretty face to me in a flash. "Did you hire any private investigators to follow me or find dirt on me? I have nothing, not even a car. Look at me. I'm not worth wasting your hard-earned money on. Call them off, because they will find nothing."

I sit in silence, my emotions simmering. Although every word and gesture feels calculated, she's right. The private investigator won't find anything on her. *If what she's saying is true.*

As my thoughts and feelings shift to Matthew on autopilot, self-reproach overwhelms me, knowing that while I am still undergoing a phase of depression, he endured far worse—hitting the deep, dark, and unforgiving slough of despondency.

"Right until I rescued him from jail, he gave me his everything, unwavering in his support. After he hit rock bottom, we supported each other and rose from the shadows, stepping towards the light, struggling, but holding onto each other."

She sits straighter, her chest jutting forward with quiet pride. "He is today a proud, sober man."

Did she rehearse this?

I can't believe that even a trained actor could maintain such calm composure while delivering this emotion-filled story—*no, a barely veiled statement of insult and a record of my shortcomings, failures and unworthiness.* There's not a single crack in her façade—as if she's impervious to the words she's speaking.

How is she doing this?

Focusing on my eyes, she asks in a caring tone, "I'm sure you don't want him to become an alcoholic again. Do you?"

What the fuck is she implying? That he'll spiral into alcoholism if he reunites with me? What's that supposed to mean?

Her choice of phrasing twists in my brain, feeding my insecurities, stirring the pot of rage and confusion within me. Her tone is caring—her words and actions are anything but.

She doesn't wait for a response, as if my thoughts and feelings are irrelevant. "I think we know the answer to that, don't we? We both want him to stay sober, healthy, and happy."

Happy. She keeps repeating that word, hammering at my skull as if it's the only thing that matters.

Why does she keep mentioning it, over and over again? I can speak for myself, you bitch.

Her poise riles me, and emotions brew in my chest—rage at her audacity, guilt nibbling at my conscience, and an overwhelming sense of worthlessness. I want to hurt her, but I'm drowning in self-loathing.

"Do you want to learn the other things that eventually broke him and drove him to drinking? Things that happened before your breakup?"

The time I had with Matthew drove him to drinking?

My thoughts fragment as her questions cleave me. A splitting headache forces me to clutch my head with both hands—my fingers digging at my temples as if I could massage away the pain. Nausea rises in my throat as her relentless speech hits me where I'm most vulnerable.

My incoherence spins further voices accusing me of destroying everything he had, that it's all my fault.

Her question sounds as if it's coming from the depths of a well. A rhythmic pounding echoes in my ears, matching the frantic beating of my heart. *God, I wish she would stop!*

"You listened to the things he lost after the breakup. Are you aware of what he lost before that?"

My breathing quickens, and each gasp is a struggle as I try to keep myself together. My hands press harder against my aching head, but it's no use. I can't stop the shame crashing over me.

Yes, I destroyed his world. I am good at nothing. Matthew, the strongest man I've met, suffered because of a costly mistake I made in haste. A sting behind my throat piles on.

"His job, his teaching career, his professional identity, dignity, and respect in the intellectual community."

Her statement is a blow—perhaps not the last, given how indomitable she appears—shattering whatever defenses I had left. I wail as my pent-up emotions explode in stomach-wrenching cries. My hands clutch at my abdomen, trying to hold myself together, but the pain is too much. I cry louder, and each sob rips me as remorse pounds over and over in a relentless assault that I can't escape.

In a gesture that makes me want to hurl her through the window to her death, she calmly hands me a box of tissues. She doesn't wait for me to take one but places the box next to me and strolls back to her seat with the poise of someone entirely unaffected by the storm raging in front of her.

In a small gap between my gasps and sobs, she continues with calculated purpose, utterly oblivious to the human wreckage crumbling before her. "Don't you want him to regain those, Alex?"

Her manipulative ask severs the air. The question isn't an inquiry—it's a taunt, a knife twisted in my already bleeding heart. I begin another guttural wail, crying with desperation—a howl that fills this empty living space. "Yes...I do...I want that...yes..." The desperate cries rip from my throat.

"Good. See, we both want the same things for Matt." Her tone is infuriating, as if this is merely another polite conversation.

I recall the day he lost his job. He took me to dinner that evening to celebrate a milestone in my career, while his own professional career had crumbled to dust hours earlier. He showed me that I was the center of his universe, that nothing else mattered to him. The memory tears at me as guilt rains down a fresh volley of punches, each one landing where it hurts the most.

Anna speaks as if she's seated in a serene garden. "I have some good news. I know you will jump up and down with delight when you hear it."

Mocking me. She must be. I'm falling apart right in front of her—teetering on the edge of a complete collapse—and she's talking about joy? Is she going to rub their engagement in my face? Their wedding? I can't take that.

My stomach tightens, bracing for the blow.

"He's interviewing with the Philharmonic. The hiring process is in an advanced stage. He excelled in the blind auditions."

The information hits like a flood of midnight sun. I wail louder, but this time my tears are pure happiness. He deserves this. He deserves to play on the highest stages with world-class musicians. But then self-loathing twists the knife deeper—the Philharmonic rejected him once because of his relationship with me.

But even that can't smother the joy that floods me with tears of delight.

"We both want that process to go smoothly, don't we?"

She doesn't bother waiting for my response. Instead, she rises gracefully, moving towards the kitchen with the effortless elegance of a deer, and returns with a glass of water. Placing the glass on the table in front of me, she gently nudges the box of tissues closer, as if it's the most natural thing in the world.

She lets a long pause hang in the air, as if she's giving me time to cry, to collect myself, to breathe. For a fleeting moment, I think she's done—that I've finally broken her cold, calculating exterior.

"But all of that..." she begins again, and her voice shreds the silence with the precision of a sharpened knife, "is not what I came here to talk to you about. There's something more important."

Her sudden, dramatic announcement momentarily pulls me from my grief. I snap my head up from my palms, glaring at her with tear-blurred vision.

Is she fucking kidding me? Did she come here to drive me insane? What could possibly be more important than everything she's already said? What more could she take from me?

She lets another agonizing pause stretch between us, and the silence is suffocating. Every ounce of strength I have left goes into pushing back the crushing weight of worthlessness that threatens to consume me. It hisses in my ears—a relentless chorus reminding me of every failure.

My heartbeat steadies. I clear my throat, and words bubble up—things she needs to hear, things she'll never understand. My bond with Matthew is sacred. It doesn't just vanish because she thinks she can barge into my world uninvited and take him from me. There are things about a father figure and ward relationship that she doesn't understand. I'll make her see that.

I gather what's left of my composure, wiping my eyes with trembling hands, sniffling as I steel myself to speak.

I open my mouth to unleash the fury, the pain, the raw truth. But she beats me to it. Her voice is soft, but the words slice through my thoughts with surgical precision.

"In some cultures, they say matches are made in heaven, signifying a blessing from God and the angels," she begins, and her tone is resolute, as if she's sharing a long held, sacred truth. "But that's a lie. The strongest bonds are forged in the depths of hell. That's where Matt and I shaped ours, as we dealt with grief and mended each other, driving out devils and demons. This is a bond that the most powerful force cannot break. It's priceless and eternal."

Her story hits me hard—a physical blow that knocks the breath from my lungs. My intellect races to process the full impact of what she's said. She's not talking about love—she's talking about something far more powerful, forged in suffering and fire. A bond born of despair that grew in the very depths of their pain—a bond I could never hope to break.

I stare at her, stunned and silent, and my earlier resolve crumbles like ash. My thoughts scatter like dead leaves in the wind. The ground beneath me is slipping away, taking with it any hope I had left.

Anna leans in slightly—her scheming gaze never leaving mine—and delivers the final, crushing blow with the kind of calm that comes from absolute certainty. "We both love him. But don't you think he deserves the best in life? We both know that he deserves someone who can be his equal, not his burden."

She delicately clutches the strap of her handbag with her porcelain hand, preparing to leave. The glint of a modest diamond on a simple band blinds me. The crowning glory of her performance—her engagement ring thrust in my direction.

The final blow.

The tears are different this time. They're tears of total, soul-crushing despair. I can't speak. I can't move. All I can do is sit here and allow myself to drown in the truth of her ultimate declaration—*that I am not his equal, but a burden.*

She watches me for a moment, as if she's merely observing the inevitable outcome of a battle she already knew she'd won. Then, with the same grace she's maintained throughout, she rises from her seat.

"I'll show myself the door," she says softly, almost kindly, as if offering me a final mercy. But there's nothing kind about the devastation she's wrought. I watch her walk away—my heart shattered, my spirit broken, my world crumbling to pieces.

The elevator door closes behind her with a quiet thud, leaving me alone in the silence with the echoes of her words still ringing in my ears.

What just happened?

I imagine the penthouse crumbling around me—steel and concrete collapsing, the once solid walls turning to dust. The glass from the towering windows shatters—a thousand sharp shards slicing the air, lancing me before burying me under the rubble.

My body feels weightless—my lucidity fragmented—as if the world is fading away. I try to grasp my thoughts but they slip through my fingers like sand. My brain is struggling to say something, to wake me from this paralyzing state. The voices in my head grow louder—circling vultures—another cruel demonstration of Doppler's Effect as they recede again and leave me lost in their echoes.

"Their bond is unbreakable."

"They are a perfect match."

"They deserve to be happy."
"Let them be."
"Move on, Alex."
"It's over."

The brutal truths swirl around me, taunting me, pushing me deeper down the chasm. Matthew and Anna were always meant to be together. Everything is slipping away, and I'm left with nothing but the unbearable weight of those final words.

PART THREE
HELL

CHAPTER THIRTY-SIX

Anna: Bàba

"**M**att...babe...I want to take your...your name," I gasp between ragged breaths, while my body is trembling and drenched in sweat as I cling to the sheets. I begin a long howl as he pounds me with relentless force, precisely the way I crave.

"What...huh?" he grunts, his breathing heavy. His brawny hands grip my neck and waist, holding my hips down by my stomach. Each thrust plunges his cock deep inside me, and my wetness eagerly welcomes him, throbbing with every mighty stroke. Pain and ecstasy electrify every nerve within my frail frame as he quickens his pace.

"Sav...Savannah...Michaels...Anna Michaels...it has a nice...ring to it," I moan with the sheer pleasure of his ownership of me. The thrill of saying the names sends every cell spiraling into a whirlwind of bliss, and anticipation builds to a fever pitch as I yearn for release. I moan the names louder—my body responding instinctively to his aggressive care.

"No..." he growls again, and his hand comes down hard on my butt, and the sharp sound of the slap reverberates around the room. I lose count as the stinging intensifies—each nerve ending aflame, creating an even deeper pleasure that diffuses through every bone, muscle, and sinew.

A new flood of pure joy overwhelms me, and fresh tears spring forth as I fuss about. "Bàba...Bàba..."

The sound of his brute roar fills the air—a raw, animalistic bellow that resounds off the walls of the small bedroom. His fury surges, and his extensive thickness rams my pussy with a ferocity that leaves me breathless. I moan with him, and our voices mingle in a symphony of pleasure and suffering.

"Bàba...Bàba..."

His actions grow wild, unrefined, and primal as his bawl turns eerie, almost frightening in its intensity. Then he moans, "My angel, my gorgeous," as I feel his dick grow harder inside my soaked pussy. His thrusts shatter me, sending me into a mind-altering orgasm. My body quakes and quivers, but he steadies me, pressing me harder into the mattress, anchoring me in pleasure. He howls as he releases, and I invite him again, "Bàba...Bàba..." I prod him further, wanting every drop of his essence, all of it.

He continues to pummel me, taking his pleasure, filling me with his semen—warm, reaching, comforting—elevating me to a cloud where I float, wrapped in the envelope of his protection.

Time loses all meaning. I lie there, basking in his aftercare, my limbs as disconnected as my thoughts. My arms, hands, legs and feet seem to exist in far-off places. My wrists and ankles tingle as his powerful fingers gently massage lotion on the areas where the ropes had left their marks, and each touch draws forth more dull aches of lingering pleasure.

My nicknames cut through the haze—each word a disjointed burst that echoes inside my head, reverberating in a comforting chaos of blissful numbness. As we settle, he pulls me closer.

"My sweet Anna," he whispers, his voice a balm to my soul. "I don't need my name next to yours to know you are mine, gorgeous."

Saturday morning begins with Matt lounging on the sofa, his viridian eyes lighting up as I hobble towards him. His quiet laugh and amused gaze send playful irritation through me. I grab a few notepads and toss them at him. When I finally give up, he sweeps me into his arms and carries me to the sofa as I let out a surprised squeal. We settle together and he feeds me breakfast—a moment of intimacy that feels more invaluable than words.

After breakfast, we dive into wedding preparations. We argue over the guest list—he's insistent my entire family attends, while his list is much shorter. I see his longing for the large family he never had, and my heart softens. My warm kiss reassures him, but practicality wins. I remind him of our budget, especially since we plan to conceive. In a week—which puts the timeline a month before the wedding—I'll be going off birth control. The thought fills us both with quiet joy.

Reluctantly, he agrees to a smaller reception. We're getting married in a small church in the New Jersey town where he grew up, with immediate family in a simple ceremony. Tomorrow, we'll meet with the priest to discuss the process and finalize details. He asks again if I'm sure I don't want a big wedding, and I dodge the question. I can sense his disappointment but choose to focus on what matters most—our future together.

Later, as I prepare tea, my thoughts drift to the two weeks of silence from Alex since our meeting. When Matt asked about it, I brushed it off, calling it a "practical chat," and he assumed she was moving on. But deep down, I know it's not that simple. Beneath her fragile exterior, I saw a will of steel—a determination that unsettles me. Broken people often rise stronger, and her intellect and resilience make her a formidable force. I hope she uses her strength to rebuild her life, but a part of me remains wary.

I have no regrets about how I handled our confrontation. I did what I had to do to protect him and the life we're building. She was like a loyal ward to him—their bond something only they can understand. To me, she's a young girl in need of help—but not the center of my world. My focus is on the family he and I will create, the children we dream of. If she reappears, I'll meet her with kindness or force—whatever it takes to protect what we have.

As I sip my tea, I steel myself. This is a lifelong mission to fight for our happiness. His paternal connection to her means she'll always be a part of his memory, but our future is what matters. Whatever challenges lie ahead, I'll be ready.

We spend the rest of the day cleaning our humble abode, and the familiar routine brings a quiet sense of contentment. As we work side by side, there's a comfort in the simplicity of it all, in the shared silence and the occasional glances and kisses we exchange. It's a reminder that, amid all the chaos, we've managed to carve out this little haven. A place that's ours alone.

During late afternoon tea, with sunlight streaming through the window, he reminds me I still haven't bought my wedding dress. A warm flush spreads across my cheeks as I imagine myself in a simple, mid-length white dress—modest, just like the life we've built. I tell him I've done my research and listed affordable options in the city. We make a plan to visit the shops next weekend to leave time for alterations. His eyes light up with tenderness, and I smile, picturing his expression when he sees me in my dress.

As we return to our freelance work, the hum of laptops fills the room, and a comforting sense of normalcy settles in. But beneath it, something monumental is on the horizon—a life filled with a wedding and children.

After dinner, we cuddle on the sofa, watching a movie. My mind drifts, lulled by the rise and fall of his chest against my back and his warmth surrounding me. When the credits roll, I kiss his cheek, and in that moment, everything feels right. The future feels close enough to touch. We fall asleep in each other's arms and the world outside fades as we drift into peaceful slumber.

As we prepare to meet the priest, Matt's phone rings, and the caller identification shows a number we don't recognize. We freeze, gazes locked. My heart begins to race, and a sudden chill grips me in a tight band. The familiar rush of adrenaline invigorates me, sharpening my senses.

I nod towards the phone, urging him to answer. He hesitates for a fraction of a second, then puts the call on speaker.

A man's voice crackles on the line, broken and filled with barely concealed sniffles. "Hi, Matthew...hey, this is Edward Cunningham...I'm..."

Matt's expression hardens instantly. His brows knit together, and his eyes harden, burning holes into the phone. "Is Alex okay?" he demands, his tone sharp, edged with impatience.

"She...she's in the hospital...I'm wondering if..." Edward wavers, struggling to form coherent sentences.

"Was she in an accident? What happened to her?" He launches off the sofa, his pacing quick and erratic. Though his tone remains steady, his resolve is a frayed wire about to snap. He casts a glance at me while waiting for Edward to respond.

My thoughts twist, frantically attempting to think of scenarios to explain what we're hearing. I collapse once more onto the sofa—my body suddenly too heavy. My chest tightens and the room feels unbearably small, stifling. Overheated air presses in on me, suffocating.

"She...Alex...she attempted suicide...she's in..."

The rest of Edward's words become an incomprehensible murmur as a vacuum envelops me. My eardrums fill with a high-pitched ringing sound, and the ambient noise is muffled. Matt stops pacing, and my heart stops in unison. Dizziness submerges me, and I clutch at my head, elbows digging into my knees as if trying to anchor myself to nonexistent strength. The suffocating heat is suddenly replaced by an icy cold that seeps inside my bones, chilling me.

My mind rejects Edward's words, but fragments of the conversation are looping in my head. Each second drags as I hear my own confusion echoing in the void, a desperate, silent scream. *No. This can't be happening. It's not true.*

A sudden jolt threatens to shatter what little composure I have left. I gasp and immediately cover my mouth as Matt collapses beside me on the sofa, his frame rigid, staring blankly. His breaths are slow but heavy, and each one is a laborious effort.

"Matthew...hi, are you there? I'm sorry to call..." Edward's speech cracks.

Matt doesn't respond. The phone has slipped from his palm and lies forgotten on the floor. I scramble to pick it up, and my fingers tremble as I hand it to him. He clears his throat, shaking his head in quick, jerky movements. He appears stunned, so deeply disturbed. My hand instinctively finds his forearm, and I squeeze it, rubbing his thigh, trying to ground him, to offer any comfort I can.

He takes the phone from me and speaks into the mic, "Is she...?" His question and composure are strained.

Edward responds quickly, and his voice is thick with emotion, his words punctuated by sniffles. "She's alive...doctors say her vitals are stable."

Matt releases a quick sigh of relief. He covers his face, massaging his temple as if trying to ease the pain of the crushing news. "What happened? When did this...when did she..."

"Two weeks ago..." Edward falters, the distress in his words traveling into this disintegrated living space.

Matt lurches from the sofa. "Two weeks? And you only call me now? What the hell is going on?" His eyes widen and his mouth hangs open as his breaths come faster until he is nearly hyperventilating.

Edward's tone breaks as he pleads, his words stumbling over each other. "Matthew, please, can you come to Manhattan St. Michael's Medical, the

Charles Cunningham Block, and ask for Trauma Care Wing Seven? Please? I'll explain everything once you get here. I'll wait for you."

"I'm coming," Matt says, almost devoid of emotion, as he cuts the call.

We stare at each other as what we've heard settles between us—a heavy fog stiffening with each passing second. I crumble, and tears spill down my cheeks as I rush into his arms, my palms rubbing his spine in a futile attempt to comfort him. For several long moments, he stands still—unresponsive, as if the shock has turned him to stone.

Then, slowly, he tightens his arms around me, holding me closer. We stand rooted in place. Our disbelief is unrelenting, and I will this to be a nightmare from which we'll wake in a cold sweat. Outside, the sun disappears behind gathering clouds, casting the living room in a shadowed gloom.

As I cling to him, shaking and quivering, my brain races, desperate to make sense of what I've heard. I need to know specifics to understand that this is real. My sobs grow heavier as I think of the unimaginable pain he must be in. The thought breaks me, and I tighten my hold on him, wishing with all my heart that I could take some of that torment away.

But then, amid my grief, a thought pierces the chaos—I must recover and stay resilient, for him. I force myself to be steady, to prepare for whatever lies ahead. That first step feels impossible to take, but I know I must. I shake him gently.

"I have to go," he says, as if the words are being torn from him. I can feel his heartbeat drumming at my ear pressed against his chest.

Without hesitation, I pull away and straighten, wiping my tears with trembling fingers. "I'm coming with you," I tell him, my voice fractured. I grab my bag and take his hand in mine.

We ride the subway in silence, arms locked. My other hand rubs his bicep, and I rest my head on his shoulder, giving comfort with the simple contact. But he remains still—stare fixed on the wall of the subway car, lost in his own silent torment for the entire ride.

The Charles Cunningham Block is a towering hospital building donated and established by Alex's family. Inside, the air reeks of disinfectant, and the harsh fluorescent lighting reflects off the white walls, making everything painfully bright. The soft drone of air filtration fills the space, and every sound seems amplified—the beeping of monitors, the shuffle of feet, the squeak of shoes on linoleum.

Trauma Care Wing Seven, on the seventh floor, is much less crowded, but still hums with urgency and sterility.

We're escorted to the waiting area by a nurse whose warm voice is a contrast to the cold environment. The floor is busy with staff moving like clockwork—their efficiency at odds with the chaos unfolding around them. I cling to his hand, struggling to anchor myself. My thoughts are suffocating, the same feeling I had when my dad died and when Matt left me for her.

The pressure in my chest grows, and I'm overwhelmed with nausea. Despite going through the motions and getting to this clinical environment, part of me refuses to accept that this is real.

Edward appears in the hallway, eyes bloodshot and hands deep in his pockets. His shoulders are slumped. I remember Matt's stories—Edward's controlling nature, his violent outburst toward Matt. Now, he's a broken man.

Matt doesn't waste time on pleasantries. "Take me to her," he demands, his voice firm but laced with desperation.

Detectives and officers stand nearby, speaking in hushed tones. It's clear that this particular trauma care wing is restricted—a private area cordoned off exclusively for Alex's case. Edward wearily turns to Matt. "Only you can come in. The doctors and police are restricting access—it's protocol."

I nod at Matt, offering a comforting tap on his forearm. "Go. I'll wait here for a bit and then head home. Don't worry about me."

He hesitates, then kisses the back of my hand before following Edward. The doors close behind them with a finality that roots me in place.

The situation presses down on me, and my simmering headache flares with violent intensity. I barely make it to the bathroom before I collapse on the floor of a stall, retching violently into the toilet. Each spasm feels like my insides are being torn apart, and the pain in my head becomes unbearable. I clutch my skull but my body betrays me—punishing me for something I can't yet face.

I feel as though I've been sitting in the stall for a long while. My thoughts are still unclear, but they settle on a few key areas.

First, I have to support Matt during this tragedy, to look after him and be there for whatever he needs.

Second, I can't help but wonder what this means for the tangled web Alex, Matt, and I are caught in. I thought we had finally untied ourselves, but it seems we're still entwined, our lives more knotted than ever.

Third, the wedding plans have to stay on track, for everybody's sake. *He and I have come too far and we can't afford to let our marriage plans slip. That would destroy the dreams we've started realizing. The wedding could also serve as the final signal Alex could do with, for her to move on, with her family's help.*

I'm desperate to calculate what I must do to ensure that we get married as planned. The dizziness returns, and my stomach churns again. I clutch my breastbone and mouth, trying to massage away the ache as I stifle the wail that's been building inside me.

My logical self, though ragged and beaten, begins to emerge from the chaos, still determined to find its footing.

Let's learn what happened. Lay the facts on a timeline. Add supporting factors, context, and effects. Analyze each point and fact, plot the scenarios and courses of action. You've got this, Anna. Look at how far you and Matt have come. You will get through this. But rise now, and harden yourself. Collect as much information as you can.

I repeat these thoughts to myself as I continue to cry, though more silently now, in this suffocating stall. I bury my face in my hands once more, but this time I focus on trying to relax. My breaths slow as I work to separate the tangled thoughts crisscrossing in my head. I sniffle and wipe my nose, as my sobs gradually cease. The heaviness in my chest lingers, but the pain slowly begins to subside.

Emerging from the stall, I nearly collide with a kind nurse who asks me warmly if I'm okay and if I need any help. I thank her for her kindness and proceed to wash my face and mouth. The headache remains, but it's not as sharp and piercing as it was earlier. I notice how pale I look in the mirror.

You've got this. Slow down and focus on one thing at a time. I close my eyes and take several long breaths, steadying myself before leaving the bathroom and returning to the ordered chaos of the trauma care wing.

CHAPTER THIRTY-SEVEN

Matthew: The Blanket - I

My footsteps echo loudly in the sterile, silent corridor, each one faster than Edward's faltering steps. He's sluggish, but I can't slow down—I won't. My heart pounds with desperation and anxiety, and my muscles tighten with every hurried step. My mind is a whirlwind with a single, relentless question: *Where is my precious girl?*

Impatience claws at me—body heat rising, breath growing heavier and more erratic. The air reeks of disinfectant, alcohol, and medication. The cold, clinical smell strips away my patience, leaving urgency. I can feel my grip on control slipping, as every instinct screams at me to shatter whatever stands between me and her.

Edward hobbles beside me, and his grief sinks his shoulders and slows his steps. I can't afford to feel sympathy for him right now, but guilt stabs at me, so I do. Despite my frustration, I throw my arm around his shoulder, steadying him as he stumbles. His weary gaze meets mine briefly, but I barely nod, already surging ahead. I round the corner in three quick strides, only to find another long hallway and more white walls stinging my eyes.

"What the hell? Where is Alex?" I lash at the walls as my urgent questions boom across the corridor, startling a nearby nurse. She glances at me with pity and concern, but her sympathy irritates me.

Edward leads me to a door marked "Dr. Henrietta Robbins," but the long list of qualifications beneath the name does nothing to ease the rising tension in my chest. Every muscle in my body quivers. The urge to break this door, to demand answers, to shake Edward until he tells me where she is, overwhelms me. My self-control is hanging by a thread, and I'm ready to snap if it means getting to her.

As if on cue, a kind-looking woman opens the door. She scans the hallway briefly before her eyes land on me, widening slightly before relaxing. She extends her hand while the other reaches for my arm. "Hi, I'm Dr. Robbins. I wish we were meeting under different circumstances." Her voice is soothing but it does nothing to ease the fire inside me.

"Hi. Can you take me to Alex?" I try my best to keep my impatience disguised as I make an effort to sound polite.

She motions for me to follow her inside her office, her movements quick and responsive, which I appreciate—but it's not what I'm here for.

"Mr. Michaels," she begins, her tone gentle yet firm. "I want to prepare you for what you'll see when I take you to her. She won't be who you're used to seeing. For her own safety and health, she's been put in restraints, is sedated, and is being monitored closely. She's still on suicide watch."

She pauses, and my movements arrest and her next words sound muffled to me. "She also has a feeding tube."

Her kindhearted updates fade to the background as something hammers at the back of my head, knocking whatever poise I had left. *Restraints? Suicide watch? Sedation and feeding tube?* The words ricochet in my mind, each one a brutal blow.

She continues. "No one is allowed near a patient under suicide watch. Certain...exceptions have been made for the Cunninghams—not solely because of their wealth and influence, but also because they are the major donors to this hospital." Her gaze holds steady, unwavering, as she adds, "Even so, I need you to follow my direction and all protocols—legal and medical. For her sake."

The words hit, but I barely hear them, and the phrases fade into a distant hum as my head spins. *Restraints? Suicide watch? My little girl?* A surge of adrenaline shoots through me. Before I can think, I storm out of the office, hurling the door open. I look left and right until my glare lands on the station nurse and back at Dr. Robbins.

Then, without warning, her expression tightens, her features pinched with tension. She crosses her arms over her chest and exhales a heavy sigh. Frustration coils around her voice as she says, "You need to calm down, Mr. Michaels. The hospital and I have made enough compromises."

I pause, her sudden shift and sharp words stopping me in my tracks, halting my desperate urge to break down doors to find Alex.

Dr. Robbins scrunches up her face, then smooths it out, visibly trying to regain her composure. "Alex is here of her own volition. I wanted to transfer her to a psychiatric facility, but she insisted on staying here and asked for you," she says, then throws a pointed hand toward Edward. "Money talks, and her family...the Cunninghams have power in this city." She lets out an impatient sneer before continuing, "We've already broken several protocols to accommodate her wishes."

Edward massages his temples, leaning back against the wall. Dr. Robbins briefly closes her eyes, takes a deep breath, and rolls her shoulders slightly, trying to shake off the tension.

She meets my gaze with a pitying look, then points to my left. I barely register the soft footsteps of the doctor and Edward behind me as I reach the door at the far corner.

A uniformed police officer stands outside the room, which bears no name or label. Opposite him is the nurses' station, with an array of computers and monitors, staffed by a lone nurse. The officer steps forward to stop me, glancing behind me as if seeking confirmation. Dr. Robbins waves her approval, and the police officer lets me pass. I can hear Dr. Robbins and Edward catching up as I push open the door and step into a dark, expansive private room. The walls appear a dull gray under sparse lighting that makes the space feel cold and unwelcoming.

I know it's still around noon, but the curtains are drawn, plunging the area into near darkness. Four dim lights, as good as nonexistent, are fixed in the corners of the ceiling. Cameras appear to be attached to those lights—their lenses dark and watchful, with a single red dot blinking on each. It takes a moment for my vision to adjust to the lack of light, as the gloom presses on me and yanks me to the depths.

The entire wall to my right is lined with windows but heavy curtains cover every inch, sealing off the outside world. The faint hum of the air filtration system and the cold rush of the air conditioner hit me square in my breastbone. My sensitivity is heightened since the doctor spoke to me in her office.

My gaze is drawn to the array of monitors beside the bed. More monitors are mounted behind, and their dimmed displays flash faint blue, green, and red lights, like beacons urging me forward. The mellow beeps of the machines in sync with the pulsing lights do little to calm my racing heart, but they're insistent, pulling me closer.

Finally, my eyes having fully adjusted to the dim light, I see the figure lying on the mattress. It's my little one, wrapped in a blanket. The sight of her, so small, so fragile, shatters whatever resolve I had left. She's petite, but now she seems even smaller, diminished. The only other sound in the suffocating chamber is the soft thud of my footsteps as I approach her.

When I reach her, the sight is too much to bear. I fall to my knees with a thud, and my voice breaks as I choke, "Jesus...no."

The blanket has slipped, exposing her wrists and ankles bound by fleece-lined, heavy-duty leather cuffs that are bolted to the underside of the sturdy bed—iron and steel holding her in place. Her face is turned away from me, but I recognize every feature of her profile. She appears shrunken, and her weak frame rises and falls as she breathes under sedation—the action a blunt contrast to the rapid, erratic beating of my heart, which might be on the verge of collapse. Still kneeling, I clutch the sides of my head and release a loud gasp.

For a fleeting moment, I wish Dr. Robbins or Edward would tell me I entered the wrong room in my desperation to find Alex, that this isn't her, that it isn't my dear girl covered by that blanket.

But they are behind me, silent, as if guarding a fragile being, the last of her kind. I feel the gentle hand of Dr. Robbins on my shoulder, and her touch is almost reverent. My ears are ringing with a shrill, unrelenting noise that drowns everything else. Then it fades, giving way to the muffled thud of my heartbeat and the pulse roaring in my ears. I hear myself whispering, "No...no."

A stronger hand grips my shoulder, pulling me upright with a struggle. I wipe my face several times, trying to erase the evidence of my misery. My hands clamp over my mouth and nose as I keep glancing at the girl lying on the bed—my eyes are unblinking, and the pressure behind them is stinging, burning.

Dr. Robbins moves to cover my baby's limbs, ensuring her comfort, and turns back toward me.

"Matthew," she whispers, and the sound is almost too soft to hear, yet it resounds in my ears, "let's talk outside."

Edward places a hand on my shoulder but I strike at it, unable to bear any touch that might anchor me to this moment.

Outside, a tornado of loose, incoherent thoughts rips through my mind, but one concern rises above the chaos, clear and urgent. "Dr. Robbins, get her out of the restraints, now." She calmly gestures toward a small seating area with four chairs and a table.

As I slump on a chair, she explains, "Two days after she was admitted, she somehow pulled out her IV and tried to stab her neck with it. The attendants caught her before she could do serious damage," she says, and our gazes lock. Her speech is pitched low for only the three of us to hear. "She refused to eat or speak. I had to put in a feeding tube. The only person she would speak to was me, and all she has said so far is to ask for you."

Adrenaline surges, and every muscle is tensing with the urge to rush back to Alex, to take her away from all of this. Dr. Robbins's last words barely register, drowned by the pounding in my head. I lurch to my feet—driven by an unstoppable force—and implore her.

"Dr. Robbins, get her off everything. The feeding tube, the restraints—I'll take care of her." My mandate and assertion are louder than she likes, drawing the attention of the police officer and nurse who snap their heads in our direction. Dr. Robbins smiles at them reassuringly, then turns back to me, her calmness unshaken, and gently asks me to sit.

"No. There are protocols, legal and medical. She triggered the round-the-clock supervision and suicide watch with her actions. This entire wing is on high alert, as you might have observed," Dr. Robbins says, her clarification steady. Her kind expression offers a solace that I'm too distraught to fully absorb. I clutch my face, as my mind desperately seeks ways to help Alex. But as Dr. Robbins speaks, reality sinks in. The pieces start to fall in place—each word from her and Edward, every observation I've made since arriving at this hospital—clicking together like a grim puzzle.

Dr. Robbins finishes, her tone shifting to the practical as her pager goes off. "Matthew, I asked Edward to bring you here because after two weeks, we're desperate to try other measures to get her to function, even if it's just to eat normally. Let's meet later for a more involved discussion. I'll have the nurse schedule something."

I nod, though my thoughts are trapped in the sphere of torment with Alex. The doctor gives me a reassuring pat on the back as she leaves, her footsteps echoing in the sterile corridor. Edward, slumped in his chair, stares blankly at the ceiling, his body limp, as if all the strength has drained from him.

"Hey, Edward, hey!" I snap him out of his daze, my tone harsher than intended. I need answers, timelines, details—anything to make sense of this nightmare—so I ask him to recount what happened.

The white walls press in, and the faint hum of the hospital machines drifts from beyond the door. Edward has said little so far and I see the strain on his face and the tremor in his limbs. He attempts to collect himself, preparing to give an account of the most harrowing day of his life.

The evening after Anna met Alex, he visited the penthouse.

"She was...in the tub." His vocal cords crack. Edward's never been the emotional type, but he's unraveling piece by piece, right in front of me. "Blood. There was so much blood." He chokes on the words, his breath catching as if he's reliving the agony.

"Edward…" My throat aches, but I have to know everything. "What happened?"

He squeezes his eyelids shut, shaking his head. "I thought…maybe she was…alive. I called her name, over and over." His hands clutch his knees, white-knuckled. "She didn't move. She was so still. I…" His speech falters. "I saw the blood pooling around her. It was everywhere. She…cut…herself…her wrists."

My heart pounds, and my pulse resonates deafeningly in my ears.

"Jesus, Edward," I manage, unable to keep my tone steady. Picturing the events unfolding as he describes makes me dizzy. He mentions something about her texts and voicemails, but my attention drifts to the texts she sent me, the late-night phone calls and voice messages she left me when my phone was on 'do not disturb' mode.

My thoughts immediately race next to the last contact I had with her—it was a phone call in which I warned her to leave Anna alone, suspecting Alex was behind the stalking. I replay that conversation, recollecting my roughness and anger when I talked to her. A piercing ache starts at the top of my skull. *I scorned her the last time we spoke. Oh, dear God!*

I visualize her frail body in a tub, surrounded by pools of blood. A nauseating sensation starts in my stomach, and I think I might throw up. That further aggravates the acute sting in my crown, which emanates to other parts of my head. I press my clenched fist to my mouth, making an effort to remain stable as I listen to him.

He swallows hard, fighting to keep control, but his eyes are glassy.

"I called 911. I…she was barely breathing when they got there. I thought she was gone." For a moment, I think he's going to break. "They…they brought her back in the ambulance. And then she collapsed again."

The Cunningham security wing acted swiftly, ensuring she was transported discreetly to St. Michael's, where the seventh floor was cordoned off and secured.

Imagining what he experienced and felt as he rode in the ambulance with the near lifeless figure of his sister wrenches my gut. I run a hand over my face, trying to keep my own emotions from boiling over. A sudden weakness forms in my limbs.

Edward nods, his gaze distant, haunted. "They told me if I'd found her five minutes later…five minutes, and she'd be gone." His voice quivers, becoming a whisper. "I almost lost her."

My stomach twists violently, a sickening ache spreading in my torso. "She—did she write...a note?" I ask, not sure if I even want to know the answer.

Edward reaches into his pocket for his phone and stares at the screen for a while. He shows it to me, his hand trembling.

"Yes." The note is with the police, but they let him take a picture.

I take the phone and stare at the image, the words blurring together. I read them once, and then again—the meaning sinking in and punching my belly.

> I want to sleep. When I wake up, I want to be in a world where I am free of troubles, free to be with the man I love.

Breaths leave me in hurried spurts, and my vision narrows. It's as if the floor is claving beneath me. My mind races, and my is heart thumping, trying to escape my ribcage. *Free to be with the man I love.* It reverberates in my skull, and I can't stop it.

"Matthew...I'm sorry. I...I should have gotten there sooner."

It's not his fault, but I don't respond. I can't with my limited attention solely fixating on Alex. I can't move, can't breathe. All I can hear are her words echoing in my mind. She was ready to die. *To end it all.*

A mental fog encapsulates me and the seconds blend, distort, and slacken as I try to imagine the ends of despair that she found herself in when she attempted to take her own life. My dizziness intensifies.

Edward stifles a sob. I watch him, but my mind is piecing together the events with a growing sense of dread. My own composure is crumbling. For several moments, I stare blankly at the sterile wall in front of me, struggling to hold on.

Then from deep within, that familiar voice—of an eight-year-old Matthew—urges me on, cutting across the fog of despair: *"Hey. Rise and move forward. Do what you must do to survive and help your family."*

It's the guidance and push that has kept me on track since I was a child, taking care of myself and my family when no one else could. Being afraid was never an option. That voice—my lifeline—kicks in, steadying me as fear threatens to swallow me whole. Fear of the unknown, of death, of failure—it all melts as my innate being grows stronger, saying, *"Fear blocks understanding. Understand first, then you will not be afraid anymore."*

I compartmentalize, pushing everything else aside. Clarity returns, piece by piece, though the affliction lingers at the edges. But the eight-year-old in me teaches me to manage it, to keep moving forward.

I spring to life, quickly moving to sit beside Edward. He's always been a force. But he's crumbling—his hands shaking as they grip the arms of his chair. I clasp his shoulder firmly.

"Edward," I say softly, forcing my tone to stay steady. "You did everything you could. You saved her." I lean in. "She's still here because of you."

He shakes his head, his features dipped in anguish, as if he's been ripped open from the inside. "I...I should've known," he whispers, his speech cracking. "I should've been there sooner. I should've—"

"You can't blame yourself for this." My words sting because I'm fighting the same guilt.

I squeeze his shoulder, trying to pull him back from the edge. "You were there. You were there, Edward. You found her. You called emergency. You did everything right."

Slowly he nods, but I can see the doubt still eating at him. He's a powerful personality, always in control, but he's crumbling under the pressure of tragedy. I search for something to ease his distress.

His breathing slows, and I see the tension finally lift from his face, just a little. He clings to my words as if they're the last thread holding him together. He nods again, this time with more conviction, and a flicker of hope returns to his eyes. It's small, but it's there. *I'll help him rebuild, help him find the strength I know is still inside.*

"I will make sure she is okay, that she heals from this," I declare, more to myself than to him—my paternal instinct kicking in as I feel my innate need and responsibility lift me.

Edward shares what's happened in the ten days since the incident—the devastation sweeping through their family and the business empire, the ripple effects just beginning to show. Her father, once a pillar of authority, is drowning in alcohol and shutting himself away from the world. Her mother, strained and exhausted, is caught between the estate and the hospital, holding everything together through sheer will. Ted, the eldest brother, and Ms. Rea-McCall have taken over the business affairs, but grief clouds every decision.

Sebastian and James, always the stoic ones, have fallen silent—their strength shattered. They're trying to support Alex and steer the business, but their efforts are fragmented. Even the wives of Edward and Sebastian—already stretched thin with their own responsibilities—are doing what they can, but it's not enough.

The company, once a fortress, is in crisis mode. The acting CEOs are scrambling to keep it afloat, but the market response has been brutal—stocks plummeting, investors rumbling, rumors swirling. The empire is teetering, with no straightforward way out.

Evie is the only one still at the hospital with Edward, alternating shifts to stay by Alex's side. I give Edward a half smile as he recounts the details. Gratitude and sorrow fill me as I think about how much she used to resent him. "The Enforcer," she used to call him. But now, the man before me is not the hard-nosed protector, but a broken brother, giving up everything else to be with her.

CHAPTER THIRTY-EIGHT

Matthew: The Blanket - II

We sit in silence for several moments—the weight of all that's happened smothering and suffocating us. I absorb the information from Edward, slowly acclimatizing to the sterile hospital surroundings. My inherent control rises from the abyss of shock and confusion. I am not sure what I'm going to do yet—hospital protocols, legalities, and law enforcement restrictions all stand in my way. But this is certain: *I'm going to be there for my Alex. No matter what.*

I clutch my head, trying to shake off the image of Alex in that room, but it's burned in my mind—a reminder of how fragile everything I hold dear truly is. The floor beneath me feels as if it's shaking, threatening to swallow me whole. My grip on control is slipping.

The voice of the eight-year-old Matthew anchors me. I can't fall apart now. *Alex needs me.* She needs to survive this.

I check my phone and read a couple of texts from Anna.

Anna

> Hey! I know you're trying to make sense of everything and being there for her. Do what you have to, babe!

> I'm heading home. I'll wait for you. Take care and… Matt, everything's going to be okay. I love you.

I close my eyes and whisper a note of thanks to Anna, my heart warming. I feel a tug at my heart as I think of her heading to an empty apartment with a lot going on in her head. But I need to compartmentalize and take things slowly, one at a time.

> *Hey, angel! It's not looking good. I'm learning things slowly. I'll update you soon. Take care. I love you too.*

With that, I take a few moments to think of the next steps, covering my face and steadying my breathing.

I rise, motioning for Edward to follow. We walk toward the coffee machine. I hand him a steaming cup, and he takes it, murmuring a quiet thanks, and his hand trembles slightly as he sips. I offer him a half smile, though my thoughts are miles away.

"Listen...about that night...I'm sorry I—" Edward's voice falters, his apology barely more than a whisper.

"Don't worry about it." I cut him short, brushing it aside. There are far more pressing matters to deal with. *Like Alex under that blanket.*

"Thank you for being here, Matthew. I know it's going to make a difference to her treatment..."

But the gratitude does little to cool the anger simmering just beneath my skin. My voice sharpens, steady but firm. "You should have called me the day this happened. Why didn't you?" My finger jabs in his direction as the frustration tightens my chest, and my fists itch to lash out, to break something—anything.

Edward swallows hard, sounding strained. "Oh...come on...you know how it is between you and the family. That got worse after your breakup. Nobody believed it was a good idea to invite you or even inform you. Dr. Robbins advised us to wait."

That's not an explanation, it's an excuse.

He looks resigned as he continues, "But Alex wouldn't eat and wouldn't talk to anyone but Dr. Robbins. When she did talk, the only thing she asked for was you."

I shake my head, looking away as anger threatens to boil over. But I know I must keep it together—for her, for what's coming. I must nurse her, get her out of those restraints, and bring her to a functional state. But first, I need to talk to her, for which I'll have to wait until morning when they bring her off sedation. I mull over a plan loosely forming in my mind, and Edward's updates become background noise.

"Then, finally, the doctor recommended that we call you in, noting how she was regressing."

"I'm going to sit with her for a while," I announce, my tone clipped. I turn on my heel and hurry without waiting for a response.

The moment I step inside, every ounce of strength I've been clinging to crumbles. There she is—my sweet baby girl—lying in tatters, bound by restraints, tethered to machines, covered in a blanket that resembles a shroud. My knees buckle, and I drop to the floor beside her bed.

"I'm with you, my baby. Daddy's by your side," I murmur, the words catching in my throat.

A deep ache throbs in my chest, a longing to hear her call me Daddy, to see her blue eyes light up and her face beam. For weeks, when she was trying to intrude on my life with Anna—sending texts, calling me—every time she called me Daddy, it reawakened that inbred feeling in me—the paternal instinct, a need to protect her. It was something I couldn't ignore, no matter how hard I tried to bury it.

Never did I imagine I'd be sitting in a dreadful hospital room, facing a nonresponsive Alex, rescued from the brink of death. Still on my knees, I clutch the sides of my head as a dull headache takes root, threatening to overwhelm me. I force myself to stand and pull a chair close to sit by her bedside. I watch her fragile form twitch slightly, her slender frame rising and falling with slow breaths. Then I wait, frozen in place, for a long while.

A soft knock on the door disturbs the stillness, piercing my mental fog. A gentle voice says, "Matthew, hi, it's Evie."

I wipe my face. My eyes are dry from staring at the figure on the bed for what feels like hours. Evie silently motions toward the door.

We step into the small seating area. Evie looks like she's been through a war—her skin pale, eyes bloodshot, her movements slow and unsteady, like she's barely keeping herself upright.

For the next hour, Evie recounts Alex's time in Sweden, sparing no detail. Each word is a blade to my heart. I realize how much I missed, how long Alex has been battling grief all alone. The depth of her suffering was unbearable, and yet she was still fighting.

As Evie tells me how Alex nearly lost herself in a nightclub, how she clawed her way to happiness and hope just before leaving Sweden, I feel the pressure in my gut tighten. The reality of what Alex has endured hits me like a freight train. She was struggling, and I wasn't there. The realization crushes me.

For a few moments, I let my guard down completely, cradling my face in my hands, shaking it as if I could somehow turn back time. The pain threatens to consume me, but I snap out of it. *Where's the eight-year-old Matthew?* Bringing my essential self to the forefront and keeping him there is key—I understand that. He is required, now more than ever.

Despite the darkness pulling me under, I must confront the challenges in front of me, put Alex on the path to recovery, and maybe help her family in the process.

Edward joins us, bringing a small bag. Evie distributes small boxes of food. I have to be strong physically too, so I eat the simple pasta dinner, thanking her. As I chew mechanically, Edward hands me the bag and says, "Hey, I apologize for making assumptions, but I thought you'd want to stay the night here…"

"Of course I do. I'm not going anywhere until I talk to Alex," I respond, though a tug at my chest interrupts my conviction. *Anna.*

The bag contains a few essentials, and Edwards tells me to ask him if I required anything else. I nod and finish my meal, then thank Evie again.

I rise from my seat in a flash and check my watch. It's already seven in the evening. The image of Anna waiting for me at home tightens my chest. I leave the area, find a quiet corner, and dial her number.

"Babe…hey. How are you? How is she?" Her mellow voice betrays her tears. She's making an effort to remain calm, to be strong for me, and it sends fresh pain through my ribcage.

"It's bad," I begin, and then I unload everything—Dr. Robbins' clinical breakdown, Edward's grim account, and Evie's heart-wrenching story. Anna listens, and her occasional hums of acknowledgment ground me. Her calm presence, even over the phone, soothes me.

When I tell her of my plan to spend the night at the hospital, Anna goes silent. The silence stretches.

"Anna, I need to do this. I won't be able to…" The words catch in my throat.

Without further hesitation, she says, "Matt, I understand. You don't have to explain. Just take care, and keep me updated? Tell me how I can help."

I promise to reach out if I need anything. She is struggling too. This isn't easy for her. We've both weathered our own storms and emerged stronger together, only to face another battle now—caring for Alex and managing the fallout of her behavior. My heart stings as I think of the state she must have been in—abject desolation—when she picked up the knife.

Our three lives seem to knot more tightly with every passing moment, and trying to process it all wears on me. The call with Anna, brief as it was, leaves an ache—a longing to be with her, but a compelling need to stay by Alex's side.

I find a lone chair by the water cooler and sink into it, and the hard plastic creaks under my weight. The day's events rush in—a relentless blur of emotions, each memory fraying the edges of whatever composure I've managed to hold on to. The pull of duty to both Alex and Anna, the love I feel for them, the sharp paternal instinct tying me to Alex—everything threatens to tear me apart.

Images flash—the sterile hospital wing, the grim faces of the detectives, the endless lines of machines beeping and blinking in their unfeeling rhythm. But it's the sight of Alex lying so still under that blanket that haunts me the most. Edward and Evie's somber faces, the unraveling of the Cunningham family, Alex's haunting suicide note, the bloodstained images of her in that bathtub, the dark path she walked alone in Sweden—it all burns through me, leaving nothing but anguish.

The day sinks into my bones. The dull ache in my head sharpens to a piercing pain. My breath comes in shallow gasps.

It takes a moment to realize I'm still sitting when I thought I'd stood. I press my palms into the armrest, force myself up, and make my way to the nurse's station for an aspirin. The shift has changed—even the police officer has switched out. Dr. Robbins has to make a call to get me access again.

Evie is seated by Alex's bed with a book in her hands, and the soft glow of a reading light illuminates her face. She looks up at me, wearily but warmly, and turns off the light with a nod and closes the book. "I'll be outside," she whispers before slipping out, leaving me alone with my thoughts and the faint beeping of the monitors.

With deliberate movements, I pull the chair closer to the bed and sit. For several moments I remain still, letting everything—the sounds of the machines, the flickering lights from the monitors, the rolling graphs on the screens, the hum of the air filtration system—soak me. The whirlwind of emotions settles, replaced by an unsettling tranquility. *I'm going to help you heal and get you out of this chamber of torture, Alex.*

The aspirin takes effect gradually, and the haze in my mind lifts, easing the headache. My eyelids grow heavy. I drop my forehead to the bed, gently holding her small hand in mine, her fragile wrist bound by restraints. I run my fingers over her skin—each touch a quiet promise. My heart, full of hope as I set out with Anna to meet the priest, now aches for Alex to return to normal.

And then there's the blanket. Something about it unsettles me. It's wrong. It's not right for her. I study it, trying to understand why it bothers me so much.

It hits me. That blanket isn't the protective envelope I've always given Alex. If she were awake, it would feel foreign to her—cold, constricting, and prickly—like a reminder of everything that's gone wrong. She would have fought against it, just as I would have.

Fatigue tugs at me, but my mind races. The pain and confusion swirl, but eventually exhaustion wins. As sleep overtakes me, I whisper to her, "Why didn't you call me at the time, my precious girl?" The words echo—a mantra of hurt and helplessness fading into the silence as sleep finally claims me.

CHAPTER THIRTY-NINE

Alex: Balloon - I

My eyelids are iron weights, but with significant effort, I manage to lift them—only to be met with a blur of shapes and shadows. It hardly matters. The room is nearly dark until morning, when my care team arrives, promising to help. My eyelids close again, dragging me back into the abyss, which is unwilling to release me.

I try to open my eyes again. The world is a smear of dim lights—distorted and hazy. My thoughts are sluggish. I want them to ease up on the sedatives, just enough to remember who I am. But the haze pulls me under, and my eyelids fall shut once more.

Darkness threatens to swallow me whole—until a noise. Unfamiliar, sharp. My eyes snap open, the reflex sharp amid the fog. My gaze darts, struggling to clear the blurriness. The dim lights flicker. I blink, but they grow painfully bright. I shake my head—if I could just focus, if I could just make sense of it.

The sound is coming from the bathroom. *The bathroom? Why is that what I'm thinking about?* It's too nice for a hospital, with its marble tub and polished chrome fixtures. *Why am I remembering this? Why is my mind dredging up details of a bathroom when I can't hold a thought? What was I...where was I before?*

There are sounds coming from the bathroom. *I should probably think about that.* Only I use this bathroom, and an attendant is always present. She says she's helping, but all she does is take me there, wait until I'm done, then make sure I clean up, brush my teeth, and wash my face. She tells me to shower, but she's lenient if I skip a day. The sedatives are too strong. *Today I should request to lower the dosage. Wait, didn't I already try that? Wasn't it rejected? Maybe I should keep trying, talk to Dr. Robbins...*

Wait. How did I get here? Why am I thinking about this?

The noise from the bathroom snaps me out of my haze. *Yes, that's right…the bathroom. Nobody uses it but me.* The janitors come in during the day around noon. *So, who could be in there at this hour? Am I hallucinating? Is there an intruder? Should I alert the policeman? Why are there policemen anyway?* Wyatt comes and goes, but he's not allowed to linger. Medical professionals, police, and family are allowed in this exclusive care area and everyone else is denied access. *Is my mom coming today? It's been a while since I saw her. No…that's not true. Didn't she come the day before yesterday?*

What is this blanket of darkness? Oh, dear God, the blanket is prickly. The sedatives are too…

One by one, yes, your hands work magic, Daddy. It feels so good. Did you know that every time you massage my fingers, I never stop gazing at your emerald—I mean, vivid viridian eyes? Have you noticed? You may be talking or even watching a movie, but I ogle you, admire you—

With a loud gasp my upper body heaves upward, quickly yanked down by the restraints that bind me. Pain stings at my wrists and ankles. *But what's this?* An echo, followed by a muffled voice—Matthew's. *No, dear God, please make this stop. This illusion feels too real. Please, end it this instant before it becomes another memory to haunt me. Maybe I should ask the doctors to increase my sedatives so I never dream.*

"Hey, my baby. Can you hear me? Are you okay?"

There it is again. The fantasy continues, and I know the torture that will follow. I want to cry, but my feelings are detached from my body. I'll probably forget that I wanted to cry. Then it happens a third time—his touch on my hand, his fingers gently caressing my cheek. *Maybe I should let this dream play out. What's the harm in feeling good for a little while? Yes, let it go on.*

"My dear Alex."

I gasp again, louder, and the doors swing open. A small army of people clad in scrubs rush in, moving with the efficiency of robots. One expertly undoes my restraints, sits me up, then refastens the cuffs. Another reads my vitals aloud. A sharp male voice asks me how I'm feeling, but my thoughts fixate on the last few minutes.

I'm not insane…I felt Matthew's hands on me, and I heard those words. Those words are an activation switch. They're my soul, my sense of purpose, my belonging, my worth. And there's but one person who can wield such power, and he isn't a physician.

Ignoring the medical staff's questions, I turn to the left. He's standing in the shadows—Matthew, as I know him. It must be a lingering remnant of my hallucination. The sedatives are wearing off, but all I feel is the usual pain and the longing stirred by my dream—so lifelike it's cruel.

"You can talk to her," the doctor says, directing his words to the Matthew figure. *Wait, what? The doctor is in my figment too? Where did he come from?* I hear the nurse say she's going to open the curtains and that I might experience discomfort, that it's normal. But I lock my gaze on the figure in the dark—the man in the shadows—Matthew.

An essential and instinctive howl rips from my throat, reverberating around the large room as the curtains are drawn.

Golden light floods the space, revealing the figure standing in the shadows. He is bathed in ethereal morning light, and the rays cling to every feature as if they had been held captive behind the curtains, waiting to feast on him. My howl grows louder as I watch him move toward me with his hands covering his flawless nose and mouth, shaking his head. The black and gray streaks in his lush hair, which has grown a bit since I last saw him, dance with the joyous rays of sunlight.

The blue scrubs with the stethoscope taps my hand, urging me to calm down, while the fancy pink scrubs starts rubbing my back, trying to soothe my quivering body. *Oh, dear God...is this happening?*

Matthew's husky, baritone voice arrests my howling with a simple, "Hey, Alex, I'm here."

Hearing him, seeing him, feeling him beside me makes me weightless. A warmth spreads through me, and my mind empties of everything but him. My senses sharpen, and every discomfort fades.

This isn't a dream. His hand grounds me. I squeeze it, and my heart flutters. *Daddy is here.* I close my eyes, anchoring myself. The nurse's touch adds to the rush. I'd take it all over again for this connection with him.

Impatiently, I call out to him, "Matthew..."

He squeezes my hand and gives me a half smile. I beam back—tears spilling, heart racing. His touch stirs me, and my body hums with life.

He asks to sit next to me, and when the doctor approves, he wraps his arm around me, steadying my shaking body. I rest my head on his chest, and the familiar feeling grounds me. I breathe, and my heart slows as the beeps of the monitors fade.

First, I remind myself why I'm here. The hospital and doctors can't keep me here against my will, but I choose to stay—in this manner. In fact, they wanted to discharge me and transfer me to a psychiatric facility, but I had other plans. The only time I spoke to my family after...the incident, I asked them to persuade the hospital administrators to let me stay. The Cunninghams get what they want. *Adding another hospital wing barely makes a dent in our wealth.*

The staff and the doctor speak, but their words are distant. What matters now is the steady beat beneath my cheek. I stay there, letting his presence fill me with peace. *I will not move from this position.*

The hospital crew leaves, but one attendant lingers.

"Sir, I'm going to take her to the bathroom. You can wait here or outside. It's up to you," she says softly but firmly, her gaze flicking between us.

"Matthew, wait here," I plead, tilting to see his face. He smiles, and it's as if the sun has broken through the clouds. His perfect teeth make an appearance, one of his greatest hits, as I remember.

That grin is the answer to everything. There are no questions, only affirmations of a bond that defies understanding, and thus destruction.

I rush through my morning routine with an urgency the nurse isn't used to seeing. I want to look my best for Matthew, and the thought propels me forward. The warm water from the shower feels like a baptism that washes away the lifeless days.

When I ask for a makeup kit or anything nicer than the dreary hospital gown, the nurse gently declines, and her firm tone offers no room for negotiation. I do the best I can—smoothing my hair into a neat ponytail and patting my cheeks to coax a hint of color to my pale face.

"You look beautiful today," she says with a soft smile, but her words barely register. I'm not seeking her approval.

As I glance in the mirror, a flicker of something unfamiliar stirs inside me—hope. The memory of those empty, lifeless days fade, replaced by the thought of Matthew waiting for me. I square my shoulders, forcing a smile. After weeks of numbness, I finally feel alive.

The nurse cleans the area around my feeding tube and helps me into a fresh hospital gown. My attention drifts toward the door, anticipating him. When she finishes, she pats my shoulder and guides me to the bed.

Lying down, I flinch as she secures the restraint around my wrist. My gaze locks onto him, and his face is shadowed. His eyes flicker between me and the restraint, his face contorting.

"Nurse, please, is that necessary? I talked to Dr. Robbins yesterday..." he says. His tone is calm, but it carries a demand that thrills me, igniting familiar feelings of his care, possessiveness, and protection.

She, however, is unyielding, her retort firm, "Sir, please do not interfere. All changes to protocol must be issued by signature from Dr. Robbins and the Head of Trauma Care. Please, step aside and allow me to care for Alex."

Fuck you, bitch. A surge of anger flares. *How dare you talk to my daddy in that tone?* My pulse quickens, and the shackles suddenly feel more confining, as if they're reacting to my rage, restraining me from launching at the pretty face wearing flowery pink scrubs.

He turns away, and his shoulders are inflexible as he watches her render me immobile. I note his unease—the way this act disturbs him. When the nurse finishes, her demeanor softens as if she's putting on a new mask.

"You can be with her now," she says, her tone saccharine. Then she says, "We will monitor via video and tactile monitoring systems, in addition to the medical monitors."

Oh, you sly hellcat. Are you threatening him? Her words are a reminder of the control she still holds over my body.

Then he smiles at her, and for a fleeting moment, I swear her cheeks flush. I seethe with jealousy, and fresh heat rushes through me, sharp and bitter but oddly comforting. This is a twisted sense of normalcy, as if we're back to when the world made sense because he was mine, and I was his.

I want him beside me on the bed, to shield me from this cold, sterile place. Instead, he takes the chair next to me, but his hand clasps mine. That simple touch is a lifeline, offering me warmth. My chest rises with a deep breath, and my eyes flutter shut as his protective presence wraps around me. I tilt my head back, swallow hard, and try to steady myself.

"Alex, I'm going to get you out of here, okay?" His gravelly tone reminds me of the reality of my situation. I meet his gaze and observe the way his forehead wrinkles and his eyebrows rise.

"Daddy, I...I was struggling and I...I couldn't take it any..." My speech falters.

Before I can finish, he climbs onto the bed and wraps his arms around me, pulling me close until I'm nestled in my rightful place against his torso. "Shh...don't say anything. We'll talk only about the future and never reference the past. Understand?"

The familiar control envelops me like a warm fleece blanket, soothing every nerve, calming every fear. My chest tingles with warmth and relief—this is a heavenly feeling, the singular thing that makes sense. A few tears of joy escape, and I nod against his pectorals, whispering, "Yes, Matthew." *History is nothing but misery, and I don't want to have a conversation about it.*

He continues to hold me like a delicate glass sculpture, and time loses all meaning as we rest—the world outside forgotten.

CHAPTER FORTY

Alex: Balloon - II

A soft knock interrupts my reverie, and I mentally hurl a hellish curse at whoever dares to interrupt this moment. Matthew gets off the bed and moves to open the door, which seems miles away in this cavernous room.

I retract my curse immediately—it's my mom.

They exchange pleasantries, and the tension between them is hardly noticeable now. I can't help but think back to that disastrous family dinner, when he vowed never to forgive her for slapping me during one of the interventions over our forbidden relationship. But now they're cordial, and he follows her to my bed with that respectful demeanor of his.

She and I, on the other hand, exchange the usual formalities, the kind that always feel rehearsed. An awkward silence stretches between us. I know she wants to have a conversation—to break through the walls I've built—but my walls are impenetrable.

Her presence is both comforting and upsetting. She's my mother, and a part of me will always need her close. But she doesn't understand the bond I share with him. I sometimes picture a future where I can tell her about the unique bond I have with him. But not now. Not at nineteen. That conversation is too far off, and it would never be understood in the present.

He stands a few feet behind her, watching. He walks toward the door, presumably to leave us alone.

"Matthew, where're you going?" I call to him, breaking the stillness.

My mom is startled and lets go of my hand. She quickly regains her composure, and her voice trembles ever so slightly as she uses her poise to conceal her emotions. "You don't have to leave," she adds, her tone almost pleading.

Just as the tension hangs in the air, a few soft knocks sound at the door.

Dr. Robbins enters, followed by the nurse who administers my meals through the feeding tube. Everyone but me exchanges casual greetings, a normalcy that feels almost surreal.

The doctor comes closer, but before she can ask how I'm feeling, I beam at her, forcing a cheery smile. "Dr. Robbins, I feel wonderful today. Light, happy. I wish I could wear a nice dress instead of this hospital gown. Maybe even a makeup kit in my bathroom—what do you think? How are you? I'm sorry I don't ask that more often."

Her eyebrows raise, and I see my mom mirror her expression. I laugh, wanting to push the lightness I'm feeling onto them, to shift the mood. It works. After a beat, the doctor laughs too. My mom smiles wide and then paces the room, murmuring into her cellphone as if giving orders.

Dr. Robbins resumes her professional demeanor, saying, "Alex, after we're done with your feeding this morning—"

Matthew's demand cuts through the air, commanding everyone's attention. "Dr. Robbins, I spoke with you about this yesterday. Remove the feeding tube. She will eat normally."

Yes, I will. Warmth floods through me, bolstered by his protective and controlling stance. It's been so long since I've felt this—a primal awakening surging within me. *How I've longed to submit to him.* My focus locks onto the vibrant green of his eyes, following them like a satellite in orbit.

My mom, hurriedly ending her call, moves to my bedside. A heavy silence falls. Dr. Robbins matches his intensity. "What exactly are you proposing? I can't remove her feeding tube without following procedure—she hasn't eaten on her own since she got here. That's two weeks."

He covers his nose and mouth and exhales, the puffs of air audible. He paces in short spans, shaking his head and rubbing the back of his neck. Then, he fixes his gaze on me, and the connection roots me in the present.

He draws a breath and releases it before speaking. "Bring her a proper breakfast," he says, his ruling firm. "Plates, bowls, glasses. I'll make sure she eats."

His authority is absolute. My mom stands frozen, her arms slack by her sides. Dr. Robbins speaks in hushed tones to the nurse, who promptly exits.

Silence blankets the area. Dr. Robbins tries to engage me with a series of questions, and I try my best to focus and answer her, though my attention keeps drifting towards him.

"Wow, Alex. This is the most we've spoken since you've been here, and I'm glad you're talking," Dr. Robbins says, as the nurse returns with a tray of breakfast.

"Dr. Robbins, ask them to take the restraints off," he demands, his tone definite but almost pleading. *No, Matthew, you don't plead.* My frustration spikes. *Take the fucking restraints off, as he asked you to, you doctor-whatever.*

She meets his demand with equal firmness. "That's against protocol. We have a meeting scheduled later today, and we'll discuss it then." She glances at my mom. "Victoria, you should be present as well, and we'll decide what's best for her. Until then, you must respect both legal and medical protocols," she adds, turning to him.

Oh, 'they' will discuss what's best for me. I sit here, invisibly seething. *Hey everyone, I'm right here. But I know why they're deciding, and not me. My actions two weeks ago called for it.*

Matthew tilts his head up toward the ceiling, wiping his face a few times before taking the plate of food. He sits on the bed and feeds me.

Tears threaten to spill as I remember all the times he's fed me—cradling me in his arms or sitting with me at a table. But I stifle them. I can't let them see me break. I want everyone to see us—him and me—happy together, in a natural bond that defines us. I eagerly eat the oatmeal, bland but sweet, under his care. Dr. Robbins pats my forearm, nods at him, and quietly leaves with the nurse following behind.

Mom stays, watching me like I'm a stranger.

Matthew stands and says, "Ms. Cunningham, I'll wait outside. If you want to talk to Alex..."

I offer my mom a smile. Maybe she'll be the first to understand what he and I are. I hope she's getting the support she needs from the rest of the family, especially with my dad retreating into his own dark world. She looks at me and strokes my cheek, her gaze lingering. She kisses my forehead.

"I'll see about that dress and makeup kit, honey. I've already called for them but let me get the permissions. Talk later?"

We exchange smiles. Her appearance brightens, and despite her tears, she grips my hand tightly. She nods at him and leaves, closing the door softly behind her.

The air feels lighter now. Today's conversations—less protocol, less process—have made the room brighter. My heart swells like a balloon tethered to the bed, eager to dance among the clouds.

After she leaves, Matthew sits on the chair and takes my hand in his. I give him a look of disappointment. "Hey, come sit beside me?"

"I will. But first, I want to talk to you." His voice is full of purpose.

Oh, no. Please don't bring anything heavy down on me. My heart stops, and a tiny gasp cracks the air between us. I go completely still.

"Hey. Remember what I said and don't fret. We're never going to talk about the past."

Lightness manifests as a broad smile. *God, I am so full of energy now. I can feel the adrenaline. Put me on the track, and I'll run a 10K.*

"Show your usual determination. In my meeting with Dr. Robbins, I'm going to ask her to release you from these restraints and the feeding tube. I need you to start eating on your own. Got it?"

That is no big deal. I'm here to obey him. I nod a million times and follow up with a, "Yes, I will."

His lips curve wide and become a full-fledged smile, and his visage lights up, competing with the sun's rays. His already high cheeks rise to alpine levels, and the balloon tethered to the hospital bed fills with a lightness that can't be contained.

The entire world is cast in a divine glow as he says, "You're such a good girl, Alex."

The warmth in his voice wraps around my soul like a soothing balm. My chest tightens with the overwhelming rush of being seen, cherished. *Good girl.* My breath hitches, and I feel a deep ache—a yearning that borders on blissful surrender.

Yes, I'm a good girl. I feel weightless and heavy all at once, and my body trembles with the intensity of my emotions. His gaze holds me steady, and I cling to those words, clutching them tightly in my heart as if letting them go would shatter me completely.

Tears are a thing of the past as I beam at him. In this moment, I'm whole again—his submissive and obedient ward, his Alex.

True to his word, he comes and sits on the bed, though it's awkward since my arms are spread at my sides, fastened to the bed frame. Despite that, he holds my shoulders, and I let my head fall onto his chest.

"Tell me about your next brilliant idea to shape the world for the better," he says, giving my shoulders a shake.

Oh, dear God, is this really happening? Thank you! I've been bottling up my ideas, and that bottle has been floating somewhere in the vast ocean of my brain.

I start by sharing my thoughts on combining solar and wind farms, then discuss the opportunities in wave energy. A corner of my intellect tugs at my passion for wildlife and rainforest preservation, so I think aloud with him, exploring how I might channel some of my brainpower in that direction even though it's not entirely physics-related. I believe math can solve any problem, so I talk about how algorithms might pinpoint ideal urbanization locations without encroaching on nature. Although piano was his major, I know he studied math during his Yale years, so I feel a spark of connection as he follows along, understanding the key points of my ideas.

As I speak, my mind rejuvenates, and with it, my body. Positive energy pulses from my heart. He already has me wrapped in an envelope of protection and warmth, and now that warmth creates a cocoon of intimate comfort, safety, and security. I want to stretch this incredible moment and make it last forever.

But questions and doubts hover, lurking in the shadows of this bright cocoon. *What's next? Are we together again? When is he going to leave that bitch of an ex-wife for good, or has he already, upon hearing of my near death? Should I ask him? How will my actions affect our relationship going forward? How does my connection with my family change after this?*

More questions compound those already circulating, but I'm not ready to confront them. *Not yet.*

I don't have the luxury of options or choices here, and that leaves me trapped. My brain calculates possibilities, and I feel a desperate need to find answers. The less-than-ideal situation I am in leaves me flustered. My stomach tenses as I second guess what action to take next.

All I long for is a semblance of stability, something solid to hold onto. I yearn for lost love, found and recovered—the familiarity of the past combining with the promise of a future I can cling to, and a peaceful life going forward.

He is next to me in this hospital bed, in a scenario born of misfortune, but like he said, I solely want to look forward. *For now, can I rest in his care, please?*

I've withstood eight months of suffering. I'll tackle the challenges and unanswered issues soon. *Let me have this moment with him.*

I nestle deeper in his chest, desperate to pin him down, to keep him close and never let go. But he shifts and pulls away slightly, much to my disappointment. He gets up to sit on the chair, still holding my hand. "Hey, I have a meeting with Dr. Robbins. Your mom will also be there. I'll return in about forty-five minutes. Get some rest, okay?"

A wave of warmth born from the comfort of familiarity washes over me as I instinctively respond, "Sure."

But as I watch him leave, something inside me clenches. My heart is being dragged away with him, tugging at my chest. An invisible cord is severed by the closing door. I struggle to manage the sudden emptiness, exhaling as I try to soothe the ache of his absence. The chamber darkens, and shadows creep back in, threatening to pull me under. But then I remember his promise and his instruction. They gave me a call button, so I press it, and the attendant from earlier comes in.

I'm almost certain this hussy blushed and ogled Matthew, even if only for a fleeting second. She'll go on my burn list, but for now, I require help. "Hi. I'd like to sleep. Can you lower the backrest for me, please? And no more sedatives, I beg you. I can sleep without them." I try to keep my voice stable. The thought of those drugs makes me wince.

To my surprise, she responds kindly, "Dr. Robbins has already paused the sedation." As she flattens my bed and adjusts my pillows, I breathe a sigh of relief. I thank her softly, burying my head in the inviting pillows as the weight of the morning eases off my shoulders.

As she quietly leaves, I reflect on the most refreshing morning I've had in nine months. Positive thoughts and hope swirl in my brain, carrying me gently towards the waiting arms of blissful sleep.

A squeeze of my forearm is all it takes to rouse me from the delicious laziness of sleep. I hum, savoring the lingering warmth of slumber, and my eyelids remain closed a little longer.

Since this morning, a single thought has been drifting around, bobbing up from the depths of my mind like a buoy.

The thought surfaces again, carried by gentle waves of comfort: *"Our bond defies understanding, and thus destruction."*

I awaken to the sight of his radiant face, and his mathematically precise features reassure me I am perfect—and exactly where I am meant to be.

"Did you sleep well?" His raspy speech resonates, banishing the last remnants of sleep. I nod, and his smile broadens—a sight that never fails to fill me with contentment.

"It's lunchtime, and I want you to show your strength."

I gaze at him as he kneels next to me. He doesn't wait for my acknowledgment, and that simple assumption of my compliance sends a thrill from head to toe.

"They're going to take your restraints off. You will eat lunch on your own. I'll sit with you. Are we clear?"

He raises my backrest and carefully adjusts my pillows. I note every movement of his body as he moves with delicate precision, and each of his touches makes me feel whole again.

"How did they agree? What did you tell them?" I ask, wary of false hope or temporary solutions.

"Dr. Robbins agreed to a controlled release of the restraints—at mealtimes, only if someone is present, and on the condition that you eat on your own." He sits on the bed, rubbing my shoulders with a tenderness that grounds me.

"Show them what you're made of, Alex." His words are a command, an affirmation, and the shine on his features brightens the surroundings. Suddenly, I feel hungry—ravenous.

"Can I have a burger and fries? And a large soda?"

He bursts out laughing, and I can't help but join him. Our laughter fills the space—a shared moment of joy that lingers in the air. My stomach aches from the force of it, but we keep laughing, letting the sound wash over us.

The nurse enters with my lunch, hesitates, then grins at us. Another follows, and they join in conversation with him. I monitor for any flirtation. Though their professional demeanor remains, I catch their glances flicking toward him. *Three nurses on my burn list.*

Dr. Robbins arrives and instructs the second nurse to remove my restraints and help me sit up. The first nurse sets my food in front of me. Without waiting for direction from Matthew, I dig in—the plain chicken and rice is a far cry from a burger. He sits beside me, his attention briefly shifting to the doctor as she prepares to leave.

"I have a patient I must attend to, but I'll check on you when I'm free. Eat well, Alex. I hope you're feeling okay?" Her tone is warm despite the urgency in her movements.

I nod enthusiastically, beaming at her, and my whole body bounces on the firm hospital bed. She smiles at us before leaving. The first nurse follows her, leaving the second one to monitor me.

Matthew and I chat about the hospital kitchen's menu, making fun of the dishes. My mom soon joins us, and I squeal with delight, "Mom! Come here, want to have some of this amazing spread from La Grand?" I joke, laughing loudly. Her eyes are soft and glazed with emotion as she sits, sandwiching me between her and Matthew.

The three of us talk, and he carefully steers the conversation. We cover light topics—more ridiculing of the desserts on offer by the kitchen, the coming fall season and places I want to visit after I am discharged, and my project ideas.

When she hears me talk of traveling after I leave the hospital, her body quivers, and her lips curl as she bites them. Her tears make an appearance, but they don't spill. She gracefully disguises her emotions, leaving no trace.

Then she shifts the chatter to one of our favorite subjects—clothes and shoes. She points to a bag she brought with her. "Honey, I got you some clothes. The nurses approved some light dresses with long zippers in the back. Your makeup kit is restricted to a few essentials, but that's plenty. Rules are that you can change and put on makeup in the presence of a nurse."

I drop my plastic spoon and fork, squealing in delight as I throw my arms around her, hugging her tightly.

Outside of my time with Matthew, I can't remember a more poignant moment than being nestled between my mom and him. The warmth and safety of this moment engulf me, and a part of me wishes time would stop right here, even though I know it's a wish I dare not speak aloud. But I mean it, and I hold that thought close, cherishing the perfection of this moment.

"Mom, Mom, please...can you talk to the nurses, doctors? Can I change and wear makeup now? Please? Pretty please??" I beg her—my petition tinged with a childlike desperation—but she's already on her way to speak with the eagle-eyed nurse stationed by the door.

"Ma'am, do not disturb me while I monitor your daughter. Please talk to the head nurse," the unpleasant harpy who dared to gawp at Matthew responds curtly, her gaze fixed on me. *Oh, she's definitely on my burn list.*

After a few minutes, Mom returns with two more nurses in tow. One clears away my finished lunch tray, while the other guides me to the bathroom. Mom follows with the bag of dresses and the makeup kit, but the nurse bars her from entering. I catch her fleeting look of frustration before I'm led inside.

In the bathroom, I savor the sensation of warm water cascading over me. I take my time washing my hair, grateful for my poker-straight strands that dry in no time, freeing me from the wait. After applying some light makeup, I select a simple dress in white—his favorite color. *Thanks, Mom!*

As I style my hair and make a low ponytail, my reflection momentarily reminds me of someone—a vile bitch I'd rather forget. My memory won't allow such luxuries, so I forcefully shelve that image in a far corner of my organized memory banks.

When I step out, Mom gasps. She wraps me in a tight embrace, and her voice trembles as she whispers, "Oh, honey, you're so beautiful. Love you, darling." Her vulnerability tugs at my heart, seeing this strong-willed woman break. From the corner of my eye, I notice Matthew lingering near the watchful attendant. I wish she'd keep her distance from him.

I focus on Mom, kissing her cheeks and giving her my brightest smile. "Thanks for this!" She wipes her tears away with practiced ease as her composure returns. *How does she manage that?*

The nurse leads me to my bed, where the eagle-eyed attendant returns to fasten my restraints. Once the nurses leave, Mom and Matthew sandwich me on the bed again. We watch mindless television, and our light conversations are interspersed with comfortable silences. After an hour, she kisses me and says she needs to check on Father, her eyes shadowed with concern. I nod, not wanting to dwell on that conversation.

After she leaves, Matthew shifts to his chair, much to my disappointment.

"How do I look, Daddy?" I beam at him, but he doesn't respond, his attention glued to a pointless basketball game. *Oh, dear God, yes!* This feels familiar—his indifference and how it ignites a spark of arousal within me. I ask him again, but he raises the volume on the television, and the shrill sounds resonate with the tingling sensation he stirred in me.

When the program finally ends, he turns his attention to me, completely ignoring my question but saying softly, "How about you get an afternoon siesta?" He smirks, and though my face doesn't smile, my heart does. *Fine. Whatever you say.*

He lowers my backrest and rubs my fingers as I embrace a much deeper sleep than a nap—powered by laughter, lightness, and his touch. As I drift off, I hear his angelic whisper, "You are beautiful, Alex."

CHAPTER
FORTY-ONE

Alex: Balloon - III

C onversation fills the space as I chat with Evie and Edward—their presence making the sterile hospital environment feel homey. Matthew stands against the wall, observing us with that protective gaze. They're all carefully avoiding any mention of the past or the present. It's obvious, and I'm grateful. I suspect he ordered Evie and Edward to keep things light.

As evening falls, Dr. Robbins enters for her final check of the day. Everyone quietly leaves at her request.

"I want to soar high in the sky, Dr. Robbins, like a hot air balloon. I could run a marathon now," I respond eagerly to her question about how I'm feeling.

But instead of the enthusiastic response I expect, I see a flicker in her expression. Not that I'd be able to decipher the emotions of the world's foremost psychiatrist. She offers me a half smile, her tone placating.

"Alex, would you feel the same way if Matthew wasn't around?" Her words are deliberate, as if she's trying to wrap me in a protective blanket.

But that blanket itches and covers me in darkness. Her question draws the curtains, blocking the light. My body suddenly feeling leaden, like I'm sinking in a swamp. Pricking sensations in my ribcage and belly intensify into a dull pain. I can't breathe.

"Dr...Dr. Robbins...but he is here...he looks after me. Thank you for bringing him to me...he won't leave me," I whisper, my voice barely audible.

She gently shakes me, and her voice is a lifeline pulling me to the present. The room slowly comes back into focus, the lights warm and soothing.

"I want you to relax. We'll talk more tomorrow. You have more family coming to join you while you have dinner. How does that sound?"

I try to hug her, only to be reminded of the restraints. "Yes! Perfect, Dr. Robbins!" My chest catapults out of my control as the balloon inside me fills with warm, comforting air. I'm ready to fly, to travel the blue skies as expansive as Matthew's heart, free from worry.

She pats my arm, and her touch grounds me once more before she heads to the door to speak with a couple of nurses.

"Oh my God. Oh my God. Oh my God, nooo...nooo...yesss..." I shriek and yelp as all my sisters-in-law and Lillian enter, followed by Matthew, whose alpine cheekbones and radiant smile outshine the lights.

Two nurses enter, one carrying a plate that looks like—*are you kidding me?* A burger and fries with...just a small soda—but that's okay. *Surprise goodness!* Matthew throws his head back, laughing and running his hands through his lush black and gray hair. The sight of him, so blithe, fills me with a joy I thought I'd lost forever. The nurse undoes my restraints and returns to the door.

My sisters-in-law and Lillian gather around me, and their hugs are tentative, as if I might break. Lillian—the youngest and soon to be my fourth sister-in-law—breaks down, wrapping her arms around me in a fierce embrace. The others form a protective circle, and their whispered reassurances blend into a soft chorus of love.

As the initial wave of emotion subsides, we start chattering. My gaze keeps drifting to him, drawing strength from every glance. Being surrounded by him and my family while eating this juicy burger and crisp fries is the best medicine.

No one brings up the past—likely under Matthew's orders—so we indulge in some girl talk. The conversation eases the tension in the room. But eventually, the topic moves to me and my care. Each of the women offers their support with genuine concern and determination to help me through my recovery.

The talk then drifts briefly to business, which I imagine is suffering because of my actions. Before it can weigh too heavily, Lillian—with a surprising forcefulness beneath her fragile exterior—steers the conversation back to my care and the future.

As we talk, our bond deepens, strengthened by shared tears, laughter, and the understanding that we're all in this together. This evening with these incredible women has been another lifeline, tethering me to the world outside this trauma care wing, to a future I'm determined to reach.

My heart is full, dense with elation. Lingering memories of the chatty dinner under Matthew's watch swirl in my mind. As evening transitions into night, the world begins to quiet, and the bustling energy of the day gives way to stillness. The curtains are drawn. He hovers near my bed—checking my pillows, adjusting my restrained ankles and wrists, and tucking me under the blanket.

I note the anguish in his features, the way he rubs the nape of his neck, and his pained stare. His skin bunches around his eyes. He is unable to settle in one place and periodically clenches his fists. He hates seeing me bound, monitored by machines, and put to sleep with drugs. *But I know we'll be out of this place soon.*

He sits on the chair and slides his hand under the prickly blanket to grasp mine. His touch calms me.

His gravelly voice rises above the hum of the air circulation systems and the steady beeps of the monitors. "Alex, they're going to sedate you in a few minutes. Stay strong. I need you to have a great night's sleep. Is that clear?"

I give him a warm, assuring smile. "Yes, Matthew."

His presence, the lively conversations, and the burger and fries have left me in a state of euphoric calm. Everything seems right. The hospital, the circumstances—none of it matters because he's with me. Everything else is background noise, fleeting stops on our journey. *We'll walk this road together with him leading the way.*

A nurse enters, presses a few buttons on the machine, and dims the lights in the corners of the ceiling. I clutch Matthew's hand more tightly. The room darkens, casting his face in shadow. I catch the faint glint in his eyes and the silhouette of his perfectly shaped head.

As the medication pulls me into the depths of sleep, my senses fade. With all the strength I can muster, I voice the words that have become the purpose of my existence.

"I love you, Daddy."

CHAPTER FORTY-TWO

Anna: Blessing and Burden - I

The dim light from the lone lamp barely penetrates the shadows of our apartment, casting a muted glow over my desk where I sit with my laptop and monitors. I'm mindlessly clicking on icons and documents, pretending to work. The air conditioner, still groaning and rattling away, hasn't been fixed by the building administrator despite my repeated calls. Fall is around the corner, but for now it's stuck at a stifling seventy-seven, adding to my growing irritation.

Every time I think I've finally organized the million considerations about the chaotic life Matt and I have and attempt to bring some semblance of order, the clunky unit jumbles them again. It's not the unit's fault, though. Ever since the news about Alex and her—the incident, my concentration has slowed to a crawl, tangled in the unanticipated issues her actions have thrust upon us.

It's the one scenario I hadn't foreseen—her attempting to take her own life. I had an entry if she were to threaten self-harm or suicide. Our planned response was to alert her therapist and family.

For all my careful strategizing, my meticulous planning, and my thinking three steps ahead—it hadn't occurred to me she would actually do it without a warning or a threat. I reasoned that obsession would drive her to attain her goals using any means at her disposal. She would use her brain as if she were finding the answer to a complex math problem. I theorized she would go to extreme lengths—like murdering me—to reclaim Matt.

Every plan, every response he and I prepared, was obliterated, reduced to smoke and ashes.

I'm rebuilding a strategy from scratch, no longer ahead of the curve. I'm struggling to keep pace. I know I'll regain my footing, that I'll be steps ahead again soon, but I'm floundering. There's a question I'm not ready to confront but it keeps dragging me back when I examine my thoughts and feelings.

My violent reaction in that bathroom stall. Why did my body react so vehemently to the news of her attempted suicide?

The memory claws at me—that same sickening sensation which refused to leave even after I came home, where I retched and vomited again. Merely thinking about it brings on nausea and a dull headache. I shake it off, trying to will the thought away.

Matt's text said he'd be home at ten, which is still an hour away. I wasn't sure he'd come home at all, thinking he might choose to spend another night at the hospital.

A ripple of unease undulates through me. A longing for things to return to normal takes root. To regain the rhythm of life together—work, plans to have children and the wedding.

My hands are icy despite the warmth of the room. My fingers absently twist the edge of the notepad in front of me as I try to push away the worry that's settled deep in my bones. All I can think about is how much I want him here so I can listen to him, pacify him, encourage him, and remind him we still have a life outside of all this.

The new planning notepad I started is mostly empty, save for a few scattered notes to ponder later. The one thing I need, that we all need, is for Alex to recover—to become healthy and to stay that way for the rest of her life. The initial plans he and I should discuss must help her achieve that, not only for her sake but for everyone her life touches, including her business empire.

I've been reading the Markets Herald, diving into the Cunningham Energy Conglomerate's business and financials, and it's not good. The abrupt appointment of acting CEOs across their major companies, given her brothers' reclusion, has shaken their market position. Speculation is swirling, fueled by the absence of Alex's father in the boardrooms, despite his chief of staff and eldest son trying their best. One newspaper linked Alex's absence during the president's address at the climate summit last month to the family's current turmoil, spinning a fresh thread of rumor that's sure to catch fire as time goes on and the situation deteriorates.

But my thoughts keep returning to Matt. I can't imagine how he must be feeling. Seeing Alex like that—restrained and on a feeding tube—must have sunk him. I shudder at the thought. *He needs me, and I'll be there for him.*

Questions linger beneath the surface, and they elicit an unease I can't shake.

How will this dreadful incident shape his and my life from here? How will it affect the plans we have for children, marriage, and beyond? What's the first thing I must do? What should he do?

This isn't healthy—for my body, my intellect, or the life he and I dream of together. If I'm not well, I can't look after him or protect what we've built. With effort, I force myself from the spiral of doubt and despair threatening to pull me under.

I open an editor on the screen and start typing lines of code for my freelance project, working based on pseudocode I had previously written. The distraction is welcome—a temporary reprieve that refreshes me. For a few minutes I stretch, soothing my tense muscles, and the crack of my knuckles is comforting. It's past ten—he should be here any minute.

I hear the lock turn, and I make a dash for him. I reach the door as it opens, and the sight of him weary and drained tugs beneath my ribcage. I steady myself, determined to fulfill my mission—to care for my king, who has returned from an unimaginably exhausting battle.

His dry, raspy voice draws me to his embrace. "My gorgeous." I haven't seen him since I left him at the hospital yesterday morning. He pulls me in for a tight hug, and his arms wrap around me with an intensity that feels almost desperate. His kiss is deep and torrid, and I reciprocate, needing to connect with him.

This hug is tighter than usual, as if his hands are the ropes binding him to me. His embrace is a reminder of how foreign the past two days of loneliness have been, how much I've missed him, how much I've needed this.

His clothes smell of the hospital, sterile and cold. The familiar comfort of his natural scent is buried beneath the reminders of where he's been, of what he's seen, heard and undergone in the past two days.

He hugs and kisses me for longer than usual—not that I am calculating—then finally lets me go. I sense the reluctance in his hands, in the lingering brush of his lips, and sense something deeper stirring within him. Something is not quite right. I decide to let things unfold naturally, but that decision triggers a feeling of being underprepared for the situation.

He strokes my cheeks with the back of his hands, and the touch is soothing but heavy with the exhaustion he's carrying. His eyes linger on mine, searching, and his low-pitched voice, laced with fatigue, breaks the silence. "Have you been crying, Anna?"

Of course he knows. He always finds out. I swallow the lump in my throat, refusing to let my composure waver. This moment isn't about me. I want to be his anchor, not another problem for him to carry. I press a kiss to his cheek, lingering long enough to feel his warmth.

"A bit," I admit softly, brushing my thumb across his hand. "But it was a while ago."

His gaze holds mine, and I can see the concern etched in the lines of his pursed lips and drawn eyebrows.

"I'm worried, Matt," I confess—vulnerability seeping forth despite my efforts. "But everything's going to be okay."

I pull back enough to make sure he hears me—really hears me. "We're going to handle this," I say more firmly, grounding myself in the truth of our bond. "The issue with her, the wedding, the future..."

I squeeze his hands gently, feeling his familiar strength beneath the exhaustion. "Together," I whisper, bringing his hands to my lips. "As always."

For a moment his eyes close, and he exhales slowly. His shoulders relax slightly, and I know he's still here with me. *Holding on. We both are.*

We nod and touch heads, savoring this brief, grounding moment. We both needed this—a quick pause to reconnect. His tired eyes hold mine for several moments, and he wears a slight smile that warms my chest. He kisses my forehead and presses my head into his chest tightly again, the gesture both comforting and intense.

"Do we have dinner? I'm not hungry, but I think I should eat—"

I don't let him finish, gently taking his hand and leading him to the bathroom. "Shower and change, babe. Hot soup and bread will be waiting for you." I kiss him on the cheek and leave him there.

When he emerges, he seems brisk, dressed in shorts and a light T-shirt that clings to his frame. His clean-shaven face and perfectly maintained hair, slicked back with a bit of gel, make him look refreshed, yet the tiredness in his eyes remains. His hair has grown a bit, and the thick black and gray strands catch the light and soothe my heart as if they were stroking it with a feather. I am unexpectedly aroused—a stark contrast to the gloomy situation we're trying to manage.

I close my eyes and heave a sigh—my carnal feelings can wait until he is ready. He will claim me himself when the time comes.

We finish dinner and clear the plates. He rests on the sofa and pulls me close. Each gesture carries overt signs of something unsettling that's driving him, or perhaps disturbing him. He holds me tightly again, and his embrace conveys a need that I can't quite decipher. As he fills me in on the events at the hospital during Alex's dinner and after, I listen intently. A feeling of watchfulness creeps over me, growing stronger with each passing moment.

He finishes by recounting the moment he left her under sedation. His eyebrows relax and his features soften, but the pained look remains.

"I wrote her a note, asking her to be as strong tomorrow as she was today, and let her know I'd visit in the evening." He tries to smile, but that fades. He swallows with difficulty, as if a heavy lump is blocking his throat. His limbs shake minutely. *It was not easy for him to leave her like that.*

We sit in silence for a while, letting the day's events settle.

A sudden impatience for all of this to be over overwhelms me. A quiver travels through my stomach and speculation in my head points to an unsettling conclusion that I can't quite grasp. *Something feels off, terribly off.*

A shadow casts a pall of doubt over my understanding of her. This unease is entirely different from what I felt when I predicted Alex's return to Manhattan. *This is something darker.*

It strips away my confidence layer by layer, because I don't have a good grasp of what's really going on, or of what's about to happen. My confidence is about to go up in smoke when I think about the impact this tragedy could have on our wedding plans.

I can't sit still any longer. I jump up—startling him—and shake my head with a few jerks, as if I can physically dispel my confusion. He asks if I'm okay, and I force a bright smile and assure him I am. But inside, I'm anything but okay.

I make a mental note to intentionally recompose myself now and then—every few seconds if necessary—during this stressful time, even if I am composed. Every nuance in the environment, the problems Matt and I are trying to tackle, is a potential threat—or at least I must view it that way until I can determine otherwise. My senses are already heightened, and my awareness is sharp, but I need to elevate them further, to process details using filters of rational thinking, validating them with my plans...

But what plans? I've noted many actions—to support him and give him the warmth of home to return to every day—but very few handle this unpredictable scenario. That's what he and I should discuss—how do we prepare and respond to the demanding situation we are faced with?

Is it too early? Should I give him time, and gather information—especially on Alex's treatment plan—before we formulate a response?

In the meantime, I can draw mind maps and decision trees, charting the various paths this situation could spawn. *Yes, that's what I'll do.* I want to go to him with solutions, to offer him clarity rather than risk stressing him further.

That would stress me out first—not having a plan. I decide to let things unravel as they will, resolving to fill my notepad with ideas tomorrow.

As we head to bed, Matt notes that we missed the meeting with the priest, and pain pulls at my chest—it's the first wedding preparation task we've missed. The significance weighs on me—a reminder of how our plans are being disrupted by forces we can't control.

"Anna, I don't think I can go to work and function effectively. I'm going to take the week off," he says, exhaling a long-drawn breath. I pat his cheek, feeling the rough texture of his skin, and nod in agreement.

He fires quick emails to the recording studio and La Grand Élégance, and his fingers move with an urgency that belies his exhaustion. He also texts a couple of his musician friends, letting them know they can sub at the restaurant if they want to. I watch him, wondering if he is trying to regain some semblance of control to manage what little he can in a world that feels increasingly chaotic.

Then he asks me if I can take leave for the week too, to focus on wedding preparations. The question lightens my chest, and I find it difficult to suppress the wide smile that spreads across my face.

"A week is difficult," I tell him, my voice tinged with regret. "We have a high-profile case. But I can take tomorrow off so we can visit the priest in the morning and then go shopping for my wedding dress." I try to keep my tone light.

I pull him in for a kiss, wanting to shower him with my love and support. When he pulls me deeper as we kiss, I perceive the intensity of the disturbance within him.

The night settles, and we curl up in bed—his grip on me firm.

I gently ask him about Alex's treatment plan, and he releases a slow breath. When he answers, his voice is low and deep, each word measured. "I'm not clear on that, angel. I don't think even the doctors know it yet. She wasn't talking to anyone or eating by herself...not until I got there yesterday."

He takes a breath. "Dr. Robbins had a short session with her in my presence, and another with her alone. I don't know if that gave her enough information to create a treatment plan."

His words hang in the air, heavy with uncertainty, and his worry oppresses us both. But I don't flinch—I hold him, and he holds me tighter.

I can't help but think of how he gave Alex, her family, and the doctors a brief reprieve by waking her from an inert, distant and uncommunicative state to a show of strength and joy. *Had he inadvertently given them false hope?* I keep this thought to myself.

Like the doctors, he and I have no choice but to wait and see how she responds.

I tell him how a detective spoke with me for an hour once he and Edward had gone in to see Alex. He jolts upright, and surprise flickers across his tired features as he asks me repeatedly if I'm okay, his concern evident. I reassure him and summarize the interaction, though I can see the tension in his eyes as he listens.

Apparently, I was the last person to see Alex before she did what she did. The incident happened the day after my meeting with her, but the police were still eager to talk to me. I gave the detective details of my alibi—I was working late at the LLP. Then I told him the truth—that I went to ask her to let Matt and me have a new life together.

He asked countless questions, most of them about Matt's relationship with her. I didn't hold back. I told the detective what I knew—her texts, her phone calls, suspicions of her stalking Matt and me, and that my visit to her apartment was a last resort, given how close the wedding was. The detective seemed satisfied with my responses, gave me his card, and asked me to contact him if I thought of anything else.

Matt absorbs this information, and his breaths are deep and measured. He pauses for a moment before telling me that the detectives want to speak with him too. He plans to go there tomorrow afternoon after we meet the priest and shop for my wedding dress.

The mention of Alex triggers unease within me, a creeping discomfort that I can't quite place—*something is off*. But I push it down, resolving to support him as he does what he's convinced he needs to do to give him and her peace. I tell him I'm going with him, and he responds by rubbing my arm and stroking my hair. His touch is a balm as the night deepens and the heavy hands of slumber and exhaustion slowly smother us.

The talk of the detectives and the trauma wing lingers, dredging up the memory of the violent bodily reaction I had in the bathroom at the hospital, minutes before I met them. My body quivers slightly. I glance at Matt's face, shadowed and dimly lit by the trace of streetlights filtering through the blinds of the bedroom.

My eyes linger on him, searching for any signs of what he might be thinking, but he's staring blankly at the wall, lost in his own ocean of thoughts. Then he snaps his gaze to me and pulls me closer, and his hands resume their comforting rhythm of rubbing my arm and stroking my hair.

"Hey, what happened? What's bothering you?" he asks, and his voice carries that familiar note of protection that always tugs at my heart.

I shake my head and pull him in for a quick kiss before I respond, though my voice trembles, and moisture slowly fills my eyes—which I hope he doesn't notice in the dim light. "Matt, thank you for not asking what Alex and I talked about."

When I met him on the street as I left her penthouse building, I had told him simply that she and I had a frank girl-to-girl chat. He didn't press for details.

My body trembles as I wait for his response. I'm unsure of how he'll react, knowing what she did the next day.

To my surprise and relief, he doesn't push me. He doesn't comment, save for a quick shrug and a dismissive, "I don't care. How does it matter?" His gaze returns to the wall.

I'm not ready to delve into the depths of whatever is lurking beneath my reaction to the news of her attempted suicide. *Not yet.* I hug him tighter, seeking refuge in his embrace, trying to retreat from the feelings that I can't face.

His warmth is the only anchor I need. As exhaustion claims us, we fall asleep entwined in each other's arms. My final thought is about how tightly and forcefully we are clutching each other.

CHAPTER FORTY-THREE
Anna: Blessing and Burden - II

The secondhand Honda barely fits Matt as we drive to New Jersey to meet the priest. After Alex left him, he sold his beloved Land Rover LR4—the SUV we had bought together. Now, watching him squeeze his six-foot-seven frame into the driver's seat—his thick-soled sport shoes awkwardly pressing against the pedals—I can't help but laugh.

He gives me a glance, narrowing his eyes in mock disapproval. But soon his lips twitch, and he joins in, laughing loudly. It's surreal—this kind of joy has been rare lately. The sound of our laughter spills into the warm August air.

"I'm not sure I'll be able to get out of this thing," he jokes, his deep voice vibrating with mirth. "The priest might have to come meet us in the car!"

I clutch my stomach as the laughter bubbles up, as the tension of the past few days is momentarily forgotten. My sides ache from sheer joy. "Do you want me to drive?" I offer, still giggling. But I know better. He has this strange quirk—he gets carsick if he's a passenger. It's tied to his need for control, though he'd never admit it.

We continue poking fun at him, savoring this rare moment of lightness. For a brief time, we leave the chaos of Manhattan. Our hands are united, and our dreams carry us toward the church where we'll be married.

The meeting with the priest lasts an hour. He explains the rituals and the support available. I pull out my notepad with questions, and we get answers. As the priest talks, Matt and I exchange a look—a subtle smile, then a wider grin. The anticipation of the wedding fills the space between us, making my heart flutter.

But the lightness is quickly replaced by a tightness in my stomach. *I want everything to be perfect on our wedding day.* But then I glance at him, and the nervousness slips away. His confidence fills the room, even reassuring the priest.

After a prayer, the priest blesses us, and we start the drive back to Manhattan—the weight of the world a bit easier to carry.

As we approach the Lincoln Tunnel, worry begins to gnaw at me. Manhattan looms ahead—its towering skyscrapers both daunting and inviting. It's a place where you can feel alone, lost, or invincible depending on the day. The city challenges you, but it also offers a strange comfort. It is home.

Dress shopping always lifts my spirits, and I'm eager for that. We walk, arms locked, to the affordable shops I'd researched. In the third store, I find *the one*—a simple yet charming midi-length dress with an off-shoulder corset of lace, a sparkly pleated skirt, and tulle cascading just below the knees. I slip away for a quick fitting, make a few notes for alterations, then return, satisfied. We leave the shop and head to a street food vendor for a late lunch.

We savor each other's company as we stroll, chatting and window shopping. I'm grateful he suggested this plan. My chest expands with each breath, and my steps are light. This day has been a brief but much-needed respite. As we wait at a pedestrian crossing, I realize he hasn't let go of my hand all day.

In the subway, I lean my head on his shoulder, rubbing his biceps as he grips my hand. The silence between us is heavy—neither of us wants to talk about what's awaiting us at the hospital. Worry and nausea swirl inside me but I steady my emotions, drawing on our shared confidence. I take a deep breath, determined to stay strong.

As we near the station, I look up at him with quiet resolve and say softly, "Babe, everything will be okay. She is going to be okay." He nods, offers a half smile, and grips my hand tighter.

The hospital wing feels unchanged. The sterile smells and the hum of machinery are suffocating, and the staff move like cogs in a well-oiled machine. The detective who spoke with me earlier is nearby, chatting with another officer. He waves, and I offer a polite smile.

Matt passes through the secured doors after a quick check by an officer, and I return to my seat. Edward walks past on his way to the patient area. When our eyes meet, I expect a brief acknowledgment but he gives me a cold stare. It's as if my presence here is an affront. His silent judgment turns my stomach. *Is he blaming me for what happened?*

I shift in my seat, trying to shake off the nausea, reminding myself that we're all here to help. But his icy gaze makes everything feel worse.

After an hour, I spot Matt approaching. A flicker of hope fades as I see the gloom on his face. He looks as if something monumental has crushed him. He slumps into the seat next to me—his body folding under an invisible burden. The familiar tight grip of his hand is gone, replaced by a limp, lifeless hold.

I stay silent, giving him space, knowing he'll speak when he's ready.

Finally, he wipes his face and lowers his head. "Alex has regressed. She's just like she was two days ago—not eating, not talking, still restrained, still sedated. I thought my visit yesterday gave her the strength to hold on. But it wasn't enough."

He cradles his head in his hands again as exhaustion settles into every line of his face. After a long pause, he says quietly, "I want to stay here tonight and check on her in the morning."

His voice is empty—the warmth drained from his eyes. I feel his sorrow and my own unease growing heavier. I can't hold in my next question. "Is there an alternative? You can't be there for her every day like this," I ask softly.

I don't press further. I sit beside him, caressing his spine. Inside I'm crumbling—the uncertainty fraying my resolve, the familiar nausea and headache threatening to overwhelm me.

He rubs his face and squeezes his eyes shut as if blocking the world out. When he finally turns to me, he looks apologetic. His voice is cracked. "I don't know. All I can think of is her on that iron bed, restrained, sedated...that feeding tube. It's disturbing."

He trails off, and I can feel his helplessness. My heart aches for him. His paternal instinct to protect her is consuming him, and I can see how deeply it's affecting him.

This isn't the time for questions, but for quiet support. I'll let him process, give him space, and, in the meantime, prepare for what comes next. *Together, we'll figure it out.*

I press my hand firmly on his shoulder, giving it a shake and the encouragement I know he needs. But his face remains a blank mask. My heart tightens as I prepare to leave, but I push my sorrow aside, determined not to show him how much this weighs on me as well.

As I rise, I give one last piece of advice, my voice steady. "Babe, talk to Dr. Robbins and the medical team about Alex's treatment plan. Let's figure out how we can support her together."

He takes my hands, and his fingers are warm but limp—not the tight grip I'm used to. It's a touch that speaks volumes—not just of his exhaustion, but of how much of him this situation is draining. I want to pull him close, but I release his hands and step back.

A new detective approaches us. She introduces herself and asks if Matt is ready for the interview. He nods tiredly. He hugs me, pressing his lips to mine briefly, before he steps away to shake hands with the detective.

Out of the corner of my eye, I spot a woman approaching us. Her graceful stride is marred by the fury written all over her face. Her eyes bulge, and her brows are drawn low. Her rage radiates in every sharp, angry step.

"You?" she shouts, voice dripping with venom. "How dare you come near Alex? What do you want here?"

The detective moves to intercept her, but she pushes past her, jabbing a finger in my direction. "You devil! What did you say to my sister? What poison did you pour into her ears?"

She is yelling. Matt stands between her and me, trying to soothe her. "Evie, please, control yourself. Why're you attacking Anna? Stop it! We should be inside with Alex, caring for her, by her side. Come on, let's go. Please."

The shock of Evie's outburst rattles through me, catching me unawares. Standing on the sterile floor of the hospital wing, I feel a chill travel all over my body as I shake and tremble. The current surges inside me as my stomach and chest harden.

"Care? We wouldn't be in this hospital if it weren't for that woman. Detectives, take her away. Put her on the no list. I don't want her venomous air anywhere near this hospital. Do it!" Her yelling and physical gestures seem to have crossed the threshold of tolerance for the detective. She calls for a lady police officer to come over and escort Evie to the patient wing.

Matt embraces me snugly, enveloping me in his arms, but that gesture can't stop the tremors wracking my body. The comfort of his arms is no match for the stinging pain that spreads like wildfire across my chest. My back aches, making me feel as though my upper body is bending backward, breaking under the pressure. My voice is lost, swallowed by the shock of Evie's accusations, and her words—a cruel taunt—still echoes in my ears.

The nausea and headache rise faster than ever, overtaking me completely. I barely excuse myself before stumbling into the bathroom where I collapse, retching uncontrollably. The sickness is worse than it was two days ago, as if my body is expelling not just the contents of my stomach, but the very essence of the emotional torment that's gripping me. I clutch my head tightly, trying to keep myself from shattering, and spend a while trying to recover.

One word repeats in my mind: *burden*. It circles relentlessly—an echo in my foggy mind.

I fight to collect myself. *Matt doesn't need to carry my weight tonight. He's already shouldering the world for Alex. I won't add to his burden.*

I take deep breaths, forcing myself to settle down. After splashing cold water on my face, I touch up my face with shaky hands. My reflection shows the surface—composed, even if everything inside is a storm. I nod, giving myself one last push to appear strong.

When I step back into the hallway, he is waiting outside the bathroom, his expression a mixture of concern and exhaustion. I smile as I walk to him and wrap my arms around him, and my resolve hardens even as I fight the tears behind my eyelids.

"It's okay," I say, my voice steady, though my heart is breaking. "Evie's just worried about Alex. This outburst...it's understandable. She's close to her."

I pull back, squeezing his forearms gently. I meet his gaze, giving him all the strength I have left. "We need to be strong for Alex, for both of us. Let's do that, okay, babe?"

He stares at me for a few moments—his expression weary but filled with kindness. Then he nods slowly and clasps me in another secure hold. He kisses my forehead, and walks with me to the elevator. I tell him I'll text him when I get home, and he nods as the elevator doors close.

I move on autopilot to the subway, finding a quiet corner. As the train jerks forward, I crumble. I bury my face in my hands, trying to stifle the sobs. A few strangers glance my way, but I'm too lost in my grief to notice. Everything—Alex's suicide attempt, the uncertainty of her treatment, Evie's outburst, Matt's struggles, and our shattered plans—crashes over me. And the question I'm too scared to confront presses against my chest.

The train moves through the dark tunnels but my mind splinters as each thought slips further away. The relentless motion of the train contrasts my crumbling self, lost in yet another tragedy I must survive. I perceive myself standing in the middle of an endless tunnel, swallowed by shadows with no direction or hope of escape.

CHAPTER FORTY-FOUR

Matthew: False Hope - I

A s I walk with the detective through the sterile hallways to the conference room, two images keep replaying in my mind. One is of my little girl lying in that cold, clinical room—hooked up to a feeding tube, restrained, sedated, and wrapped in a hospital blanket that feels more like a shroud. The other is of Anna, the woman I love—yelled at, trembling, sick to her stomach, walking alone on the streets, heading back to an empty apartment.

My heart feels like it's being pulled in two directions by ropes that keep tightening. One rope drags me deeper into abiding love, and the other tugs me toward the sacredness of fulfilling responsibility. Neither direction offers solid ground, and I'm stuck, pulled apart by duty and love, both demanding something I'm struggling to give.

Meeting with the detective does nothing to ease my mental agony. I recount my history, starting with my marriage to Anna, the divorce, Alex, then Anna again, then Alex again after she returned to Manhattan.

My tone is steady, but it's as though I'm being gouged with each word. I don't tell her about the father figure and ward nature of my relationship with Alex—not because I want to hide it, but because it seems a truth too delicate to expose to the harsh light of this interrogation. If she asks, I will answer, but I keep it guarded, as if the bond is a priceless relic.

Fear grazes over me as I avoid mentioning Adam. I watch for any signs that she might bring his name into the conversation. But she doesn't. The fear recedes, leaving behind a bitter residue of self-loathing. I hate myself for even entertaining fear.

Where the heck is the eight-year-old Matthew? The one who took control of his happiness and forged ahead with unyielding resolve? Of late, with everything going on, that command and control needs to be forced now and then, instead of being my involuntary breath. I hate myself for that too.

The detective seems most interested in the circumstances after my breakup with Alex, so we discuss that part of my story once more, but in greater detail. Her questions are probing, as if dissecting every moment, every decision. Then she asks where I was the evening of the incident. I tell her that both Anna and I were working late. I played for an extra hour at La Grand.

When she asks if I was surprised by what Alex did, my whole body freezes. The question stabs like a blade, cold and precise, piercing the layers of my composure and bleeding me deep in my ribcage.

I stare at the detective. My throat tightens, and my mind blanks for a moment as I grapple with the disbelief that has yet to release its grip on me. *Of course I was shocked—how could I not be?* She stunned everyone. I tell the detective that, and my throat is parched, making each word a struggle. My eyelids shut as Alex's action pushes me under. I cover my face, trying to shield myself from the reality of it all.

She asks questions about Alex's habits and behaviors, but I answer them on autopilot—my mind still reeling. Finally, she closes her notebook, and the sound is jarring. I ask her what's going on with the investigation, given that nearly three weeks have passed since Alex was admitted to trauma care.

"It's protocol to investigate suicide cases to rule out foul play," she explains, her tone almost detached. "This is a high-profile case—a family that routinely receives death threats from enemies, both business and beyond—so we're being thorough, working to rule out foul-play."

Her responses are mechanical—routine for her—unknowing that for me, Anna, and Alex's family, what happened is a tragedy that has upended lives. The detective even smiles as she pats her notebook, stands, and opens the door for me. "We'll be in touch. Please be available for any follow-up interviews," she adds in a firm tone, handing me her card.

Before going to see Alex, I need a private moment. I lean against the cold wall near the water cooler, letting its chill seep into my spine, grounding me. I close my eyes, slide my hands through my hair, and rub the sides of my nose.

I've been running on empty ever since Alex returned to Manhattan. I'd tried not to show it, but the mental fatigue has caught up. Anna is exhausted too, but she processes emotions faster. I've always been good at letting my need for control dominate, but when I do let emotions in, they hit me like a bus, knocking me down hard.

I barely slept last night, clinging to Anna. I felt the same as when I started my recovery from alcohol addiction—gripping to her for support. Because without her, I'd have picked the bottle up again, trying to drown my sorrow instead of managing it.

I'm forty-two. By now, I should be better at managing my emotions, but the truth is, I'm not. False hope lingers in my thoughts as I try to gather the strength to brave what lies ahead.

I need the eight-year-old Matthew at the forefront. The fearless child. I feel him coming to life as I tell myself that I need to be strong—not just for myself, but for everyone around me. For Anna, and for Alex. I sense the control taking over, the confidence lurking just beneath the surface ready to be unleashed. I remind myself to rely on my core traits—to manage my emotions, block them if needed, and be there for the people who need me most, starting with Anna and Alex.

I approach the water cooler and gulp down a few cups, each one a small act of renewal. I rub my forehead for several seconds, feeling refreshed, and walk towards Alex's room, bracing myself for the harrowing sight awaiting me inside. I let my command drive me forward, and a steely resolve settles in my chest.

I'm going to get that hellish blanket off my precious girl and I will get her out of this hospital. She doesn't belong in this trauma care wing. No one does. Only Matthew, the in-control Matthew, can do that.

On the way, Evie approaches me with an apologetic expression. Her usual elegance seems fragile—a thin veneer barely concealing the turmoil beneath. She says, "Matthew, I disrespected you and your fiancée. You came to help, and I wasn't thinking straight. I'm sorry for my—"

I stop her, my tone slowly returning to full strength. "Evie, don't worry about it. None of us are thinking straight right now. We're all exhausted and on edge. I appreciate you and Edward staying strong and being with Alex during this time."

She covers her mouth and nods, her whispers of gratitude barely audible.

I step closer to her and lower my voice. "But don't ever attack Anna again. That's a warning." I retreat, straightening my frame, and my stern gaze locks onto hers. She looks stunned, but she quickly acknowledges me, and the tension between her and I dissipates.

A part of me felt distraught at seeing a woman of sophistication like Evie crumbling and hurling insults at Anna in public. But another part of me wanted to strangle her for treating Anna that way.

As we walk, Evie clears her throat, her pitch cracking as her words spill in a torrent of pent-up anxiety. "Are you giving Alex and the rest of the family false hope? Can you truly make her better? Are we just dreaming? You can go now if you think you can't make her better. No hard feelings—it's unfair to put you in this predicament. We'll understand, and we'll be happy that we tried. It's not right—our intruding on your future with your fiancée."

Her tone reveals how profoundly disturbed she is by everything happening with Alex. Yet, her feelings are clear—she's questioning my role, my ability to help.

I stop her about twenty-five feet away from Alex's door. The silence stretches as I think for several seconds before speaking.

Fixing my stare on her, I finally respond in a measured tone, "I don't make promises, Evie. But I will get Alex out of this hospital."

I pause, watching her reaction—a pained look, and a hopeful nod—before continuing, "We're going to leave this place, and she will heal."

I soften my speech as I say, "You, I, Anna, Edward...the whole family—we're all drained."

I exhale and finish on a resolute note, "Let's not push each other."

A flicker crosses her features, then she glances downward and releases a weary sigh. "You're right. Now get some rest. I know you need to see her first." She forces a smile, a small, fragile gesture.

Edward approaches and offers me a private room within reach of Alex's. I decline, stating that I want to be by her side. He mentions that my small bag with essentials is next to Alex's bag with her dresses and makeup kit.

Dr. Robbins has left for the day but has ensured that I have access to Alex without restriction. I thank them both.

Exhaustion grips me as I walk briskly to watch over Alex. The dismal scene of her frail body restrained and sedated greets me. *That hellish blanket.* My fortitude crumbles under the agony of the scene in front of me, but with each step towards her bed, I resurrect my grit and determination, vowing to make her better.

"Sleep tight, Alex. Tomorrow is going to be alright."

"I'm going to be with you."

"Just sleep. Don't worry about anything."

"I'll help you heal, my dear Alex."

"I'll take care of everything for you."

I murmur these pledges, hoping they will somehow reach her beyond the haze of sedation. My head feels heavy, and I rest it on the edge of the bed as I sit on the chair beside her. Before my eyelids surrender to the pull of exhaustion, I hold her hand gently but securely.

"Daddy's with you," I whisper, the words barely escaping my lips before sleep overtakes me.

I stand by, watching silently as the doctors and nurses bring Alex out of sedation. Her waking comes in stages—each one a small battle against the haze. One nurse opens the curtains, letting the morning light flood the room. Alex turns toward me, and a fleeting jolt of life sparks in her eyes as she sits upright. For a moment, I see a glimmer of the girl I know, but then it fades, and her countenance recedes behind the shadow that has taken hold. She slumps, allowing the medical professionals to move around her, and her posture is one of resignation. The doctor's glance darts between Alex and me. Neither Alex nor I speak. I move closer but Alex avoids my gaze.

The doctor announces that her vitals are good, and I force a smile but it feels hollow. He reviews the day's protocols, addressing the nurses and Alex, but she keeps her head turned away, staring beyond the window as the morning light fills the space.

I can sense the depth of her despair, and it twists my heart. It's not even seven in the morning, and the day is pressing on me. I think of how alone she must have felt waking up yesterday morning in this cold, sterile area, surrounded by nothing but walls that confine her. I'd hoped she'd find some strength in the time we spent together the day before, but that was naïve. I should have known better, known that she would need more than just a day of my presence to feel whole again.

I understand how she's feeling now, and I'm going to fix it. Not just for today, but for her future.

The nurse takes her to the bathroom, and on the way, she asks for her bag of clothes and makeup kit. After forty-five minutes, she emerges, dressed in a beautiful red summer dress, with light makeup. But her movements are slow, and she doesn't look at me even once. *Not a single fleeting glance.*

She returns to the bed and allows the nurse to fasten the restraints and cover her in that dreadful blanket. At the sight of the blanket and restraints, I turn away and exhale a long breath. The nurse leaves, mentioning something about returning with breakfast, but Alex remains silent, her glare fixed on something outside the window.

When the door closes, I sit beside Alex's bed and reach for her hand. She flicks it away, and I see a flash of defiance in her blue eyes. Undeterred, I put her palm on mine, holding it this time. "Alex, look at me." She tries to pull away, but I tighten my grip—my order is clear.

I know she'll obey.

Her head snaps towards me, and her eyes are filled unshed tears threatening to spill, her anger on the edge of release. "Why did you leave me all alone, Daddy?" she barks, her lips trembling with emotion.

I release her hand and bury my forehead in my palms, my elbows crushing my knees. Instead of feeling defeated, warmth blooms in my chest and spreads to every part of me. My heart drums in my ribcage, and my breath quickens as a surge of adrenaline courses through me. My senses are on hyperalert, and my body is fueled by a heightening stimulus—a stir that has escaped me for a day.

My chest expands.

It's because of that one word—Daddy. Hearing it from her lips reminds of the innate sacred duty I feel for her, grounding me in a sense of purpose that nothing else can provide. Every time she calls me by that title, it ignites something primal within me, something that makes me powerful—a man in the most fundamental way.

The world and all its troubles fade to insignificance. Confidence, command, and control resurface in me effortlessly, as natural as breathing.

Daddy. I feel accomplished as a male, as a man.

With my strength renewed, I lift my head from my hands and meet her gaze. Her face is streaked with a single tear, shining as if it were a fragile thread of pain.

"Did you hear my question? Why did you leave me?" she asks, the tremors bare, and her emotion is gushing as if a dam were broken inside her. I hold her hand, intending to ground her, to offer comfort before the difficult conversation ahead. Her resistance melts, and she grips my hand, seeking the reassurance she desperately needs.

"I had some personal work to attend to," I begin, my voice steady. "Alex, I had hoped you'd stay strong, as you were the day before. That you'd listen to the doctors and follow their instructions."

I pause, watching her carefully, waiting for her reaction. I need her to know that I'm being honest with her. But I also expect an answer.

Her features harden, brows furrowing, "What personal work? With her? Your ex-wife?"

I remain unfazed—my focus on the longer-term goal of getting her better and on a path to healing. With calm resolve, I respond, "She's my fiancée, and we had appointments to keep."

She snatches her hand from mine and jerks her head away. I watch her closely, noting the pain and confusion in her features. Gently, but with authority, I instruct her, "Look at me."

She sniffles, tears wetting her cheeks. She turns, and her lips part to speak but I signal her to stop, and my expression softens as I wipe her nose and eyes. I motion to her, urging her to stop crying. It's a struggle, but I know she will try—she always obeys.

As I sit, she continues to chide me, gaining strength with every word. "If you're going to abandon me after I go to sleep for the night, you might as well leave now. You have no idea of the pain I was in when I woke up and didn't find you beside me. Ask these nurses and the doctors—they'll tell you what they witnessed yesterday in this torture chamber."

I massage her fingers, trying to stabilize her. "If I go, will you stay strong as I asked you to, and go to therapy with Dr. Robbins? Eat by yourself? Show them your resolve?"

I stroke her cheeks and eyebrows. "Slowly get yourself off these restraints? Until you're ready, maybe you can even work from here? Start a new project? How about one of the ideas you shared with me the other day?"

Her voice rises, sharp and cutting, as she barks at me, "None of your business. Just leave." Her body trembles as she clenches her teeth.

I return to massaging her fingers—my touch gentle yet insistent. "It is my business. How can I leave if you don't tell me you're going to be a brave girl?"

Her tone, though still loud, has gained composure. "None of my business. You decide. Period."

As I caress her fingers, I give them a tug. "What does that mean?"

She pulls her fingers away sharply, and her brows narrow. "If you stay, you stay with me—completely. But if you walk out that door, don't bother coming back."

That line lances through me as its familiar sting echoes the pain from the weekend when she left me. I stand, straightening my posture and crossing my arms as I meet her gaze. Her expression is a mix of defiance and vulnerability. "I'm not going anywhere until you tell me you're going to be okay," I say softly, yet with demand.

Her response now carries a subtle tremor, and her chin and lips quiver as she speaks. "I've accepted my fate—on restraints, feeding from a tube, mute—for the rest of my worthless existence. I'll be okay. Fine? Now go."

My forehead wrinkles as I glare at her. I lean in, and my muscles tighten under the impact of what she said. In a stern tone, I ask her, "How can I go after hearing that?"

There's a knock on the door, and the nurse enters, ready to administer her food. I ask the nurse for a couple of minutes, and she nods, stepping away to allow privacy. I turn to Alex. "How about we talk after breakfast? Will you eat your food on your own? I'll ask them to uncuff the restraints."

She softens, and her acquiescence is both soothing and piercing as she replies, "Okay, Daddy."

I give her a half smile before making the arrangements with the nurse.

With the nurse observing closely, she eats her breakfast. Each bite brings a little color to her cheeks, though every motion seems to require an immense effort. I sit beside her, trying to anchor her. When she finishes, Dr. Robbins enters, and her warm smile is a welcome contrast to the sterile environment.

"Good morning, Alex. Matthew," she greets, her tone soft but professional. "Alex, are you ready to talk today?"

To my surprise, she brightens with an exuberant smile. "Yes, Dr. Robbins. But only if Matthew is present."

Dr. Robbins glances at me, and her expression asks a silent question. I meet her gaze, but my expression is blank—uncertain of the best course of action. I want to support Alex, but I'm also wary of how much I might be enabling her dependency.

The doctor and she talk, and I stay in the room.

Alex—*oh dear Lord*—is confident, as if she's returned to her usual self. She speaks to Dr. Robbins with poise and authority. She could be in the Cunningham boardrooms or addressing an intellectual audience at Harvard. It's a striking transformation that fills me with a flicker of hope, though what she says next causes that hope to waver.

"My path to recovery is through Matthew," she states clearly, her voice steady. "I'm not trying to make life difficult for anyone. But if he's not in the picture, just restrain me, and please go about your business. I will say no more about this."

I watch her with my arms crossed, betraying no emotion. I focus on the ground as I absorb her declaration. She is making it clear—without me, she will not fight for her recovery. It's an ultimatum that leaves me feeling both needed and trapped.

Dr. Robbins finishes her conversation with Alex and approaches the corner where I'm standing. "Would you follow me? Let's have a word in my office," she says, her tone firm.

I nod at Alex, who is being restrained by the nurse. She returns my nod with a smile, and her head tilts sideways slightly as she blinks slowly in a silent plea for reassurance. I force a smile and nod, though I'm churning with conflicting emotions. I follow Dr. Robbins, already bracing for what she might say.

CHAPTER FORTY-FIVE

Matthew: False Hope - II

S he doesn't waste a moment. Before she even sits at her desk, she jumps right
in. "Well, what are you thinking? What else did she tell you?"

I smile, though there's no genuine joy behind it. "My conversation with her
had a familiar air. I was reminded of the weekend she left me. She gave me an
ultimatum."

Dr. Robbins nods, still moving towards her desk as she sets her things down.
"Ah! Nobody likes those," she says, gesturing for me to sit. There's a softness in
her voice, but it's undercut by a firmness that tells me she's fully aware of the
gravity of Alex's stance.

"Perhaps it was wrong of me to ask you to come," she continues, and her
voice takes on a more reflective tone. "I put you in an impossible situation. But
I was desperate." She chuckles. "Doctors get desperate too, sometimes. I was
hoping you could convince her to accept treatment because I know she listens
to you."

For a moment, silence hangs between us, and the tension is palpable as we
maintain eye contact. It's as if we're both waiting for the other to say something
that will tip the balance.

*Is the doctor also pressuring me? She must have understood the connection Alex
and I share, which is why she called me. But is she expecting any specific action
from me? Encourage Alex to enter treatment—is there anything else the doctor is
demanding from me?*

I glance away, gathering my thoughts before I look back at her. My pitch is
low. "So you're aware of the complicated nature of my bond with her."

Dr. Robbins doesn't miss a beat. A smile crosses her face, almost dismissive.
"Of course. I figured that out in my second session with her, long before she
broke up with you."

She pauses, then continues in that same measured tone, "You are her father figure, and she sees herself as your daughter."

We sit in stillness, as unspoken demands and unasked questions settle between us. Dr. Robbins glances at her watch—a subtle signal that her next appointment is close. "Anyway, I'm glad we tried this approach, Matthew. I don't want to impose on you any further."

I look at her questioningly, and she continues, "I think you should get back to your life. It's my recommendation, not merely as a doctor, but also as a friend and well-wisher."

My life, with Anna. Anna. A pang of longing—for things to be restored to normal, and for Alex to find her own happy path in life-persists. *Talk to the doctors about her treatment plan, Anna said.* My alertness triggers me as I address the doctor.

"Doctor, what is your plan for Alex's treatment? Short- and long-term? Surely there must be something you can try." I stare at her with an expectant look.

She is unfazed, although she appears to think for a minute. She addresses me sympathetically, "I understand you want answers. Unfortunately, the options are slim to none."

A rock falls on my shoulders, and it takes all my strength to remain standing. My mouth parts slightly and my breathing becomes heavier as I stare at her.

Dr. Robbins adjusts her glasses, and the slight tilt of her head betrays her hesitation before she continues. As she flips through her notebook, her voice softens with a restrained sigh. "Alex hasn't spoken to me at all, save to ask for you. Every time I try to bring up the day of the incident, she shuts down entirely. Since the moment she was admitted to trauma care, she's been silent—you're aware." Her words land heavily, as a somber edge creeps into her tone. "It's possible that she may not even remember what happened."

Her statement hits like a cold draft. I force myself to keep looking at her, though my mind reels and my chest tightens. "She...might not remember?" My voice is strained, and my brows furrow as I search her face for clarity.

Dr. Robbins meets my gaze steadily, her expression neutral. "To protect her, her brain might have blocked out that memory—the moment she...used the utility knife, and perhaps even the events leading up to and following it. It's a psychological defense—one way the brain shields someone from unbearable trauma."

I try to formulate a response, something logical. "But doctor...she has a photographic memory. She's...remarkable. How could she..." My voice cracks as my confusion breaks through my composure.

She gives an understanding nod, sensing my struggle. Her voice softens further. "I'm not diagnosing her. Not yet. But if she's not talking, I can't fully assess her. I just want you to know that memory suppression is a possibility. She might have blocked it out to survive the shock."

She exhales lightly and pauses before continuing. "That's also why I wanted you to visit her. It'd been two weeks, and she hadn't opened up. I hoped that with you there to support her, she might feel safer, and we could move forward with therapy sessions—conversations that could begin her healing."

My thoughts spiral. I had told Alex not to discuss the past—to only think of the future. I was trying to protect her, to shield her from the pain that haunted her. *But now...this?*

My stomach twists. Part of me wants this conversation to stop—wants something to distract me from the possibility that Alex, my Alex, might have truly forgotten what she did.

Forgotten what she did. Could it be good for her, at least in the short term?

I know Dr. Robbins and the team will push for her to remember, to process the issue so she can heal. But right now, I need her to survive. She can tackle those memories when she's stronger—off these restraints, free of the feeding tube and that blanket. *That's my goal. To free her. Then we'll deal with the rest.*

"Unless she starts talking to me, no progress can be made. That brings us to where we are today, and where we were before you came in. I have not conceded—never will—but she has surrendered to what she thinks is her destiny." Her composure falters as she sits down and lets out a sigh. Then she reverts to her unruffled self.

"It's not what anyone wants to hear. But she has resigned herself to a life without you, on her own terms. In a sense, it's bravery."

On her own terms. Bravery. My mind spins as I imagine what a torturous life that would be. For the rest of her existence. *She is only nineteen, for God's sake!*

I slump on the chair, and the sting in my belly intensifies. I call upon my inner Matthew again, for this is not the hour to sit still and not act. I prepare to give her a piece of advice and ask her to get on with her job.

She preempts me by sitting upright and smiling briskly. "Anyway, don't think we—the medical professionals—have folded! We will try all protocols and methods. But you should return to your fiancée and the future the two of you are embarking on," she says, spouting the sentences with vigor, clapping thrice.

The core of Matthew is intact and ready to act and help Alex.

I stand and place my hands on my hips, staring at her with an amused, incredulous look. Shaking my head, I respond, "You say you understand my relationship with her—yet you think I can simply walk away from her after hearing her say she will spend her days mute and restrained? Fed through a tube?" I attempt to disguise the tremor in my speech as I finish.

Dr. Robbins' tone is matter-of-fact. "Everyone's life doesn't have to suffer because of Alex's circumstances. I hear your wedding is approaching—congratulations! You deserve to be happy with the woman you love." She beams at me. Her expression is encouraging, but it deepens my conflict.

A sudden pang of pain finally releases and stabs at my chest, leaving a tingling sensation in its wake. I close my eyes, feeling the sting as I think of Anna and the wedding...

Then I tell her, "Please stop this, Dr. Robbins. I'm not moving an inch from here until I am convinced Alex is going to be okay. And by okay, I mean leading a normal life."

She falls silent, and her demeanor shifts. "What are you proposing?" Her tone is serious, almost challenging.

"Give me a few days. I'll talk to her, bit by bit," I respond.

Dr. Robbins raises her pitch. "It's my professional opinion that she won't change, but you're welcome to try—I'd never stop attempts to improve her life. But don't promise her—or her family—things you can't deliver. You don't have unlimited time, is that clear? Days, at most."

I nod as I rise and thank her, but her words linger as I exit.

As I sit on the chair by her bedside, Alex asks me about my meeting, and I tell her that Dr. Robbins asked me to leave. A shadow flickers on her face before it floats away, only to return. She sniffles, twisting her lips as she looks away. I squeeze her shoulder.

"What did you say?" she murmurs.

"The same thing I told you," I reply, towering over her as I gently lift her chin to face me. "I am not leaving until there is a plan for your recovery, and you start healing."

She pulls away, turning her face from me for several long moments before meeting my gaze again. "We're looping in circles. I'll only be okay if you're with me," she says, unwavering.

I stare down at her. "Is that an ultimatum?" I ask grimly.

Her tone remains calm. "No, it's not, because I am asking nothing of you. You are free to go."

We are repeating ourselves. This seems like an excellent opportunity to take a break from the discussion—not that there was one—so I suggest we park the topic until later. She asks when, and I smile, promising I'll raise the issue when it's right.

I bring over the tablet from her bag and sit beside her on the bed, reading two chapters of a book to her. Then we watch a movie in silence. She eats lunch by herself with the restraints off, and I sit next to her. After lunch, I suggest she take a nap.

When Alex falls asleep, I find a quiet waiting area to call Anna. Before dialing her number, I clear my dry throat. My throat feels constricted, and the imagery of a gloomy forest in which two vines are pulling me apart floats in my mind. My need to control the situation, my protectiveness, my unwillingness to leave without ensuring Alex's well-being—all these emotions descend on me as I dial Anna's number. I cut the call almost immediately, needing a moment to regain composure.

Tension knots in my stomach, and I feel trapped. I thought I was prepared for this conversation. I had mapped an action plan to spend a few days stabilizing Alex, to find solutions and a treatment option that could work, but when it comes to Anna, my heart sinks. This is a decision I'm making without consulting her. The thought of calling her with news of what I'm thinking about next steps seems as though I'm slapping her in the face.

None of my options here are easing my concerns about Alex's well-being. Desperately searching for answers, my mind races through possibilities. But the answers revolve around me and my actions. I have to make some tough decisions, and Anna won't like them.

My mind drifts to another image that haunted me last night—a tattered tent being pulled down by two ropes, searching for solid ground in a murky forest of entangling vines.

Taking several deep breaths, I steady myself and summon the resilience of my eight-year-old self. I dial Anna's number. Her soft voice on the other end threatens to tear down the fortress I've built, but I hold on.

"Anna, the doctor and Alex both asked me to leave. But I can't. She shows no signs of improvement, and there are no guarantees that she will if I leave."

A long silence stretches between us, filled with unspoken pain. The stillness thickens, and I wait—my breath caught in my chest. Finally, she speaks, her voice fragile yet laced with incredible strength. "I understand, Matt. I want to help you. What do you need? Or do you already have a plan?"

Her sniffles are audible, and my heart sinks further. I remind myself of the big picture—the chaotic entanglement of Alex's, mine, and Anna's lives, Alex's family, a business empire, my love, my wedding, and a dream future with Anna. *I must find a way to resolve this.*

"I want to spend a few days at the hospital. To talk to Alex and get her to accept treatment and make a recovery plan she can stick to." I squeeze my eyelids shut and steel myself, and my breaths slow as I wait.

The suffocating silence returns. Then, incredibly, Anna's firm tone emerges, composed despite the weight she carries. "Tell me what you need. Can I bring your clothes and essentials in a bag?"

I mute the phone, gasping, marveling at her strength. *I could learn from her.* Composing myself with greater difficulty this time, I tell her I'll come to the apartment and collect them later. A dull ache settles in my chest, and a knot forms in my belly as I wallow in regret at putting her in such a painful position.

I thank her profusely, and she cuts me off, telling me to stop. I have faith that she will understand, because Alex, Anna, and I have a good grasp on what suffering is. *We're experts in it at this point.*

Late in the afternoon, three bodyguards from the Cunningham security branch gather outside Alex's private room, checking protocols and chatting among themselves. A fourth joins them, laptop in hand. Wyatt and Flint are there too. Wyatt shoots me an unimpressed look, frowning when he sees me. We were partners in crime, but that doesn't seem to matter anymore. None of them seem eager to interact, so I offer a mock flourish, "Gentlemen, no handshakes today?"

I stroll back to Alex, chuckling. She laughs along, and the sound is light in the sterile air. Then her face softens. "Matthew, they're being protective. It's out of love."

"I understand, my sweet Alex," I say, waving it off.

The atmosphere shifts as a detective and two police officers arrive. The scene now resembles a high-stakes trial. Edward and Evie join, conversing with the authorities. I sit beside Alex, and we start playfully critiquing the crowd, turning the tension into comedy. Her laughter grows with each joke, and her eyes are twinkling with mischief. A few glances come our way, but no one seems to care.

Edward remains focused, phone glued to his ear. Evie's the only one who gives us a brief, reluctant smile.

Dr. Robbins enters with nurses in tow. Her gaze lands on me, unamused. "Matthew, thirty minutes. You'll follow all instructions from them." She gestures to the security team. Alex and I exchange a glance, struggling to suppress our laughter. It bursts out, echoing off the walls. Dr. Robbins glares for a moment before her attention shifts to Alex, and her expression softens.

Once we compose ourselves, a nurse removes the restraints from Alex's wrists and ankles, while another stands by the door with the security team. I take Alex's hand and guide her outside for a walk.

After pushing Dr. Robbins to allow us some fresh air, she finally agreed—much to the frustration of the security team. They'd charted an isolated path for us that included grassy areas and covered walkways around the Charles Cunningham Block.

Flanked by the nurse, security, and police, I lead Alex to a quiet spot. She grips my hand more tightly, savoring the warmth of the sun. She takes deep breaths, relieved by the fresh air after weeks of the sterile hospital atmosphere.

When we reach a small pool, I suggest we stop. The security team protests, but I plead for five minutes. They agree with a warning.

Through her sunglasses, I can see Alex's blue eyes glisten with unshed tears. I pull her close, whispering, "You will not cry." She sniffles and nods, pulling me even closer.

"Matthew, don't give me false hope. If you're going to leave, go now. If you want, I'll tell you I'll be fine," she says.

I know her too well.

I look away, shaking my head as I watch two birds dart across the sky, then disappear behind trees. I turn back to her. "Why does everyone keep talking about false hope? And if you tell me you'll be fine without meaning it, aren't you giving me false hope too?"

We both scan the sky in silence, searching for the birds again.

"I don't need your words," I say softly. "Show me with your actions that you're healing."

She doesn't meet my eyes, still watching the sky. "Sorry, that won't happen. You'll be waiting forever."

Before security can intervene, I give her a firm, controlled directive. "Let's take it day by day. Like I asked you this morning. Today, we don't talk about this further. Understand?"

"Yes, Daddy," she replies, and her meek obedience is filled with trust. Her response melts me, but I hold steady.

At dinner, her father makes an appearance, escorted by Ted and Edward. He is clearly inebriated and trying to maintain a façade of composure. The sight is heartbreaking, and my chest tightens. I've been there—too many times to count—so I am familiar with exactly what he's experiencing. I'm also aware of how others perceive a drunk, and I won't judge him, nor will I allow others to.

As they approach, I briefly move aside, thinking he might want to sit beside Alex as she eats dinner unrestrained. But he motions for me to stay, his hand wavering slightly. Edward quickly brings him a chair, and I notice both he and Ted have bloodshot, glazed eyes—their expressions betray how profoundly unsettled they are to see the head of their family in this state.

My heart aches for her father, but perhaps seeing Alex unrestrained and eating by herself will give him a bit of comfort.

False hope, Matthew?

The thought creeps in, but I shake it off and focus on the moment, ready to help either of them.

For several long moments, the silence is heavy. She and her father don't speak—their pain fills the space between them. Finally, in a fractured voice, he asks her if she is okay. She glances at him, and tears well in her eyes before she quickly looks away. "Yes, Father," she replies, her shaken response barely a whisper.

He nods slowly, and the troubles triggered by her actions seem to press down on him—his family, his business empire, and his personal life. Ted leans in, whispering. They prepare to leave, both men looking more shattered than before. Her father bids her good night, and she acknowledges him with a small nod before turning back to her meal, mechanically pushing the food around her plate.

As they reach the door, I catch up with her father, gently squeezing his arm. "Mr. Cunningham, Alex will heal, and she will return to her old self. Please take care."

False hope, Matthew?

The voices in my head taunt me, but I push them aside, holding onto the fragile optimism that this time, it might come true.

What I said comes from one recovering alcoholic to another—someone who, I believe, hasn't yet been completely claimed by darkness and despair. When I fell, nobody gave a damn about me until Anna came along.

But Mr. Cunningham has family—and me. I feel a sense of duty to help him, as I'm helping Alex. And I will, if he lets me.

Wow, that's a lot of rose-colored glasses floating around. Which is good, right?

"Did you give my father false hope, Matthew?" she asks before I sit beside her.

Oh, come on already. Please, stop with this false hope thing. It's not false if we all work on achieving the goal, making it real. Talking without action is what constitutes unattainable expectation—false hope.

I admire her as she eats. We occasionally lock gazes, basking in each other's presence. In this moment, we're wrapped in an envelope of my making. The nurse at the door fades away, and so does the reality that we're in a trauma wing, with her on a mattress on an iron bed.

Warmth fills this envelope, and scattered images of the life Alex and I had flash before me—the first encounter at the gym, walking hand in hand on Fifth Avenue, her body in ropes and cuffs, mornings entwined under the sheets, the touch of her hand, the warmth of her kiss, her calling me Daddy, the evening by the riverfront, the night by the Manhattan Bridge, her crying on my chest after Adam violated her, the vacation in London, and her head on my lap as I played the piano for her. The warmth builds, and a familiar comfort takes hold.

She shakes me out of my trance with playful punches on my biceps. That feels familiar too—I let her punch my shoulders, chest, even my face countless times.

369

"Hey! Did you hear me? I asked if you gave my father false hope." She looks at me, waiting for an answer.

I shake my head and curve my lips into a gentle smile. "No, I didn't."

She presses, and her gaze is unwavering. "How are you sure I'll recover and be my old self again?"

I grin at her now. "Because you're my good little girl."

She scoffs, turning back to her dinner. "Sweet talking won't help. I need to see some action," she says, mocking my steady tone and mimicking my mannerisms.

We both laugh.

What just happened? What is this I'm feeling?

Contentment and joy fill me and escalate into an elation I haven't felt in a long while. I feel lighter, more powerful, complete, and...buoyant. *But what am I encouraged about?*

I don't want to know the answer to what made me feel this way. But I can't ignore the question, or it's going to present itself and catch me unawares.

Right now, I feel content.

Edward arranged for a spare bed to be placed in Alex's room, at the far corner diagonally opposite her bed. He also brought me an overnight bag, including night clothes and a change of casual wear. It seems Alex told Evie my sizes when they stole a quick moment during lunch to talk. I shake my head and sigh, but I take the bag from him.

"It appears you and I have moved into a hospital apartment, Matthew. Should we throw a housewarming party?" Alex says, and we laugh.

She continues, "Menu: tiny cartons of milk, fruit cups, mashed potatoes, and chicken breast. Oh, bring your own salt, pepper, condiments and spices!" We are in splits, and the sounds of our mirth echo in the small space until the nurse arrives and asks us to calm down.

The nurse, though entertained, checks the restraints twice over, then places Alex under sedation. I watch as the nurse pulls that hellish blanket over her. The pressure in my chest and the dull ache in my stomach surge painfully, but I hold it together.

Sitting on the chair beside her bed, I hold her hand until she quickly falls asleep.

"Good night, Matthew."
"Good night, my baby girl."

I try to shift to a comfortable position in the bed they installed for me in the corner while texting Anna. Deep pain in my heart pulsates with each word I type. The guilt and regret for making her wait for my sake, to let me explore ways to make Alex better—overloads me. It's unfair, and I am torn all over again.

I don't have any good options here, only tough choices. I picked one, but in the process, I placed Anna in a hard spot. The anchor of guilt at having taken advantage of her kind heart ensures that my chest sinks in pain.

Matthew

> She is asleep. Restrained, sedated, watched, and monitored by machines and guards outside.

Anna

> How are you doing? Anything I can bring you?

Matthew

> No. They gave me essentials and a change of clothes.

Anna

> You're strong, babe. Do what you think is right.

Matthew

> You're tough too.

Anna

> Did you talk to Dr. Robbins about her treatment plan?

Matthew

> There is no plan as of now. I'm hoping I can help with that in a few days.

There's no response for a few minutes.

Matthew

Anna, you there, gorgeous?

Anna

Matt, don't give them false hope.

CHAPTER
FORTY-SIX

Alex: A Room and Two Beds

My new routine begins in the early hours when the room is cloaked in shadows and stillness. I lie there and allow my eyes to adjust to the low light, then strain to lift my head just enough to watch Matthew as he sleeps on the small bed in the far corner. Seeing him there brings a mixture of happiness and thrill that settles my racing thoughts. For the time being, he's here, and that soothes me, even as a whisper of doubt lingers—*am I relying on fantasies of idyllic times ahead?* Perhaps, but I cling to them, nonetheless.

The bed is too small for his frame, forcing him to sleep with his knees bent awkwardly. I wince as I note how uncomfortable he must be—*I'm continuing to make his life difficult. But...it's necessary. I'm sorry, Matthew. This will all be over soon.*

Under the dim lights, his body moves slowly, and his breaths are deep and unhurried. My breathing syncs with his, as if he's drawing me into his calming presence and coaxing me to sleep. I resist, wanting to savor these moments.

Since he sleeps with his legs facing me, I catch occasional glimpses of his divine face. My heart flutters, and a warm ache spreads through my chest as a familiar desire stirs within me—a longing to slip into his bed, to feel his powerful arms wrap around me, anchoring me to reality.

Today's the seventh day he's spending with me. The first morning, he confronted Dr. Robbins, demanding she reduce my sedation. She dismissed him, citing protocol for high-risk patients, and the consideration that a restrained patient would find it difficult to sleep without sedatives. He appeared resigned.

After a while, she agreed to a controlled reduction of the dosage, provided I showed progress towards recovery. He then beamed and assured her I would make progress, and that it's his responsibility. But then, the uncomfortable questions of false hope and long-term plans surfaced, and I saw the flicker of doubt in his eyes and in the doctor's questions. In the end, the two of them agreed to allow a week to pass, reducing the dosage by small amounts.

Because of the reduced dosage, I fall asleep a little later and wake a bit earlier.

It's during these moments—when he thinks I'm asleep—that I watch him through my barely open eyelids as he texts the whore at night. The sight is a bitter reminder of the precariousness of my happiness.

None of us—including the doctors—have clarity on what my long-term plans are. I refuse to cooperate, talk, or function when Matthew isn't around. I'm playing a waiting game, seeing where things lead, and what he decides to do when the time comes. My heart fills with joy knowing he's in this same room, putting me to sleep every night and waking me every morning.

It's not the life I long for by any means, but it's more than I hoped for a few weeks ago. I take what I can, relishing in his constant care. I want him to care for me as his ward and lover, to give me all his attention and praise, to admonish and punish me when I make mistakes—all of which is happening here in some form or another.

A rustling stirs me from my thoughts, and I open my eyes just as he awakens. He does a few stretches and then comes over to place a kiss on my forehead, whispering a gentle good morning. A lazy smile spreads across my face as I drink in the sight. Then, he heads to the bathroom and gets ready to welcome the doctors and nurses who will bring me out of sedation. This has become the daybreak routine—a small slice of normalcy in this otherwise strange life we're living.

The rest of the day follows a monotonous rhythm, dictated by rules and high-risk protocols. It is a glorified jail that I've created for myself. The doctors and Dr. Robbins refuse to make any further changes, including removing my feeding tube, unless I agree to a treatment plan that doesn't involve Matthew's constant presence—something I'll never agree to. If I do, I might lose him completely.

I could always bring him to the hospital again, when I regress, but I suspect the doctors and Dr. Robbins would grow wary of involving him repeatedly, especially if he's married to the whore by then.

I think of that evening when I took the brand-new utility knife in my hand. The morning after having been judged a worthless burden by the snake Anna, I received an email from the private investigator I had hired to find dirt on her. The email was basically an apology—saying he couldn't find anything, but also giving me a couple of informational items. First, the whore had booked a mod-est venue in midtown for a wedding reception the evening of the Mid-Autumn festival. Second, the investigator found an announcement on a church's website that Matthew and she were to be married there in the afternoon.

I remember saying, oh, dear private investigator, what you gave me is worth its weight in gold. That evening, I did what I did.

I shake myself back into the present and notice the people around me, including Matthew taking care of me. He tries hard to break the pattern—finding new and subtle ways—even if it only changes my routine by a bit. For example, he requests the nurses let me rest for a few more minutes once I've eaten. Then he pleads with them to let me walk around the bed a few times before they restrain me. Then he gets them to cuff my hands in a way that allows me to hold an e-reader, if only for an hour.

I'm thankful for these slight changes, but I can't ignore the way he uses his charm on the female nurses. Anger simmers as familiar friends—jealousy and rage—hover close by, waiting to pounce.

The days roll on, and false hope lingers over everyone. Occasionally, Evie, Edward, or Dr. Robbins will raise the issue. We'll talk about it, but then it drifts away again, as if it were a ghost haunting the corners.

Sometimes there are arguments, but Matthew silences all of them with one last question, in an irritated voice, "Do any of you have a plan for her?" Then he turns to me with a glare. "Tell me how you're going to recover, Alex." His stare remains, and I shake my head and turn away from everyone.

I wonder if I'm giving myself a make-believe by thinking he'll stay with me indefinitely. My delight at having him by my side is tainted by the doubt that this might not last. The lingering fear that he might leave eats at me, but I push it aside to enjoy the moment.

Sometimes, I mention false hope myself, asking him the question, giving him an ultimatum without giving him one. I hate being subtle and manipulative with him, but I don't have a choice.

I have no conceivable reality without him in the picture. I have no life without him.

To break the routine, Matthew asks if he can bring in a digital piano to play by my bedside. Surprisingly, the doctors and Dr. Robbins approve. Music therapy, they say, is a well-established treatment. They place restrictions on the size and placement, but otherwise, it's allowed.

True to form, Edward buys the most expensive piano he can find—what Matthew calls a "slab digital piano"—and has it installed. When he plays my favorite track, I break down because the memories are too much to bear. I remember falling asleep in his lap while he played for me in the Weehawken penthouse. The contrast between those peaceful moments and where we are now—trapped in this hospital, him struggling to bring light to the gloom—pierces my heart.

Music becomes a small beacon of normalcy in this dreary place—a small piece of the life we had before everything changed.

I also notice how my family gravitates toward Matthew. My sisters-in-law have always had soft spots for him, and Lillian bonds with him just as they did. My brothers view him as the reason for Father's decline and the business's struggles. They're cordial but blame him for the chaos. Father—sober on his second visit—doesn't yell at him as he did during that disastrous dinner a year ago.

My family sees Matthew as a stabilizing force, a hope that things will return to normal once I recover. I wonder if they're relying too much on him to fix everything.

He has become increasingly involved in my care. I see subtle changes in how he interacts with the nurses, organizes his day around me, and takes charge of my treatment. It brings me joy, but also fear—the sense that this, too, may be temporary.

He takes breaks to talk to the whore on his phone. Whenever he returns from these breaks, tension hangs between us. Jealousy and rage consume me—burning sensations that linger long after. My anger is directed at him, at her, at the unfairness of it all. She took him away from me, now I'm trying to reclaim him, but she is still in the equation. Matthew approaches me with a calm that intensifies my internal turmoil, trying to defuse my agitation with acts of care.

The uncertainty festers. Embers simmer beneath the surface of this hospital room, heating and growing redder, needing only the slightest spark to ignite and blow apart this fragile happiness I'm clinging to.

I cling to his words and find comfort in taking it a day at a time. The hospital feels less like a prison and more like a cocoon with him here, though my situation is never far from my mind—*how long will this last?*

All I can do is wait for something—or someone—to give, and it will not be me.

My plan is simple.

Matthew is with me, and we have a piano, albeit in a 'hospital apartment.' It's not the life we'd dreamt together, but it's enough. As long as he's beside me, I can endure this. I can live this way. I have him, and that's what matters.

If he leaves, I will stop speaking and let them restrain me and feed me through this tube if they must. I'll become what they all fear—mute, lifeless, unreachable. I know he can't stand the thought of my living such an existence. The guilt would tear him apart, and he would return. His unwavering love would overpower his guilt, and he would come to me, driven by his fondness for me. *He has to.*

I acknowledge that I'm hurting him. I observe the way his eyes sometimes lose their brightness. He smiles, but I notice the heaviness that pulls at his shoulders and the way his voice falters, just for a second. He's enduring the pain I've placed on him.

I'm sorry, Matthew. I truly am. But this has to happen. You belong with me, and I belong with you. We were happy in the life we had, but I ruined everything. I handed you over to your bitch ex-wife. But that is a mistake I can fix.

He and I have to get back to the fulfilled life we had. Our dreams await. That plot of land in New Jersey is crying out for the house we designed together. I can see it waiting to hold the future we promised each other. I'm impatient to start a family, to carry our first child.

All I need is for him to take that ultimate step—to reclaim me, to choose us. The future is waiting.

He'll choose me. He has to. There's no other option.

I understand what I've done to my family. I've shattered them. Edward is a shell of himself. Evie's eyes are constantly red. My father is teetering on the edge of alcoholism. And my mother doesn't speak when she visits anymore. She just sits beside me, staring out the window.

The business empire is suffering too. I don't need anyone to tell me. Matthew has kept my family from discussing it with me, but my brain can evaluate the damage. Without my father—the face of the conglomerate—at the helm, speculation is running wild. The stock prices are plummeting, and the confidence in the empire is faltering. Ted wasn't supposed to take over for years, and while he's talented, he's not ready to command the largest conglomerate in the world.

I'm sorry, family. I've broken you all. But I promise, when Matthew and I are reunited, when we're on the path to the future we deserve, I'll fix everything. I'll rebuild what's been lost and take Cunningham Energy Conglomerate to heights no one could have imagined. Project GreenWind is only a glimpse of what I'm capable of. I'll push the empire into newer, more challenging technological territories. There is potential for the conglomerate to impact every facet of human existence, not just confined to energy, and I will lead the conglomerate towards such a lofty goal.

Until then, my focus is on reclaiming Matthew. I don't dwell on the choice I made few weeks ago when I reached for the utility knife. A tool meant for precise work, which I used to carve out an escape. No one but me understands the darkness I was drowning in.

I don't need therapy. I need him. He is my medicine, my heartbeat, my reason to keep breathing.

The ex-wife doesn't matter. This isn't about Anna. It's between him and me. I have control, and my plan will work. My stubbornness will force his hand. He won't leave me to this hollow existence. I trust him, because my daddy won't abandon me to this fate.

It's just a matter of time.

As each evening passes, I find moments of peace. Even though the shadow of false hope looms, I believe in my simple plan.

As the nurse administers my sedative, I cling to Matthew's words about taking it a day at a time and try to push away the nagging thoughts of what might come next. If he's not beside me tomorrow, I know he will return soon enough. I will not give up.

As I drift off to sleep every night, the last image I see is always him lying on his bed ten feet away texting his ex-wife, anchoring me in a precarious world.

CHAPTER
FORTY-SEVEN

Anna: Edward the Enforcer

The subway car rattles, each jolt echoing my turmoil. The nausea intensifies, a familiar sting. This is my third visit to the hospital, and I already feel the bile rising, just as I did the last two times. The headache returns, and I brace myself for another difficult encounter. I don't know what awaits, but I know it won't be pleasant—except for the brief moments when I can see Matt.

What was supposed to be a few days of him caring for Alex has stretched into ten. I hide my unease, but I'm flailing—confused and helpless. I recognize this feeling. It's the same one I had when my dad's condition worsened and when Matt left me for Alex.

More than anything, I miss him—the security of his presence, the warmth of his touch, the intimacy we shared. I miss our dinners, our jokes, and the way I felt safe in his arms. The life we planned, full of love and a future together, now feels like a distant dream. The thought of planning a wedding without him deepens my loneliness.

He connects through frequent calls and texts, but they heighten my worry. He tells me what he's doing but avoids discussing Alex's treatment or recovery plans, leaving me in the dark. Recently, his updates have shifted to bonding with her family, and it eats at me. Either he's giving them false hope, or they're clinging to him as their last chance. I know they're struggling, but false hope will make things worse. If they're relying on him, what will happen when he leaves? They'll fall harder.

He hasn't been working and put the Philharmonic interview on hold. I'm unsure of what this means, and that uncertainty bothers me.

Though I have a general sense of what's happening with Alex and her family, I lack clarity on the true dynamics at play. I don't know their motivations, and that's troubling because those will shape their actions—and consequently mine and Matt's.

I've tried not to pressure him, but yesterday, I asked him when he plans to come home and resume his life. He avoided the question, saying he can't think beyond each day. His words hit me like a blow.

So here I am, riding the subway to the hospital to find out what's really going on. His updates have become less revealing, and I need more than text messages to figure out what's happening. I need to be there.

As I ride, I feel trapped in a web of motives, tangled in Alex's past with Matt and her family's needs. He doesn't realize it yet, but he's caught too. I must help us both break free from this mess so we can move forward.

As I arrive at the hospital, clutching my handbag in one hand and his travel bag in the other, memories resurface. Dad's last days hit me hard—long hours in sterile waiting rooms, the constant presence of doctors, and the devastating moment at his deathbed. I push those thoughts aside and focus on why I'm here—for Matt and for us.

Each step toward the entrance feels heavy, and my unease grows with every move. But I press on. This is the battleground, and I'm ready to fight.

When the elevator doors open on the seventh floor, a security guard—flanked by a police officer—tells me I'm not allowed on the floor. I had expected this, but the sting still shocks me. I had hoped being Matt's fiancée might offer some leeway, but it doesn't. I'm not asking for access to the restricted wing—just the general floor—but even that is off-limits.

I ask politely, mentioning my relationship with Matt, but they stand firm. The guard's explanation—that the police want to avoid another confrontation—hits me like an insult, making me feel like an outsider to everything happening here. My frustration rises, but so does my resolve. I'm here for Matt, and no rule will stop me.

I smile and comply, and the tension in my chest hardens into steely determination. The guard directs me to a conference room on the ground floor and promises to have Matt meet me there.

In the conference room, I realize this forced separation from Alex's wing might be a blessing. Getting him away from her—away from the constant crisis—will give him the break he needs. Here, we're free to have a proper conversation, without her presence hanging over us. The ten days apart have felt like an eternity, and a chilling dread settles in my bones. I breathe deeply.

"Oh, Anna, I didn't think they'd put such a restriction in place." Matt charges through the door, pulling me from my thoughts. In two strides, he closes the distance, and his arms wrap around me in a tight embrace. He hugs me like he did that first night he returned after being with her, rubbing my back all over, grounding me in his presence.

He kisses me passionately, and our lips meet with a fervor that's been building over these ten long days. We savor each other's mouths, and our whispered words of love fill the space. The intensity of his affection catches me off guard, leaving me pleasantly overwhelmed.

In this moment, all I want is to be in the apartment's bedroom, where we could fully express this pent-up passion in ways only we understand. My thoughts race, imagining the force of his control, the way he would pin me down, exerting his dominance over me...

Oh my, my mind is wandering to places I need to avoid until these issues are resolved. We have battles to fight, and I must stay focused. I indulge in a few cherished seconds of his embrace before we reluctantly break apart, hands lingering. For several moments, we lock gazes and let the calming force of the connection anchor us, rooting ourselves in love.

"I missed you, babe," I whisper, my tone trembling. He cups my cheeks and chin and touches his forehead to mine in a gesture that always centers me.

"And I missed you," he replies, and his husky baritone wraps around me in a comforting embrace. Beneath the warmth, I detect exhaustion. He grips my hands tightly, leading me to the table. We sit at a corner, diagonal from each other, still locking fingers as if we fear losing the connection.

"I'm happy you came," he says, as he gently caresses my fingers. A part of me wants to scream, *Why don't you simply leave this place and come with me? An entire lifetime is ahead, waiting for us to fill it with children, peace, love, and happiness.* But I keep that question unspoken, knowing it's the issue nobody wants to address—Matt himself, Alex, and her family. *When is Matt returning to his fiancée?* I'll be humbled and happy if the notion that no one wants to grapple with the matter is wrong—but thus far, I don't have evidence of anybody confronting that question.

I kiss his hand, maintaining the connection as we begin the conversation I came here to have.

Though he has updated me on Alex's progress, he now goes into further detail about the past few days—her slight improvements, but only when he's present, her stubbornness, and the rallying of her family around him. As he speaks, an unsettling feeling grows. *Something feels off.* His language, his tone, the way he talks about the Cunninghams—they're drawing him deeper into their web, and he may not even realize it.

I close my eyes, steadying myself, then place my palm over his. "You're getting tangled in her family dynamics," I whisper. "It feels...unclear. Maybe even manipulative."

"Anna," he responds. "I'm trying to help. You know what she means to me, and I to her. I can't walk away. I tried, and you saw what happened a week ago...she regressed."

It's been ten days, but I nod, squeezing his forearm as he continues.

"At this point, her family and I have the same duty to make her better. We all need help. I can't separate them from her," he says, his gaze steady. "I look at her father, and I see myself when I was drinking. I feel an obligation to help. It's all connected."

I nod, shifting the topic. "Tell me about her response to your care—and the psychiatrist's. I know you've mentioned bits and pieces, but I need a clearer picture."

His expression flickers as he describes her reactions—cold toward the doctors but responsive to him. I press him for more details, especially about her long-term treatment and Dr. Robbins' prognosis. Despite his discomfort, he answers that there are none, and I finally get a clearer picture of her condition.

I cover my face, trying to push away the nagging feeling that something isn't right. Then it clicks. A thread unravels in my mind.

"Tell me about the day of the incident," I ask, urgency creeping into my voice. "Edward must have shared the details with you, right?"

His brows furrow in confusion. I cut him off, pleading, "Please, don't ask why—not yet. Tell me everything. Every detail."

He hesitates but eventually begins, his voice steady as he recounts the day. I piece together the story—filling in gaps, connecting dots—my mind is racing. I ask clarifying questions so I understand her actions in detail. *Something's wrong—deeply wrong.*

Halfway through, I stand, startling him. He looks up but I urge him to continue. He finishes recounting everything Edward told him.

My body feels shaky, and dizziness hits. I slump back into my chair, trying to mask it. My pulse quickens, and my chest tenses. He grabs my arm, concern flashing in his eyes. "Anna, what's going on? Are you okay?"

I stare at him with dry, wide eyes. He repeats the questions, and his eyebrows are squishing as he leans in. We maintain eye contact for several long seconds, while my breaths alternate between shallow gasps and held pauses.

Needing a moment to calm my spinning mind, I ask him to fetch me water. I'm not thirsty but I need him out of the room to collect my thoughts before I tell him what's on my mind.

When he returns a minute later, I am standing with my arms crossed and a half smile plastered on my face. I'm far from composed—my pulse is still racing, my breaths still uneven—but I manage to maintain a semblance of control. I ask him to sit, and he does. I sit down with him, straightening my posture and covering my mouth and nose with a hand. My voice is almost fragile as I say, "I'm going to tell you something important. But first, I need you to trust me. Later, I'll ask you to trust me again, but when I do, I'll also ask that you verify that I'm right."

His brow wrinkles as he runs his hands through his hair. I see exhaustion in his eyes and sagging shoulders—but he'll have to bear with me a while longer. He clears his throat and says dryly, "What is it, Anna? I'm worried about you now. You know I trust you. Why are you—"

"Alex faked her suicide."

The words escape my lips. I'm shaking all over as cold dread races from tip to toe. I interlock my fingers in a prayer pose and brace for his reaction, hoping he will listen to what I have to say.

His mouth parts slightly, and he becomes absolutely still. His face is a blank canvas except for the stony expression, and his vivid glower sharpens, drilling me. I am struggling to process this. I can only imagine what he's feeling as he cradles his forehead in his palms and his elbows brace against the table.

But that lasts only a fraction of a second. He frowns at me. "What the hell are you saying? Explain." His fingers press on his temples as his glare turns fiercer.

I try to steady myself against the emotions threatening to consume me. Love for him, the longing to rebuild our life, and the tangled feelings of anger and empathy toward Alex all collide within me. My head feels like it might split open, but I force myself to focus. My thoughts land firmly on her.

"Matt…" My voice trembles slightly, but I push forward, "before I go any further, I need to make one thing clear—what she did was real. No one can truly understand the state of mind she was in when she…when she picked up that knife. She could have died. We can only imagine the kind of isolation and despair she must have been—"

He cuts me off with a sharp snarl—his eyes are blazing, the whites tinged with red, "Anna. Stop. Just get to the point."

I can't imagine what he's going through, and I haven't even told him all of my suspicions yet.

I swallow, steeling myself to explain. I recount the timeline to him and connect the events with careful precision—confident in my deduction but struggling to remain poised.

"She decided to fake her suicide the morning after the day I met her." My vocal cords tremble despite my attempt to stay composed. "The exact trigger? I don't know. But the timing...it's undeniable. I hope you realize too, by the time I finish explaining."

I glance at him. His brows narrow, but otherwise he's wearing a mask. I understand if he doesn't want to believe—although it hurts that he won't give me the benefit of the doubt—but I want him to let me finish, which he does. I mentally thank him, though his silence is deafening.

"Throughout that day, she texted Edward. Though her texting him was unusual, the texts themselves were casual. Merely asking how his day was going. But soon the tone shifted. She asked him if he thought she was a good sister." I pause, letting the words sink in. "Do you get it? She was planting doubt. She was setting the stage."

His jaw clenches, and his fingers curl into fists as he listens. I notice the tension in his frame—his readiness to resist the logic I'm laying out.

"By afternoon, her texts became heavier, filled with regret. She asked for his forgiveness and said she might've tainted the family legacy. It was escalating." I exhale sharply, the betrayal cutting more deeply the longer I speak. "She wasn't only texting—she was also leaving voicemails. Her voice...may have sounded desperate, sincere. She knew how to manipulate him."

Matt grips the edges of the chair. His breathing is shallow, but I keep going—needing him to understand—even if it temporarily tears us apart.

"Late in the afternoon, she sent him one final message and voicemail. A goodbye of sorts. She told him he was a good brother, that she loved him. It was designed to get him to go to her penthouse—exactly what happened next." My tone falters, and I bite my lips to curb the surge of anger threatening to choke me.

He looks at me, but his countenance is difficult to read. I understand and empathize with him. I also perceive him slipping away from me, recoiling from the plausibility of my theory, but I can't stop.

"Edward was unsettled—how could he not be? Her words, that sudden show of affection—it was unlike her. He rushed over, of course. And when he got to the penthouse...that's when he found her." I pause, while my ribcage is being hammered. "In the bathtub, in a pool of blood. Exactly as she intended."

The words hang like a dark cloud. I can't breathe, waiting for him to say something—anything.

"Babe...can't you see it? She orchestrated all of it. She manipulated him, twisted the situation to get exactly what she wanted...you."

I watch him closely, but he is hard to read—his features are a mask of disbelief and anger, as if he's fighting every word I've said. The betrayal I feel on his behalf clashes with the questioning expression on his features. *He doesn't want to believe it. He can't find it in himself to believe me. And that is what hurts the most.*

He resumes cradling his forehead in his palms, which is a relief—I don't want him to erupt yet. I have additional logic to support my theory, and if he bursts now, we'll end up arguing, and I won't get to expound on everything.

"Listen, if I'm right, she probably sent similar texts and voicemails to one of her other brothers. I'd guess Sebastian," I say quickly, my speech breaking with urgency as a powerful surge of adrenaline engulfs me.

He launches up from his position in a flash. His eyes blaze and bulge slightly, and his brows narrow. Wrinkles form on his forehead. His fists clench, and his jaw tightens. It's frightening, and the fear of Matt fills me. Caught off guard, I scramble, retreating a couple of steps, bracing for his angry response, which could turn physical.

He lets a few seconds pass—the cold, dreadful air in the room thick—before his question finally breaks the silence. It's a hoarse whisper. "How did you know she texted Sebastian?" his breaths come in audible bursts as he asks.

I close my eyes, and a few tears slip out—tears of hope and maybe relief—knowing I have stumbled onto something that could help resolve this complicated situation.

I take a moment to clear my nose and wipe my face with tissues. Sniffling, I continue, "Since she planned this down to the last detail, she would have made sure at least one of her brothers arrived at the right moment. She wouldn't have relied on Edward alone—she created a backup."

He stares at me in disbelief, and his body is rigid. I press on, "She chose the two brothers her texts would have had the most impact on, driving them to go to her. She hates those two, right? You said she calls them 'Sebastian the Manipulator in Chief' and 'Edward the Enforcer.' Edward hit you. I remember you saying he threatened to kill you and put her in isolation during the interventions."

Keeping my eyes locked on his, I continue laying out my reasoning, "It's possible she texted the other brothers, but I'm certain she wouldn't have done it the same way she did with Edward and Sebastian. Ted and James already have some kind of relationship with her. They'd have simply responded to her texts or called her back."

I walk up to him, clutching his arms as I make my ultimate point. "Matt, she never intended to die. This is her grand plan—the one scenario we didn't consider. Giving up her life to win you."

He shakes me off almost violently and starts pacing the room, his fingers combing his hair every few moments. I watch him, trying to calm my own racing heart and pounding pulse. He finally stops, facing a wall with his hands on his hips, remaining there for a while before turning to me. I regain my emotional and physical balance, and the sudden clarity works wonders.

"No, it's not true. It's all coincidental. She was apologetic and regretful in what she thought were going to be her final moments. That's all. None of what you said proves she orchestrated anything," he retorts, and the words spill out in rapid succession. His disbelief is palpable, and the anger in his tone is unmistakable. His protective instincts are flaring up and creating a tension between him and me—but I expected this when I prepared to tell him my theory.

Though I'm hurt by his rejection, I remain patient. It's natural for him to feel this way—I've dropped a mountain in front of him, and he must be struggling to process it.

"Babe, this is where I need you to trust me, but with verification," I say, imploring. "Find a way to get Edward to give you his phone. Tell him you want to listen to the voicemails and read the texts because you think they'll give you insight into how to help Alex with her healing." My confidence doesn't waver for a moment.

"She could still have died. What if Edward had been late?" he yells, and it startles me with fear. I yelp and cover my mouth, taking a few steps back as he looms over me.

With tears streaming down my face, I pause before I place the last piece of the puzzle, completing the picture for him. "She—check her phone if you can. There should be a device finder or location tracking app with her brothers' phones mapped. She's a genius, Matt. She would have timed everything. Don't underestimate her."

When I spoke to Alex in her penthouse, I saw through her façade. Despite her brokenness, there was something fierce in her eyes—a love for Matt that burned like an unquenchable fire. Afterward, the image of her reminded me of a wounded tiger waiting for the right moment to strike. I knew it would come—just not like this.

I fall into the chair, hoping he will verify and validate everything I've laid out. Then he will trust me again. I won't hold his mistrust against him.

I stifle a sob and say, "I understand she could have died. It's undeniable. Also undeniable is the gamble she took with her own life, to win you. No one can imagine her agony, but it's time to acknowledge that and put it in the past where it belongs." I take his hands. "Get her the help she needs, Matt. Verify my theory. Talk to the doctors. Please."

He paces the room, shaking his head as though rejecting the idea. He stops suddenly, and his hands clutch his head. Watching him like this tears at me, but I know I'm on the right path, even if it feels like I'm walking it alone. If I must fight this battle without his trust, I will—for him.

"Babe, please, listen," I urge, stepping closer and taking his hands. "If the doctors know what we know, they'll have a new direction. Let Dr. Robbins decide if it's plausible."

His breath hitches, and his grip tightens. Then he slumps into a chair, burying his face in his hands. "Anna, I'm confused and emotionally exhausted. I can't deal with this right now. What you're saying...it's insane. I don't know if I'll ever believe it."

The sting of his words is sharp but I hide it. I sit beside him and squeeze his arm gently. He says he must get back to Alex.

I see his struggle—torn between his duty to her and his trust in me. The idea that she is manipulating him is too much for him to process. I ache for him.

I move behind him, wrapping my arms around his shoulders. "Just go back in there. Verify my theory. It could change everything for her treatment."

We sit in silence, breaths slowing, bodies pressing together, until he finally stands. He walks to the door then turns impulsively and pulls me into a tight hug. He kisses my forehead, and his voice is tired. "Are you sure you'll be okay at the apartment?"

I nod and hand him the travel bag.

As I leave the hospital, I hope he will see what I've seen and trust me again. His trust in me has been shaken, and I can't blame him—but once he sees it for himself, we'll be okay.

Tonight feels like a turning point, not just for Alex, but for Matt and me as well. *I won't stop until I've figured out how to handle her dangerous game.*

Once again, I pause and acknowledge the sheer depths of agony Alex must have been in when she planned the events of that tragic evening and did what she did. The chilling thoughts tug at my heart and I ache for her. My heart drifts towards empathy, but then I also have to manage this situation as best I can—by getting her the right kind of medical help. That is far more beneficial than feeling empathy for her. I ponder these thoughts and calm down.

Surprisingly, I feel a surge of confidence. I hadn't planned to see Matt tonight, but something told me it was the right time. The hospital updates from him had painted a picture of unpredictability, and my instinct drove me here. My body feels lighter, and my head clearer. The nausea is gone. My muscles are energized, ready for whatever comes next.

I know what I must do now. Alex isn't the vulnerable girl who once held Matt's heart—she's a threat. Although I'm not discounting the desolate state she was in, I won't let her take anything more from us. I feel empathy for her, but life is not fair, and I am entitled to fight for my own life and happiness. The stakes are higher than ever, but I'm ready. Whatever comes, I'm prepared to face it.

CHAPTER FORTY-EIGHT

Matthew: Friends of Alex - I

"My sweet Alex, this is between you and me. No secrets, remember? If you did it, that's fine. We can talk about what's next..." I'm being gentle, almost pleading, as I search her eyes for a glimmer of truth.

"Daddy, I don't know what you're talking about, and you're hurting me with your words," she snaps at me, and her voice trembles with anger and desperation. Her eyes dart away, refusing to meet my gaze.

I make another attempt. "My precious, even I can't comprehend what you were going through when you...I won't pretend to. But, Alex, please, I need you to talk to me, now that..." Although I can't get into her frame of mind on that evening, I know her other moves, and I sense she is withdrawing. I soften my approach.

"I'll help you process this and I'll be with you every step of your recovery. I will never abandon—" My words are soothing, but there's a tightness in my chest as I try to reach her.

"For the millionth time, I have no idea why you're concocting this story about me," she interrupts, her tone rising. Tears form in her azure eyes, making them shine with an intensity that's both heartbreaking and defiant. "I nearly died, and you're insulting me? Killing me again?"

"Don't yell. I'm merely asking..." My voice falters, and my heart aches at the pain in her features. I must tread carefully.

"No. You're accusing, blaming, shaming me," she retorts. Her hands clench the sheets tightly. "Your ex-wife called me a burden, and you've gone a step further, labeling me a cheat."

"Alex, calm down," I urge. My tone is firm yet soft, as I try to diffuse the escalating tension. "I don't want the nurses to hear—"

"Did that whore poison you? Is this what you were talking about for more than an hour?" Her questions drip with venom as she glares at me—her anger barely contained.

"She's my fiancée. Show some respect," I reply, and my pitch takes on a harder edge but the weariness builds in me. "I need you to take it easy. We're talking, not…"

"Please leave, Matthew," she whispers, and her energy suddenly drops as if the fight has drained from her. She sobs and retreats inward. "I'll go back to living under restraints, mute, and with a feeding tube. At least then I had happy memories to keep me company for the rest of my existence. You just gave me nightmares."

As I laboriously make my way out of her room, each step is more burdensome than the last. The urge to delicately confront Alex with the theory is now firmly put to rest. There is no delicate way to do it. That's precisely why I had told her I wouldn't talk to her about the past, only about the future. I made that commitment knowing her hypersensitive emotional makeup.

There goes that option, which wasn't really an option to begin with. Along the same lines, interventions will make things worse. Whether it's an intervention or my delicate confrontation, the result will always be the same—she will retreat into a shell and resign herself to a cold chamber in a mental institution for the rest of her life, knowing I won't let that happen.

I need to sit down for a bit.

I find a vacant conference room and lock myself in, trying to process.

I can't let this discovery go. I must try to get her the help and treatment she truly needs. The best approach would be to tell the doctors—who can remain objective—and let them decide Alex's course of treatment. *But wait—am I jumping the gun here? Who said what Anna theorized is true? What proof do I really have?*

I need to resolve this burning in my chest—reconciling what Anna said with what I feel for her. I trust her, and there is but one kind of trust—the unconditional one. She helped rebuild me. She is the architect of our current life and the dreams we hold for the future. I wouldn't be where I am today without her. We've traversed the fire-lined depths of hell and emerged stronger as one. We share no secrets, only the best intentions for each other. Every day is spent thinking of how to make the other happy.

I trust her.

Yet, I'm still reeling from the impact of her words.

Sitting in this conference room—trying to give my chest and legs respite—I attempt to collect and organize the information Anna presented to me. There are two things that strongly suggest she might be right. First, she asked me to verify—a cautious, considerate move. Second, she accurately predicted that Alex sent similar texts to Sebastian on the day of the incident. Not to any other brother—Sebastian—and she was spot on.

Wait. What? Anna might be right? You don't trust that she is?

I trust her. Unreservedly. Period.

Oh, these voices—shut up already. Since when did I let my emotions dictate to me? *I don't have time to answer that question.*

As I cradle my forehead in my hands, clarity returns, dispelling the thick mental murk. Like fog lights piercing the gloom, the things Anna said are gradually pulling me towards the clear.

She understood the gravity of her claim and how serious it was. That's why she asked me to verify it—she was being empathetic, kind, and open-minded. *And how did I repay that?* With outright rejection, shaking the very foundation of our trust. I let her leave the hospital wounded. Although she's strong, my open distrust and harsh language must have impaled her tender heart. I should have—

Stop. The best way to compensate for that is to follow through with what she asked—no, begged—me to do.

I feel better now. I need to find a way to test her theory. *Let me talk to Edward...*

But then a fresh pain surges within me. My stomach feels as if it were a charring rock. I haven't verified Anna's supposition, but that doesn't stop these simmering feelings.

Alex? My sweet little girl? Could she really have done that to herself, her family, and her business empire? To me?

She's my loyal and zealous ward, and I understand the grief and rejection she's experienced—twice. No one can understand the desolation she felt when she picked up the knife. *But to put her life on the line to manipulate me? Should I view this as an act of desperate love, or of sheer stupidity? Was it manipulation, or love for me? If it's true that she orchestrated it, how would this profoundly reckless act change the dynamic between us? What would we become?*

The darkness crashes down again, sending me into a tumultuous spiral. I struggle to reconcile my protective instincts towards Alex with the possibility that she might have exploited me—and everyone else.

I jerk my head up from my hands and sit upright. With hurried motions, I rub my face a few times and stand with chest forward and shoulders square. Exhaling a long breath, I recall a guiding principle, *One step at a time. Let's see what I can find to test Anna's theory.*

I drink a few cups of cool water, a welcome chill to my system. As I walk to Alex's room where she's waiting to have dinner with me, I cast my chaotic thoughts, feelings, and emotions aside. The cold water manifests within me, bringing a familiar confidence. I draw strength and determine to take command of the situation. It's how we're all going to untangle ourselves from this web.

While eating her dinner, free of restraints, she is her usual bubbly self. She talks animatedly, making fun of someone on the television, and her laughter fills the space. But my focus is elsewhere. I'm trying to read her, searching for signs that Anna's theory is true. I am familiar with Alex's every mannerism, every shift of her features, every action and quirk—yet nothing remotely indicates she orchestrated a destructive game.

She stops mid-sentence, and her laughter fades. She smacks my forearm lightly, shooting me an inquiring look. "What's bothering you? Did your ex-wife say anything that hurt you?" She speaks softly, concerned, as she shakes my shoulders with her gracious, yet impatient hands.

Her eyes are darker under the warm lighting. They hold steady—pure, as I've always known them to be. Not a flicker of deception. She punches my shoulder playfully, breaking my concentration, and I pause my search.

She was alone, with no one to care for her. She was in a corner—no, in a pit from which she couldn't escape. She was drowning, with no one to pull her to the air.

I shake my head and force a smile. "I'm fine, Alex."

She resumes her chatter, bobbing on the bed, and takes my hand. As we regard each other, she tugs at my forearm, and her loving assurance is firm. "Don't worry, Daddy. You have me."

I stare at her eyes. Every emotion I've ever felt for her breaks like rapids across rocks. I mask my turmoil and smile.

However hard I try, I can't shake the feeling that I'm an intruder—a criminal. Searching Alex's belongings in the dark of night deepens this betrayal, casting me as an immoral thief.

But I can't wait until morning when Edward will come to the hospital. I grab Alex's phone, determined to read the messages she sent on the day of the incident. I'll have to wait to listen to the voicemails she left Edward, but I'm too impatient to find something to support or refute Anna's hypothesis. It wasn't merely a hypothesis for her—it was a belief. That speeds up my determination to get to the bottom of this.

Alex's phone is in the bag of personal belongings stashed away in a corner closet behind her bed. The device is dead. I plug in the charger and wait, jabbing the screen as if that'll power the device on faster. Her passcode is simple—the same as mine once was—the date I first saw her at the gym.

As I type in the code, memories flash in my mind—a young girl in pigtails staring at me, her hand touching mine, our attempts at exercising, the cheerful conversations and laughter—taking me back to one of the happiest times I can remember.

I hurry to find the messages. As I review the words, my head shakes and my face goes slack. I go completely still with the phone screen illuminating my face in this cavernous chamber. Blinking slowly, my head swivels, and I glance around.

I refocus on the phone and texts. My limbs grow heavier. Exhaustion threatens as my eyelids droop. The hum of the machines fades, replaced by ringing, and then I hear my own muffled heartbeat.

As I collapse onto my bed, my mind goes blank for a few moments, as if it's been unplugged. When my thoughts return, they race so fast it's impossible to grasp any of them. My confidence and command—the traits I've relied on—are enshrouded in a smog of disbelief, leaving me emotionally numb. Vertigo sweeps over me when I attempt to sit upright. I stare at the dim, bleak ceiling above.

Even though I'm holding evidence in my hands, I still can't believe what I'm seeing. Anna's interpretation of Alex's communication with Sebastian and Edward is painfully accurate. The words in her messages do seem manipulative.

Alex

> Edward, I've always known you had my best interests in mind, though I resisted. I'm sorry for being such a rebel and making things harder for you.

> I hope one day you can forgive me. I love you, although I'm such a disappointment.

> Edward, I'm thinking a lot about our family and how I've let everyone down.

> You're a good brother, and I don't deserve you.

... and then...

Alex

> Sebastian, if anything happens to me, know that I always admired your strength.

> Edward, if I'm not around anymore, please don't blame yourself. You're the strong one who holds the family legacy together.

She may hate her father more, but her animosity towards Edward and Sebastian runs deep. They've always seen her as a rebel, especially after our relationship started, and they each dealt with her in their own ways—Sebastian with his manipulative tactics, Edward with brute force.

My entire body shivers as I realize how chillingly accurate Anna's assessment is. It's as if she was inside Alex's head.

These texts could still be a natural course of communication during what she thought was her last day on earth, a voice deep within me screams. A small corner of my brain clings to the belief that there's innocence left in this narrative.

No, Anna is right, because Alex didn't communicate like that with Ted and James.

I flip to her messages to them—a few scattered messages, casual greetings, and general check-ins. The stark contrast between these lighthearted exchanges and the manipulative messages to Edward and Sebastian sends another icy current coursing through me.

My pulse rises as I open the location tracking app, and my breath catches in my throat when I see the four circles—Edward, Theodore, Sebastian, and James—hovering over a location on the map: the mansion in their Upper West Side estate. *Did she monitor Edward's movements and time her...dire act?*

The voices that tried to reassure me that her actions were coincidental fall abruptly silent. I search for them, desperate for rationality, but the voices seem to be leaving me alone with my discovery.

The phone drops onto my chest with a soft thump—the burden pressing on me. I lie in stunned silence, and time loses all meaning as I wrestle with the implications.

I shift positions, but comfort eludes me. My gaze drifts to Alex's bed where her slender frame lies wrapped in that blanket, sedated and breathing slow and silent. The sight hurts.

Eventually, exhaustion wins at 3 AM. Too beat to decide whether I should try to sleep or simply survive the night, I finally rest, embracing a fitful sleep born of sheer mental fatigue.

I try to read Alex again as she eats her breakfast, though my bloodshot eyes struggle to focus. She's not giving anything away, leaving me questioning whether those voices—insisting the texts could be part of a natural, albeit tragic, progression—might have some truth to them after all.

She notices my red-rimmed eyes, and her concern is clear as she asks why I look exhausted. I dismiss her worries with a casual wave of my hand, telling her I'm fine and could use a second shower. Despite my lack of rest, I'm grappling with the idea that her love and zeal for me could have driven her to do what Anna explained.

My survival instinct—honed since I was an eight-year-old child seeking safety and happiness—kicks in. The familiar takeover pushes me forward. Edward is next—I need to listen to Alex's voicemails to him that day. I need to pursue the truth, no matter how painful.

Getting Edward to give me his phone is surprisingly easy. I explain that I want to listen to Alex's voicemails to gain clues about her mindset, which would help me communicate with her better. He hands me the device, already unlocked. I had half expected him to challenge me with, "If you claim to understand her best, why do you need my phone?"

But then I see his face—exhausted like the others caring for Alex. They are desperately clinging to anything that might offer a glimmer of hope, anything that could bring them closer to a solution. The doctors—including Dr. Robbins—have begun to wear that same shadow, though they hide it better.

As I listen to Alex's voicemails, I shut my eyes, inhaling deep breaths. My calm is almost unnerving—a clarity I hadn't expected. I accept Anna's theory, as all the pieces fit into place as I listen. The voicemails mirror her texts—same messages, but with the added weight of her sobs and her sniffles. I doubt Edward heard the subtleties, but I can imagine him listening to these recordings until it hit him—something was terribly wrong, and he had to rush to her.

A weak voice in the back of my mind questions whether any of this could still be innocent. But that hope is fading, becoming weaker until only the certainty remains that Anna is right.

It's decision time. I've never deliberated like this before. Instinct has always given me the confidence to act on my intuition. But today, sitting in this locked conference room, I plan my next move with precision. The urge to move forward is overpowering. *I'll face whatever comes. I'll adjust, but I must act now.*

Before I go further, I take a moment to reconcile my feelings for Alex. I'm not angry with her anymore. I'm filled with paternal feelings for her. She's a broken child lost in her own mess, but she is still my beloved ward to care for. She is someone who needs my presence in her current situation. And as much as it pains me, I know that what she truly needs is beyond my means—specialized help from medical professionals and a recovery plan I don't have in my sights yet.

My sorrow is deep, but it's not the time for grief. Right now, it's about action—about getting her on a path to a future she still deserves. I won't let her future be defined by a moment of collapse.

Alex is a brilliant young girl—just nineteen—with so much life ahead of her. I will find a way to give her the future she deserves.

CHAPTER FORTY-NINE

Matthew: Friends of Alex - II

*T*his *is going to be the hardest conversation I'll ever have in my life. But it must happen.*

I make a quick mental list of what to expect in this meeting. A strange laughter bubbles inside me, and I smile, heightening my determination. The goal in my mind is happiness—joy for Alex and everyone around her. That vision drives me forward.

One after the other, people enter the conference room, which doesn't feel so confining and chilly anymore. Originally, I'd planned to go straight to Dr. Robbins. But driven by my instinct, I chose this audience. The conference room, tucked away in the trauma care wing, is stark and sterile, with fluorescent lighting casting a harsh glow over the plain white walls and sleek, metal furnishings. A chill lingers, though the presence of familiar faces softens the atmosphere.

With a calm smile, I address Dr. Robbins first. My tone is light, yet purposeful. "Dr. Robbins, you're here as a friend of Alex. I'm saying that so you can talk freely, separated from your role as her doctor. There are no strings attaching you to your professional obligations and ethical requirements. I will address you as a friend, not as a doctor."

She smiles and nods, though her forehead creases slightly as her brows narrow in curiosity.

Turning to the other two participants in the meeting, I continue in the same tone, "We need to have a conversation. But please, let's all keep in mind that we are her well-wishers, with the sole aim of improving her life."

The expressions on their faces differ from Dr. Robbins's. Evie offers a half smile, while Edward remains blank. I keep my smile steady, attempting to put them at ease, but they're drained—running low on energy, motivation, and hope.

I bow my head slightly, bring my palms together to my nose, and close my eyes for three seconds. Then, with practiced precision, I present my findings.

"Alex's suicide attempt wasn't what it seemed," I begin, locking glances with each of them in turn. "She staged it. The timeline shows she carefully planned the outcome she wanted. From the texts she sent to Edward, to the voicemail that sounded like a last goodbye—she arranged the events. She knew Edward would come for her. She knew how to create urgency, how to ensure that he'd act. When he found her lying in the tub and bleeding, it wasn't an act of resignation and farewell to the world. She had orchestrated it all."

Dr. Robbins leans in slightly with her brows furrowed. She appears to be listening intently—her chin supported by her interlocked fingers, elbows resting on the table. Evie gasps and covers her mouth with her hand, while Edward's jaw twitches. I continue speaking slowly.

"Before I continue, let me stop to state that no one—including me—can understand what she was going through. I am not accusing her or disregarding her actions. She still could have died. None of us can imagine the pain she was in."

I observe them, and they're static, giving me a stare that fixates. The air in the room seems stagnant. I fall back on my resolve, moving on with a lump in my throat.

"Edward," I say, my voice softening as I turn to him, "she knew you'd come for her. She wanted you to find her like that, barely in time. It was her way of manipulating all of us, and it worked."

I offer a brief pause and finish gently, "Don't take my word for it. Please, review the timeline, texts, and voicemails, and think. It's true."

Edward's features contort in pure anger, and his fists tighten. His body trembles with barely contained rage. Evie's reaction mirrors Edward's, though less intense, and her tears swell.

Edward slams his fists on the table. His body is shaking with rage, and I brace for his reaction. But I don't break eye contact. I need him to understand.

I expect what unfolds next.

Edward rushes at me, grabs my collar, and raises his fist. I stop him, restraining him with a firm grip. Dr. Robbins yelps at the sudden violence, but I calmly ask her to stay composed as I guide Edward to his chair, seating him with a gentle but decisive push. He flares again, but I fend off his raised fist before he can strike.

Evie watches, her expression hard. He shoves me and rises once more.

"You bastard!" Edward lunges at me, and his hands grip my collar. His fist shoots up but I catch it. "You dare accuse my sister of manipulating me? Who I rescued from the brink of death! How could you think she'd do that?"

I grip his wrist, my speech calm. "Edward, listen to me. She's hurting. She manipulated everyone, including me...this is her plan to win me back. I understand this is hard to hear. I wouldn't say this if I wasn't sure."

I tell them of her intrusions on mine and Anna's relationship with her texts, phone calls, and voicemails, and even my suspicions of stalking and private investigators. I explain that Alex was forced into a corner with no other option left to reclaim me.

"Shut up!" Edward shouts, his face knotted with fury. "You think you know her? You think you know anything about what she's going through? How dare you?"

Evie stands, and her expression is pale but her pitch sharp. "Matthew, get out! You and Anna are the ones who've pushed her to this point. You're the devils in her life, making everything worse. You've been suffocating her, and now you're blaming her for what happened?"

She steps toward me and shoves me toward the door with surprising strength. Her voice trembles as she continues, "Leave! You're not wanted here anymore. You're not helping her. You and your fiancée have destroyed her!"

"Stop!" I raise my palm. "Calm down. I'm presenting what I found. Alex is important to me. I care about her...why would I accuse her?"

Dr. Robbins, meanwhile, remains seated, observing the chaotic scene unfolding with a look of deep concern. I make eye contact with Evie and Edward, who flick their stares away.

I heave a deep sigh and temper my speech. I focus on Alex's state of mind on the day of the incident—searing me. "Edward, Evie, please. I'm not slighting her fragile emotional state that evening. I can't imagine it. None of us can. All I am trying to do is act out of love for her...she needs care and attention—"

Edward's eyes blaze, and his voice shakes with fury. "Love? You call this love? Accusing her of faking her suicide? What kind of love is that? You've lost your mind."

Evie stands beside him, and her voice is lower but no less biting. "You're talking about her as if she's a criminal. Are you hearing yourself?"

I don't flinch. "I'm not accusing her. I'm explaining what she did, while acknowledging her delicate mental state. I'm showing you the events, step by step. I can relate to how you don't want to believe it. I didn't either, but we can't ignore the facts."

"You're delusional," Edward spits. "You've twisted everything. You're the one manipulating us, making us doubt her."

I stand firm, my voice unwavering. "I'm not twisting anything. Look at the timeline. Look at the evidence. This isn't about hurting Alex. We must talk about the professional care she needs."

The tension within the walls thickens—their accusations nonstop—but I hold my ground. I take a breath, reminding myself of the goal—to make sure Alex is on a solid path to recovery and healing.

As their voices rise, I let their anger wash over me. "You're angry. This is hard to hear, but we need to stay focused. For Alex's sake, we must understand what really happened."

As the minutes pass, I notice Edward and Evie beginning to calm down—maybe they're tired from attacking me.

Seizing the moment, I turn to Dr. Robbins and ask her if she thinks what I've presented is plausible—that Alex could have staged this. I remind her she's here as a friend, not a doctor.

She clears her throat. "Matthew's not wrong," she says slowly, choosing her words with care. "It's plausible. Based on the timeline, and what I've seen in Alex's behavior, I can't rule out the possibility that she planned this."

Edward and Evie turn on her, their voices rising in disbelief. "You too? You're siding with him?"

She remains calm. "I'm not taking sides. I'm looking at the facts, as Matthew is, and like him, I'm not discounting Alex's emotions. But this might help us reevaluate our approach to her care."

Their voices taper off and they become silent as they struggle to process what I've presented to them. I use the pause to my advantage, softening my tone. "I understand this is painful, but we need to help her. This isn't about blame...it's about getting her the right support."

I leave them briefly and return with cups of water. "Let's take a breath. We're all in this for her. Let's make sure we're doing what's best for her."

Evie and Edward sit quietly, their foreheads resting in their hands, and I sense they might finally see the truth.

In that period of silence, I speak kindly, emphasizing that we can't rely on unpredictable, unplanned, hopeful efforts to get her better—that we have to act on what we've found.

Finally, Edward speaks—a sliver of calm breaking through the layers of turmoil. His throat sounds parched, and his voice is deep and trembling. "How does any of what you say matter? She will shut down once she learns something has changed," he says, walking toward me. "You'll leave, get married, have children—congratulations. And she'll go back into her shell—mute, on a feeding tube, and in restraints for the rest of her existence, stuck inside a room in a mental institution. Is that what you want for her, Matthew?"

Now I am confused about why they put this back on me. Pushing that thought aside, I respond calmly, "No, obviously, that's not what I want for her, which is why we're having this meeting. With this knowledge, the doctors can chart a different treatment plan. That's what Alex needs—the right professional trauma care."

He doesn't seem to consider my suggestion, shaking his head minutely at me as he walks away to a far corner. After a moment, he composes himself and walks back toward me. Fatigue drips from his posture as he continues, "Again, does it matter? Let's say your version of events is true. She's still not going to respond to treatment—not without you. It might even get worse. You're more aware of her stubbornness than any of us."

I stare at him as frustration unfurls within me. I scratch my forehead and rub the back of my neck. Glancing between Dr. Robbins and Edward, I venture in a steady voice tinged with irritation, "Come on, shouldn't we at least try? Maybe Alex will reconsider, especially between us knowing the truth and the doctors suggesting a new plan—"

He doesn't let me finish, but places a hand on my shoulder, and his grip is steady. "The best-case scenario is she'll be exactly how she is when you're not there—restrained and mute, with a feeding tube."

Why do they keep thrusting those words into my face? It hurts.

He lowers his voice. "Is that how you want her to be, for life? Can you live with that?"

Dr. Robbins exclaims with a blatant air of displeasure, "Edward, this line of conversation is not healthy."

He doesn't acknowledge her.

"Go on, answer me," he says, crossing his arms and looking unblinkingly at me.

I place my hands on my hips and exhale a long-drawn breath. I fixate on the ceiling for several seconds before facing Edward and Evie. I feel empathy for them. This has shaken them. It's understandable that they're not thinking rationally, but I'm here to help. I'm trying to steer them toward the right trauma care for Alex. Their constant refusal to see—or even consider—my point of view is frustrating.

Have they surrendered?

Have they lost all hope that mental health professionals armed with the right information can help her? I'd expected we'd be discussing the next steps—medications, therapy, maybe a controlled intervention led by doctors—but now I'm preparing to start over.

Edward approaches me with a soft smile, a stark contrast to the anger he displayed earlier. Clearing his throat, he forces back a sniffle. "Tell me I'm wrong. You know her better than any doctor. Do you really think she'll behave differently if you're removed from her life?"

His loud words echo through the room. "Whatever she did, she did it for you." The declaration stings, and the emotions I've tried to suppress threaten to spill over.

I walk away, trying to process their reaction. I'd hoped they'd see Alex's need of professional care, but this was what I feared. Suppressing my frustration, I remind myself to stay focused.

Before I can speak, Evie stands. She wipes her eyes and faces me. Her voice is shaky as she says, "Matthew, take Alex and be happy with her, or leave now—but know you'll be leaving her in a mental institution for life. The choice is yours."

Dr. Robbins interjects, her voice firm but tinged with disappointment. "Evie, that's not fair!"

Evie whips her head toward the doctor, her tone icy. "Can you fix her, Doctor? Does anyone have a plan? No. He does. He is the plan." She points at me and waves her hand up and down.

She declares, "I'm her sister, and I'll be selfish. If Matthew is who she needs, then that's what I'll fight for."

She turns to me, and her face is suddenly serene, as if she's found the answer. The calm unsettles me more than her previous outbursts. The room feels smaller as frustration takes hold. The unfamiliar sensation of losing control intensifies. Control—the one thing I rely on—slips from my grasp, but I won't let it go without a fight.

Before I can speak, Evie cuts in. "Take your beloved Alex and be happy with her, or consign her to a mental institution for life." The ultimatum hits like a slap.

Her gaze locks onto mine like we're in a battle of wills. Right now, she's winning. My need for control is replaced by a desperate attempt to stay grounded I sit as dizziness overtakes me.

Did she really just say that, or am I imagining this? My mind struggles, unsure if my exhaustion is distorting reality.

As if sensing my doubts, Evie sits beside me. She remains cold, and her tone is sharp as she repeats her ultimatum, leaving no room for misinterpretation. Time slows as I search for a reason—any reason—why she would issue such an ultimatum after I've patiently explained what's going on and my intention to get Alex the care she needs.

Dr. Robbins glances at her watch and apologizes as she excuses herself to attend to her duties. Evie and Edward rise, expressing the need for a break and to check on Alex.

In orderly fashion, they leave the same way they entered, leaving me in stunned disbelief. I stare at the textured surface of the conference table, its intricate patterns intensifying my discomfort. More than anything, I feel trapped—caught in the grip of yet another ultimatum.

As I walk in the sun, the warm rays do little to soothe the chaos inside me. My feelings are a tangled mess, and I can't even tell if frustration or sorrow dominates. Am I grieving more for Alex, or for myself?

Every time Anna and I manage to overcome an obstacle, it seems there's a tougher one waiting in the shadows as if by design. I slam my fist into the trunk of a tree, and the rough bark bites my skin and draws blood.

What am I doing wrong? Why is her family unwilling to fight alongside me? Has everyone surrendered to the idea that the only solution is for me to start a new relationship with Alex?

Desperate for guidance, I call Anna and sprint through the details of the meeting. After a moment of hesitation, I apologize for doubting her last night. "I should've listened to you," I admit, my voice low.

She answers, but there's an edge to her usual calm tone—a frustration that mirrors my own. I hear the brief catch in her throat that hints at tears.

"You need to keep trying, Matt," she says, wearily. "Try again with the doctors. With the family. Push for a second meeting. It's the only way."

I don't say it, but I can already feel the futility. Edward and Evie have made their positions painfully clear. Another meeting with them will be just as draining.

I could try talking to the doctors alone, but they're bound to loop the family in. I don't have the power to decide, and I am not a medical professional. I'd just end up back at square one. Evie and Edward will either repeat the ultimatum or kick me out, both of which will leave me further from what I want—what Alex needs.

For a fleeting second, I entertain the idea of talking to her mother. Maybe she'll offer a reasoned approach that cuts through the chaos. But the thought doesn't settle.

The image of Alex trapped in a sterile room confined to a bed for the rest of her life fills my mind, too vivid to ignore. I can almost feel her mother's heartbreak. That would break her. Worse still, it might drive her to fight harder than Evie ever could and deliver that same brutal ultimatum to me.

Edward's words echo in my head. He's right. Alex is stubborn—so much like him. If the doctors approach her with new information, she won't embrace it. She'll retreat behind those walls she's built. Stubbornness will consume her and everyone around her. *Only I can reach her. Only I can break through.*

A freezing shiver runs down my spine. That realization presses down on me, and its consequences threaten to knock the breath out of me. My mind recoils instinctively, pushing it away as I force my feet to move. The path ahead feels longer with every step, and I can barely summon the energy to keep going.

I retreat to the conference room in Alex's wing. I stare at the ceiling as disbelief washes over me. *Could she have orchestrated this situation so precisely that it's now her family delivering an ultimatum, when in reality, it's her manipulation at play?* The thought hammers in my mind, a relentless refusal to accept it pounding repeatedly.

Did Alex manipulate everyone around her, leaving me facing another impossible choice between Anna and her?

CHAPTER FIFTY

Alex: Bloodshot Eyes

*S*omething is wrong.

I feel it pulsing—an ever-present unease. The atmosphere in this stupid hospital room has turned sinister, as if the entire place has been transported to a different planet. The mood has shifted, and the energy in the air is different—off in a way I can't quite define. It's been this way for the past three days, but today it's blatant. At first, I tried to dismiss my uneasiness, ascribing the sudden change to everyone being exhausted from dealing with the burden of caring for me while juggling their own lives. But today, I'm not so sure. There's something more, something I can't ignore.

Matthew's exhaustion stands out—his eyes bloodshot and his movements slow. That's the biggest change, and it worries me the most. I can't shake the feeling that he's carrying an invisible burden—something more than just my care. A knot tightens in my stomach whenever I see him, and my mind races with questions, *What's happening? Why does he appear as if he hasn't slept in days? Is he going to leave me to get married to that bitch?*

He says he'll be back in about twenty minutes—presumably he's going to talk or text with Anna the Whore. That thought claws at my insides but I push it away, trying to focus on the present. As I sit restrained on the bed after breakfast, Evie enters.

Her presence used to be a comfort, but now there's something off about her too. She's been wearing a near-constant blank expression—one that disappears when she's smiling at Matthew or Dr. Robbins. With me, it's either a stoic face or this distracted, distant look, as if she's not really here. It stings, and I'd never have expected my beloved sister-in-law, and friend to trigger such a reaction.

She moves about, checking to see if there's anything to tidy, but Matthew always keeps things in order, so she has nothing to do. She's restless, and that unsettles me.

Instead of sitting with me and chatting as she always does, she seems eager to leave. There's a tension in the air that I can't quite place, but it's making my skin prickle. She asks me in a monotonous voice if I need anything, and her tone is a stark contrast to her usual cheerful, comforting tone. The change in her demeanor pains me, leaving me confused.

I try to fill the silence, hoping to bridge whatever wall she's built between us. I throw out compliments on her hair and outfit and add in a bit of humor, but her responses are cold and clipped—just monosyllabic answers that stick in my throat. It's like speaking to a stranger. My heart sinks with each word she doesn't say.

During the midday check-in, as the doctor and Dr. Robbins review my vitals, the room feels suffocating. The tension in the air presses against my chest, making each breath harder to take than the last. I glance around, and my eyes land on Evie to find her gaze fixed on me. Her stare is hard and unblinking. Her eyes—cold and flinty—send a jolt of unease through me.

Edward's demeanor mirrors hers—distant. Gone is the protective energy he used to radiate, the energy I had grown accustomed to since I was admitted. He avoids my gaze, and when he speaks, it's as if each word is a chore—emotionless. I feel the disconnect, the absence of warmth from my family.

What's happening? My chest is a vise that refuses to loosen. My family—the ones who should be here for me—are pushing me away. They're holding something back—something I'm not allowed to know—and it is driving me insane. I can feel it in the space between us, in the way they look at me now.

What changed? What am I missing?

One thing, however, hasn't changed—Matthew's ever-present love, care, and attention. Although he looks exhausted—his bloodshot eyes now a constant—he never falters in attending to me. His hands are always there, steady and sure, but the shadow covering his eyes is impossible to ignore. It's even there when he smiles his greatest hits at me. Those smiles that always told me the world was right now deepen the pit of disquiet in my stomach, and the veil over his features dampens the joy he evokes.

I've asked him about it gently, trying to understand what's happening, but he brushes me off, telling me everything's fine. But I don't believe him. The cold weight in my chest grows with each dismissive smile. *Something is wrong.* I keep pressing him for answers, growing desperate with each repeated question.

With an authority that drives the familiar fear in me, he commands me not to ask again. The chill runs through me as I nod, too terrified to defy him. I want to push, to demand the truth, but I don't—because submitting makes me happier. Obeying him brings a familiar sense of relief.

But I can't ignore the signs—they leave me floating in the uncertainty of what's happening around me.

The change extends to Dr. Robbins as well. She seems unusually subdued, and her presence lacks its previous warmth. Before she heads home for the day, she comes in for a chat. First, she does her routine checks, but those seem perfunctory. Matthew is present, as that's my condition to talk to anyone. She chooses her words carefully, asking if I want to talk about the day of the incident or restart therapy sessions. Her voice is soft, almost coaxing, but it makes me feel cornered.

Panic washes over me, and I deflect, clinging to the one pledge Matthew made—to focus on the future and not the past. I tell Dr. Robbins that I want to focus on what's ahead, hoping it will ease the tension that has settled like a thick fog between us. But her gaze, though kind, peers right inside me, and she leaves with a lifeless good evening. Her departure feels final, like a door she has closed behind her, and it sends a shiver down my spine.

The nurse just sedated me for the night, and I'll be drifting off soon. But the unease that has been biting at me all day refuses to let go. I'm convinced something has changed, and I can't shake my intuition that everyone is hiding something. A cold dread settles over me as I worry Matthew might leave me here in this torture chamber, despite his assurances to the contrary. The thought is unbearable, and I lie awake, trying to prolong my consciousness for fear that if I sleep, I'll wake up to an empty cell of agony again.

I stare at the ceiling, and my mind races, wondering if the life I'm clinging to is slipping away. The sedatives are too strong though, racing faster than my thoughts and pulling me into darkness...I fight to stay awake, but it's no use.

The darkness swallows me whole, and I'm left alone with my nightmares.

CHAPTER
FIFTY-ONE

Anna: Love and Grace

The look on his face says it all.

I had just opened the blinds to the morning light when he came in, the rays of the sun somehow failing to reach him at the door.

There's no, "My sweet angel," "Oh, my gorgeous," or "How's my darling?" The absence of his usual endearments leaves a deafening void.

His expression conveys his impossible choice, which he battles to articulate. His body states the heartbreak that he came here to reveal. I hope he knows he doesn't need words. He better not speak because if my world shatters any further, all that will be left is dust.

His eyes have lost their vivid viridian glow—they're a dull emerald. His disheveled hair and stubble add to the image of a man defeated. He stands hunched over, as if his decision has physically bent him. His broad, muscular chest seems deflated, like the air has been sucked out of his lungs.

But it's the glisten in his eyes in the golden light that tells me of a catastrophe. I've never seen moisture in his eyes—I'd always imagined he had no tear ducts. The image of him standing there—the embodiment of resignation with tears in his lackluster green eyes—tells me everything I need to know.

He keeps his distance. His head tilts and his lips part, but no words come forth. The mix of features on his face—quivering chin, dark circles under his eyes, hollowed cheeks—piles atop a solid foundation of exhaustion. His shoulders curl as his hands and feet remain still.

His body and expression give it away as he attempts to speak—not that he needs to. My heart sinks, beginning its long descent. My world slows to a crawl, and my thoughts disintegrate. I fall to my knees with a thud on the wooden floor of our apartment. The force of the contact echoes inside my head like a sudden clap of thunder. The impact of my fall reverberates to the top of my skull. I inhale sharply, gasping for breath as my torso collapses under the weight of what I instinctively understand.

Fragments of text conversations and phone calls from the past few days flash across my hollow mind.

"Babe...I was supposed to go off birth control last weekend. We planned a cozy vacation, remember?"

"Anna...I...Can I come talk to you later? It's difficult here..."

Matt, we missed the appointment at the reception venue.

"I...I'll call you or come to you, Anna..."

I am numb...yes, it's as if I am anesthetized. I'm floating outside my frame, disconnected from reality. His tears will have to compensate for mine because I'm unable to cry, incapable of reaction. I am wrapped in a potent detachment, a protective shell against the shattering world around me. Time slows down, and I tune out everything except the image of him, while my mind replays our recent conversations.

My skin tingles as dizziness sets in. The world blurs as I struggle to process the inevitable. After an eternity, I attempt to rise, but my legs give way, and I collapse again. He rushes to help, arms outstretched, but I stop him with a feeble show of my palms. His arms drop, and I slowly, painfully, rise to my feet, but each movement is a battle.

My eyes remain dry, my breaths shallow. I move toward the bedroom as if I were a broken-down robot. I fall onto the bed and clutch a pillow, staring blankly at the wall, which is as empty as my world has just become.

I lie there with my gaze fixed on nothing, unable to focus. Distorted images, sounds, and memories flood my mind, crashing into my consciousness. I lose track of time. Then the flood returns, swirling so fast I can't follow my thoughts, and again it vanishes, leaving me in the void. This cycle repeats endlessly, and each wave leaves me more hollowed.

My throat stings with the effort to restrain tears that won't come. I knew he was struggling, battling things I can't even begin to comprehend, and I knew he would decide soon. But this...this is not the decision I was expecting him to make. His journey through conflict, grief, and sorrow has been agonizing, but I didn't expect him to lose focus on us.

Hours later, the numbness shatters, and reality crashes in. The dam suppressing my tears bursts, and I am left howling alone in this bedroom—a place that once held warmth, comfort, love, protection, and dreams, now cold and barren.

As I weep, a cry erupts from deep within me. It is as if every drop of blood and water is being extracted to fuel this endless spate of tears. My wail is raw, a bellow filled with unimaginable pain. It's not just heartbreak—it's love lost, dreams shattered, and a future rewritten. This grief tears me apart completely.

The hours stretch, yet the tears continue to flow, a relentless river of sorrow. Each gut-wrenching cry summons more, a testament to the bond that was forged in the fiery pits of anguish.

Was that bond so easily broken?

I know—though my mind struggles to find coherence in the chaos—that he couldn't have made this decision lightly, and I hold on to that truth. But in the end he made it, and thus I am mercilessly cast aside, left to grapple with the devastating reality of a future without him.

As my tear ducts run dry and I lose the strength to even cry, I blink and glance at the time—late afternoon. Amid the chaos of my breakdown and the fragmented processing of my disordered thoughts, one truth stands like an unshakable mountain: *I love Matt.* It's a truth I can't deny—a belief that has shaped me and made me the strong woman I've become since my dad's death. Well before we were married, that fact was the foundation of my desire to become a better version of who I was, for him and for us.

That faith gave me the spring in my step, the rush in my blood, the energy in my muscles. It taught me, admonished me, corrected me, and picked me up when I faltered.

Though my world is broken, I begin to pull it together, piece by piece. There are things I need to do, and the first is to ensure that his decision doesn't destroy me. There's only one way to achieve that. What I am about to give him—the words I am going to say to him—will be to protect my fragile heart, so it doesn't shatter beyond healing.

The simple truth—that I, Anna, will never stop loving Matt—drives me forward, while the wretchedness burns inside me. There are many decisions I must make, and I've made the first one. *Onto the next.*

With great effort, I head to the bathroom, composing my thoughts and steadying my breath. I wash my face, straighten my hair, and then walk to the living room to see him.

I am determined to make this easy for him, because if I don't, it will be devastating for me. He won't get anger or bitterness from me—that will destroy me further. As I walk to the living room, each step is a reflection of our love, the life we planned, and how I will now have to pursue happiness on my own terms. Although my thoughts are scattered, the thread of my love for him remains taut and strong, guiding me forward.

Despite the burning ravaging me, I gather the strength to stay strong for him because that's what he needs most from me. He's sacrificed something he holds sacred, and he deserves to heal.

In the living room, I find him sitting on the floor slumped against the sofa. He looks thoroughly defeated. I take a seat opposite him, watching as his arms hang, heavy and lifeless. He meets my eyes with the same expression from earlier, only worse now—he's aged in just a few days, and it hits me like a punch.

Tears threaten, but I hold them back, reminding myself I must be strong. I sniffle and clear my throat, my voice tight. I take a sip from a water bottle, trying to steady myself.

His gaze stays fixed on mine, drained and empty. "Matt," I say, my voice trembling but firm. "I need you to listen. Don't speak." His features twist, and guilt, pain, and helplessness are etched into his face.

Summoning all the strength I have left, I push through the stinging grief. "I will stay on the path I chose...the life I chose. I will pursue happiness. I know it's what you want for me, what my dad wanted for me. But more than that, it's what I want."

He slaps his face with both hands—the sound sharp in the quiet room—before shaking his head, his body shuddering. Seeing him so broken tears at me, but I hold steady, unwilling to give him comfort. I want to take his pain away, but not like this—not in the way either of us would wish.

I fight back the sobs and force the words out. "I need you to not worry about me. Look at me," I command, my voice rising just enough to cut through the silence. He meets my eyes, his gaze dull and heavy with exhaustion.

In a deliberate voice, I say, "I will be fine."

I feel my strength falter as my words sink in, but I've said what I needed to. I sit still, covering my nose and mouth, watching him twist and turn in agony. He's fighting the urge to speak, and his body is trembling as if he's desperate to comfort me. But he holds back, resigned to his decision. He raises his hands, then lets them fall limply. The sight of him in such torment is too much to take. The tension in the room thickens, but I remain silent. He's torn between what he wants to say and my command, and the pain in his eyes is unbearable.

I rise to my feet and cross my arms, trying to steel myself. I look down at him as he searches my face, pleading silently, but I won't give in.

I'm in control, and I will heal on my own terms.

I take a deep breath, feeling the tears push to the surface but suppressing them with every ounce of will I have left.

I walk to the door, open it, and step aside. I stand rooted, praying he leaves before I fall apart. He hesitates, then takes one last look around our apartment. My chest tightens as he rubs his face, then runs his fingers through his hair, as his gaze lingers on me.

At the door, he pauses again, looking at me with those glazed eyes. I almost crumble under his sadness. But I hold my ground, though my breath quickens, and my heart is about to break. I'm on the edge of falling apart, but I take a step back and stay firm.

He walks out, and as I close the door behind him, the soft click feels like the world shifting under me. It sends me crashing into a dark void.

It's over.

The silence is deafening. The apartment, once filled with the promise of our shared future, is now a hollow shell. The dam I've been holding back breaks free. My cries tear through the stillness, filled with the loss of everything we could have had. It's not just sadness—it's everything slipping away.

I collapse, the pieces of my heart irretrievable.

Shrouded in darkness, I wake up to a silence that feels unnatural, a void I've never experienced thus far. My body stirs with an eerie alertness. I have no awareness of time or day, but my senses seem heightened as each one picks up on the profound stillness that surrounds me. The night is unnervingly quiet. The usual clank of the rickety air conditioner is absent, and I can't even hear my own breath. My pulse is steady—a comfortable rhythm that's keeping me anchored to my new reality.

A flicker of resolve grows within me—small and tentative at first, but gaining strength with each passing moment. I know I must go on—I must live and find happiness. If not for me, then for Matt and my dad. Despite writhing in despair, that flicker of determination builds.

I will survive this, and I will emerge stronger, even if it takes every ounce of my willpower. I can do it—I must.

Beneath the layers of torment and grief, a basic truth remains, burning as brightly as an unquenchable fire. It's the guiding principle that fuels my resolve: *I love Matt.*

And amid all this mental turbulence, a small smile forms on my lips as I remember something crucial.

The look on his face when he walked in this morning said it all: *I have his heart.*

He has sacrificed the life he wanted with me and the dreams we shared, but he left his heart safely in my possession.

He was my heart-keeper until today. From this moment on I will be his.

CHAPTER FIFTY-TWO

Matthew: Heart-keeper

Evie sits across from me, relaxing as she reads a book. I try to mimic her composure, but rest feels foreign. It's clear to me that it will be a long while until I can relax again.

We're the only two in the waiting area outside the operating room of this trauma care wing. Every now and then, Evie turns from her book and offers me a smile—warm, filled with gratitude, and tinged with an apology she can't quite articulate.

Yesterday, she broke down when I told her my decision, thanking me repeatedly and pleading for my forgiveness. Her words blurred as I struggled to process the choice I'd made—the hardest I've ever made—which continues to tear at me. I consoled her as best I could, though my words felt clumsy and inadequate.

As we wait for the surgeons to emerge from the procedure to remove Alex's feeding tube, my thoughts return to my decision and the weight that has been crushing me ever since. She doesn't know what I've decided, though her brilliant mind might have pieced it together when I told her to prepare for this surgery. However, she doesn't know that she won't be returning to the private room that has been her cavernous prison for the past month. She doesn't know that she won't be restrained to that iron bed and wrapped in that hellish blanket again. I wanted to wait until after the surgery to tell her.

I've been living in a haze of pain, dizziness, and nausea since the evening I left the apartment—a place where I could truly relax in the warmth of Anna's presence. This feeling of suffocation is worse than what I felt when making my decision. Sometimes, my heart stops altogether for a passing moment and then lurches to life. The ache in my chest is constant as I think of Anna and the life that could have been. My muscles frequently force me to sit, and when I do, my lungs make it difficult to breathe.

My mind keeps dredging up the past, going back years, trying to understand how we all ended up here. It's a feeling reminiscent of my drinking days—this questioning of everything I believed, every relationship that held meaning. And then, just as I feel myself spiraling, I jolt upright—my warning not to head towards a bottle.

I will endlessly love Anna. She holds a part of me that will remain hers forever. There's a void inside me that can't be filled, no matter how much time passes or how much I try to move forward. *But I have to. For Alex, me, and our life ahead.*

I will, in quick time, love Alex the way I did when we were a couple because my existence is irrevocably tied to hers. It always has been. It always has been her—and life taught me that in cruel ways.

Nobody will ever replace her role as my precious little girl. I will guide her through this new future. We will find each other again amid the ruins of what we previously had. My paternal instinct didn't falter—that's the core reason behind the impossible choice I made.

The image of Alex restrained, mute, and dependent on a feeding tube is an image I can't bear to live with. She's only nineteen. I am her protector, a fierce guardian and provider, who will ensure she receives all the goodness the world offers. The bond we share has always defied easy understanding. I'm certain that love will envelop us without us having to search for it—that's how it happened when she and I met in the gym twenty months ago.

As I wrestled with my decision, the confidence that had been lurking in the shadows finally surged forward. It came to my rescue when the pain threatened to consume me entirely. My senses threw a question at me, stark in its practicality: *Of the two women in my life, who would survive—thrive—without me?*

I've never wallowed in agony for as long as I did that night—tossing and turning, trying to make an impossible decision. The sting in my chest, the ache in my belly, simply wouldn't relent. It still hasn't eased. But that night, I let go. I let go of Anna, let go of the dreams I had envisioned with her.

Gathering strength, I finally went and met her. The ache escalated—compounding the torment in my mind—as I writhed on the floor in the apartment in the presence of Anna's strength and resolve.

In the end, a part of me was torn away, and a piece of Anna was ripped from her as well, leaving us both fundamentally changed. The fragments of what we were are scattered in a deep abyss from where they won't be recovered.

Yet, it's the vision of Anna's unwavering strength that pulls me back into control and reignites my command over my own life as I sit here in the waiting area, reflecting on the past and trying to self-heal. I shake my head vigorously, startling Evie from her book.

On to the future, Matthew, please.

Though the hurt and the soul-stabbing guilt will probably linger—perhaps never fully fading—they will serve as reminders. Reminders to be strong, to manage my affliction, and to be the father figure Alex needs me to be.

As I find my resolve once more, the doors to the operating room swing open, and the surgeon appears with a cheery air. He doesn't spend more than a minute talking to Evie and me, smiling as he informs us that the surgery went as planned and that Alex is recovering well in post-op. Evie and I exchange a glance, and a shared sigh of relief escapes our lips.

I meet Alex three hours after her surgery. The nurse watching over her tells me I can talk to her, then leaves. Alex smiles at me, and that instantly tells me she's alright.

She is a bit drowsy but gradually waking to alertness as she says, "Hey...I love you." I take her hand, give her my best smile, and kiss her forehead, which feels warm. I massage her hand and stroke her hair, my gaze fixed on her.

There's no need to wait any longer.

"I love you, Alex. Now, are you ready for some good news?" My voice sounds like a broken stereo bass.

She waits a few seconds, and a single tear escapes her left eye, which I quickly wipe away. She nods, and a feeble whimper escapes her lips. "Daddy..."

"We're leaving this place. I'm taking you with me," I state, trying to smooth my voice. But my tone is steady. Instantly, I'm taken down memory lane to that evening in New Jersey, in the parking lot of our favorite coffeehouse, where I said the same thing to her. I feel the same thrill I did then—a satisfying knowledge that my little girl is mine, and as her paternal figure, I'm going to take care of her for the rest of my years on this earth.

She sniffles, and sobs break free as her tears flow unhindered. I break into a smile. My eyes sting and burn from exhaustion, but my smile is unbridled. She tries to reach for me, but the position of her bed makes it uncomfortable. I step closer to bend and hug her, treating her like a delicate glass sculpture. Just as I'm about to pull away, I give her a tight embrace, then keep my smiling face on. It's a gesture that always lifts her and fills her with energy, and I feel some of that energy in me as well.

The weight, the burn, the pain—they all linger, threatening to pull me under. But I've already started on my journey of managing these sensations and the emotions that come with them for however long it takes—maybe a lifetime.

What else can I do?

Yeah, it's painful. So what? Don't overthink the agony, just manage it. Give it your best. You don't have a choice. You will manage the misery and everything else thrown at you, and you will survive. Find happiness for yourself and for others—my eight-year-old self teaches me.

"Matthew...what...I'm sorry. I don't know what to ask." Her low whimper pulls me from my brief mental trip to the command-and-control store, where I've been trying to replenish my strength. I wipe more tears from her face and cradle her head in my hands.

"I've left Anna. That's all I'll tell you. You won't talk about it, and neither will I. Understand?" My voice, still rough and broken, finds its strength—the cracks slowly mending.

My mind drifts to the first occasion I commanded her, reflecting on how much has changed since then. The feelings coursing through me at this moment differ from what I felt for her then. Normalcy will resume as she and I recover from the arduous journey to get to where we are in this instant.

She stares at me for a moment, absorbing my words. Then she gives me the response I need to hear.

"Yes, Daddy."

She nods as I cuddle her and repeat my directive, that we will only talk about the future. She nods again. I wipe away more of her tears and finally order her not to cry. Just then, the nurse comes in, saying she needs to prepare Alex for discharge. I leave the two of them together and exit, where I'm met by Dr. Robbins, her face radiant.

We share a light hug, and I thank her. Warmth and profound gratitude fill me as I address her, "Dr. Robbins, I can't thank you enough for being there for Alex. You were with her during her darkest times."

Oh, what's this new feeling?

Deep indebtedness toward Dr. Robbins rises above the pain and pressure weighing on me. If I'm going to manage what's eating me inside, I'll need to fill my days with more gratitude-filled moments like this.

Dr. Robbins waves me off almost dismissively, as she says it's her job to be there for her and that she felt a special connection to her.

After a pause, she adjusts her glasses and looks at me with a seriousness that quickly softens into a smile. In a kind, yet measured voice, she says, "Matthew, I was wrong about you." She pauses and heaves a quick sigh, then continues, "I'll leave it at that because you're going to prove that for the rest of your life." She breaks into a light laugh, and after a moment, I join her. We shake hands, and she heads in to see Alex for their last session, after which we'll leave the hospital.

This hospital wing holds memories of a dark and painful journey. But today, we'll leave all of that behind. We're going to see the last of the hellish blanket that has wrapped around her every night for the past month. It's time for her to return to my envelope, where she belongs.

Alex leads me on a tour of her new penthouse, and her steps are light as she talks about the design of the rooms. Meanwhile, her mom, Evie, and Edward relax in the large living space. From a distance, I watch them, and my expanding chest feels lighter as I see smiles on their faces after what felt like an eternity. I compare their expressions to what they were in the hospital wing, and a small smile tugs at my lips. I take in their cheerful faces, their uncurbed laughter filling the space, and for a moment, the weight on my chest lifts.

Oh, that feeling again. This time, from the satisfaction of knowing I brought happiness to people.

Her mom had a slew of housekeepers from their mansion clean and reset this vast penthouse, restocking the pantry and refrigerator. Edward had emptied the bar, mentioning he'd present a few proposals to turn that area into another living space.

In the corner of the main living area, the grand piano sits regally, its presence commanding attention. Floor-to-ceiling windows frame the skyscrapers of midtown Manhattan—the cityscape stretching as far as I can see. Alex and I exchange a glance, and we understand what's next. As I take my place at the piano, her favorite piece by Chopin, Nocturne No. 1 in B-Flat Minor, fills the penthouse, weaving through the air as though it were a familiar old friend.

The small gathering congregates around the piano, but my focus is on her as I play. I read every emotion that flits across her features, every subtle change as the notes waft around this opulent space. Her expressions speak volumes, summarized in a single line: *I am happy I found you.* A line we both said to each other during our first date.

As she talks with her family while they prepare to leave, walking toward the elevators, my mind drifts, contrasting this extravagant penthouse with the apartment I shared with Anna. The tightness in my chest resurfaces as memories of the simple pleasures she and I cherished in that small haven flood back. I gaze north, as if I could somehow see the apartment in Hamilton Heights from here—as if I could watch over Anna from this distance.

She will be happy. I will remind myself to be happy, for her and for me, and she will do the same, my mind keeps repeating, as sorrow—slowly, ever so slowly—starts to abate.

I keep staring north as the sunlight fades, searching with the knowledge that she is there in the distance.

"Anna," The single word—low, tender, and raw—escapes like a prayer. It lingers in the air, untouched by the noise around me, and everything else fades.

I close my eyes, feeling the ache settling in the space between my ribs and heart.

I chose this path. I chose to let Anna go, to turn away from the future we could have had. For Alex—for the promise I made to myself to save her from herself. But in this stillness, I feel the crushing weight of that decision.

"What're you looking at?" Alex's voice pulls me from my thoughts, and as she hugs me from behind, I gently guide her to stand in front of me. My eyes trace my admiration over her features until they lock with her blue eyes, deep and unwavering. In them, I see only love—that has never failed—a force that has defined her, consumed her, and ultimately become her. At this moment, I realize I'm not just holding Alex—I'm holding the love she carries for me.

She jumps, her lips puckering for a kiss, but I nuzzle her away with a soft chuckle and order her to fetch her journal from Sweden—that has but a few pages filled. Mumbling her disappointment, and mouthing a "whatever" while shaking her head, she pivots on her heels. She goes to her study to retrieve the journal. I laugh quietly, settling on the sofa, and my gaze drifts north again—towards Hamilton Heights, where memories of another life linger.

When she returns, journal in hand, I ask her to explain the drawing of her vision—which she sketched when Dr. Robbins prompted her to during their therapy sessions in Sweden.

She playfully smacks my forearms before lightly punching my shoulder. A frown creases her face. "Matthew, the vision is yours and mine, not something I concocted."

I laugh, the sound lightening the air, and nod. "Yes, my baby. But you put it on paper. I need you to explain it to me because from this moment on, you and I are going to work together and make it real. Understand?"

"Yes, Daddy," she squeals, bouncing on the sofa, and her excitement is infectious as she throws her arms up in the air.

We cuddle on the sofa, gazes drifting towards Central Park as the golden light of the evening sun bathes everything in a soft, ethereal glow. After ages of darkness, a sense of peace peeks from the shadows that have lingered for far too long.

The world keeps spinning, but I am still. *I have my little girl, and I will carry the memories of Anna in my heart.*

CHAPTER
FIFTY-THREE

Alex: Cunningham

His usual wake-up routine has changed. In the two weeks we've been living in the penthouse, he awakens around seven in the morning, instead of five-thirty, which is the same as my body clock. I suspect it's due to the exhaustion that drained him over the time spent in that wretched hospital. I have recovered more quickly. Thus, in the early hours of this Sunday morning, I lie on my side, my hand propping my head as I watch him sleep.

I shouldn't be ogling him. But I can't help it.

Stop it, Alex. Let the man get his rest—what's happened over the last nine months has been taxing on everyone, including you.

Yet I can't stop admiring his body, the way his chest rises and falls in slow, steady motions. The mountain of muscle, bone, and limitless heart—my beast and I finally returned to our bed, where we both belong.

He hasn't fucked me yet. At first, I let it slide after making subtle suggestions. Then I made more explicit advances before finally demanding sex. Every time, he chuckled, his viridian eyes crinkling with genuine amusement, and told me we needed to wait. He said it was because I was recently discharged from the hospital, where I'd undergone two surgeries in the span of a month, to say nothing of the emotional struggles.

But they were minor surgeries, Daddy. And emotionally? I didn't really have much to worry about once you arrived to nurture me. I'd have happily spent the rest of my life in that hospital as long as you were with me. I worried you might leave, but when you returned the second time, I knew you wouldn't ever abandon me.

I run my fingers through my hair, desperate for relief from the restless, chaotic energy pulsing through me. My hand drifts between my thighs, seeking release, but it makes the ache worse, and the sensation throbs in time with the anticipation building in my chest. My breathing is shallow, and I can feel my heartbeat in my fingertips. I sigh—a sound that feels like it could bring this entire skyscraper crashing down. My eyes close, but the darkness makes the rush of thoughts more overwhelming. *Focus*, I tell myself, but my mind's a hurricane.

I glance at him—just one more look—and then I'm up, scrambling off the bed to distract myself from the carnal thoughts that keep slamming into me. I hasten to the kitchen, trying to keep my breath steady, fighting the need to scream, but the tension stays coiled tight in my gut.

The sound of the coffee machine cranking to life is reassuring, and the smell of coffee fills the air, rich and inviting.

I know he's holding back—he's only a few days out of his life with Anna, a woman he loved with a passion I can't understand. *And yet, here we are. Together.* I cling to that thought like a lifeline, ignoring the sharp ache in my chest when I think of them, of her. I don't want to think about her. I can't. But then her perfectly poised image flashes—she was his, they were a couple.

They forged a bond in suffering. And bitterness churns inside me because I can't understand it fully. But I see the way he looks at me now, and it's real, and he's mine. *So why do I still feel her shadow?*

She's gone. She's gone. She's gone. I repeat it like a mantra, trying to convince myself. But the dizziness is back, and my head pounds.

Focus. Focus. I shake it off. I can't let her steal my peace. *She's out of the picture.*

I walk around and pause at the spot where she and I met. The memory slams into me, and my chest tightens with a jolt of fury. *I hate her.* The thought is instantaneous. My pulse thunders in my ears. I want to shatter the memory of her, but instead I bite my lip so hard it hurts. A hot, sickening rage floods my veins. I can feel my nails biting into my palms. *Why—why does she still haunt me like this?*

And then in the same breath, relief. *She's gone.* That thought hits like ice water, but the relief feels fleeting. It always is.

I breathe deeply and push thoughts of her aside, focusing on Matthew and on what we have. *We'll be okay. We'll be okay.*

I force myself to remember his command to think about the future. *Speak only of the future. Think only of the future.*

I tear my eyes away from that cursed spot where she broke me. I'll remodel that space, turn it into something that doesn't have her in it—something that's just his and mine.

And then I remember tonight—the reunion. The family, along with soon-to-be-Cunningham Lillian, will gather to celebrate a new chapter. It's a joyous embrace of the future, but the knot in my chest tightens all the same.

I'm anxious to be the disciplined girl Matthew needs me to be—the one who never falters. But the fear of failure clings to me—a constant shadow. It can be a motivator, but it often crushes me under its weight. *I'll not let him down.*

There's also the thrill—and the trepidation—of managing a household of my own. *Will I be able to handle the challenges, or will I stumble? Will I meet Matthew's expectations and my own?* The questions leave me both keen and uneasy.

And then there's the business. The pull to dive back into work is overpowering. I can feel the gears of my mind turning, envisioning new ways to innovate and expand. My latest idea—tapping into wave energy—is just the beginning. I want to leverage the conglomerate's global reach to launch large-scale projects to curb deforestation. I've even begun drafting plans to use advanced mathematical models to design sustainable urbanization options, incorporating renewable resources and preserving ecosystems. The possibilities are endless, and I feel the fire of determination burning bright within me.

Yet, above all is my yearning to start a family with Matthew. The vision of our life together—beginning with the dream house on that beautiful plot of land he purchased last year—reigns supreme in my heart. Building a home, a family, a legacy with him is the ultimate goal that shapes all others.

Tonight's family reunion is an inauguration of sorts—a launchpad for everything Matthew and I plan to achieve together.

My family all love him. But I also know their previous resentment will take time to lessen. In their minds, they might still think he's the reason everything went to hell—that his arrival in my life set everything in motion. *But now they've accepted him.* They've seen firsthand what he and I are to each other, and even though they may not fully grasp our relationship. *They've accepted us.*

I should be overjoyed, but I can't shake the unease. *Will this last? Will everyone continue to hold Matthew in high regard?*

Then there's Edward the Enforcer. He sees him as a savior. He's Matthew's biggest fan, talking about being friends. *Friends!* That's the highest accolade anyone could receive from the Cunninghams. Even Father's approval pales compared to Edward's. Edward, who once threatened to kill Matthew and punched him on the chin. It's surreal.

This is my home. I'm supposed to be the Lady of the House.

Thus, I attempt to assume the role, strutting into the kitchen and bossing the chefs around. But it doesn't take long for them to bark at me, asking me to leave with a polite but firm "please" tacked on at the end.

I stomp my feet and mumble curses under my breath as I leave, my mood darkening. My mom's laughter makes it worse as a sharp pang of embarrassment cuts me. I watch her approach, resigned to the idea that I have more to learn. *I can never become what my mom is, but I want to get close.*

She sees my frustration and leads me to the kitchen, guiding me with gentle, whispered instructions and deftly avoiding the chefs as she teaches me how to ensure the best spread for a memorable dinner. She assures me the chefs know what they're doing, and there's no need to worry. But her reassurances do little to soothe the anxiety in my chest. *Will I be able to maintain a household? Will Matthew be disappointed in me, given my inexperience?*

My sisters-in-law and Lillian join us, teaching me the etiquette of reception, the distinct stages of engagement, and how to gracefully socialize before dinner. I've been a participant or an observer on many such occasions, but today I'm learning how to organize a formal dinner, step-by-step. Despite their kindness, a creeping sense of inadequacy settles in. I'm supposed to be in control, but instead I am a novice, fumbling and trying to appear composed.

Evie is conspicuously absent from this educational discourse. She's with Ted and the men, and their voices fill the penthouse with jovial chatter and bursts of loud laughter. But despite the racket and babble, I can feel her glower on me. Unease arrests me as I catch her staring at me from across the living area, as though she were an eagle eyeing her prey. Her gaze is unnerving, and I can't shake the feeling that she's constantly waiting for me to slip. *What the hell is her problem?*

I don't know what's changed, but something has. Edward is the same, keeping his distance and avoiding conversation, while his glare tracks my every move with cold detachment.

Something happened in that hospital wing—something involving Edward, Evie, and possibly Dr. Robbins—but I'm at a loss to even guess what their issue is. *Wasn't I nearly dead? Doesn't that deserve kindness?* They were showering me with grace until the last few days. *What the fuck happened then?* My mind spins with confusion as more frustration bubbles inside me.

When dinner finally begins, the atmosphere shifts. Conversations flow, smiles are exchanged, and laughter drifts around the table as Matthew engages with everyone equally. It should be comforting, but the tension between me and Evie lingers—a shadow I can't quite shake.

We all clink glasses of sparkling water, and Matthew surprises me by proposing a toast to the future of the Cunninghams. It's a rare show of sentiment from him—one I wasn't expecting. In all our dinner dates, it was always me who toasted to things that defined the bond we share. Seeing him make a toast at this table, surrounded by my family, brings a bittersweet pang to my heart. *Is he trying to mend the cracks that I caused, or is this his way of reconciling with the life he's chosen with me?*

Evie, despite the tension I've felt from her, makes this gathering shine, elevating it to a moment none of us will forget.

She stands at the head of the table, next to my seated father, with tears shimmering in her eyes. Her voice rings as everyone holds their glasses, "Matthew, you are now a Cunningham. Here before you is a fragment of the large family you've always wanted."

He goes still, absorbing her words. Then, slowly, his face transforms. He smiles radiantly. It's the greatest hit I've ever seen on him, a beam that reaches deep in my soul. He mouths a heartfelt, "Thank you," as his eyes lock with each family member, gratitude pouring from him.

"Hear, hear!" everyone cheers, raising their glasses in unison. Overcome by the moment, my head falls on my mom's chest, and I release a wail that's been building inside me for years. *Finally, my family has accepted Matthew, and they embrace us as a couple. But what a toll of devastation that has taken.*

As I cry, images and memories flash in my mind—interventions, insults, accusations, judgments, the dismal dinner last year, Edward's outburst at the penthouse, my desperate return to the mansion when I left Matthew, the events of the past few months. It consumes me, but this time, I'm surrounded by love.

My family embraces me, and their warmth is soothing, heartwarming. Lillian leans in, comforting me with gentle hugs, while my other sisters-in-law—except Evie—humor me and bring me back to the present.

Ted rises, glass in hand, and with a grin that further brightens the gathering, jokes, "Let's hope Matthew doesn't regret wanting a large family after he meets our extended families." We erupt in riotous laughter, the kind that shakes the walls and fills every corner with joy. James, who's usually more reserved, jumps in with a mischievous glint in his eye, adding, "Especially since Lilly's folks will join the clan soon." Laughter explodes, and the decibels are high enough to shatter glass.

Lillian's skin flushes red as she hurls a few spoons and napkins at James, who ducks with a grin. When she's about to throw a plate, my mom steps in, stopping her with a firm hand, which makes everyone hysterical. Lillian tries to maintain her indignation, but soon she too is laughing, albeit red-faced, as James apologizes and tries to comfort her.

Amid it all, I laugh and cry, overwhelmed by love that fills my home. It's a beautiful occasion, where the past's pain and the present's joy collide, leaving me hoping that, maybe, just maybe, everything is going to be okay.

As everyone follows Matthew to the grand piano, eager to indulge in music, conversation, and views of this magnificent city, I feel a forceful tug at my elbow that prevents me from joining the rest of the group.

It's Evie.

"Can I talk to you for a minute?" It is more of a command than a request, and her tone is devoid of warmth and filled with purpose. Without waiting for my response, she strides toward my study, clearly expecting me to follow. A fleeting urge to snap, *"Screw you, bitch,"* and head straight to Matthew crosses my mind, but curiosity gets the better of me. I want to know what's crawled up her butt.

She stands behind the desk with arms crossed, her posture rigid, and her gaze piercing. I linger near the door and train my scowl on her, trying to decipher her game. The silence stretches until my patience wears thin.

"What do you want, Evie?" I ask, my voice tinged with irritation.

Her cynical laugh echoes around the study. I've had enough. I pivot on my heel, ready to leave, when her laughter cuts off like a door slamming shut.

"I know what you did," she says, emotionlessly, as if a switch has flipped off.

I freeze mid-step, and my heart skips a beat. Slowly, I turn to her, but her smirk twists a knife in my chest. The urge to physically hurt her simmers beneath the surface. She moves closer—her stride precise, her high heels clicking against the floor in an eerie countdown.

She stops a foot away from me, leaning in so close I can feel the heat of her breath. Her smirk remains and her eyes burn mine with an intensity that makes me flinch. "And I'm here to make sure you don't manipulate anyone in this family ever again."

Her words strike hard, but I remain poised. She retreats and perches on the edge of the pristine mahogany desk, her arms still defiantly crossed.

"It's very simple, Alex. Be a good girl to Matthew and to this family. Don't take anyone for granted. Respect him," she pauses, and for just an instant, I see tears. She continues, "And remember the sacrifice he made for you." Her voice is firm. She lifts her chin, and her expression demands a response.

But I remain silent, unwilling to give her the satisfaction. Unfazed, she presses on, "Victoria is not your mom. From this point on, I am your mother. I'll be watching you like a hawk. You don't have an eldest sister-in-law or a friend anymore. Evie, your sister, is dead. I've taken her place. Tell me you understand everything we've discussed."

Discussed? You talked, and I endured your fucking Prévoir-clad presence, you bitch.

She takes a few steps toward me, the to-and-fro movement calculated to instill fear. Her biting smile is replaced by a hardened expression that makes her an intimidating figure—a living embodiment of a baleful warning. In articulate tones laced with betrayal, she says, "We stood by you and walked with you through hell—for seven months in Sweden and another agonizing month in that hospital. We sacrificed our personal and professional lives without a second thought—all for you."

Her voice drops menacingly, so uncharacteristic that it chills me to the bone. "We'd do it all over again, which makes this warning more necessary. Don't take family for granted, my child. Don't take Matthew for granted." It's both a threat and a twisted kind of nurturing being delivered in this uncomfortable moment. She retreats, and her face wears a caustic expression, the warmth gone.

Message received and acknowledged and I understand what you all did for me, with thanks. But how dare you mother me, you harpy?

The door swings open, and Edward steps in with a casual, "Hey, no apologies, and I hope I intruded on your conversation. Evie, is Alex clear on our statutes?" He pauses before continuing, "Knowing she can never win trust back?"

Great, as if this evening couldn't get any worse. While I appreciate his help during my tragedy, I wish he would leave this country and be with his UK companies.

Their eyes meet, and they share a smile that sends a bone-chilling stab of pain through my entire body. I remain rooted to the spot—my only movement the frantic darting of my eyes between the two of them.

These two are working together? To parent me? They don't have the slightest clue who they're dealing with.

"Oh, I think she gets it, Edward. Isn't that right, Alex?" Evie's cynical laugh pierces the air, and her voice is laced with a dark satisfaction. The two of them close in on me as if they're intent on pinning me to the walls of this study, leaving me nowhere to escape. Edward's expression is a mirror of when he threatened to kill Matthew and punched him in the face.

He-he is-he is scary.

My breath catches, and I take a shaky step backward as my hand fumbles for anything to grab onto for support.

Edward leans in closer, his glare fixed on me. His voice is an omen as he warns me, "Alex, this is one case where you don't want to find out the answer to the question, 'What's the worst that could happen?' So, you will behave, my little sister."

He steps back with a cheerful spring in his step, clapping his hands a few times as if this were all a game. "Oh, Alex, Matthew has been asking for you at the piano, bless him. Let's go give the kind man an audience, shall we?"

Both smirk at me, and their heads nod in unison as they lock arms and walk out of the study together. I follow them, my unblinking eyes fixed on the back of their heads, walking deeper into an inescapable trap.

Matthew's breathing is deep in the rhythm of sleep. I silently slide out of bed, my movements precise, and enter the shadowy embrace of my study.

Relax, you genius. Don't panic.

Calm is my companion as I move with the ease of someone who has rehearsed this a thousand times in her mind. When I was planning how to reclaim Matthew, I explored certain dark corners of the web. In those depths, I created layers of aliases and subnets, contacting a few individuals who offer...services. Services for impairment, cross impairment, and elimination—which I had planned to use on anyone who kept me from him, for example, a certain ex-wife and whore.

I did end up using one of their lower-tier services—stalking and driving fear into the bitch. My contact suggested that it would make me appear innocent if Matthew were stalked too, for an extra cost. It would give the impression that Edward was doing this—to drive Matthew and Anna out of the city in fear. I agreed under the condition Matthew wasn't to be harmed. I didn't stipulate the same condition for the snake, but my contact was a pro—he stuck to the terms of engagement.

I sit at my desk—the only light the faint glow from my laptop screen, which I've positioned perfectly to shield any light from leaking into the penthouse. My fingers move efficiently, retrieving the notes I've stored and the conversations I've had. I casually ping my contacts, and my heart is steady as they respond immediately, eager for the hundreds of thousands I promised them. They don't need to know much—just enough to execute certain 'assignments'—missions I might one day need them to undertake at a moment's notice.

I push the backrest as far as it will go and stretch my interlocked hands above my head until I feel the satisfying pull of my muscles. I drop my hands to my lap and release a controlled breath.

"It's simple, Alex," I murmur, the words a dark melody in the stillness. "If Edward or Evie ever try to tell Matthew what I orchestrated that day, or if they even think of it, all I have to do is click send on these instant message drafts."

Yes, I faked my suicide, but it's my secret to tell, not anyone else's.

I stand and walk to the front of the desk, leaning against it just as Evie had earlier. A sardonic laugh bubbles to the surface, resonating within the study's walls, threatening to seep into the rest of the penthouse.

I pat myself on the shoulder. "It's the same with Anna, isn't it?" I whisper, the thought more comforting than chilling. "That whore might have figured out what I did—her sharp mind probably pieced it together." I wince, feeling a sting of jealousy, then quickly amend, "Well, maybe slightly sharper." I let out a sinister laugh that echoes in the silent study.

"Pity those who try to take Matthew from me," I say, my voice a cold promise. "Or dare to taint the love I have for him."

I pause, feeling the fire spreading through my veins like molten lava. *They don't know me. They don't know the lengths I'll go to...for him, for us.*

A surge of possessiveness tightens in my chest, an unyielding resolve. *They'll learn soon enough.*

The world keeps spinning, but I am still. *I have him, and I win.*

CHAPTER FIFTY-FOUR

Anna: Good Night

The morning light filters through the curtains, brushing softly against my eyelids, but I've been awake for a while. It's quiet with just the gentle hum of the city outside, a far cry from the noise that usually fills my mind. I turn onto my back, eyes tracing the lines of the ceiling, and the first thought that crosses my mind is Matt. It always is.

I miss him. I miss him so much it's like a dull ache that never goes away. *But I can't dwell on it.* I take a deep breath and remind myself that I'm strong, that I can do this. It's what he would want, what he always wanted for me—to be strong, to be happy, to move forward. And so I do.

The alarm on my phone buzzes softly beside me. I'm already awake, slipping from under the covers, letting the cool air greet my bare feet. There's a strange comfort in the routine, in knowing what comes next. Coffee, shower, work—it's not much, but it's mine.

I move across the small apartment—a new one in a different area of Manhattan, a space I've made my own. It's not luxurious, but it's comfortable. It's enough. The coffee machine clicks on, and the smell of freshly brewed coffee fills the kitchen. I close my eyes and inhale deeply, feeling the warmth spread through me. It's the little things that keep me going—the simple pleasures that remind me life can still be good.

As I pour myself a cup, I glimpse my reflection in the window. I look...different. Stronger, maybe, or merely more resolved. I miss him with every breath—I miss him especially every morning when I wake up alone in bed, but I know he would want me to keep going, to find joy in the world I've built. So, I try.

Work at Hudson & Greene LLP is busy as always, and I welcome it. The constant buzz keeps me focused, grounded. Today, it's more than admin tasks—a partner has a tech issue, and I'm the go-to problem solver. My fingers fly over the keyboard as I troubleshoot with practiced ease. It's a small thing, but it makes me feel useful. This job isn't glamorous, but it's fulfilling, and I take pride in the work life I've built here.

My colleagues congratulate me on last month's raise, and I smile, thinking of the compact car I bought with it. Every time I slide into the driver's seat, it feels like a small slice of freedom. This isn't the life I imagined with him, but it's mine, and I've worked hard for it.

Even in the hum of my day, Matt lingers in my thoughts. I wonder what he's doing, if he thinks of me too. I know he's with Alex now, building their life together. And while it stings, I want him to be happy—in the end, that's all I've ever wanted for him, for us.

When I get home, the city lights shimmer against the dark sky, New York's pulse vibrant and alive. I park my car and take the elevator upstairs, savoring the quiet simplicity of my routine. In the apartment, I trade my office wear for something more comfortable, prepare a quick dinner, and sit at the small table by the window. The stillness soothes me, yet a part of me wonders if he is taking care of himself.

After dinner, I curl on the couch with a book. It's a novel about love and loss, and the words resonate with me in a way that feels too close to home. But I keep reading, letting the story pull me in, letting it remind me I'm not alone in what I've been through. Other people have loved and lost like I have. And they've survived.

Later, when the city is wrapped in darkness, I stand by the window, looking at the skyline. The lights twinkle like stars, and I wonder if he is somewhere in one of those skyscrapers, searching for me, trying to make sure I'm okay, thinking of me too.

When I close my eyes, I can almost feel him beside me, his arms holding me close. It's a memory that's comforting and painful—a reminder of what we had and what we lost. But I hold on to it because it's all I have left.

I compose myself and look at the stars. My dad is up there, watching over me. I know he's proud of me, of the life I've built, even if it's not the future I thought I'd have. And Matt is watching over me too, in his own way. I can feel it.

I whisper a quiet prayer to the night sky, asking for strength, for guidance, for the courage to keep moving forward. I'll need it in the days to come, but I also know I'm strong enough to get through this.

Before I head to bed, I take a last look at the starry skies of the night. The city is quiet, the lights soft against the dark sky. I imagine him somewhere out there, gazing at the same stars, wishing me a happy life, just as I wish the same for him.

Our love will never fade, I know that. It's been tested and forged in fire, and it will endure, no matter what. I hold on to the strength it gives me, to the peace it brings.

I turn away from the window and slip into bed, where the warm sheets are a welcome comfort. I shut my eyelids and exhale a deep breath, letting the day's thoughts drift away. As I drift off, I think of him one last time, sending him a silent wish for happiness.

And as sleep finally takes me, I know I will carry him in my heart forever, just as I know he will carry me in his.

The world keeps spinning, but I am still. *We're forever—Matt and I.*

EPILOGUE

I'm Nora. My full name is Eleanor Henry Cunningham. It's really long, so everyone just calls me Nora. My sister's name is Katie. Her full name is Catherine Victoria Cunningham. It's big too. Sometimes when Mommy is angry, she uses our whole names. But Daddy never gets angry with us. He tells us to do things, but he's always happy. I'm happy too. Katie is happy too.

I don't always like her, but I like playing with her. She's my little sister, so I have to take care of her.

She's really good at playing the piano. He teaches her every day. Every key on the piano has a name. She knows all of them. He is a piano teacher and teaches other people, using a computer where he can see them play.

I sit on the floor and draw what I see. That's my superpower. I can draw anything. I remember everything I see too. Mommy says Katie and I have the same superpower because we never forget anything.

"I'm going to beat you!" Katie runs past me, squealing. We're having a competition.

Mommy taught us numbers and how to count.

"Remember, girls, this is not a competition," Daddy says, putting us both on his lap. We kiss him on the cheeks.

Mommy asks us to add some numbers, one after the other. Then she asks us to add them, skipping one number in between, without looking again. Today's competition is easy. Sometimes Katie wins, and sometimes I win. She cries when I win. Then Daddy takes her on a helicopter ride on his shoulders, running around our big house until she can't stop laughing. Then we all laugh together on the sofa.

Mommy reminds him that our birthday is coming up. They say it's our fourth birthday. We scream and jump up and down because we want dresses and shoes and wands. Aunt Evie and Grandma Victoria are the best. They take us shopping, and Daddy goes too. Mommy doesn't go because I think she and Aunt Evie aren't friends. Most of the time, Katie and I get the same dresses.

451

He says we're twins because we look the same. I was born ten seconds before her, so I'm her big sister. I will take care of her.

"Daddy, why is Mommy's tummy big?" she asks when we're reading our storybooks.

"I told you, that you're going to get a baby brother," he says and laughs.

"But I'm bigger than Mommy's tummy, and Nora is as big as me. Will Mommy's tummy get bigger? She'll burst, Daddy," she says, and he laughs again. He falls back on the sofa, holding her up in the air. She screams and laughs. I jump on his chest and tickle her. She squeals and laughs more, and he throws her up and catches her with his strong hands.

He is very strong. He does exercises in a big room in the house. It has a lot of machines. Everything there is heavy, and Katie and I can't lift anything. Mommy and Daddy have to exercise to be strong so they can take care of me and Katie.

Daddy and Mommy always kiss each other on the lips. That's because they're adults. They're always smiling and laughing.

He takes care of her. Mommy has a big company. She's very important. She comes home tired after working and making money. He takes care of her when she's tired. He even carries her to the bathroom and gives her a glass of wine, which is a juice that only adults can drink.

I drew pictures of them laughing. They say the pictures I drew are lifelike. That means they can hang them on the wall. My picture is next to a photo of them in wedding clothes, and there is a big party and they are dancing. I drew a picture of Katie too, and they put it on the wall.

Mommy keeps asking me to draw in color, but I don't like that. I like graphite pencils. Daddy got me the best pencils from a special shop. He says they're artist pencils. I like them, and I draw with them. My hands, fingers and face get so dirty when I draw with them, but he cleans me with towels and tissues. Sometimes I'll draw in color, but only if I want to.

Mommy says the picture I drew of them will look good in color. That's because they have beautiful eyes. Daddy's eye color is the same as mine. It's green, but Mommy calls it something else that I don't know how to say. Katie's and Mommy's eyes are the same blue color.

"Daddy, can I play music? The song you taught me?" Katie asks, jumping up and down.

"Did you do your C major and A minor arpeggios in piano staccato first?" he asks back, patting her cheeks.

She stomps the ground with her foot and goes to her room. He got her a small piano and put it in her room. But it has all the keys like the big piano in our big room with the big windows. So she goes to practice, I think, and I cuddle with him as he watches me draw this big park that we can see from the window.

Today is Sunday, and Daddy is taking us to a concert! That means people will sing and play instruments like the piano. There will be lots of other people there. They'll sing and dance too. It's noisy, but it's fun. The concert is in the big park, the one we can see from the top of our big house. He took us there before, and Katie and I remember everything. It's our superpower!

Sunday means Mommy has a holiday. She doesn't have to go to work and make money. But right now, she's in the room she calls a study, and the door is closed. Katie and I are jumping up and down, tugging on Daddy's shirt and shouting at the same time.

"What's Mommy doing in there?"

"I want to go to the park! I want to hear the music. Will there be a piano today, like the one in my room?"

"Daddy, ask Mommy to come out..."

He picks us both up in his arms and gives us an airplane ride around the house. We scream and laugh, and then he takes us to the kitchen for juice. I like orange juice, and Katie likes watermelon juice. He always makes them fresh for us.

"Girls, remember what I told you? Mommy is trying to save the trees so people don't keep cutting them down. Isn't that important, my darlings?" he asks, giving us our juices in cups with straws.

Katie and I nod our heads really fast.

"So she's in a work meeting with the people who will listen to her," he says, hugging us both tight.

"We love the trees, Daddy," Katie and I tell him. Then we drink our juices because he won't let us get off this chair until we do.

"Where are my sweetie pies? Where are my cupcakes? Who took them?" Mommy comes charging out of her room, making scary faces and noises. Katie and I jump up and try to run and hide, squealing and screaming.

In the park, Daddy carries us on his shoulders. He's so strong that he can put Katie on one shoulder and me on the other. He dances, and we're shaking and screaming, holding onto his hair and his hands. He has lots of hair, so we grab onto it tight. Mommy's tummy is big, so she can't dance, but she takes lots of pictures of us. I'm going to draw some of them when we get home.

The sky is so pretty today, with purple, pink, and orange colors, and lots of yellow too. I think I'll use the color pencils Grandpa Henry got me to draw the picture when we get home.

People are dancing, singing, and laughing. The people playing the music are happy too. I like all the colors today. The grass is green, like my eyes and Daddy's.

While we're dancing on Daddy's shoulders, I see a woman in the middle of the crowd. She's very pretty. Her eyes are black, and her hair is long and black too. She smiles at me and makes funny faces. I laugh, and she keeps making funny faces, so I laugh and scream even more. Daddy and Mommy ask what I'm laughing at, but when I point to her, the pretty lady isn't there anymore.

After the concert, Daddy takes us for ice cream. There are these people in black and blue suits with dark glasses who go with us, and there are a lot of them. Daddy says they're our bodyguards, and they take care of us.

"But why do we need them, Daddy, when you and Mommy take care of us?" Katie asks.

He says there are some bad people in the city, so the bodyguards are like the police who'll catch them.

We have a big car, and Daddy always drives. He puts Katie and me in our special chairs first. Mommy and he love this city, and they teach us the names of the buildings while he drives. The car moves slowly, even though he is awesome at driving. It's because there are lots and lots of cars on the road. She asks us to watch TV on the screens in front of us, but I want to talk to them.

I tell them about the woman in the park who made funny faces at me and made me laugh. I also tell them she blew me a kiss with her hand. Mommy laughs and says, "You girls are just too adorable." It means we are cute. She says people like us so much that they want to tell us we are beautiful.

Daddy is quiet. Then he asks me to tell him what the woman looked like. So, I do. After that, both Mommy and him go silent. I think it's because they're tired, and he is trying to drive with all the cars on the road at the same time.

When we get home, they go into the kitchen to make dinner, but they're not talking. I think it's because they're still tired. But they look sad.

I'm not happy now.

I take out a sheet of paper and my graphite pencils. I draw the picture of the woman I saw in the park. At the dinner table, I show them the picture. Katie jumps up and down, shouting, "Daddy! Mommy! It's the same woman I saw! She made funny faces at me, she smiled at me, and she was so cute, Daddy! She blew me a kiss with her hands too..."

I'm happy now because I showed them the woman I saw. It's the truth, and Katie saw the same woman, so it's double truth.

He takes us on his laps and feeds us dinner. But Mommy is angry because she shouts at him and tells him to put us back in our chairs so we can eat by ourselves. He puts us back in our chairs, and we all eat quietly. Nobody is talking. He still feeds us a spoonful now and then, and Mommy closes her eyes.

After we brush our teeth, Katie and I walk hand in hand back to the living room. We see him and Mommy hugging, but they aren't saying anything. Her head is resting on his chest. I think adults have their own way of talking without using words.

Then they see us and come to us with open arms. Daddy lifts me and Katie up, and Mommy puts her arms around us, hugging all of us together. Since it's Sunday night, we get to sleep in Mommy and Daddy's big bed. It has lots of space.

Katie and I sleep on either side of him. We hold on to his arms and fall asleep on his shoulders. Mommy lies next to us and usually reads us a story. But tonight, because she's tired, there won't be a story. Instead, Daddy asks us to look at the stars through the big windows and tells us a small story about how the stars are like bodyguards, watching over everyone on Earth.

Katie makes noises when she sleeps, so I know she's asleep. Daddy knows too, so he presses a few buttons on a remote control and the windows close. It's dark, and I'm about to fall asleep.

Mommy is making some noises that sound like she is crying. Then she talks to him. "It's her, Matthew. You know that." Now I think she is angry.

His voice is soft but strong, and when he speaks, his body shakes, so I'm shaking too. "Alex, it doesn't matter. We have our own peaceful life now," he says.

Mommy makes more noises, and I think she's crying more because her voice sounds different. "You know how I feel about her."

I clutch his arm tighter, as tight as I can.

"My dear Nora, I know you're not asleep, isn't that right?" he whispers. He shakes his arm slightly.

"Are you and Mommy fighting, Daddy? Are you sad that she's angry?" I'm sleepy now, but I want to make sure they're happy.

"She's just tired. She has to save the trees, and she's also carrying your baby brother, remember? We must be kind to her. Isn't that right, Nora?"

"Yes, Daddy. Good night, Daddy. Good night, Mommy," I say as my head drops on his arm.

When they talk like adults, I don't understand much. But I think Mommy is getting off the bed because the bed shakes. I hear her say, "I'll be in the study."

The door to the bedroom shuts softly, and I fall asleep.

THE END

Dear Reader,

I can't thank you enough for investing your time in reading my work—it's truly humbling. As an independent author, it would greatly help if you could spend a few extra moments leaving a review or rating on your favorite book-review platform. Even just a quick click to rate the book would make a meaningful difference!

I'd love to hear your thoughts or chat about the book. You can find me on social media as **@avamilns**, or reach me directly at **avamilns@avamilns.com**.

Thank you once again. I wish you and your loved ones the very best.

Warmly,

Ava Milns